Praise for *Here Comes Another Lesson*

"These are amazing, fearless stories—wild dreamscapes that take place in our very own world, with its murderous brutality, impenetrable mystery, and tender beauty. Whether he's working in the fantastic or the familiar, O'Connor is an artist of the unpredictable, a supreme talent."

—Joan Silber, author of *The Size of the World*

"'Love,' my favorite in this book of wonderful stories, says it all about the author, who exhibits throughout this collection a true mastery of the form; along the way, Mr. O'Connor, in his passion for language and storytelling, not only forms a bond between the reader and himself, but also leaves one with a feeling of gratitude—and yes, perhaps, even an affection—for his gifts."

—Oscar Hijuelos, author of *Beautiful Maria of My Soul*

"In these odd, funny, touching stories Stephen O'Connor plants himself in a great tradition of surrealist writers. He's not afraid to take whacky risks with his material and move us at the same time. I don't say this lightly, but there's a through line from Gogol to Kafka to O'Connor—writers who find that the seemingly ordinary and everyday can be the strangest thing of all."

—Mary Morris, author of *Revenge*

"The world as conjured by Stephen O'Connor—with its apocalyptic skies, its extravagant dispensations of feeling, its beautiful bestiaries full of minotaurs, untenured professors, and other lonely big-headed creatures—may feel like some wondrous dream, a funhouse mirror for our most primal yearnings and fears. But it's neither more nor less strange than our own. For all their riotous warps and woofs, these stories achieve an aching reality, a full-throated *human*-ness rare in American fiction. Like all the best art, they can't be summarized, only experienced. So what are you waiting for?"

—Robert Cohen, author of *Amateur Barbarians*

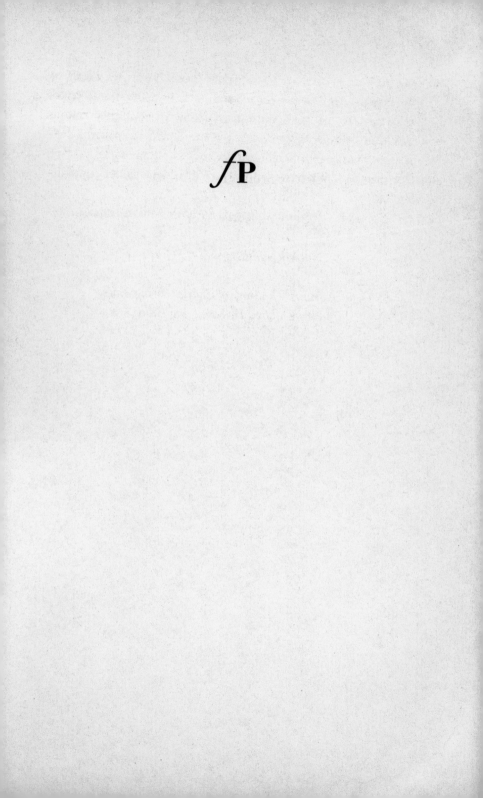

Here Comes Another Lesson

Stories

———◆———

Stephen O'Connor

Free Press

New York   London   Toronto   Sydney

FREE PRESS

A Division of Simon & Schuster, Inc.
1230 Avenue of the Americas
New York, NY 10020

First Free Press trade paperback edition August 2010

FREE PRESS and colophon are trademarks of Simon & Schuster, Inc.

For information about special discounts for bulk purchases, please contact Simon & Schuster Special Sales at 1-866-506-1949 or business@simonandschuster.com.

The Simon & Schuster Speakers Bureau can bring authors to your live event. For more information or to book an event contact the Simon & Schuster Speakers Bureau at 1-866-248-3049 or visit our website at www.simonspeakers.com.

Designed by Carla Jones

Permission credits appear on page 305

Manufactured in the United States of America

1   3   5   7   9   10   8   6   4   2

Library of Congress Cataloging-in-Publication Data
O'Connor, Stephen.
Here comes another lesson: stories / Stephen O'Connor.—1st Free Press trade pbk. ed.
p. cm.
I. Title.
PS3565.C65H47 2010
813'.54—dc22   2010005545
ISBN 978-1-4391-8199-7 (pbk)
ISBN 978-1-4391-9500-0 (ebook)

To my mother, Alix Euwer, 1925–2009

Contents

Contents

Ziggurat

The new girl sat at the computer in the corner playing Ziggurat, Panic! and U-Turn. This was in the pine-paneled section of the Labyrinth, which is where the Minotaur had been hanging out lately, mainly because he didn't remember ever having been there before, and he liked sleeping on the pool table.

The new girl was smaller than most of the others. Peanut-colored. Her shoulders shook. Her fingers twitched on the computer keys, making noises like munching rodents. Her eyes were filled with rhomboids of white, then blue, then red. Yellow. Then red again. Lots of red. And they were separated by two wrinkles that said to the Minotaur, Go away! I'm too busy for you!

It is true that the Minotaur was very strong and that his head was nearly as wide as his shoulders. But, in fact, he didn't really look like a bull. He had no horns, no ring through his nose. He was just very, very ugly. His lips were fat and earthworm pink, his eyes were asymmetrical, and his eyebrows were like forests of black wire. The same with the hair on his head, and on his cheeks—which was indistinguishable from the hair on his body. He didn't walk like a normal person; he lumbered. That was just the way he was born.

All the other girls had run when they'd seen the Minotaur. The women too, and the boys. Some of the men had tried to fight—not that it mattered. The end had always been the same: The Minotaur patting his belly, pulling a sucked femur from between his slick lips. No one had ever been too busy.

He watched the way the new girl's shoulders sometimes rose as high as her ears, and how, at other times, she leaned way over to the right or left. But always that jerky twitching, always that smacking of rodent lips. After a while he went right up behind her and leaned down close enough to savor her smell. She didn't cringe. She didn't even glance away from the screen. Just: twitch, twitch, twitch, clickity-clackity-click, click-click-click. "Oof!" she would say. "Oh my God!"

On the screen a square tower rose stone by stone. The stones were carried by angels. Red devils would attack the angels and the angels would drop the stones. Sometimes a big blue hand would come down out of the sky and sweep away one or more levels of the square tower, or even the whole thing. Every time the tower was reduced to rubble and dust, the face belonging to the hand would appear. It was a sad face, blue, with big round glasses and a mustache like a pair of bluebird wings. "Oof!" said the new girl.

To the Minotaur, humanity consisted of loud noises and a series of cowardly and craven acts. Running, etc. Curses, self-soiling. It was not uncommon for one human being to push another into his path, or even to kill that human being and stretch the cadaver out on the ground as an offering. Human beings would needle the Minotaur with knives. They would sprinkle his hide with lead. They would pound him with their fists the way flies pound themselves against windows. They would attempt to reason with him. And sometimes they would get down on their knees, and weep with their hands clasped in front of their chins. They would kiss his feet. None of this made any difference, of course. Wham! Crunch. Splurt. Hmm. Hmm. Tasty.

"Oh, no!" the new girl said. "Oh, shit." Her smell filled the Minotaur's sinuses and engendered slobber. At one point he brought his lips so close to her shoulder that he could feel his breath bounce back off her skin. Why not? he thought. Why not right now? There's not a reason in the world. But he didn't. Instead he went and leaned against the pool table. He would wait a bit. He wanted to see what would happen. His life was not exactly what you would call variety-packed, and he had the feeling that something unusual was in the works. Clickity-clackity-click. Twitch-jerk-twitch-twitch-twitch. "Oof!" He noticed how the new girl's hair swung heavily, like a velvet curtain. Dark brown, but also red. The color of old rust, only shiny. He noticed how parts of her jiggled, and how he could see every knob of her vertebrae except for two between her shoulder blades. Thunder rumbled from one side of his gut to the other. Drool wet his belly. Finally he got up and lumbered off to a tile tunnel where he could always find a skulking dog or two, sometimes whole packs. He baited a dog until it lunged. Then he snatched it mid-leap and ripped it in half. As he returned to the pool table a warmth spread from his belly through his chest and into his massive shoulders. He burped. Nothing had changed. Click-clickity. Twitch-jerk-jerk-jerk. He stretched out on the pool table and was soon asleep.

"Are you really the Minotaur?" the new girl asked when he opened his eyes. She was leaning over him, those same two wrinkles between her eyebrows, but this time they said, Hunh—weird! "*Are* you?" she asked. "When you first came in here, I thought you were, and I just kept on playing that game because I didn't want to see what you were going to do. But then you fell asleep." The new girl was silent awhile. Then she said, "I probably shouldn't be standing so close to you. I mean, you might just grab me and gobble me up. Right? If you really are the Minotaur, I mean." She took a step away and folded her arms across her chest. The lines had disappeared from between her eyes. There was a twist in one corner of her mouth, as if something were not right in her stomach. "So are you?" she said.

The Minotaur swung his legs around and sat up on the edge of the pool table. His head was at least a yard higher than hers; four of her could easily have stood between one of his shoulders and the other. As she waited for him to speak, she took another step backward. Whatever was not right in her stomach got worse, or so it seemed to the Minotaur.

"Yes," he said.

"Whoo-boy!" She swallowed. "I guess my goose is cooked."

He looked at her for a long moment.

Then he slipped off the table and said, "Excuse me."

When the Minotaur returned there was a trickle of blood descending from the corner of his mouth and pinkish flecks of gristle in his beard. The new girl was back at the computer, clicking away at the keys. She glanced up, and the Minotaur could tell from the way her eyes reverted instantly to the screen that she had seen something disgusting on his face, but she didn't say a word. Jerkity-click, click, click. Her eyes went yellow, then blue, then red. The Minotaur ran his hand over his beard and felt the flecks of gristle. He brushed them away, and licked up the blood trickle with his exceedingly long purple tongue. Then he stepped up beside her and looked at the screen. There was the sad-faced man with the bluebird-wings mustache.

"What are you playing?" the Minotaur asked.

"Ziggurat," the new girl told him, and when he didn't say anything in reply, she told him about all the other games she had discovered on the computer. And then she said, "Basically, they're all disappointment games. Except this one. This one's about ambition. You're supposed to build the Tower of Babel before God knocks it down. But that usually ends up being a disappointment game too." And when the Minotaur still didn't say anything, she said, "Basically, this is a pretty stupid bunch of games."

"Then why do you play them?" the Minotaur asked.

"Just . . ." The new girl blushed, then went pale. "Well . . . you know. It's like I said before." After that she put her hands in her lap, became very quiet and seemed to shrink to half her size. The Minotaur figured that this was her way of telling him the time had come for him to eat her. But, just as his big lips went glossy and he was baring his shovel teeth, she said, "I like to play pool, though. Pool's a great game. Do you like to play pool?"

The Minotaur looked over at the table, which, he was embarrassed to discover, had been stained by many nights of drool, as well as by other secretions. He wasn't quite sure why this embarrassed him, however. Embarrassment had not played a big part in his long life.

"I don't know," he said. And when he saw that the new girl did not fully comprehend his answer, he said, "I've never played."

"Do you want me to teach you?" she asked.

The Minotaur shrugged.

The new girl beat the pants off the Minotaur three times in a row. Even though he didn't particularly seem to mind, she worried that he might get irritated or bored if he kept losing, so she decided to acquaint him with a more advanced level of strategy. She gave him tips about wrist action, momentum, angles of incidence, about which part of the cue ball to hit when, and about the need to care just enough that you noticed you cared, but no more than that. The Minotaur turned out to be a fast learner. On their fifth game, he beat her fair and square.

Against the wall beside the pool table was a half-size refrigerator jammed with beer. "Oh, wow!" the new girl said. She looked at the Minotaur and pulled out a bottle of Rolling Rock. "Want one?"

"Thanks." He took the bottle and held it up a few inches from the end of his nose. His bristling eyebrows buckled in a way that made him seem excessively stupid, like a caveman examining a lightbulb. When he saw the new girl twist the top off her bottle, he did the same, and when she took a sip, he did too. "Oh!" he said, and examined the bottle even more attentively.

"Something wrong?" the new girl asked.

"No," he said. He took another sip, which he kept in his mouth a long time, his eyebrows parting, moving up his forehead, then shooting back down into a collision of uncertainty. When he swallowed, he seemed to be paying acute attention to the fluid's descent along his esophagus and into his belly.

"Haven't you ever had a beer before?" the new girl said.

"Not exactly."

"Not *exactly*?"

"I mean no, I guess."

"Wow!" the new girl said. "You've never shot pool, you've never played computer games, you've never drunk a beer—what have you been doing with your life?"

The Minotaur shrugged. "I don't know," he said. "Wandering mostly."

"Wandering?"

"Yeah." His big lips formed an upside-down U, expressing something between defensiveness and disappointment.

"Just wandering?"

He glanced up at the ceiling and tilted his head noncommittally. "Of course," he said, "I'm always . . . You know: hungry . . . I mean—"

The Minotaur stopped talking.

The new girl didn't say anything either.

After close to a minute of silence, he said, "Sorry."

"Don't worry about it," she said, but didn't meet his eye.

There was another long silence.

"Just so you know," the new girl said, "I'm not actually a virgin. That was just something I . . . I mean, who likes to talk about that kind of stuff with their mother, you know? So I just let her believe whatever she wanted to, and . . . Well, maybe that wasn't such a hot idea. . . . Anyhow, the main thing is, you might not like the way I taste. Too tough or something. You might get indigestion from me."

She laughed nervously.

The Minotaur made a small noise deep in his throat, and looked away. Then he drew the back of his hand across his lips.

Their half-empty bottles stood on the edge of the pool table. They were playing another game. "What's a virgin?" the Minotaur asked.

"*You* know," she insisted.

He didn't.

"Yes you do. They always told us virgins were like . . . you know: like your favorite—" She couldn't say it.

When the Minotaur still seemed confused, she gave him a hint. Then she gave him a bigger hint. Finally she just explained the concept of virginity straight out.

"Huh," he said. And then he said, "I can't see why that would affect the taste." Then he didn't say anything else.

The new girl stood the butt of her cue stick on her big toe, and looked down at the floor. She was shrinking again.

What is the Labyrinth but so much human junk? That's how the Minotaur saw it. Cathedrals, bus stations, diners, bowling alleys, subway tunnels, endless basement corridors—they all seemed profoundly pointless to him, not just because they were generally empty and unused, but as a basic fact of their existence. He could tell that humans didn't share his opinion. He would find them on their knees in the pink and purple pools beneath stained glass windows, their brows dark with grief and desire, their lips rippling with unvoiced words. He would find them looking impatiently at classroom clocks, unable to keep their feet still beneath their desks, or sitting atop vinyl-covered swivel stools, savoring their own tasteless and puny repasts, or intertwined in bed, making all the chest and throat noises of aggression. Idiocy. All of it. None of the things they yearned for would come to pass. All their beliefs about destiny and justice, all their rituals, injunctions, inhibitions and plain-as-the-nose-on-your-face truths: trash, irrelevant, wrong—and always had been. This was shocking news to his victims. He could see it in their eyes. How could they be so stupid?

The new girl asked a human question: "What's your favorite part of the Labyrinth?"

The Minotaur's unequal eyes went still for a moment; then he shrugged.

"Come on!" the new girl said. "You must have a favorite place!"

Here came that embarrassment again, that sweatiness at his hairline, that prickling in his armpits, that heartsurge that was like a form of strangulation. Why was this happening?

"Come on!" the new girl said again. "I know you're thinking of one! I can tell! Don't be shy!"

The new girl's face was like a soap bubble in candlelight. Her voice: like the slow plinking of a music box. Her smell: Every hair on his body stood upright.

The Minotaur turned and lumbered down the tunnel.

Walking behind him, the new girl called out, "Do you want me to follow you?" And when he didn't reply: "Where are you taking me?"

Before all else, the Minotaur was the agent of his own appetite. But, sometimes, in philosophical moods, he would think of himself as a messenger bearing this ultimate truth: You were created to be destroyed. That was it. Simple. And such a shame none of his victims had time to benefit from this insight.

The Minotaur led the new girl down tunnels that seemed to have been gnawed in stone by giant worms: wobbling tunnels, dark, cylindrical; their walls oozing and their ceilings hung with long strands of algal slime that slapped the new girl wetly in the face, and adhered to her cheeks, her neck, her fingertips. There were pipe-filled tunnels so hot the inside of her nose cracked like the bottom of an evaporated lake. Tunnels lined as far as her eye could see with toilet stalls and urinals, many of which had overflowed onto the floor. One tunnel connected a vacant basketball court to a walk-in refrigerator, while another was paved with glossy pink marble and smelled of incense and candle wax. In yet another tunnel, the slapping of her own feet and the Minotaur's echoed and re-echoed so that it seemed as if whole nations of bats were flapping angrily around her head.

The new girl was lost. Within minutes of trotting after the Minotaur, she had realized that she would never be able to find her way back to the room with the pool table, beer and computer games. She would never be able to find her way anywhere. At every turn the geometry of the world was reinvented. Her footsteps were wholly digested by the past.

Whenever the new girl and the Minotaur entered a diner, there were always two cups of steaming coffee waiting on the counter. And nearby, two little stainless steel pitchers of half 'n' half, always brimful and cool, even though there was never anyone else there: no customers, no staff.

"Where is everybody?" the new girl asked, and instantly regretted the question, because she already knew the answer. And when the Minotaur started to speak, she put her finger on his lips and said, "No."

The Minotaur saw the new girl's eyes narrow in a way that he couldn't interpret. Fear? Pride that she alone had been spared? Some variety of awe? He didn't dare ask.

"Haven't you ever tried to escape?" asked the new girl.

"Escape?" said the Minotaur.

"You know, get outside."

"Outside what?"

"This," she said. "The Labyrinth."

The Minotaur was silent for a moment. A dew of sweat materialized on his fingertips.

"How do you know there's someplace to escape to?" he said.

"Because I remember it."

"Tell me one moment you remember."

"Okay," the new girl said.

She looked with the in-turned eyes of memory, but it was like looking into a house with every wall painted black. And all the lights out. And every shutter down. The new girl was puzzled: Why was her brain so blank? She felt her way along the corridors inside her mind. She went in and out of rooms, up and down stairs. Black and black and black and black. Finally she saw a chink of light. She walked toward it, down a long, long corridor, and gradually the chink became a door and the door became a room, and inside the room her mother was sitting in a rocking chair before a white fireplace, and her father and her little brother were lying on a rag rug, playing chess.

She started to tell the Minotaur.

He held up his hand. "Wait a second." He was lumbering again. "Follow me."

He led her left, then right. In total darkness. Up and down stairs. A long, long corridor. Finally they were in a room where there was an oak rocker. And on the seat of the rocker, a needlepoint cushion that the new girl's mother had made herself, portraying a smiling lamb jumping a fence. There was a white fireplace in which hooks of orange light leaped silently from wood to blackened brick. There was a chessboard on a rag rug. The king on her father's side of the chessboard had just fallen over. Its bottom rolled around the pivot of its top, then went over the board's edge and stopped as it hit the rug. The rocking chair was moving too: back and forth, back and forth, as if her mother were still in it.

"Is this what you were talking about?" the Minotaur asked.

The new girl didn't answer. After a while she said, "What happened to my family?"

The Minotaur pretended not to hear her question, then glanced around the room as if he had lost something.

The new girl tried to escape. She ran down tunnel after tunnel. She turned left. She turned right. But every turn was entirely arbitrary. And every tunnel only took her to dozens of other tunnels, some of which went on for miles, and ended in points of light so distant and pale they were like stars in other galaxies. She hid in the back of closets where mothball gas brought tears to her eyes. She hid under cars in subterranean parking lots, her cheek resting in gritty-slick splatterings of motor oil. She buried herself under heaps of orange, yellow, and aquamarine laundry. But no matter where she hid, the tectonic rumble of the Minotaur's footfalls would mount and mount, until finally the door behind which she cowered was wrenched from its hinges, or the wall against which she had pressed herself was reduced to noise, dust, nuggets of mortar, and shattered brick.

"There you are!" the Minotaur would say. He would hold out his anvil-heavy hand, and the new girl would let herself be led away. Maybe he's not so bad, she would tell herself. Maybe everything I've heard is wrong.

But then, in the night: those screams, that weird whistle of tearing flesh. And in the morning, everywhere she went: that fetid stink, those heaps of sucked white femurs, fibulas, tibias, skulls, ribs.

One time the new girl asked the Minotaur, "Why haven't you eaten me?" His answer: "Because I'm not hungry."

The Minotaur was a novice of arc and swell and dip, a new-minted connoisseur of smooth and tender and sway. That little snippet of bird-peep that entered the new girl's voice whenever she got excited, or when she thought something she had done was stupid— he wanted to put that in a box, tie it up with a leather thong, and keep it always around his neck. That way she had of elbowing him in the ribs, rolling her eyes, slapping herself on the top of her head, and saying, "Only joking!"—why did his cobblestone feet always do a shuffling dance when she did that? Why did his shoulders squinch together and his floppy lips twist up at the corners? To his embarrassment was added shame, and the Minotaur found that he could bear his message of ultimate truth only on the sly, when the new girl was asleep, or when she was looking the other way. He took to wearing a kerchief, and giving his lips a hasty wipe after every meal.

Then one day the new girl was gone, and the Minotaur worried that, in a moment of thoughtlessness, he had gobbled her up. When he didn't see her for several weeks, he could think of no other explanation. A year passed, and then a century, and new girl-lessness became a fact—as simple and discrete as other facts. In a way life became easier for the Minotaur, as easy as it had been before the new girl's arrival. But only in a way. In another way, the Minotaur began to wonder if he was getting too old for his job. His vocabulary increased. To "embarrassment" and "shame," he added "joyless." He added "regret." He added "lost."

There were sections of the Labyrinth where the walls were so far apart that if you stood beside one, you could not see the other, and where the ceiling rose so high that wads of illuminated water

12

vapor drifted beneath it, and a ten-thousand-watt sun was dragged across it on nearly invisible tracks. In the middle of such a place the Minotaur constructed a square of rocks a mile across. On top of this square, he constructed another, and then another and another, until what had merely been unlikely geology became four walls, and what had been four walls became a tower. Centuries passed and the tower rose to such heights that to look up at it or down from it was to become dizzy. There were collapses that began like a massive clearing of the throat and ended like a prairie shuddering under the hooves of gigantic cattle. But the Minotaur developed new technologies, perfected his technique, and worked day and night, never pausing even for a moment's rest.

Gradually it became clear that the tower was a pyramid, diminishing at every new level by a space just broad enough to accommodate the Minotaur's feet. And with every new layer of stone, the air got warmer and began to smell, at first something like a laundry hamper, then more like inside the mouth of a sun-baked cadaver. Eventually the Minotaur discovered that the ceiling was not the translucent blue plastic he had always assumed it was, but blue-painted plaster, cracked and warped by age. When his tower was high enough that he could touch his upraised elbow to the ceiling, he went all the way down to the bottom and climbed all the way back up, carrying a long stone roughly the size of his leg. He used this stone to knock a hole through the plaster, lathing, and masonry of the supposed sky, and when the stone rattled off into emptiness on the other side, he reached up into the hole and pulled himself through.

There he was: belly-down in a cinderblock tunnel. But after only a few yards, the tunnel became panelled in wood, and floored with a charcoal gray indoor-outdoor carpet. Not long afterward, he found himself in the pine-paneled room where he had first met the new girl, only the pool table had been gouged repeatedly (the felt was ragged and upstanding, a corona of slate dust spewed from every gash) and the half-size refrigerator was on its side, door open, empty of beer. He left the room and wandered for a long time down a series of corridors so dark he could find his way only by memory.

He saw the face: Blue. That bluebird-wings mustache. Round glasses. Eyes transcendently sad—with the welling sadness of an infant. The sadness of what-have-I-done? The sadness of this-can't-be-true. The blue-faced man was sitting at a desk on which there were two stacks of crinkled, smoothed-out paper that had obviously been rescued from a trash can. In his lap rested a battered leather briefcase from which more papers stuck up like pale, petrified flames. He clutched a single piece of paper in each of his upraised hands.

"Excuse me," the Minotaur said.

The blue-faced man lowered the piece of paper in his right hand onto the left-hand stack, transferred it instantly to the right-hand stack, then lifted it once again into the air.

"Excuse me," the Minotaur repeated.

Only now did the blue-faced man look in his direction.

"I was just wondering," said the Minotaur.

The sadness of I-can't-take-it-anymore. The sadness of what's-the-point?

The Minotaur felt his heart go weak, and his hands.

"I'm sorry," the Minotaur said, and for a long time he couldn't speak, deprived utterly of strength.

"I was wondering," he said at last. "I was wondering if you had seen—"

"Leave me alone," said the blue-faced man.

"I'm sorry," said the Minotaur.

"Please," said the blue-faced man.

Hammers, chains, ice picks, and tire irons. At the intersection of four corridors, a gang of new arrivals made short work of the Minotaur, and left him stretched out on the paving stones, so much hacked meat. When he opened his eyes the new girl was leaning over him, two lines between her eyebrows. "Why didn't you fight back?" she said.

"I don't know," he said.

Then he said, "I didn't want to."

"Hunh," said the new girl. "Weird."

The Minotaur closed his eyes again, and when he opened them, he was alone. Utterly. Where the new girl had been there was nothing but a twist of phosphene, peanut-inflected; a stirring of empty air.

He rolled onto his hands and knees, then stood up. Blood trickled from his fingertips, belly, and chin the way water trickles in a cave. Echoing drips. Minute gurgles. He took one step. Then another.

A day or two later, the new arrivals went after the Minotaur again, but this time everything was different: Crack of skull against skull. Clang of falling weapons. Pleading eyes. Teeth tearing air. Slice, rip, slurp, burp. It was all over before the Minotaur even noticed.

The Minotaur wandered drafty spaces that smelled like a paper mill. All that pounding. So much muck on his feet. Sometimes a yellowish light laminated the wall at a bend in the tunnel, and the Minotaur was sure the new girl was hiding just around the corner. But, as his footfalls shook dust streams from the ceiling, the lamination would dwindle to gossamer cross-hatching, to a golden web, to a few glowing strands, to winking glints, and then, finally, to only the possibility of light. On and on and on. The central aisle of an airliner, the backseat of a car (stale popcorn crammed in cushion cracks), a coal mine, a hospital waiting room, a long tunnel in which a breeze blew hot in one direction, then cold in the other. So many varieties of emptiness. For centuries. Millennia. But, every now and then, just ahead: the patter of footflesh striking wet stone, or the lip and tongue smacks of very small mouths. And so, once again, the Minotaur would start to run. Every time. He couldn't help himself. "Oof!"

Nights, when his eyes were closed, the new girl came to lie within the hollow created by his arms and legs. But always she was silent. Never a word. Her warmth was there. His sinuses were filled with her smell. His memory was able to adhere to her smoothness, to her rough parts, to her every swelling and concavity, but only in a way that was like an ache—or like a hunger trying to feed upon itself.

It was a mystery: Mountains of skulls with stoved-in crania, ulnas protruding from eye sockets, mandibles cradling shinbones, swirling heaps of sucked, yellow ribs, like the nests of enormous birds— the Minotaur could not help but recognize his own, distinctive handiwork. It was everywhere he went, and yet he remembered none of it . . . so much so that he began to wonder if, somehow, he had turned so many corners that he had come, at last, to a part of the Labyrinth that didn't actually exist. Or if, at some intersection, he had accidentally turned right and left simultaneously, and thereafter wandered ever farther from himself. Or if, in some other way—only just beyond the limit of his comprehension—he were not, in fact, the one who had spilled the blood with which his lips and hands were stained.

A train station with breath-grimed marble walls and an arched ceiling portraying the night sky in sapphire tile and bits of gleaming gold. A vast hangar, in which a fully inflated dirigible, gondola doors open, gangplanks lowered to a wooden embarkation deck, hovered, humming, awaiting passengers. A stadium, klieg lights glaring, the playing field radiant, shimmering: like an acre of low green flame; and the surrounding parking lot so enormous that the Minotaur felt sure he was coming again to that place where he had built his tower. On and on. One foot in front of the other. The walls receding to such a degree that they might as well not have been there. The ceiling growing higher and higher, until finally it was obscured by the blueness of empty air. Sounds arrived from great distances. Indecipherable. No echo. On and on and on. The Minotaur lumbered across a rusty bog empurpled with heather. Then sun—all at once. A clean, salty breeze. Golden sand. Dune after dune, rising and falling beneath his feet, then finally falling, falling, falling—all the way to a gray-green-blue vastness, riffled, glinting, and crossed by the cloud shadows as far as the eye could see.

The Minotaur stopped for a moment on that last sandy crest. The wind buffeted his ears. A line of pelicans glided prehistorically just above his head. After that, the sand fell away beneath his lunging feet. He grew smaller and smaller. Every now and then he would vanish, only to reappear on a lower incline of the dune, and then upon another even lower. Until at last—there he was: A tiny figure moving up the shore. A minute silhouette against the mirror sand. A wavering speck. Then smaller. Ever smaller.

White Fire

So the first thing is I get out the gate and there's this big crowd. Mostly it's women and kids. But also there's. I mean. Parents. And signs. And everybody's yelling and everything. And. You know. Welcome back! Our hero! Stuff like that. So I'm looking for Trudy, and it's like there's so many people, and everybody's jumping up and down, screaming. So for a long time I can't see her. Then all of a sudden, there she is. She's. You know. Just like all the rest. Her hands up in the air. Her mouth open. Like this is after some football game, and we're the victorious players coming out the locker room. Like we won the championship and everything. And when I get closer, I see that she's crying. Her cheeks are all shiny with her tears. And. Well, here's the thing. I just hate her when I see that. I just. Well. Hate her.

And she comes running up to me. She doesn't even say anything. Just. You know. Throws her arms around me. And she's squeezing herself up against me. And finally she whispers in my ear, "Oh, Davy, I'm so glad you're home!" So I put down my bag and I wrap my arms around her too. And I'm squeezing her and squeezing her. "Me too," I say. And then I say it again, "Me too." And I think if I just say it enough, it'll start to be true. I'll feel it, I mean. I'll feel it like it's really true. Something in me will just. I guess. Open up. But it doesn't. And I got my arms wrapped around her ribs. And. Even though I already seen how she lost weight and everything. Been running herself ragged, like she said in her e-mails. And she looks good. Practically like she did when we was in geometry class. But all I can think is how she's like this big bundle of. Like organs and everything. Bones and muscles and. Well, meat. That's when I have to let her go. And I'm like, "I love you, Trude. I'm just so—" But the words cut off in my mouth. I just can't say them.

So now we're standing apart and everything. And she wants to hold my hand. So I let her. But at the same time I bend down and pick up my bag, hoping that maybe. You know, she won't notice. But she does, of course. She knows me too well. So then there's like this big kind of silence. And I'm like. You know. I want to tell her I love her. Just say it. 'Cause I can see she's all like, Aw fuck. Like when we're just about to have a fight. And I can see her tears. She's wiping them off her face with the end of her sleeve. I know she isn't crying just because she's happy to see me. I know that she's, you know. That she's fucked up too. That she's been going through her own thing while I was away. That I'm not the only. But the thing is, I just don't care. You know? I mean, I know I should be compassionate and everything. That I should feel her. What she went through too. But I was just. Well, what it really is, is. Well. Shit. You know? Just shit.

So finally I'm like, "Where's the car?" That's all I can say. I mean, I noticed Ashley and Clarry aren't there and everything. But I can't even say, you know, "Where are the girls?" Just, "Where's the car?" And she's got this worried kind of hopeful little bad dog smile on her face. And she's like, "This way," she says. "This way. Over here." And then she reaches up her hand and puts it along my cheek, and she's like, "It's okay, ma-honey." And she's. I mean, she's really trying. And I can see how. Well. We had our problems and all. But I can see how we were right to. You know. Married and everything. Kids. But I don't say anything. Just silent. A rock. I mean, how can a man tell his wife he can't stand the feeling of her hand on his cheek? How's a man gonna say that?

In the car it's better. Mostly I pretend to sleep. That way I can give myself a talking to. You know: This is a whole different situation, man. You're *home*. Ain't nothing can happen to you here. Shit like that. Turn over a new leaf. And after a while. I don't know. Maybe it just starts to seem like it's true. I mean hope and everything. The only thing is Trudy says, "Do you have to do that?" And I'm like, "What?" "Your leg." And that's when I realize I been bouncing my leg up and down like it's the end of a diving board after somebody jumped. So I'm like, "Sorry." And I stop it. But after a while it just starts up again. All by itself. I can't do anything about it. So it's like this really long time and she's not saying anything. And I'm pretending to sleep. And finally she just says it like we been smack in the middle of a conversation. Just, "I don't want to hear about any of it until you're ready to tell me." That's what she says. But I know that what she really wants is for me to start talking right then. You know? Like, "Explain to me what the fuck's the matter with you." So I just don't say anything. Just pretend like I didn't even hear her. Asleep and shit. And then there's this other big long silence. Until finally she's like, "I only want to know why you stopped calling. Not even any e-mails." I just let that set there in the air for a little bit. Then I say, "You just told me you didn't want to hear about it." And that's pretty much it for the rest of the drive. Maybe an hour after that.

Trudy already explained how my parents was there. Picked up the girls from school and everything. Taking care of Jimmy. So I'm like prepared for it and all. But still. You know? I mean, *man!* So, anyhow we're not even in the driveway when the door pops open, and there's little Clarry running down the steps, that white-blond hair of hers flapping around her head like the color of spaghetti. And I don't know what Trudy is. You know: *doing*. 'Cause she just swings around into the driveway and doesn't stop. And there's Clarry running right in front of us. And I'm like, "Trudy!" And she's like, "Sorry! Sorry!" And I'm like, "What the fuck!" And the car's already stopped and everything. You know: The dust we drug up the road is already blowing past us. And Trudy's got her head down on the steering wheel and she's like, "Sorry." But Clarry's just standing there shouting, "Daddy! Daddy!" She don't even know how close she come.

So I get out the car and I say, "Hey there, Clarabelle! You got to watch out, little Ding-Dong!" And, I don't know. Maybe that's the second Clarry figures out what nearly happened. Or maybe it's just. You know. Finally seeing the real me. Too much for her, I mean. Anyhow, she just suddenly gets all quiet. Looking down at her sneakers. And I'm crouching down. Gonna. You know. Take her in my arms, give her a real hello. Then boom! Something hard hits me from the side. All I can see is like this spidery blackness. And I'm like. It's like. You know. I mean it just nearly sets off something inside of me. I almost.

And then I see it's Ashley. And I just let myself be knocked right over. Just fall down flat on the dust and gravel. And Ashley's all, "Daddy! Daddy!" And I'm just lying there looking up at the sky. Thinking. You know. Until finally it's like Ashley's voice gets a little funny. And I see Trudy just standing there looking at me. So I hold up both my arms and say, "Ash-Trash! I fooled you, hunh? I fooled you!" And she throws herself on top of me, just like she rammed me from the side. She's only five, but she's all muscle and bone and wiggle. And her headbone knocks my cheekbone. And I'm like,

"Whoa! Watch it there! Gonna have to call you Ash-*Bash* from now on! You watch what you're doing." So I get up on my knees and I scoop her up. And then I scoop up little Clarry. And I'm like walking toward the front steps. And, you know. That really does feel good. Makes me feel like I'm a real father. I look over at Trudy. And she's just standing there. Still looking at me. And I give her this smile. And she gives me this smile back. And then my parents are all over me. Dad's got this Abraham Lincoln thing going. With the beard. Trudy wrote me about that. And Ma's face. It's just like a plum exploding with its redness. It's just like tears exploding out from her eyes. And she says, "Look, Davy! Look! Little James!" And she holds up this blanket that's all wrapped around this other exploding red thing.

What it looks like to me. I mean, I know he's just having a poop and all. But what it looks like to me is a heart. A human heart. Only it's more like raw muscle, just kind of twitching around itself. You know? And my ma is like, "Look, little Jimmy! Meet your daddy! That's your daddy, little pea!" Then she's holding up the blanket for me to take. And I'm like, "Hold on a second, Ma." And I bump up the two girls I'm already holding. My arms're full and everything. And she's like, "Oh." And I'm like, "Let's go inside."

So I lead the way and there's. I should have known it. But still, it's like this shock. I mean. First there's this big sign going all the way across the living room. It's like all Christmas colors and everything. Every letter cut out of a different piece of red or green paper. My mother must have done it. Not Trude. That's not her. You know. And it's like, WELCOME HOME DADDY. And hanging off of the H and the O in HOME are these two drawings. One's just an orange-and-black scribble. The other's got these blue stick people holding hands. Three have skirts on. And the other one's holding what looks like a broom with a trigger on it. And they're all crammed up into one corner. In the other corner, way down at the bottom. There's like this red stick figure, lying on its side. A big red dot for its mouth. Two little dots for its eyes. And there's this smoke coming up from its mouth. Just like these two letters over and over—WAWAWAWA—going right up to the top of the page. But that's not the shocking thing. The shocking thing is in the middle of the table. There's like all these glasses and silverware on it. Set up for lunch and everything. And then there's this photograph of me in my National Guard uniform. In this shiny brass frame. And on the top it says AMERICAN in these sort of like fat psychedelic letters. And at the bottom it says HERO.

So the first thing I do is put the girls down, pick up the photograph and stick it in the drawer where Trudy keeps the dishtowels. And everybody's like. I mean. You know. But nobody says a word. So then my mother. Her face is like she got this really bad news for me. And she's holding up little Jimmy. And I'm like, "Hold on a second. I'm all dirty. You know? Better go wash up." So then I'm walking out the room and I hear Trudy saying in this soft voice, "Dave's kind of tired. Long flight."

I get to the bathroom. And. I mean, I don't even know what I'm doing there. Don't even have to pee. So I pee anyway. Then I wash my hands. Just. You know. For the hell of it. And that's when I notice how much I changed. I look in the mirror. And. Well, I'm twenty-six. But that dude in the mirror there. He's forty-six. All bones and sunburn and these little lines and everything. Stubble. Sweated off every drop of fat in that 120-degree heat. You know? And that awful food. So I been seeing that face for months, of course. But this is the first time I *really* see it. I mean. Like in my own bathroom mirror and everything. With them same old purple flowers on the wall behind me. This is the first time I see how much I changed. And what I'm thinking is that what I got is the face out of a mug shot. You know how them faces always look a little tilted? Like the bones don't line up exactly. And there's always something off about one of the eyes? That's how my face is looking to me. So I decide, Fuck my hands, I'm gonna take a whole damn shower. And that's a good idea. You know? Like it's a cleansing or something. Finally getting all that sand out of me. Out my ears. Out my hair. Out my asshole even. That sand's not like real sand. It's like this dust. Gets in everything. It's in your spit and your snot, twenty-four seven. So I wash my hair three times. Even rub in some of Trudy's conditioner. Then I use her armpit razor. All my shaving stuff is still. You know. In my bag. In the living room.

So then I get out the shower and I can hear Jimmy's wailing. But not just like normal crying. It's like some kind of cosmic. I don't know. Rage. And then I'm thinking, Oh shit. I bet he's colicky. I bet that's what Ashley's picture is all about. The red baby going WA and everything. Shit, you know. Trudy didn't say anything about that. But shit. Fuck! That's all I need. So then I'm turning around in circles. And finally I just stuff my uniform into the hamper. Thought about burning it. Wanted to burn that motherfucker. But. Well. So now I'm out in the hallway in my bath towel. And Jimmy's still crying. But not. I mean. All the time. It keeps being interrupted by that Three Stooges noise. You know? That *gnargnargnargnar* babies make when they're feeding. So I go into the bedroom and there's all my clothes hanging in the closet, all neat and skinny. Like Trudy sent them to the dry cleaners while I was gone. You know? And my underpants are all folded up in stacks. And my tee shirts. And it's like she did all this work for me. Like she put in all this effort. And I'm thinking I got to thank her for that. I got to remember to thank her. But what I like best about what she did is that they don't seem like my clothes anymore. It's like they're the clothes of a different me. A better me. The me I would have been. If. I mean. So, I put on a pair of black jeans and a black Pantera tee shirt. *Pantera,* man! Home.

By the time I get out there, everything's quiet. And everybody's just sitting at the lunch table. You know, waiting for me. "Jimmy got tired," Ma says. And I'm like, "I know. I heard him." And Trudy's like, "Perfect timing!" She's up by the stove, putting the chicken on people's plates. "He'll be down for at least a couple of hours," she says. "We'll all have time to talk." And she looks at me. But I can't really tell what's on her mind. So, anyway. There's my usual place set for me. At the head of the table. Between my mother and my father. So I sit down. And soon as Trudy sits down, my father. He takes hold of my left hand. And my mother grabs hold of my right. And my father's got. You know. His deacon voice on. And he says, "I think we all need to say a special grace today. 'Cause the Good Lord's seen fit to bring our Davy back to us." And soon as he says that, it's like my head starts pounding. 'Cause I know just what he's going to say. But I don't say anything, 'cause Trudy fires me one of these looks. Like, *Just you hush!* And I figure, you know. She had to make her own kind of peace with these people. With them helping her out and everything. And me being away. So I'm just like, I can sit through this once. Just once. What the fuck does it matter anyway? What the fuck does it matter?

And so, of course, my father says everything I knew he was going to say. Talking 'bout fighting terrorists and everything. Saving the country. And of course he's like, "American Hero" this, "American Hero" that. Even my mother thinks that's. You know. She just does this little thing with her breath. But he keeps at it. The usual God-bombing that he's always doing. In that Abe Lincoln beard of his. And I just keep my mouth shut. Don't say a word. But also I don't say amen when he's finished. And he gives me this. You know. Like this glance. Like he used to do when I was little. The kind that meant, *Just you wait!* And sure enough. Soon as we're all eating, he's like, "I hope you was talking to Jesus when you was over there, Davy." And I just keep chewing on my chicken, even though it's making me sick and I can hardly swallow it. "'Cause you know, that's the time a man needs His guidance most. When the bombs're falling and there's an enemy on every side." My mother hisses, "Henry!" And my father puts on this boogle-eye look that's supposed to be all innocence and everything. Like he's *shocked,* you know. Just *shocked!* But really it's like that's almost his most angriest expression. And he's, "What! What did I say?" And my mother's like, "I just think maybe Davy doesn't want to talk about such things his first day home." And my father's like he's more shocked than ever. "Can't a man even talk about his son's mortal soul? Can't a man talk about things that matter? Davy knows what I'm talking about. He knows how a man can get so confused in the heat of battle that he can't tell what's what and what's not. And how, 'less he asks for Jesus' help, he can carry that confusion home." Trudy sees what's was coming, and she tries to stop it. She's like, "Grampa, there's a time and a place—" But I had enough. I had all I can stand. So I'm like, "The thing is, Dad, you don't know what you're talking about. You don't know one blessed thing about what happened over there. So I think you should just keep your mouth shut and let me eat my chicken." And my dad's working himself up to be shocked all over again, but my mother won't let him. She's like, "Give it a rest, Henry. Give it a rest. We should just all be happy we're together again." My father's mouth opens and closes a couple of times. Finally, he just starts gnawing on his chicken bone and doesn't look at anybody. My ma pats my hand. And I look at Trudy, who's got a headache on her face but seems relieved. Ashley's looking all big-eyed over her chicken leg like she's hiding behind it. And Clarry's waving a thighbone in the air. You know, conducting an orchestra and everything. Trudy grabs her hand and presses it down to the table. "No."

So after a while the girls can't stand it anymore. And Ashley's like, "Can we go outside?" And Trudy's, "Sure, honeybun. You just take care of your sister, okay?" And I sit there a little longer. Trudy and Ma talking about how Tiffany Delgado made so much money last week selling baskets to the neighbors. How her son's, you know. Biggest pothead around. And my father's just chewing on his bone, staring into space. Like he's having this private conversation with Jesus. And Jesus is telling him, "Don't you worry, Henry. They're all going straight to hell. I got it all worked out. Just straight to hell." Finally, I stand up. Bring my plate to the sink. And I'm like, "You know, I think I'm gonna go outside. See how the girls're doing." And Ma is like she thinks that's a great idea. You know: Spend some time with your children. Her head going up and down. And Trudy looks at me with this like, Don't abandon me! But I can see how she's resigned to it. You know: Spend time with the children; that really is what he ought to do. So, I'm, "Don't anybody touch them dishes. Okay? I'll get to them myself when I get back inside." And, of course, my ma makes this kind of click in her nose like that's ridiculous.

Soon as I'm out the door, there's. Well, it's like this big noise cuts off. Like a motor or something. A car alarm. Then suddenly there's just this quiet. It's like the quiet's this *thing* suddenly. You know? And you can appreciate it. Instead of it just being. I don't know. Just another kind of nothing. Also there's the air. It feels like that's the very second I take my first breath of American air. Fresh. Cool. And since as it's about halfway between Thanksgiving and Christmas, the air's not. You know. So hot anymore. And there's this smell of grass. Peat moss. Trudy's planted these four skinny trees at the edge of our property. Put peat moss all around them. I never realized how much I like them smells. And water. You can *feel* the water in the air. Soft on your skin. Comfortable. Not like that sandpaper air. You know? Like the wind out of an oven. Not like that. So I just stand there for a long time. Just. Well. Breathing. And I'm thinking, Maybe this is how it will begin. You know? Me, I mean. I don't know. Normal and shit.

Ashley's like jumping up and down on this itty-bitty trampoline thing she got for her birthday. Trudy told me about that. Like a truck inner tube with this cloth across it. Like a rolled up condom is what it is. And I'm thinking. You know. About this girl there. Another soldier. From Florida. I suppose I got to tell Trudy about her. For a while there things started happening. But. I don't know. That's all over with. That girl got. You know. Fucked up. This guy's brains all inside her mouth. Sniper. Maybe I don't have to. You know. It's all over with. So anyhow. Clarry's just sitting there in the sandbox. Bucket between her knees. Shovel in her hand. But, not doing anything. Just sitting there. Like somebody turned her off. And Ashley's just going up and down, up and down. Ash-Trash. Both of them are looking the other way. So neither of them knows I'm right behind them. Watching. "Hey you two!" I shout, like they're in trouble. And then they're both looking at me. Ashley just turning around slowly, one jump at a time. Sort of like she's one of them spin-around ballerinas on the top of a kid's jewelry box. "You wanna go to the playground?"

Normally we drive over there. But this time I just feel like walking. Of course that means I got to carry Clarry most of the way. Half a mile. Playground's over to the new middle school. Behind the ball fields. Where the old Armitage place used to be. And while we're walking, it's already getting dark, you know. Gray sky. It's not even four. But there's already like this definite change going on inside the clouds. You can feel how there's just a little more darkness in there. And a few minutes later there's like. A little more. Night comes so early this time of year. So, even before we get to the school, I'm thinking this is a mistake, you know. Walking home in the darkness. Cars going so fast and everything. But the girls just love this playground. Swings. They got this whole jungle gym there. Made out of tires and such. Chains. Really, it's like this mountain of tires. All made into tunnels, rooms. Some of them hanging off like swings. One time I spun Ashley around so much on one of them tires she got sick.

So anyway. We get there, and the place is like. Deserted. First thing is the girls run straight over to the regular swings. And I'm, you know. Pushing them both at the same time. Pushing them really high. Like, "Can you touch the sky? See if you can put your feet right up against the sky!" And I never really pushed Clarry this high before. But I'm watching her hands. And I can see she's holding on just fine. She's like three and everything. And she's loving it. Laughing and laughing. But then they had enough of that and they're off to the tire mountain. I sit down on one of the benches there. And I'm wishing I brought along a basketball so I could shoot a few hoops. 'Cause one thing I already know is it's no good when I got nothing to do. Got to keep my mind *occupied*. Just do stuff, you know. All the time. So after a while I hear Ashley calling out, "Daddy! Clarry's going on the top." "So what?" I say. And she's like, "She's not supposed to go on the top." "Don't be such a spoilsport," I say. And she's, "But she's not supposed to." "You're just jealous!" I say. And at that very instant I see Clarry's little blond head stick up from the mountain. You know, like she's this little burp of yellow lava coming out a volcano. "Hey, Clarabelle! Look at you, big girl!" And. I don't know. Maybe she was going to wave at me or something. But soon as she looks up over the edge of that tire, her head disappears. And Ashley starts screaming. "Daddy! She fell! She fell!"

And what really scares me is I can't hear Clarry crying.

I'm up them tires in half a second. And it's, you know, like basic training. I'm ready to dive in one of them holes soon as I know where she is. But I don't see her till I'm right at the top, looking down through the hole she disappeared in. And she's just lying there on her back. Six-eight feet down. Not doing anything. You know. Her eyes all filled up with blue and just staring at me. And she's maybe twitching her hands a little bit. And I'm. You know: Fuck! Shit! It's like for a second I just die there. I go all weak. Can't move. Fuck! Shit! My little baby! And then it's. I mean, boom! Kicks out her foot and starts crying. You know, like she just got the wind knocked out and shit. So then I'm down there hugging her. And I'm all quivery and everything. Way overreacting. Like I'm gonna faint. So Ashley helps me get her out. And then we're all rocking on the bench and I'm saying, "It's okay, little Clarissa-pie! It's okay, my little Ding-Dong." Her little fluffy head right up against my chin. And I don't know. Even though she's a big girl now. Her head's still got. Especially when she's all crying and everything. Hot. It's still got this *baby* smell. That's the most beautiful smell there is in the world. I always loved that smell. But I don't know. This time. Somehow. She's still crying and I say to her, "There, there. Got to stop crying now. Be brave. Got to be brave like a soldier." And that's when it starts.

I don't know why I say it. Sort of like I can't help myself. But I know exactly what I'm saying. So, I'm like, "You know, where I just was, the little kids was soldiers too." That does it. Her tears stop just like that. She's all ears to what I'm saying. Ashley too. I can feel it. So I say, "It's true. They was soldiers. Just like the grown-ups. Only thing is, they was *enemy* soldiers. And sometimes they stepped right in front of your truck. To make you stop. So that their daddies. Or their brothers. Could shoot you. Or blow you up. That's what they wanted. That's why they would stand in front of us. And. So, you wanna know what we did? We just ran them right down. Like they weren't even there. Their mamas too, sometimes. And. Well. We just had to. If we didn't, they'd shoot us. And we would die." I stop talking then. I can't say any more. And it's like the whole world. It's like God takes this big deep breath, and he's holding it. And he's not going to let it out. It's. You know. Like long as he's holding his breath, nothing is going to happen. So then I say, before either of the girls can make a sound, "Ice cream time! Let's all go home and have some chocolate ice cream! You girls haven't even had dessert yet. You all deserve a treat!"

I watch the girls as we walk home. And mostly they're pretty much normal. Maybe a little quieter. I have to carry Clarry most of the way. And she falls asleep on my shoulder. When we get home my parents are just leaving. So there's goodbyes and everything. Then Trudy doesn't want the girls to have ice cream. Says it's too close to dinnertime. But I say I promised. You know: a special treat. Daddy's home. So she gives them both bowls and puts them on the floor in front of the TV. *Pete's Dragon*. Ashley's favorite. Soon as they're settled, Trudy goes to the cabinet over the refrigerator and gets out the china bowl with the rolling papers in it and the weed. "Thank God," she says. "That was a torture." I just shrug my shoulders. "I swear," she says. "For a while there I wanted to hit Grampa over the head with my fork. I'm serious! Wanted to stab him in the cheek." "He's a trip," I say. I don't want any marijuana, so I go to the refrigerator and get myself a beer. Tecate. My first real beer in six months. I sit down at the table opposite Trudy. She lets these jets of smoke out her nose and smiles. "So now you're really home," she says. I raise my bottle. You know: sort of a toast. She reaches across the table and rubs the back of my hand. "You doing okay?" I shrug. "Don't worry about it," she says. "I been talking to Lucile Gordon. I told you about how Pauly's come back? Only one leg? She been telling me what it's like and everything. Said there's this wives group I could join if I want to. You too. They got all kinds of groups for soldiers." She takes another long toke. When she lets it out she says, "We'll get through it." Then there's this sadness on her face. She looks like her mother. Then she smiles. "Come with me!" She takes my hand.

Just before Jimmy was born, my father. He's always been like a handyman. He builds this wall in the girls' room. Right down the middle of the window. You know. So both rooms have light. Air. So, anyway. Jimmy's room is hardly bigger than a closet, really. Just big enough for us to squeeze in next to his crib. And his changing table. Trudy takes a last toke on her joint before going in. Puts it down on the bathroom sink. Then she's like, leaning over the crib. "Look," she says. The room's all. You know. Baby-breathing, diaper cream. So then there's this little guy lying there with his butt up in the air. His cheek's all pressed down against the sheets. And he's got no nose worth mentioning. Know what I mean? So Trudy's like, "That's our son. We *did* that! That's our little boy." Then she points again. "You see that? That's your ear! That's exactly what your ear looks like." And I'm like, "Oh yeah," even though I don't have a clue what my ear looks like from the side.

So then, you know, most of the rest of the evening's not so bad. Normal mostly. Me and Trudy have time for another beer and a joint. Then Jimmy wakes up. And I get to feed him a bottle. I'm holding him. And it's just like when I used to hold the girls. I can do it, you know? What was I so worried about? And then I'm changing his diaper too. Which isn't really like changing the girls, of course. I realize, smack in the middle of it, that this is the first time I'm like. Touching somebody else's dick. Which is. You know. But anyhow, it's just this little pink thing. So then there's dinner. And more TV. And then the whole family's in the bathroom. The girls are having a bath and everything. And I hold Jimmy out over the water. And he's kicking it with his little pudgy feet. And the girls are all laughing and. You know. Loving it. And I'm thinking. Just. I mean I'm thinking. Maybe. Just maybe. You know?

Then finally, the day's over. It's like ten thirty. Me and Trudy are sitting on the couch and she's opening up her shirt. Getting ready to give Jimmy his last feeding and everything. But then Clarry calls out from the bedroom. She's like, "Mommy! Mommy!" And Trudy's like, "Go to sleep! You should have been asleep hours ago!" And Clarry's like, "I can't sleep. Ashley's crying." So Trudy gives me like. This look. And she puts Jimmy in my arms. And she's, "Hold him for a second. I'll be right back." But this time I can't hold him. I mean I can't stand to. I just got this. Like this whole feeling in my body. And I guess he can tell. Or maybe it's just he's hungry. So he starts wriggling around the way babies do. Cranking his head around. Looking for titty. His arms working. You know. All spastic. His legs pedaling back and forth. And he's getting all red again. And I can tell he's just about. You know. So I'm like, "There, there, little Jimbo. There, there, little man. It's gonna be all right. Mommy's coming." But he's not having anything of it. And I don't know what I'm going to do if he starts to scream. Crying and everything. So I stick my pinky in his mouth. And for a while, that's okay. For him, I mean. That satisfies him. But me. I'm starting to get that feeling. I'm shaking all over with it. You know. What I can't stand is how hot the inside of his mouth is. How slippery. Wet. How he's just sucking on my finger.

So, finally I pull it out. And that's when he starts to cry. It's just a little at first. Just cranky. And I'm, "Shhh, shhh." But it's no good.

And then he's wailing. You know. Screaming. And that's it. I just can't stand it anymore. So I get up. And I don't know what I'm going to do. I'm just. You know? Walking around the room. So that's when I see his playpen. And I put him down inside it. And then I go out the back door. I just have to get out. Get some air. Get away. But even outside I can hear the crying. Jimmy in the living room. And now Ashley *and* Clarry in the bedroom. I don't know. Maybe Trudy too. The whole house is just full of noise. So I don't know what to do. And I'm running around in circles. Then finally, I just grab on to one of them skinny trees Trudy planted. And I'm like trying to rip it out of the ground. You know. Then I'm trying to break it off at its roots. But I can't. It's just too strong. Too green. So then I just sit down on that trampoline. My back to the house. And I'm trying to cry. Trying to make the tears come out my eyes. But I can't do that either.

That's where I'm sitting when Trudy calls my name. She calls it again but I don't answer. I don't look around. She goes back inside. Jimmy's still crying. But then he's quiet. And the girls are quiet too. And now I can hear this one cricket doing his deedlydee next door. And in this big old black oak tree at the corner of the yard, a squirrel makes that kissy-laughing noise that I always used to think was a rattlesnake when I was little. And far, far away. Like it's coming from everywhere. Like it's the sound of the whole world. There's this big, quiet. Like roar. From traffic on Route 57. Maybe Route 36 too.

After a while the back door opens again. And I hear Trudy walking toward me. Fast. Like she knows exactly where I am. I don't turn around, but she keeps walking till she's standing right in front of me. "*What did you say to those girls?*" She says that in a whisper, but it's like the sort of whisper that rips out your mouth. At first I don't answer. Then I say, "Nothing." And she's like, "What did you say? They wouldn't make that up! Why did you say that?" "I don't know what you're talking about. I didn't say anything." I was sitting down when I started saying that, but now I'm standing up. And that's when I notice she's carrying Jimmy. You can hear these like. These little cat noises he's making. But I don't know whether he's sucking or just dreaming. It's too dark. All you can see is like these sort of gray clouds. You know: Faces. Shoulders. And then Trudy makes this noise deep in her chest. It's like the closest to a growl that a human being can get. And she says, "David, I'm willing to put up with a lot. I figure it's my duty. As your wife. But I am *not!* Do you hear me? I am *not* going to let you do *anything* to harm my children!" "Shut up!" I say. "Just shut the fuck up! I didn't do anything! I don't know what you're talking about!" *"I will not let you harm my children!"* "Oh, Jesus, Trudy! Jesus Christ!" And then she says it: "It's *true* what they said. That *is* what you did. You *did* do it, didn't you? You *did* it!"

And that's when there's like this explosion of whiteness inside my head. The whole night sky lights up with whiteness. The house. The trees. Everything. Everything burning in white fire. And it's like. You know. I'm not there. Or I am there, but it isn't me. And I don't know what's happening. Or what's going to happen. But I know it's going to be. You know. Very bad.

All in Good Time

◆━◆

They always held the fair down by the water, near the Mobil plant. Pink, yellow and aquamarine confetti trampled in the mud. That hog smell. Root beer coming out of your nose. But this time there was something wrong with the music. No one knew what it was at first.

The banners said, GO SLOW, TAKE TIME TO MEASURE. I guess they were a comfort to some people. My sister's boyfriend got THIS IS EVERY-THING tattooed on his forearm. He said it was because of the comet.

My sister was a Corn Dog Queen. She looked so beautiful in her silver bathing suit, with the pompoms on her boots. But on the way over, she made Dad stop the car so she could vomit into the ditch. "Do you think you can still do it?" he asked. "Do I have any choice?" she said. She did that thing with her lips as she marched, so that she always seemed to be smiling. And she kicked her knees up so high. But the band sounded like it was playing underwater, and you could tell that most of the people watching really wanted to look away. They were trying so hard to be decent. It was killing them.

———

Green apples had lost their whitish dots by then. And rose was the only color in the sunsets. No golds, no oranges. Really it was mostly blue, that blue which is a form of gray.

When William got off the Tilt-A-Whirl his little face was yellow, his lips were white. At first I thought it was nausea, but when I took him into my arms, I could smell that sour nutmeg on his breath, and I knew he had a fever. I put my lips on the back of his neck and it was like kissing a coffee mug. Dad gave me the keys and I brought the little boy home and put him to bed. I called Chuck and said we would have to stay another night. "Do what you've got to do," he said. But I could tell he was hurt. I was so tired of hurting him.

I went down to check on my mother. She was sitting upright in her chair, like she was in an airplane making an emergency landing. Her glasses were on crooked. Her oxygen machine was making its outer-space pings and whooshes, but she'd let the tube fall out of her nose. It was lying on her chest, like one of those Fourth of July necklaces, but with the glow gone out of it. "You know what I've never liked?" she said.

"No, Mom, what?"

"Caviar. Caviar is a cliché. Like pretzels and beer. I hate pretzels. I don't see how anybody can eat pretzels. I don't care much for beer either."

"I kind of like caviar," I said.

"I'm not talking about you!"

She spoke the word "you" with such force, her glasses slipped right off the end of her nose.

"I didn't think you were."

My sister came home after two a.m. It was pouring rain. She was still wearing her silver bathing suit, but she had a raincoat on too.

I saw her in the hall light, and said her name, but she didn't poke her head in my door. A little later I rolled over and lifted the blinds with one finger. People were running, jumping and shouting in the playground. They had no shirts on. Most of them were my sister's friends, I think.

William woke up at five thirty in the morning. He said he was freezing. He said he'd seen a beagle on top of the dresser. He said there was a purple witch in the corner. I popped aspirin into his mouth: one, two, three, four. I rubbed his shuddering body with a cold washcloth. Then I lay beside him on the bed until he went back to sleep.

My sister was at the breakfast table in her silver bathing suit, which had grass stains all over the butt. "I think you should take him to the emergency room," she said. "If he gets like that again, I think you should take him to the emergency room."

"People want so much. They want all those selfish things. They are filled with their hate and their jealousy and their fear, and so they are vile and disgusting. But somehow they still want to be good. They want to be good as much as they want everything else. And they want all those selfish things to stop punching each other in the nose, pulling out each other's hair, and just sit down for once and smile like a family portrait. That's what they want more than anything else, I think—just one single moment of peace."

My mother said all this to no one in particular.

And then she said, "Don't you think that's pathetic?"

When William was lying on the bed in the emergency room, his right leg began to wobble like it was a rolled-up carpet that some-one was shaking from one end. His foot bounced up and down on the paper-covered Naugahyde. "Mommy!" He threw his arms around me as if someone had grabbed on to that foot and was pulling him down a hole. "Mommy!" Then his eyes went veiny-white and his whole body became hard as a plank. His arms no longer clawed at me. They were like tree branches.

"Wise not to want," Chuck said.
"Fuck you!" I said. "William needs you! *I* need you!"
"Oh, God!" Chuck said.
"I need you, babe."
"Oh, God," Chuck said.
Then he told me he'd been on the computer the whole time we were talking and there were no flights.
"Can't you go standby?" I said.
"No. I mean there are no flights."
I didn't say anything.
"They say they're going to close the airport. It was on the news."
"Oh, God," I said.
"He'll be all right," Chuck said.
"Oh, God," I said. "Oh God. Oh God."

They had to tie William's arms down to do the MRI. "Normal," the doctor said. "Everything is completely normal. We don't know what this is."

That sweet dust when the rain starts—gone. That weird electricity thing aluminum does with your fillings—nobody felt that anymore. The air had begun to thin, and stars were becoming visible in the afternoon sky. People had stopped talking about the suicides, but spontaneous sidewalk conversions were increasingly commonplace. Stands were set up. Hymns to God's gentleness dribbled through tinny loudspeakers. And as for that orange light before thunderstorms—over. History. Defunct.

———

I was looking out the window at the conch pink apartment building rising above the treetops. One of the nurses had told me she lived there.

"Mom."

William was sitting up on the edge of his hospital bed, his little body lost in a blue hospital gown, his hair upstanding and pillow-mussed, his eyes wide, eager and clear. I thought he was going to leap from his bed.

"Don't," I said.

"What?" he said.

"You need your rest."

"I want to go home." He slid to the floor and crouched to look under the bed. "Where are my clothes?"

"William, you have to lie down."

He was over by the closet, where I had hung his pants and his shirt on the solitary hanger.

"Please, William."

He gave me that look I remember from breast-feeding, then smiled with such tender sorrow.

He slung his clothes—still on the hanger—over his shoulder and walked toward me, his right index finger through the hanger hook, his shoes dangling from his other hand. I had never seen him walk so confidently—like an athletic young man, a gymnast. He tossed his clothes onto the bed and stroked my arm.

"It's okay, Mom. I'm all better."

I didn't know what to say.

"Really," he said. "There's nothing to worry about."

I called Chuck, but he had already hit the road. Just in case, I tried his cell: No ring. No message. Nothing. I wanted to tell him he could stay home, but when I hung up I was glad I hadn't reached him. He would probably arrive the following afternoon—by dinnertime at the latest. I imagined him, road-weary, worried, shambling up the path, and was surprised at the intensity of my emotion. I would wrap my arms around him. I would squeeze him so hard. I would apologize.

"I hope you can forgive me."

I heard those words in my head.

At last an explanation arrived: The octave now had only seven notes—C was no longer possible. A panel of experts deemed that the new music surpassed the old for beauty and flexibility. When the radio interviewer asked why nobody was dancing at parties, the panel's spokesperson answered confidently: "All in good time." And then he said: "There's nothing to be concerned about." William and I were listening in the car. Not two seconds later we passed WISE NOT TO WANT written in white plastic letters on the black felt notice board outside the Lutheran church on Maple Avenue.

My sister's boyfriend was hurrying out the front door. He seemed so embarrassed to find William and me standing on the porch that he couldn't speak. At first I thought he would go to our left, then to our right. But then he just stopped and held out both hands, palms up.

An instant later he was gone: not a word, not a grunt, not a sigh.

My sister was seated at the kitchen table wearing a man's tee shirt and nothing else. Her head was down, the back of her hand pressed to her brow. Her hair was like a tangle of tree roots, her lips swollen and red.

I touched her shoulder with two fingers. "You okay?"

She lowered her hand and looked over at me as if she had only just realized I was in the room.

I spoke her name. She just shook her head and said, "Whoa!"

Then she looked me in the eye.

"How can this be happening?" she said. "Is it like this for you and Chuck? I just can't get over what it feels like nowadays. You know? Is it like that for you?"

Then she glanced at William.

"Sorry," she said.

The newspapers said the seas would be glassy, and tonight would be our first without the moon. William and I were out in the garden, picking basil for the salad, when Dad shouted out the door, "Mom wants to go see the closing ceremonies! I'm gonna pull the van around the side of the house. Could you help me with her chair?"

Normally the high school band plays in the gazebo and then there are fireworks, but this night the fairgrounds were empty and the only sound was a low murmur down by the water. The whole town was there, stretched out on blankets or sitting on stumpy beach chairs. Some people had coolers. I saw plates of chicken, and sliced watermelon, but nobody was eating, and the only talking I heard was like people muttering against one another's cheeks at the movies. It was impossible to push my mother's chair across the sand, so Dad, my sister and I lifted her chair into the air and baby-stepped it down toward the water. William walked ahead carrying the blankets.

The newspapers were wrong. The water wasn't glassy. There were waves—though it was true they were more like lake than ocean waves. The comet was so much bigger here. It seemed to take up a quarter of the sky. Perhaps a third. This electric blue fist swinging across space, trailed by streamers of pink, yellow and aquamarine. "Will you look at that!" my mother said, when we first put her chair down in the sand. "Oh, my!" she said. "Oh my-oh my-oh my!" When a few people sitting near us glanced around pointedly, Dad put his hand on her arm and she became quiet. None of us said a word.

The Professor of Atheism
Here Comes Another Lesson

———◆◆———

The professor of atheism is in despair. The book by which he had hoped to get tenure has been revealed to him, by his own careful analysis, as a tissue of stretched points, bogus premises, and pretentious posturing, written in prose that is the linguistic equivalent of a mudslide. *Where Madness Lies: The Rise of American Pantheism*. His life's work. Eighteen years in the making. Rejected by forty-seven academic and commercial publishers. And now he knows why. He pours himself another glass of bourbon.

The professor of atheism is being confronted with a moral challenge: Through the soot-shaded window across the airshaft he sees a woman holding a frying pan over her head and a man holding a butcher knife. They are members of an ethnic minority and they are shouting in a language the professor does not understand. The man lunges and the woman falls against the refrigerator. Now she alone is shouting. She has raised the frying pan even higher. No blood, thinks the professor of atheism. Not yet. The professor's name is Charles.

———

Charles has always believed that an atheistic morality is the only true morality because an atheist does good neither in obedience to commandment nor to achieve eternal reward, but only for its own sake. The problem with atheism has always been motivation. It is a moral position conspicuously short on saints. Atheists, as a group, tend to be much more interested in ambiguity than action. And, at this very moment, Charles is wrestling with this tendency in his own nature.

He has won. He is pounding at the door of the apartment down the hall. The one with soot-shaded windows that shares his airshaft. The shouting stops. Charles hears two sets of footsteps approaching the door from the depths of the apartment. The rhythm and timbre of the footsteps suggest to Charles that only one of the four approaching feet is shod. The door opens. The man and the woman are standing side by side, both panting heavily, both wearing tee shirts that are transparent and fragrant with sweat. "Are you okay?" Charles asks the woman. "You can't do that," Charles says, pointing to the knife in the man's hand. "Leave us alone!" says the woman as she brings the frying pan down on Charles's head. She is wearing one golden flip-flop.

The professor of atheism is about to have a vision: He is back at his desk, the eight hundred pages of *Where Madness Lies* stacked in a neat, squat tower. There is a single drop of blood on the title page, just below the last letter of his last name. He is holding six ice cubes in a dishtowel against the top of his head. He remembers hearing shouts as he staggered down the hall. A door slammed. The shouting continued. Now everything is quiet. He wonders if this means he has performed a good act. He looks across the airshaft. There are no lights on behind the soot-shaded windows. No motion, anywhere. And this is when it happens.

The sky is blood and gold. Ranks of silhouetted angels stream across it like bombers in a Technicolor war movie. Row upon row upon row.

Sunset? thinks Charles. How did it get so late? One angel has become lost. He is flying erratically and so much lower than the others. Lower. Still lower. Maybe he is falling. His wings have become entangled in the clothesline on the roof of the building across the street. He is saved. He won't fall any farther. But no, his wings detach. And even though the clothesline is in the middle of the vast roof and the angel is falling straight down, he slips right past the verdigrised cornice as if he were sliding down a photograph of the building, and disappears from sight behind an enormous ginkgo. What exactly happens when an angel falls from the rooftop to the sidewalk? Charles stands on top of his desk and presses his forehead against the window, but still he cannot see.

In the morning the sky is windswept blue, and the apartment across the airshaft is still silent and, apparently, vacant. Tangled in the clothesline of the building across the street is either a pair of crumpled cream-colored comforters or a set of angel wings.

Charles is nearly hit by a car as he crosses the street. He is determined to prove to himself that last night he was hallucinating, and that his imagination has worked its tricks on a pair of comforters. He doesn't know anybody in the building. He rings a dozen bells and shouts "Me!" every time a new voice asks who's there. "Me, me, me, me, me." The door buzzes and, too impatient to wait for the elevator, he runs up seven staircases. By the time he reaches the top floor and the roof staircase, he is panting, his eyes are stinging with sweat. The roof staircase is dark. The walls radiate heat. When he pushes the bar on the roof door, his ears are machine-gunned with sound from the red bell directly overhead. The sound does not quit when he is out in the open air, but it no longer ricochets inside his skull. Comforters! Thank God, they are comforters!

But they are not comforters. They are classic angel's wings: cream-white feathers, soft as mouse fur, almost lighter than air. Charles will never know why he thinks to do this, but he presses the wings, one after the other, to his shoulders, and they stick. Through his shirt. He can fly. He is standing on the roof cornice. And just as his feet lift off the tar, the building's super comes running through the ringing door with a drawn pistol. "What the fuck do you—" He falls to his knees before the vision of Charles hovering eight feet above the naked clothesline. "Jesus-Mary-Joseph!" says the super. He drops the gun, crosses himself and wails, "Lord forgive me!" Charles laughs. The wind from his wings is messing the super's silver hair. How is it, Charles wonders, that I am already such an expert flyer? He circles the super as effortlessly as a buzzard on a thermal draft. Then the roofs of the city begin to race beneath him and the super grows smaller and smaller, until finally he is such a tiny speck that he could just as well cease to exist, and he does.

Somehow Charles has not remembered that he was once married, but there he is, standing on the sidewalk, talking to his ex-wife. He does not remember ever having seen this woman before, but she knows everything about him. She is telling him what a torture it was to be kept awake every night of their marriage by his snores. She is telling him that at all those dinner parties where he regaled the table with funny stories, the guests had only laughed because they pitied him. And when the guests had a moment alone with her in the kitchen or hallway, they would always take hold of her hand and say, "You poor woman! How are you ever going to get away from him?" And then it turns out that his ex-wife is an editor, and when she was sent *Where Madness Lies,* she had found it such a despicably insightless piece of tedium that she set fire to it in her waste basket and then invited strangers from the office corridor to come in and urinate on it. At this point, Charles has had enough. He unfurls his angel's wings and fills the street with wind and light. As he rises into the air, his ex-wife cries, "But you never believed in God!" "I know," he shouts back. "Isn't it amazing!"

Charles flies down city street after city street, his wings stretching from fire escape to fire escape, and everyone who sees him falls to his or her knees in awe or prayer. Traffic stops. The entire city is quiet.

What is he to do with this tremendous power? A classic question. Charles begins patrolling the city from high above, like Superman, looking for a crime in progress: a bank robbery, ideally, but a mugging will do. To his astonishment, given the notoriously high crime rate of the city, not once, after days and days, maybe weeks of such patrolling does he happen upon the scene of a crime. Tabloids glare up at him from every newsstand: CITY GOES TO DOGS . . . WILL THE KILLINGS EVER STOP? . . . "YOU'RE NOT MY DADDY!" SHE CRIED . . . Whenever, drifting past apartment windows, he catches glimpses of the evening news, the screens are awash with blood, the red-illumined faces of viewers deformed by horror and disgust. But everywhere he goes: peace. Everyone he sees: law-abiding. It's a profound mystery.

At last: A cat stuck in a tree! A little girl weeping, "Please come down, kitty! Please come down!" No sooner does he dive in the direction of the tree than the cat leaps into the little girl's arms. But her joyful squeal dies in her throat the instant she catches sight of Charles, hovering overhead with a patronizing smile. "Ghost!" she screams, and runs away. Charles is troubled by this incident for hours and days afterward, not merely out of frustration, but because it makes him wonder if the only reason he has these wings is that he has died.

He is sitting in a wooden chair beside the bed of a sick old woman. His radiance lights the walls and suffuses the old woman's face with a glow that is very like health. She is dying. As soon as he came into the room, the weariness and fear left her withered features. He doesn't quite know what to do, so just sits in the chair, smiling in a way that he hopes is comforting. Soon an answering smile appears on the old woman's face. "Now that I have seen you," she says, "I am no longer afraid of death." "That is good," says Charles, and he means it. "May I ask you a question?" she says. "Of course," says Charles. "Will I be seeing my husband soon?" Charles looks at his watch. It is five p.m. She waits for him to speak, happy expectancy bright in her yellowed eyes. He says nothing. The expectancy fades. "So?" she says. "What?" he asks. "My husband?" "Oh." Charles had been hoping she would forget her question, because it places him in a moral dilemma. He knows what she wants him to say, but he cannot bring himself to utter false consolation. "I don't know," he tells her at last. Her disappointment pains him. "Well," she says, "can you at least tell me if there is an afterlife?" Pushed to the wall, Charles finally decides to stand by his principles. "No one can say for sure," he tells her, "but in my opinion, life after death is utterly impossible and the widespread belief in it pathetic self-delusion." A small noise of pain escapes the sick woman's lips, and her eyes begin to glisten and go orange. "There, there," says Charles, reaching out to take her hand. But no sooner does his fingertip touch her pale and silky palm than a shudder passes through her whole body, her eyes close and a long sigh eases out of her lungs. Charles pulls back his hand in horror. He has never seen someone die before. In the end, however, it is not the blackening of her lips or the startling inertness of her hair that causes him to fling himself out the window, but the almost incomprehensibly awful thought that he might, in fact, have become the Angel of Death.

Somebody whistles. Charles is flying through a run-down section of the city, where rats lounge on garbage can lids and yellow vapors rise from puddles in the gutters and on the sidewalks. "Yo!" somebody calls. A man in a woolen hat, with a short, scruffy beard, is leaning out a window on the fifth floor of what Charles had thought was an abandoned building. "Yeah, you!" says the man. "What?" says Charles. "You're amazing." "Thank you," says Charles. "Do you mind if I paint your portrait?" The man backs away from the window and Charles flies inside. He is in a large room filled with what must be huge canvases, but they are all covered with burlap. The man is already standing at his easel, paintbrush in hand. "This won't take long," he says, and indeed it doesn't. Charles works hard to maintain a suitably angelic pose, but when he looks at the finished canvas, he sees himself lying naked on a bed, wings and legs spread, clutching an enormous red erection in his right hand. "Why did you paint me like that!" he cries. "Because I am an artist," says the man with the scruffy beard, "and you are a cliché." "*That's* a cliché," says Charles as he dives through the window.

CRISIS WORSENS . . . HATERS AMONG US . . . SUICIDE WAVE FEARED . . . Charles decides the only thing to do is to offer his services to the Mayor. He is standing just inside the Mayor's office window. The Mayor is bent over his enormous desk, scribbling furiously on a piece of paper. He is a tiny man, so tiny that were it not for his gleaming, bald head and bushy mustache, he could easily be mistaken for a child. Charles clears his throat. The Mayor looks up. "Yes?" he says. "I've come to offer my assistance," says Charles. "What can you do?" asks the Mayor. "I can fly," Charles offers, but the Mayor shakes his head, "Sorry," and goes back to scribbling. "I can also inspire people." At this, the Mayor stops and sticks his pen, point first, into his mouth. After a moment of cogitation, he hops down from his chair and disappears behind his desk. When at last he emerges on the near side of the desk, Charles notices that his pants cuffs drag on the floor; his sleeves entirely cover his hands. "Inspire?" the Mayor asks. Charles nods. "Okay," says the Mayor. As he leads Charles toward two French doors so tall their tops are lost in echoing darkness, he asks, "You can fly, you said?" "Right," says Charles. "But can you hover?" asks the Mayor. Charles: "Of course." The Mayor: "Good. Do that while I talk. Right over my head." The Mayor flings open the French doors and steps out onto a balcony, beyond which the city plaza is thronged with people, going back for a good half mile. As the tiny man raises his hands over his head, a sound like gravel spilling down a chute echoes off the neoclassical facades of the buildings that surround the square. And when Charles rises above the Mayor's head, and keeps himself aloft and motionless with undulating wafts of his broad and beautiful wings, awe silences every single member of the crowd. "My friends," cries the Mayor, his voice filling the silence like thunder, "I bring you hope and inspiration in this troubled time! As you all know, haters stalk among us, and disbelievers, who would have you question everything we hold to be most holy. But, as you can see from the divine radiance shining down upon my shoulders, our cause is just and our mission the very will of the Lord. Bow down, my beloved people, bow down and praise the merciful Lord who will not rest until he has slaughtered every last one of your enemies!" At first Charles is rather happy with the Mayor's speech, but then it goes so wrong so fast that by the time he has gathered his wits enough to cry out, "Don't listen!" his words are obliterated by the blasting of hundreds of machine guns firing down from the rooftops on the crowd.

The revelations come thick and fast, but every one in the form of a question: What earthly good is this tremendous power? Am I, in fact, any more powerful than a sparrow or hummingbird? Why is it that I never need to eat or sleep? Was my book really so bad that it deserved being urinated upon by strangers? If there is no God, then why do I have these wings?

At last, a robbery in progress! A pocketbook snatching! As Charles hurtles down out of the sky, the thief drops the pocketbook and flees into an alley. Charles is in the alley in less than a quarter of a second, and finds no trace of the culprit. Actually, it is a rather neat alley. Its cinders have been raked very recently. Every speck of litter must have been put into the three pristine galvanized steel garbage cans that stand in a row against the wall. Apart from these shining items, the alley is entirely empty. No doors or windows open onto it. And the fence at its far end—which is not all that far—is so tall that Charles can't even see its top. Most puzzling of all, there are no footprints on the newly raked cinders. None. Charles settles onto the sidewalk just outside the alley. The woman and her pocketbook have both vanished. There is not a single other person on the street or in any of the windows. There are parked cars, but no moving ones. The only sound to be heard in the entire city, it would seem, is the hush of air moving in and out of Charles's lungs, and the faint, sandy whisper of his sneakers on the sidewalk. "Hey, Professor!" Charles turns around to see a very short, very wide man stamping and scraping his feet on the cinders. His blunt, wide head is lowered beneath his mountainous shoulders, and a massive nose ring loops between his snorting nostrils. "Who are you?" asks Charles. "I'm a *real* angel," says the man. "Then where are your wings?" "Don't be stupid! That's just a cliché." Even before these words are out of his mouth, the man has begun running toward Charles, ramming his blunt forehead into Charles's solar plexus and knocking him onto his bewinged back. It is a moment before Charles can catch his breath. He sits up and asks, "What did you do that for?" "To teach you a lesson." "What kind of lesson is that?" "What other kind of lesson is there?" It is a long time before Charles can think of a response to this one. Finally he asks, "Who sent you?" "Who do you think?" "God?" The man laughs. "Satan?" The man laughs even harder. "You know," he says, "you're so pathetic I almost hate to do this." The man slaps his hands together and begins stamping and scuffing again. "Okay," he says, "here comes another lesson!" He lowers his head and charges, but this time Charles manages to dart to one side and grab hold of the man's gigantic head with both of his arms. There is a sickening crack, and the little man falls to the cinders, his head twisted at an impossible angle. Charles hears a voice: "You killed him!" Then another: "Murderer!" Charles turns around. A torch- and shotgun-bearing mob has filled the street outside the alley. A rock strikes Charles on the cheekbone. As his whole head is absorbed by pain he hears, "Let's get him!" and is relieved to feel that the ground is no longer beneath his feet.

ANGEL PSYCHO, reads one headline. WINGED TERROR, reads another. DEATH FROM ABOVE, reads a third. And every single tabloid and news program also features the scruffy artist's portrait of Charles, in colors that are even more lurid than the original. Photocopies of this portrait are plastered on every bus shelter and lamppost and thumbtacked on every post office and public school bulletin board. Thinking that there is security in numbers, Charles spends the day roosting on a cornice with a flock of pigeons. He keeps his wings up over his face and, from time to time, even utters a plaintive coo. He intends to flee the city as soon as darkness falls, but is prevented by a nonstop barrage of green and purple lightning, and a constant downpour that is like a series of oceans falling out of the sky. His feathers are singed by the lightning and his wings nearly wilt beneath the rain. The pigeons, however, hardly seem to notice the weather. They continue with their bobble-headed walking, their flappy mating, their rich, rolling coos, and Charles is moved to marvel at their hardiness and determination. Then, all at once, just before dawn, the clouds are swept away on a chilly breeze and Charles seizes his chance. Soon he is high above the city and circling higher. He loves to embrace the wind with his enormous wings, to dive and bank and circle higher still. And the more altitude he gains, the more he can see of the blue earth, and the more beautiful it seems to him. And gradually, to anyone looking up from the ground, he grows smaller and ever smaller, until finally he is such a tiny dot of light that he could just as well not exist.

He Will Not See Me
Stopping Here

—◆—

The snow began to fall while Allison was driving down Route 26. Just scattered fat flakes, fluttering like moths—but worse was predicted. She knew she ought to have canceled. Several times she had walked back and forth in the kitchen, arguing with herself; several times her hand had hovered over the telephone keypad, but she had hung up every time without calling. She would keep her eye on the weather. If the snow got heavy, she would just leave. The trip took only forty-five minutes. The snow couldn't possibly fall fast enough to keep her from getting home. And maybe the weather reports would be wrong. Maybe this was all the snow that would fall.

Here is the problem: Inside the motor's drone there is another drone. It is a man's voice, talking. I will pretend to love you, but I will not love you. I will not love you. Do you want to know why? The snowflakes rush at your face, then rise. Here is the problem: You lie. And inside your lie is another lie. It is the rabbit's brown eye, watching you over the arrow. You hold the arrow. The arrow is in its neck. You say: This is not my arrow. You lie. You are holding the arrow. So here is the problem: You must eat the rabbit. And you must think about eating the rabbit. Always. So here is the problem: I will not love you. You lie. You cannot lie.

Lisa lived down the block from the restaurant, and was already at a table with an open bottle of wine when Allison arrived. There was only one other customer, an athletic, gray-haired man sitting at the bar. Exposed brick. Dim lightbulbs in globes. Extravagant arrangements of dried flowers and weeds.

"You made it!" Lisa said, standing beside the table. "I called you to cancel. But I guess you'd already left."

"It's not so bad." Allison touched her right cheek to Lisa's. "Just a few flakes."

"It's supposed to be a blizzard. I was sure you were going to cancel."

This was just the kind of thing Lisa always said. Allison hadn't even taken off her coat and already she was furious at Lisa. "I prefer to be an optimist," she said.

"Well, let's keep our eye on the weather," said Lisa, "just in case."

"That's exactly what I was planning to do."

Lisa looked hurt. She had known Allison for sixteen years. She knew everything about Allison—although, it was true, she hadn't seen Allison for months . . . No—for more than a year. "So, what's new?" she said.

Allison put her hand over her glass as Lisa lifted the bottle of wine. "I'm not drinking," she said.

A baby lies under the ice water in the long bathtub. Her body is glistening with Vaseline. Ivy climbs the wall like snakes, like snakes sprouting dark pentagonal leaves. Leaf after leaf after leaf. Like flies. Furious. Flies. When you strip everything down to what cannot be doubted, what's left isn't good for anything. Is it? Flies. Even truth. Flies. And the baby sitting at the bottom of the deep pool moves in slow motion, waving her arms. She sighs. I will be true to you, which is to say I will lie. Lies. I will be true to myself. What else can you do? Look at the veins in your eyes. Cars. The canals on Mars.

"This is very good," said Allison, holding up a forkful of risotto with porcini mushrooms.

"Yeah. The restaurants in this town are just getting better and better."

Lisa took a sip of her wine. Allison took a sip of her ice water.

"So?" said Lisa.

"How's Glenn?" said Allison.

"Oh . . ." Lisa frowned and looked over Allison's head. "You know. Fine. He's getting a lot of gigs in the city."

"Oh?"

"He's down there a couple of days a week, at least. Also, he's started working in a recording studio. So sometimes he's down there for a whole week."

"How's that make you feel?"

"We're thinking of moving back to the city."

"Really?"

"This country life isn't what it's cracked up to be. For us, I mean."

"I love it."

"Well, you've got. I mean, the library. Time to think. For me, it's isolating. I don't give a damn about work. And . . . Like this blizzard. I might be housebound for days, and Glenn's in the city."

"I love it. I love the peace."

Lie down. Take off your clothes. Who told you to take off your clothes? Take off your clothes. The bed is on fire. Lie down because the bed is on fire. Who told you you could get out of bed? Look in the mirror. Do you like what you see? The people who have done this, they are just like you and me. Smell my fingers. Go on, I said. Smell my fingers. Does that smell anything like smoke to you? I'm sorry, but it's true. They did it just the way we do. They love their families. They love their God. They want to do good—don't you? Get out of bed. Who told you you could get out of bed? There's a fire in my bed. So much pain. Go to bed. Unending pain. Go to bed, I said.

Allison had poured herself a glass of wine. "I was at the rally," she said. "And everyone around me was chanting. The pressure was tremendous. I wanted to chant along with them. I really cared about it. I believed everything they were saying. But I couldn't do it. I just couldn't chant along with them."

"Why not?" said Lisa.

"I wouldn't have been chanting because I believed what I was saying but because I wanted to go along with the crowd. That would have been the main reason. The *real* reason. Because I just wanted to do what everybody else was doing. And I couldn't do that."

"But if you believed—"

"That's the point. I didn't know what I believed. I thought I believed what everyone was saying. I *believed* I believed, but I didn't *know*. Maybe it's the same with all my beliefs. Maybe I only believe what I believe because I want to go along with everybody else."

"But all you have to do is think about it. I mean, how could you support this war?"

"It's not just a matter of thinking. Of logic and evidence. Evidence has weight. And arguments have weight. The more weight, the more likely we are to accept them. But that weight doesn't come from the evidence or the arguments alone. Mostly it comes from what we want to believe. Or even what we have been told to believe. So I had beliefs, but I didn't know if I really believed them. If they were what I *should* believe. So that's why I had to be alone."

"What about James?" said Lisa.

"James." Allison looked down at the table and poured herself an inch more wine. "What about James?"

You could have a conscience. Well, that would be nice. I care. I do care. I'll do anything for you. I'll sniff your hair. I'll run you through. This is it: The pink worm in the red meat. This is it: I am glossy with the juices of your body. This is all you see, all you know. This is your body. Down on your knees. On your hands. I am yearning with my hands. It is the sharp itch that twists through. Eat me. I will do anything for you. I want. I want you to. Eat me. Except that. When you make me, when I am only meat before your knife—that's all the peace I know. It's not a crime if no one knows. It's a thought. It . . . Is . . . So . . . Much.

"I never loved James," said Allison. "I only said I loved him because I wanted him to fuck me, and I didn't want him to fuck other women. Also, I wanted to keep him around me, so that I could feel good about myself, and not feel lonely, especially on Friday and Saturday nights."

"*Excuse* me," said Lisa. "You wanted him to fuck you? And not fuck other women? He made you feel good? And when he wasn't around you were lonely? Doesn't that sound a lot like love?"

"It doesn't sound anything like love. Because I didn't give a damn about him, really. I just pretended I did. I listened to hours and hours of his complaints about his job and his family, but only so that he would listen to mine. That was all I cared about. I'll tell you the truth: I was even happy when bad things happened to him, because that way I could feel better about myself. You call that love? I called it love mainly so I wouldn't have to realize what a selfish bitch I really was. And so he wouldn't recognize it either. I wanted to make him feel guilty for feeling exactly the same way about me as I did about him. If that's love, who needs it?"

"I don't know," said Lisa. "I remember a certain dinner when those eyes of yours were all full of sparks 'cause you were telling me about this great guy in your economics class, who was so smart and so cute and you were pretty sure he liked you. And then there was that night when you were sobbing on my living room floor, because he'd dumped you and you thought it was all over."

Lisa was being condescending. Sort of. Had anyone else condescended to Allison like that, she would have been furious. But this was what she liked Lisa for. Lisa always gave her resistance. Lisa always stood up for the other side of the argument, sometimes as a matter of principle, sometimes only for the fun of it. Lisa was fun. And that was why their friendship had lasted so many years—including years in which they wouldn't talk to each other.

Allison had poured herself one more inch of wine. She took a sip. "I never said I didn't want him. I wanted him for all those reasons I said. I wanted him very badly at times. But that's not the same thing as loving."

"All I'm saying is that it was a little more complicated than that."

"And all I'm saying is—" Allison laughed. "Well, I guess I can only speak for myself."

"Uh-oh," said Lisa. Her eyes were turned toward the restaurant window. Snow was swirling so densely it was impossible to make out the buildings on the other side of the narrow street. "Guess we should have kept a better eye on the weather."

Have you found the point of intersection? It is a dance in which one is both partners, and that beautiful number one hears is the music of the spheres played by Good Man and Arm Strong, and it is all chiffon and rose water, isn't it? Did I say bathwater? Don't pay attention to the color. Only you never had to learn because you knew it all along. This step and that. And while everything is coming apart—the tiny pieces of glass, some of them speckled with blood, and that great wind which is the will of God—you have finally become one. You have won. You are in the bath, which is where everything comes together, and no one needs to think, Is this good? This is simultaneous climax. It is rose. It is surrender. Not thought. Surrender. Speckles. Mere atoms. No matter. Come.

Cold. Hard wind. And white. Lisa helped Allison shovel out her car. And then, turning red in the taillights, Lisa stood in the middle of the white street, waving.

"Stay with me," Lisa had said.

"That's okay."

"It's dangerous," she had said. "I've got a nice bottle of wine."

"I'll be fine."

Then Allison had seen that expression come up in Lisa's face, that condescension Lisa liked to pass off as love.

"Really," Allison had said, then touched Lisa's shoulder. "*Really*. . . . Now help me get out of here."

You are yourself, but you are also your mother. And you are sitting at the dinner table with your father. Except it is not really a dinner table; it is a card table, and everything else is darkness. Your father is talking, but you do not know what he is saying. You see your face from the outside, and you are your mother, and you are looking down at your empty plate and you are saying, "I don't understand." But, in fact, you do understand exactly what your father is saying. He wants you to come around the table because he has something to show you. And you are afraid. You are very afraid that if you don't come he will stand up. And you know that if he stands up it will be the same thing as dying, and you are so afraid that you are now in an aviary. And it is filled with red-winged blackbirds. Hundreds of red-winged blackbirds. And they are flying all around your head, from bush to bush, branch to branch, and they are flinging themselves against the net that keeps them from flying off into the sky. Some of them get caught in the net and struggle, but there is no hope. At first you are standing, but now it seems that you are lying and you cannot move and the birds are walking all over your body and one of them walks across your chest and you feel its tiny, needle-toed feet on your neck and then on your chin and then you know he is going to peck your open eyes.

Allison had been driving for two hours and was almost home. Another twenty minutes of grinding over packed snow in second gear and she would just drop into bed. She wouldn't even wash.

As the temperature had fallen, the snowflakes had shrunk to the point that, even to the naked eye, they were clearly ice crystals, glinting in the headlights, striking the windshield with so many tiny clicks that, collectively, they seemed to fizz. Twice she stopped: Once because she saw a deer, just at the edge of her headlights' illumination, standing up to its globular knees in a field of white. An instant of startled attentiveness. Then the deer leaped and was so immediately obscured by falling snow that Allison was not sure it had ever been there. The other time she stopped was when she had felt a sudden slippery emptiness under her wheels and watched as her car veered, of its own volition, toward the ditch. She had had to back down to the bottom of the hill and reclimb it in first gear at a steady three and a half miles per hour.

She traveled at seven miles per hour along the hill's broad flat crest, but decided it would be safer to descend at three. Her toe touched the brake, and she felt that slippery emptiness again. But this time the car was not veering toward a ditch. Rather, the rear end was swinging slowly around to the front, so that for a while she was going sideways down the middle of the road, then backward, then sideways again. Nothing she did with her foot or her hands had any effect. Soon it was the road that was veering right, while the car continued in a straight line toward a grove of tall trees. Allison thought that if the car would only stop rotating while it was facing forward she might just pass between the biggest of the trees, and be safe. But the rotation didn't stop. The car went off the road sideways, and lurched into a ditch with such violence that she was sure she was overturning.

Then the car filled with a Brahms string quartet—very loud.

The car had stopped. The big trees were still many yards away. Safe.

She turned down the radio. The snow fizzed.

The car was parallel to the road, and facing the direction from which she had just come. Her left wheels deep in a ditch, her right wheels out of it, her shoulder leaning against the snow-splattered window.

She turned the radio off and put her foot on the gas. A sound like the engine tearing itself apart. Black mud and leaf fragments shooting across the snow. No motion. Not a twitch. She put the car in reverse, but it was the same.

The door was smack against the bank of the ditch. She clambered across the stick shift and got out on the passenger's side. Standing in the open air, she realized that her entire body was muggy with sweat. Salty droplets were running into her eyes. The cold felt good, and so did the strong wind, even if the snowflakes bit her cheeks.

It was well after midnight, and Allison couldn't make out a single light or any other sign of human habitation. She had passed a farmhouse, about a half mile back, with a light on in one of its upstairs windows. That was probably her best bet. As far as she could remember, there wasn't another house for a mile or more in the direction she had been driving.

She had to get down on all fours to clamber up the embankment to the road.

She had no gloves or hat. Within minutes her fingers were flaming with the cold, even inside her pockets.

The motion is toward the true. You must. And the good. You must get this right. The corruption of everything is in the caring. Is in the idea. Can you be like that glass on the windowsill? Empty and transparent. Can you? Like the winter sun? White with so much darkness inside. You will never get there if you try.

Cats everywhere. Pine paneling. Gnomes on either side of the stone fireplace, and honey brown foam rubber showing beneath the frayed edges of the couch cushions. "Call them back," the old woman was saying. Yellowed pink terrycloth bathrobe. "Wouldn't you rather wait here? Call them back and tell them you'll wait here. It's cold out there. I can make you some tea. They might not come for hours."

"That's okay."

"It's so cold. You were blue when I opened the door. Your teeth were chattering."

"I'll be all right. The engine still runs. I can keep warm and listen to the radio."

"But they might never make it with all this snow. I wouldn't be surprised if they never showed up. Not till morning."

"They will. They will. They said they would. I've troubled you enough. Thank you. Thanks so much."

And a little later she was back on the road, teeth chattering, a wad of slushy snow gathering at the point where her lowered head met the brunt of the wind.

We are making progress here, toward the particulate white, toward the fierce purity of all that lacks intention, what can be praised but never condemned. This is it. Now. You've almost made it.

Bestiary

—◆—

Paul has strong feelings. Strong feelings are the only thing between him and the woman at the next table.

Sometimes Paul wonders if it is wrong to be naked in bed when
he is alone.

That is Paul, on his knees, peering at the large black ant tapping
the floorboards with its antennae.

The woman's name is Bea.

On the day pink electricity cracks down out of green and orange
clouds and the wind has gathered such a great quantity of water
that it is as if a river has chosen to fly sideways through the air—
and trees are falling everywhere—the female snapping turtles
see their chance, lumber to the top of the highest hill, penetrate
the rain-softened earth with their clawed, clubbed feet, turn and
ease themselves down into the mud, where they remain for hours,
droplets slapping their beaks, and release their eggs. One turtle
and then another and then another and then . . .

———

See that? In the window? It's Paul. Watching the turtles. He's barely moving.

Bea has seen a duck-size bird fly under her window, a dollop of red on top of its head, and a very long, very sharp beak. "A pileated woodpecker," says Paul. They are standing in the long corridor. "It must have been a pileated woodpecker. You're lucky. They're very shy. You almost never see them." Bea smiles. "I saw a great blue heron," says Paul.

There is a complication. The woman Paul has nearly married has come to visit. She is a tall woman. And she is wise. The ant is back. Over dinner she tells him how Picasso used to sit in an easy chair, holding a spoon, wanting to fall asleep. And when he did fall asleep, the spoon would drop from his hand, waking him as it clattered to the floor. Immediately, he would get up and paint whatever image was in his mind. The ant is carrying something about half its size. In the candlelight the woman's eyes seem iridescent, like the wings of moths or the necks of birds. And in his room she kneels on the bed, her face down, while he stands behind her, thinking it is very good that they are to be married. Is that the abdomen of another ant the ant is carrying in its pincers? The light is bad. Paul cannot see. But he does see that when he frustrates the ant by putting his finger in its way, the ant rotates its burden and plunges its mouth into it—eating, clearly eating. That can't be another ant's abdomen, thinks Paul. Can it? He is not sure why he is so eager to discover that ants are cannibals.

Paul saves energy by keeping the lights off until he can no longer read.

It is hard to see Bea around his strong feelings. Sometimes he waves to her. He can see her eyes but not her mouth, so he doesn't know what she is thinking. But she always waves back. Her waving hand is like a fish fin flashing into the sunlight, then disappearing beneath the water. It occurs to Paul that she might be shy.

Paul is sitting on the terrace, reading. That is Bea at the bottom of the sloping lawn, looking at the fountain. Her hands are clasped behind her back. From this great distance it looks as if her hands are the head of a pink pushpin on which she is impaled, like a collected butterfly.

As Paul leaves the dining room, he passes Bea coming in. "Hello," he says cheerily. "Hi!" she says. "The food's great tonight," he says, and then he is past her, entering the lonely corridor. I'll go back and pretend I haven't eaten yet, he thinks. But that, of course, is impossible. The corridor is lonely, and very, very long.

There is another complication: "I work at a publicity firm," says Bea. "Most of our clients are airlines. I'm here for the mud baths." "I'm writing a book," says Paul. "That's so exciting," says Bea. "What's it about?" "The coming ice age." "Ice age?" says Bea. "I thought this was global warming." "It is. The earth will warm. The cloud cover will increase. The clouds will reflect sunlight. The earth will cool and a new ice age will begin." "In our lifetime?" asks Bea.

Paul will say, "Hey, I was just thinking, would you like to go into town for a beer?"

Paul will take a mud bath. He will be the only man.

He will run into Bea at the pool, where he has already seen that her belly button is a vertical oval, as if it stretched as she grew. They will be in the water, she leaning against the wall, he standing in front of her. He will move closer. He will say, "I think you are an extraordinarily attractive woman."

The woman Paul has nearly married is a philosophy graduate student, but she earned her way through college by modeling women's underwear in catalogues.

Bea is not, in fact, beautiful. Some people might think her face looks like a knuckle. This means nothing to Paul.

His strong feelings are a hairy beast that keeps him from sleeping. They chase him through his would-be dreams and finally drive him from his bed to urinate mournfully in the dark. This makes no difference. When he is back in bed, everything is the same.

Paul is absolutely certain humanity is doomed. Not fire. Not ice. Garbage. We will bury ourselves in excrement.

It has actually happened: Paul and Bea are walking around the lake. If you look carefully, you can see that she smiles a lot more than he does. He smiles too, but, in between, he looks worried. Her smiles become more and more frequent, but also begin to seem more and more fake. Paul can't help thinking that the leaves on all the trees are made of leather. The lake mirrors the sky in a cloud of green leather leaves. It is immensely quiet.

There is a part of women that Paul loves best. It is the part where belly becomes pelvis becomes thigh. And it is very important to Paul that this part is bordered by pubic lushness. This is not the part that Paul imagines when he is alone in bed. But when he is not alone, it is the part where his hands and eyes most love to graze.

———

"Hey!" Bea cries, "I'm over here!" He can just see her, peeping around the edge of his strong feelings. He runs after her, but she disappears. He runs and he runs, but she is constantly just beyond the edge. "Yoo-hoo!" What is that? Look at that mischievous grin! It is Bea, just behind him. But now she is gone! How can she run so fast! Why are his strong feelings always coming between them? He sees a bare foot, a bare leg. Can it be that Bea is naked? No! She is wearing an olive mackintosh and a plaid beret. "Catch me if you can!" she shouts. And she's gone.

Now the moment has come. Twice, as they circuited the lake, their hands touched. They had each felt as if electricity had jolted through them, but it was a soft electricity, almost cool. Once, their eyes had met. "Sorry," she said. And they had both laughed. But now they are at the very point in the long corridor where they always say goodbye. But they are not saying goodbye. They are talking about mosquitoes and different types of bug spray. Slowly, very slowly, almost imperceptibly, their bodies are moving closer together. The electricity is making the hair on their arms stand up. Even the hair on their heads is growing more radiant and odorous.

So how is it going to happen? Will he finally say, "I think you are an extraordinarily attractive woman"? Will she look up at him, stop talking in the middle of a syllable and moisten her parted lips? Will some practical joker yank the hall rug out from under them and send them toppling into each other like skittle pins?

For some reason, Paul keeps thinking the interior of the ant's abdomen is Styrofoam. But that can't be. It must be mushy, like mashed potatoes. No, there would be membranes, tissue, wet, resistant to the teeth, but not too resistant, like fish, like salty haddock.

———

For a moment, Bea seems shy about letting him undress her. But when she is lying under him, on his bed, she writhes and makes long, low moans, like some sea mammal, beached and in despair. Afterward, she curls up with her forehead touching his chest. "That was wonderful," she murmurs into the hollow between her lips and his solar plexus. But not long afterward, he feels motion and moisture, and realizes she is weeping.

In her last letter, the woman he has nearly married wrote: "We have seen all of this before, but in less elegant terms."

As he lies in the dark, he knows what is wrong, and he asks her. Bea gets out of bed and crouches beside her pocketbook in the middle of the floor. Her pale skin is blue in the moonlight. He hears the click of her pocketbook opening, then the click of her purse. Something black comes out and she holds it upside down over her cupped hand. She rejoins him in bed and shows him the ring. No, there are two rings.

"Turn around," he says. He slides against her back and moves his hand down her belly. "Pretend you are all alone."

In the morning she will not meet his eye. When he comes out of the bathroom, she has already dressed; she would have been gone had he taken a moment longer. And, in fact, he wishes he had taken that extra moment.

Later in the same letter: "A beast acts like a beast and a man acts like a beast: What is the difference?"

But now that he is here, she presses her clothed body up against his naked one. "Thank you," she says, "for not being angry." That wrinkled brow, that bunched-up little face: Yes, she does look like a knuckle, he thinks.

A little later they are both naked on the edge of his bed. Their feet flat on the floor. "I guess we should make some decisions," she says.

And so begins the long shame.

Man in the Moon

—◆—

You stay away from them, Mama said. They don't like you. You've got your big head friends at the school. That's enough. You just stay here.

Mama didn't know anything.

You got a big head, the girl said.

No I don't.

Yes you do. It's gigantic.

No it's not. It's exactly the right size.

Your head is so gigantic, if it wasn't attached to your body it would float away. You better be careful, or somebody's going to tie a string to your head and give it to a little kid to carry.

My head is exactly the right size to be my head.

The girl just squinched up her eye and looked at me. After a while she gave her head a shake like she was so, so sorry. Then she said, Don't you have any brains at all? You got all that head and no brains inside?

That's what they told us at the Big Head School: Your head's exactly the right size to be your head. There's no such thing as a normal head, they said. Don't let anybody tell you different.

They were all big heads at the Big Head school. The only little head there was Alf. And his head was so little it was more like an elbow. Golf-ball little. They made him do all the stupid work. With the toilet brush and the litter stick.

You walked in the door and there was a gigantic sign: THINK BIG.

There were signs everywhere: BE BROAD-MINDED. BIG HEADS ARE MADE FOR BIG IDEAS. THE BIGGER THE HEAD, THE BIGGER THE HEART.

That was the main way you could tell it was a big head school. Everything else was normal. The blackboards. The desks. The trash cans.

That and the doors. They were all coffin-shaped.

Why'd they have to do that? You know? Why couldn't they have made the doors lightbulb-shaped? Or keyhole-shaped? Coffins! You know what I mean? *Coffins!*

Get out! the man from another country shouted. You are scaring my customers!

All I want is a doughnut, I said.

Go away! Nobody wants you!

Please. Just a chocolate twizzler.

You are scaring the children!

The man from another country grabbed a hammer from the box under his counter, and ran around the counter with the hammer in the air. Look what you did to that little boy! the man from another country said.

It is true that little boy started crying when I walked into the store. What would be the point of denying that? And now his face was blue-red and he was screaming into his mother's neck. And she had, in fact, clapped her hand over his eyes so he wouldn't have to see me. But, even so, the person *she* didn't want to see was the man from another country. She didn't want to see what he was going to do with his hammer.

One chocolate twizzler, I said. I'll go if you give me one chocolate twizzler.

I will give you my hammer on your head, said the man from another country. I will give you two seconds and then my hammer is coming down.

One, the man from another country said. Two. Go now, or I will make a hole in your head with my hammer.

Please, I said. Just one.

With a head like that you should never have been born. Why did your mother give you birth?

I put a simoleon on the counter.

The man from another country made a clicking noise to his wife. He pointed with his nose, and she threw a chocolate twizzler out onto the sidewalk.

Go! the man from another country said. Fetch!

Can I touch it? said the girl. Then she said, It's warm! It feels like there's a fire in there. She hit me two times with the point of her knuckle. Is it hollow? She pressed her ear against my temple and she hit me two times again. Huh, she said. I bet I can't even reach my arms around it. I bet it's too big.

She pressed her chest against my forehead and her arms went out on either side.

Wow! said the girl. It's ginormous! Not even halfway!

I didn't want her to move.

Mama called them the ant heads. The ant heads don't like you, she said. They want to put your head in a garbage compactor. If they saw a boulder bouncing down a mountain straight at your head, they wouldn't say, Watch out! They would cheer.

Mama is a little head.

Why did you marry my father? I said.

Because I thought he was the moon drifting through the trees.

Because I thought, There really *is* a man in the moon! I thought, Now *that* is a man who is *going* places! If I am married to the Man in the Moon, I will see everything. My home will be in the sky. I will have stars for earrings, clouds for slippers, and the sun will be my crown!

It's called the hate of love, they told us at the Big Head School. Inside the hate is the love for big heads. Bigger is better, is it not? It is because in the days before before, the little heads used to worship the big heads. They used to drape the big heads in fur and jewelry. They used to spray perfume into the air when the big heads went out for a walk, because they wanted the big heads to always think the world was beautiful. The reason they did this is they thought the big heads could see the future. They believed that the heads of the big heads were so big because they were stuffed with everything that hadn't happened yet. This was all nonsense, of course. It is true that thoughts travel faster in big heads, but they have farther to go. So it all evens out. Eventually the little heads discovered their mistake, and felt betrayed. No more gold and fur and perfume. The big heads felt betrayed too. What? they said. What! Why is this happening? The lesson is: Never worship anything. The lesson is: The love in the hate and the hate in the love. The lesson is: It all evens out. If we are lucky. If we wait long enough.

They don't know anything at the Big Head School.

It was the day after the men with torches and picks came to the Big Head School. We all got sent home for a surprise vacation. Because of all the repairs. The new roof and such.

So, do you want to know what home is to me?

Television twenty-four seven. The smell of those little see-through socks that look like stockings for fat dwarves. Parrot shit. Parrot squawks. Mac and cheese.

Trees and more trees and trees again. Our house was a hiding place in the trees. Nobody knew it was there.

Mac and cheese. Mac and cheese.

Mama would walk a mile to the shop of the man from another country, but she wouldn't go a step farther. All he sold was doughnuts and mac and cheese.

She hadn't been into town since I was born, even though the man she had disgraced herself for had long gone.

Couldn't hold on to him any more than I can hold on to the moon, was what she always said.

So that day she said, Why don't you just stay home? They hate you anyway. Why don't you see your friends from the Big Head School? What did I send you to the Big Head School for if you don't see your big head friends?

Mama didn't know anything.

I didn't have any friends at the Big Head School. The truth is that big heads are not very nice people. That's just a fact.

So that was the day I started wandering through the trees like my father. Up over the mountaintop, down the other side. Nothing but trees and more trees. And I'm not paying attention to where I'm going. Just all brain-scattered and foot-tumbling.

And that's when I saw the girl for the first time. I followed my feet to the edge of the bluff, and there she was, just below, lying on a rock, her head leaning out over a stream.

At first she didn't see me. Maybe it was because of the noise of the water. So I just watched her. She looked to me like she was just about ready to start being a woman, but not quite. So maybe twelve. I was eleven. She was playing with this piece of stick. She'd let it go with her left hand. It would drift downstream and she would catch it with her right hand. Let it go. Catch it. Let it go. Catch it. That's all she was doing.

Then one time she missed it.

I must have air-sucked, because her head jerked up and she was looking at me.

She was a fat face girl. You know? One of those girls who look like a professional boxer. Or her face got stung by a million bees. All swollen-browed and mushroom-nosed and slug lips. No eyes to speak of.

Who are you? she said.

And I guess I said what I said because I saw how the shadow of my head just perfectly covered her whole body, even though she was mostly lying down:

The moon.

No, you're not.

Yes, I am.

Then how come you're dark?

I'm always dark in the daytime. That's why you can't see me.

I can see you now.

You're not supposed to.

She squinched up her eye and I could see she was trying to figure out if she should believe me.

Gotta go, I said. Big night tonight. Need to get some sleep.

See ya later! she said.

So after that I came down to see the girl every day. And sometimes I would see her playing her floating stick game. Or making a dam. Or just taking a nap on that rock. But she would never see me. I stuck leaves all over my head and crouched in the bushes. And I was careful never to suck air or sneeze or fart. Sometimes I would wait and wait and she wouldn't come, so I would go down and play the floating stick game myself, my head reflected like a cloud of cotton candy on the swirly-dimply surface of the water. Once I watched her the whole time she was lying on the rock playing her floating stick game. And I went down to her rock as soon as she was gone, and I put my hand down flat where she had been lying. And I could feel it. The heat from her body coming back up to me from the rock.

———

So then the Big Head School got all fixed up again. And the teachers told us to put our heads in a ring and do a Chinese Whisper of Hope for the little heads. The big head boy on my left said, I hope the little heads go to hell. And I said to the big head boy on my right, I hope they go to the moon.

That year the Big Head School canceled summer vacation. Our surprise vacation was enough, they said. In the school lobby they put up a new gigantic sign: BIG HEADS GET AHEAD.

The girl didn't come out to the stream in the winter. So I didn't see her until more than a year had passed, and we finally had another summer vacation. This time it looked like, ready or not, she'd mostly started being a woman. And I was mostly thirteen.

She still liked to play her floating stick game and make dams. But she also liked to lie on her rock and make big sighs. Sometimes she would make quiet noises that I think were a song. Then it was back to sighing again.

I used to call that being moony. She's moony today, I said.

One day I lay down on the far bank of the stream with my head under a bush. I am one of those lucky big heads with a little-head face right at the bottom of my big head where I am mostly neck. I figured I wouldn't be so scary if she only saw my little-head face first.

Hello! I called out when I heard her sit down on her rock. Who's there?

Foot-splash. Foot-splash. Foot-splash.

Who are you? she said, looking down at me.

Remember me? I said. I'm the moon.

No you're not.

Yes I am.

Why are you lying there?

I'm resting. Big night ahead. But now it's time to rise.

I had planned to say that all along. I thought if she thought my head was the moon rising in the trees maybe she wouldn't be so afraid. Maybe she wouldn't run away.

You got a big head, she said.

No I don't, I said.

Yes you do. It's gigantic.

No it's not. It's exactly the right size.

The day she pressed her chest on my forehead and stretched out her arms came and went. Then there was another day when she said, They say the bigger the head the bigger the you-know-what.

Heart?

No, she said. You know.

I didn't know, so she pointed with her nose.

Oh, I said.

So, is it?

I don't know.

Show me, she said. Then a little later she said, I'll show you mine if you show me yours.

I said I guessed that would be okay.

So that was what we did.

Then she said, I guess that's pretty big. What do you think?

I don't really know, I said.

Neither do I, she said.

So she let her dress fall back down and I pulled up my pants.

Then there was the day I said, Why aren't you afraid of me?

It's because you're the Man in the Moon.

No I'm not, I said. Why doesn't my big head make you cry?

It's because you have little hands.

I do?

You have little baby angel hands. Who could be afraid of those?

Look, she said. She took one of my hands and she touched it to her mushroom nose. See? she said. Your hand's as soft as an angel feather. Then she put my hand on the top of her head. It's like a fly footstep. On her cheek. A mouse whisper, she said. Then for a long time she just held my hand in the air like she didn't know what to do with it. This way and that. Up and down. Then finally she put my hand on her belly.

What is that? I said.

My belly.

No. What does it feel like?

Nothing, she said. That is the exact feeling of something that never happened. And never will. That is the softest feeling in the world.

She smiled.

Why should I be afraid of that? she said.

Then one day: Up over the mountaintop and just foot-in-front-of-foot down into the valley, and there I was at exactly the right stream, under exactly the right bluff, at exactly the floating stick game place, but the rock the girl used to lie on was in three pieces, and all the pieces had been spray-painted. One said, BIG HEADS = BIG BUTTS. The other said: WHY DO BIG HEADS HAVE BIG HEADS? BECAUSE THEY DON'T HAVE ANY ASSHOLES AND THEIR SHIT HAS TO GO SOMEWHERE. And the last one said, WHY ARE YOU ALIVE?

So after that it was television and parrot stink and parrot conversation:

My mother saying, Who loves you, snooky-wooky?

And the parrot saying back, Who loves you, snooky-wooky?

And then the parrot saying to me, Who loves you, snooky-wooky?

So I would lie down in the yard and look up at the stars and wish I could put my head into a garbage compactor myself.

And my mother would say, Don't worry. This vacation can't last forever. Soon you'll be back with your big head friends.

But the welcome-back-to-school letter kept not coming. And just when I was sure it was going to come, it wouldn't come again. Every time.

Then one day: Bang, bang, bang.

I opened the door and it was the president of the Big Head School.

I regret to inform you, he said, that the Big Head School has burned down again and we are too tired to keep on rebuilding it.

Oh, I said.

The good news, he said, is that from this moment on, you are on permanent vacation. Congratulations!

Mac and cheese. Parrot shit. Mac and cheese. Parrot shit. Mac and cheese. Parrot shit.

Then Mama turned blue and fell to the floor in front of the television and there was a sound in her throat like the last little bit of water going down the drain.

Get Doctor Hand, she said. Quick.

She was giving me a beached whale look.

Quick, she said.

So it was up over the mountaintop and then what? I had never gone into town by myself before. I had only gone in the Big Head School school bus. I knew that the girl came from the town, so that meant the town was on the other side of the stream.

Maybe.

Anybody have any better ideas?

The theme music to *Million Simoleon Lunch with Patti Kake* had just come on when my mother fell down on the floor, blue. When I finally walked into town, the light was going powder orange all over the tops of the stores.

You could still hear the crackling of the cinders. Everywhere in the rectangle of black that used to be the Big Head School twists of smoke rose up into the sky like the ropes in swami rope-climbing tricks, only without the swamis. Someone had stuck a sign into the singed lawn that said, GOOD RIDDANCE. Somebody else had dragged out the gigantic sign and changed it: BIG HEADS GET DEAD.

Children were screaming and hiding their faces in their mothers' skirts.

No! said the woman at the Visitors' Information Booth when I asked her, Do you know where I can find Doctor Hand?

Then she slammed down her metal window blind and I could hear her punching telephone buttons.

Sic 'im! said the man walking the big tooth dog when I asked the same question, and slobber from the big tooth dog's mouth splattered all over my leg.

Sic 'm! said the man. Sic 'im!

But the big tooth dog just bent itself into a pretzel going all snarly and snapping-tooth ballistic after its own rat-skinny tail.

The man was a pin eye man, but even he wasn't fooled by the leaves I had stuck everywhere but my little head face.

And then I was lying on the ground.

And the man who had just hit me with his big stone hand was holding his hand in the air like he was going to hit me again. And his friend the big foot man had put his big foot on my chest.

Please! I said. Doctor Hand!

The man with the big stone hand and his big foot friend just laughed.

Please! I said. My mother! Mrs. Moon! She's blue! She might be dying!

It was hard to talk with the big foot man's big foot on my chest.

The two men only laughed louder.

Why are you laughing? I said.

Doctor Hand! said the big stone hand man, wiping tears from

his eyes with his little skin hand. Then he laughed so hard he had to cover his mouth with his big stone hand.

What? I said.

Hand! said the big foot man. Hand! That's his name!

Are you Doctor Hand? I said

The man with the big stone hand couldn't stop laughing.

Are you Doctor Hand? I said.

Now I knew why the girl was a fat face girl. She was the big stone hand man's daughter, and both of her eyes were black, and her nose was squashed flat and her lips were fatter than ever.

Is this the one who did it to you? said the man with the big stone hand.

Anyone who cared to look could tell the girl had a baby coming and that the baby's head would be a big head.

Her voice was so soft the man with the big stone hand made her say it twice. Yes, Daddy, she said. And then again, Yes, Daddy.

Now get out of here before I throw you into the garbage compactor instead of him.

Yes, Daddy.

I knew we'd catch you, the man with the big stone hand said when his daughter had gone. It was just simple mathematics, he said. I knew that if we just kept at it long enough, one of you would turn out to be the one who did it.

Did what? I said.

The man with the big stone hand laughed. Then he said, You just wait right here. When I come back I'll teach you more than you ever learned in that big head school.

Later that night I heard a noise outside the bars of my window. I couldn't move but I could talk. Is that you? I said.

Yes, said the girl.

Are you going to help me escape?

You can't escape, said the girl.

Why are you here, then?

I'm praying.

What are you praying for?

For all the people who should never have been born.

The night I married your father, my mother said, all the tree leaves turned silver as we drifted over, and all the rivers and lakes showed us their silver faces. Chimney pots, too, glinted in our light, and the shingled roofs were triangles and squares of night-white gray. We drifted over mountains, seas, islands. And in almost every field we could spot the moon-glow bodies of at least one pair of lovers. Sometimes they would leave off what they were doing to lie on their backs and watch us cross the sky, and sometimes they were too distracted by one another to pay us any mind.

We drifted and we drifted.

The wind filled my veil and the skirt of my dress, and I discovered that no mattress on earth was as comfortable and soft to lie on as the sky. Stars were floating all around like unblinking fireflies. Your father gave me one for an earring. All the rest were sparkling in my eyes.

Why is everything so beautiful? I asked your father, my mother said.

Because this is the world that you were made for, your father said, and the world that you will live in from now until forever.

And I believed him, she said.

The Professor of Atheism
Paradise

——◆——

Apparently Charles was in Paradise—or so everybody said. The guidebook even identified the tree whereof Eve ate the apple, only it wasn't an apple tree; it wasn't even a fruit tree. The fruit of the Tree of the Knowledge of Good and Evil turned out to be a gigantic nut, shaped exactly like a woman's hindquarters. The problem was you needed a hatchet to open it. The guidebook said it wasn't really worth the effort, but Charles wanted to give it a try.

Charles was on sabbatical, and had come to the island to work on his magnum opus, *The Moral Ruler: Calculating the Virtue of the Great and Powerful*. But the suitcase containing his computer and the manuscript was confiscated at the airport by a customs agent in jungle-camouflage battle fatigues.

"What!" Charles exclaimed as the agent tossed both his carry-on and his regular suitcase onto a rubber conveyor belt.

"Regulations," said the agent. For a long moment he and Charles watched the two bags trundle off to their fate. Then the agent turned to Charles and smiled wearily. "You won't need any of that here," he said.

"What are you talking about!" Charles exclaimed.

A look of perplexity crossed the agent's face.

"You can't do that!" Charles declared.

The agent's perplexity deepened. Then all at once he thumped his own forehead with the heel of his hand. "Right!" he said. "Of course! Here we go again!" He reached into a recess above his desk and slapped a glossy brochure onto the counter in front of Charles. "You signed this, didn't you?"

Charles recognized the brochure from his travel agent's office. The words "Your Passport to Paradise!" were superimposed in yellow script over a photograph of an athletic couple in silhouette against an ocean sunset. The customs agent flipped the brochure open and jabbed his index finger down on the bottom of the last page. "Isn't this your signature?" Indeed it was, complete with the smudged final letters that Charles's pinky had brushed as he lifted his pen.

"I thought that was just an advertising gimmick," he said.

The customs agent shook his head slowly as he refolded the brochure. "Didn't anyone ever tell you to read a contract before you sign it?" He stapled the brochure to Charles's passport and flung them both over his shoulder into a large laundry bin.

"Welcome back!" said the smiling young woman waiting beyond the customs desk.

"That man stole my passport!" Charles told her.

The young woman smirked pertly as she scribbled something on her clipboard. "Here," she said, and handed him one of those "HELLO! My name is . . ." stickers commonly worn at conventions. In the blank space left for his name the woman had written, "Adam."

"What is this?" Charles held out the sticker as if it were contaminated.

The young woman gave him another smile—also pert—and said, "It's the only ID you'll ever need here."

Charles was ready to remonstrate fiercely, but just at that instant he noticed the young woman was extraordinarily beautiful—perhaps the most beautiful woman he had ever seen in his life. Her skin was reddish brown—the color of brick dust—her eyes hazel-gold, her hair as glossy and black as bear's fur, and hanging down well past her waist. Her camouflage shirt had been rolled up and tied with a neat knot directly beneath her breasts, and her pants were slung so low on her hips a sigh could send them sliding to her ankles. "Follow me," she said, and Charles did as he was told.

She led him down a corridor of cream-colored panels, each studded with a nickel-size post-office-box lock. "These are our wishing rooms," the young woman explained. She seemed to be counting the panels as she went and, about two thirds of the way down the corridor, she stopped, smiled, and commenced cheerily, "This one is . . ." Then her fingers rose to her lips and a tremor of distress crossed her beautiful face. "Oh! I'm sorry. I am *so* sorry!" She hurried down the corridor, looking left and right, and Charles wondered if she were about to burst into tears. But after only a few steps, her pert smile returned: "Here it is!" She plunged a tiny key into the little lock, and the door—only a section of acoustic paneling on an aluminum frame—flopped open. "You can hang up your things in here," she said, wiping the corner of one eye with the back of her hand. "When you come out, I'll apply a little lotion to those parts of your body that are not used to the sun. You'll only need it during your first day. The sun here is actually very mild."

"Things?" said Charles.

"There are hangers inside," she said, "and a rack for your shoes."

She pushed him into the phone-booth-size room and closed the door.

"Everything?" Charles called out to her.

"Yup!" she said. "Socks too!"

When at last Charles emerged, his breaths were coming in quivery fragments and he thought he might faint. The young woman pointed at his groin: "Just leave that inside. You won't need it here." She was referring to his wallet, which, together with his HELLO sticker, he was clutching with feigned casualness at the lowest latitude both hands could reach. "Go on!" she said. "Just stick it in your pocket. It'll be perfectly safe." Once he had done as she had instructed, she locked his "wishing room," tucked the key into her breast pocket and pulled a tube of sun lotion out of a holster on her belt.

"You don't have to be embarrassed," she told him as she applied the lotion. "You have returned to the prelapsarian world. The only thing forbidden here is inhibition. You can do anything you want."

"I'm sorry," said Charles. "It's all just a little hard to get used to. I didn't expect any of this."

"Many new arrivals feel that way." The young woman stood up, having finished her work. She pulled a Handi Wipe out of another holster and began to scrub her fingers. "That's why we've opened up a branch of the Eden Lounge just outside the door. You can stop off and have a drink before catching a cab to your hotel."

The door closed behind him and Charles heard the young woman turning the key. In front of him, as promised, was the Eden Lounge, a bamboo and palm-thatch affair, of the sort that was popular in the years just after Hawaii became a state. Like most survivals of that era it was tenanted exclusively by the jaundiced, the red-faced and the barrel-bellied, none of whom were made any more appealing by the fact that they were entirely disrobed. An air conditioner rattled above the door, blowing dust-darkened streamers into the dimness. "New York, New York" was playing on the jukebox.

Charles's first instinct was to flee the bar as fast as he could, but the mere thought of walking out onto the airport sidewalk and hailing a cab made half his face go numb. (His hands were still hovering unnaturally a few inches below his belly button.) Eventually, he took a seat at the least-populated end of the bar and was about to order a white wine, but then suddenly had a yearning for a piña colada.

Charles was not happy to see his glass filled from one of those multichanneled barroom hoses, but, after a sip, he felt he had never tasted a fresher, tastier piña colada, and was instantly delivered to that sad-and-beautiful-life state of drunkenness so prone to poignant revelation. He hadn't taken more than a couple of sips, however, when he heard the sound of buttocks peeling away from a barstool, and looked over to see a portly man of about sixty, with a shaved head and full-arm tattoos, sliding his beer along the bar.

Stopping at the stool right next to Charles, the man said, "Do you mind?"

Charles pursed his lips in a manner meant to signify indifference but that distinctly evoked the image of a constipated rectum.

The man applied his buttocks to the stool, and smelled powerfully of salami. "How's it goin'?" he said.

Charles gave the same pursed-lip expression, this time accompanied by a heavy nod. There was a long silence that Charles finally felt compelled to end by asking, "You?"

"Can't complain." The HELLO sticker affixed to the man's hairy pectoral read "Adam" in what was clearly the young woman's handwriting.

"How long you been here?" Charles asked.

The man released a long, garlic-scented sigh. "Oh . . . Ages."

"How long you planning to stay?"

The man looked Charles in the face for the first time, his brow dented by incredulity. "This is Paradise, man. Who the fuck ever leaves Paradise?"

Charles's cab got stuck in the middle of a street demonstration. Hundreds of people—every last one of them in camouflage battle fatigues—were carrying kelly green flags and posters featuring a photo of a neat, white-haired man whose expression of priestly beneficence had been defaced by a scribbled goatee and devil's horns. As Charles and the cabdriver waited, the crowd chanted, "The people! United! Will never be defeated!" And then: "Hey, hey! Ho, ho! Greed and sloth have got to go!" Eventually these demonstrators were swept out of the intersection by an even larger crowd carrying red flags and pristine photographs of the same white-haired man, and chanting, "Hell, no! We won't fall! Not a second time!"

"What's going on?" Charles asked.

"Bullshit," the driver muttered. "Elections. You know." When it became clear that this had not been sufficiently enlightening, the driver added, "We been, like, this socialist dictatorship here since . . . I don't know: forever. Then six years ago, a bunch of people got Spinelli to agree to elections. The first one was just a sham. But this time people are saying Spinelli might actually get thrown out on his ass. I'm not so sure. I haven't really been following it."

"What are the issues?"

"The usual. Corruption. Incompetence. Spinelli wants to buy another casino in Singapore. It's all bullshit. I mean, what's the point of democracy in Paradise?"

The bellhop didn't seem to mind that Charles had no money with which to tip him, but he did lock the door to the room from the outside when he left. This was when Charles first saw the tourist guidebooks: about forty of them, arrayed in a sort of fan across the coffee table in front of the king-size bed. They were each in a different language, but, as far as Charles could tell, they all had the same title: *Welcome Back! Your Guide to Paradise.* He took the English guidebook out onto his patio, sat down on a bamboo-and-cane chaise longue and did a little belated research on this surprising place he had spent so much money to come to. He had, of course, tried to buy a travel guide before his departure, but his local Barnes and Noble hadn't stocked any to what he had been calling "Paradiso" at the time, so Charles had touched down at the airport with nothing more than his travel agent's enthusiasm to go on.

Amazingly, although his glasses had been confiscated along with his briefcase, he had absolutely no trouble reading the guide, even the footnotes and maps. He was reassured to find out that there were no serpents in Paradise, nor any other poisonous or otherwise dangerous, noxious or inconvenient animals or plants of any description—not even mosquitoes. Yes, there were lions, tigers, rhinoceroses, and polar bears, but these were all as good-natured and companionable as elderly Labradors, and would rush to his aid if they ever sensed he was in trouble. A sidebar entitled "Personal Touch" informed him that he could rename any animal he encountered and that this new name would become the one by which the animal would be known for all perpetuity unless he himself changed it. It was in another sidebar that he found out the fruit of the Tree of the Knowledge of Good and Evil still grew in Paradise, but that for "obvious reasons" it was both no longer forbidden and "of no interest to anyone but paleobotanists."

The patio of his hotel room opened onto an immaculate, dew-fresh lawn, shaded by massive mango and apple trees, that descended gently to the edge of what can only be described as a primeval forest. Soon Charles was walking amid vegetation of such gigantic proportions and fecund profusion that he felt as if he had shrunk to the size of an ant—not that the going was ever laborious. It seemed that, in whatever direction he took a fancy to travel, there was always a clear path of springy moss or talcum-smooth sand heading exactly that way. Never once did he step on a pebble or thorn or stub his toes against roots. Every now and then a mist of rain would drift amid the lofty branches and enormous leaves, but it was never anything but refreshing, and never lasted longer than a minute. The returning sun would dry Charles within seconds, but was no hotter on his bare flesh than a lover's caress, even when he was walking across an open field or along a beach. Utterly unfamiliar birds in various combinations of turquoise, school-bus orange and birthday-cake green flitted constantly from branch to branch or darted across the open sky, and as he encountered each new variety, he gave it a name: ghost robin, squigilum, happyflap, Terpsichore crow. When he startled a pair of gorillas snacking on each other's lice by the side of the trail, he proclaimed, "Henceforth your species shall be known as Gladys." A leaping trout he deemed "carburetor," and he designated a piebald hedgehog "squintypuff."

After two or three hours of such contented astonishment, Charles realized he was hungry and, at that very instant, walked into a grassy clearing where a waiter in a camouflage tuxedo with a white towel across his arm stood beside a small, round table resplendent with antique silverware and crystal. As Charles approached, the waiter pulled back the chair and said, "And what would you like this afternoon, sir?"

Charles took his seat. "What do you have?"

"Anything you want."

"*Any*thing?"

"Anything."

Charles grinned. "Okay . . . I'd like a Persian truffle salad garnished with lime-and-coconut-oil-marinated hearts of palm, harvested exclusively from the palms on the beach at Ipanema. I'd like that followed by a moist grilled Rocky Mountain carburetor, seasoned with Tuscan thyme, garlic, and oregano on a bed of butter-glossed spinach sprouts from my mother's garden at Sixty-four Potter Avenue in Glenwood, New Jersey."

"Very well, sir," said the waiter, and within a matter of minutes began to bring out the meal exactly as it had been ordered. While Charles couldn't be sure of the provenance of most of the ingredients, there was no mistaking the delicate piquancy of his mother's spinach sprouts. Everything was done to perfection, the trout so flavorful and moist that he nearly swooned at the first bite. And all of it was washed down with a 1995 Louis Roederer Cristal champagne—the waiter's recommendation—that, like the piña colada, instantly delivered Charles to a sublimely philosophical state of inebriation.

The field in which Charles's table had been placed looked out over a bluff toward the sea, where three humpy islands made purple silhouettes against the setting sun. "What are those?" he asked the waiter, who had just brought him a quivering mango-and-sour-cherry blancmange. "They aren't on the map in my guidebook."

"What?" asked the waiter.

"Those islands?"

The waiter glanced in the direction Charles was pointing, shrugged, and said, "Haven't a clue. I never noticed them before."

Charles lingered over his dessert and a snifter of brandy until well after dark, and would not have been able to find his way back to his hotel room were the correct paths not illuminated by strands of successively blinking lights like those on the floors of crash-landed airplanes.

A hot, rose-scented bubble bath awaited him in the tub. The towels were so thick and soft he could have slept on them. The toothpaste seemed to have been made of lime and coconut liqueur. No sooner did he place his cheek on the eiderdown pillow of his king-size bed than he was as solidly asleep as a newborn, and did not stir until he was roused by crystalline sunlight and the liquid twitters of birds.

Charles rolled onto his back and stretched, groaning with contentment. Only once this exercise had been satisfactorily completed did it occur to him that the edge of his left foot had brushed something solid, smooth, warm, and decidedly unlike his bedclothes. Sitting up, he found a woman sleeping peacefully beside him. The HELLO sticker affixed to the flesh just above her left breast read "Eve."

"Holy shit!" said Charles, instinctively withdrawing to the far edge of the mattress.

A shadow of discontent darkened the woman's brow. Then her eyes fluttered stroboscopically, opened, and fixed on Charles's. In an instant, she had flown from the bed and was crouched behind a wicker rocking chair. "Who are you!" she cried. "What are you doing in my room!"

The woman appeared to be about fifty—a few years older than Charles—and was of Rubensian proportions, with limp, shoulder-length, obviously dyed auburn hair. Even as she peered at him, horrified, over the wicker chair back, Charles felt there was something familiar about her, but he couldn't think of where he had seen her before.

"I was about to ask you the same questions," he said at last.

"What are you talking about?" she said.

"All I know is that when I went to sleep last night, I was alone. And now you're here."

The woman's name was Eve. "No, it *really is* Eve," she said. "Eve is my *real* name." Charles told her his own real name, then peeled the HELLO sticker off his chest. She did the same with hers. It seemed that her plane had arrived late last night and that she had spent rather a long time—she didn't know how long—waiting for her husband at the Eden Lounge. With their three children finally all in college or graduated, Eve and her husband were taking their first extended vacation alone together in twenty-five years. ("We've had a very happy marriage," she informed Charles.) When she had become concerned by her husband's failure to join her at the Eden Lounge, the bartender had handed her a phone and suggested she call the hotel. "The desk clerk knew who I was before I said a word," she explained. "He told me that my husband had checked in hours ago and was waiting for me in our room. So, naturally, when I came in last night and noticed there was a man asleep in the bed, I assumed it was my husband."

"Naturally," said Charles.

"I was very tired and the lights were off."

By this point in their conversation, Charles and Eve were having breakfast at a marble table on the patio, her meal consisting of a croissant and a grapefruit, his of sausages, eggs, and toast. They shared a pot of coffee.

"I suppose that as soon as we are done here I ought to call up the front desk and find out where my real room is."

"Good idea," said Charles.

And that was the last word either of them ever said on the matter.

Eventually their conversation got around to their hometowns, and it turned out they not only lived in the same city, but on adjoining blocks. "I thought you looked familiar!" exclaimed Charles.

"Me too!" she said. "As soon as I saw you, I was sure I had met you someplace before."

They both laughed, and all at once Charles knew exactly where he had seen this woman: Not only did they live on adjoining blocks, but her building was the one directly behind his. One night, Charles had been gazing idly out his kitchen window and had seen Eve, exactly as naked as she was now, come up to a window in her own apartment and tug the curtains shut. For months afterward he had hoped to catch sight of her again, both in her window and on the street, but she had seemed to vanish off the face of the earth . . . And now, here she was, right across the table!

"How weird!" he said, and made no other reference to what he had remembered.

Eve also seemed to be savoring a memory, but only said, "Amazing!"

When Charles showed Eve the picture of the fruit of the Tree of the Knowledge of Good and Evil, she laughed and said it looked just exactly like the tip of a penis. "No it doesn't!" he said.

"Yes it does!" She lifted his penis so that he could see for himself.

Charles wasn't convinced, but didn't argue.

Although Eve wasn't especially interested in tasting the formerly forbidden fruit—"It doesn't sound like it's worth it"—she was more than happy to join Charles in his quest for the Tree of the Knowledge of Good and Evil (oddly, the guidebook said nothing about its location). So they spent the day clambering in the mountains, moving from rain forest to pine forest, to birch grove, to tundra, emerging regularly onto promontories with utterly stunning and absolutely distinct views: now of a tree-carpeted valley, now of an aquamarine ocean, festooned with whale spume, now of a red desert, lifeless as the surface of Mars, stretching out to the smudged horizon. Whenever they were thirsty, there was always a waiter standing by the side of the trail with two glasses on a tray and a dripping pitcher of ice water in his gloved hand. Whenever they were tired there was always a hammock for them to lie in. And any snack they wanted—from grapes to "sour cream 'n' dill" potato chips—could be plucked off the end of a branch.

When at last the sun began to set, they found that they had made their way back down to the beach, where a table draped in a blue-and-yellow Provençal cloth, and set with Queen Anne silver, Waterford crystal, and Yuan dynasty china, awaited them.

After the waiter had opened their second bottle of Margaux,

Charles wrinkled his brow philosophically and said to Eve, "Do you mind if I ask a personal question?"

"Not at all."

"When that young woman met you after the customs agent—"

"It was a young man. Agent Raphael!" Eve's eyes lifted dreamily; she ran the tip of her tongue along her lip.

"Oh," said Charles. "Yes. Of course." He smiled. "Anyway, did he tell you anything was forbidden here?"

"Inhibitions!"

"Right. That's just what my agent said to me." Charles took a quick swallow of his wine. "Now, here's the personal question: When Agent Raphael said you were forbidden to have inhibitions, what was the first thing you imagined yourself doing?"

Eve opened her mouth but didn't speak. Her face seemed to grow even more deeply crimson than it had already been in the red-and-gold illumination of the never-ending sunset.

"If it will help, I can tell you what I thought of," Charles offered. He didn't wait for her response. "I saw myself in bed with three nubile and extremely enthusiastic young women."

Eve's mouth was still hanging open. Even her eyes hadn't budged since Charles had asked his question.

"I hope that doesn't embarrass you," he said.

"Of course not!" She laughed and raised her glass to him.

"So what about you?" He clinked her glass with his own.

"Adultery."

"Adultery! Perfect! So, here's the thing: All day long, from the first instant we set eyes on each other to this very minute, we have been . . . Well, let's just say we're in a situation where it would be very easy for you to commit adultery." A small, faintly perplexed smile appeared on Eve's lips, but she said nothing. "So now what I want to know is, have you given a single thought to actually doing it?"

"Well—" Once again Eve's mouth hung open wordlessly.

"You don't have to worry about hurting my feelings. I'm sure I already know your answer."

"Well then: No, not a thought."

"Same with me. You're a fine-looking woman but . . . If you'll excuse me: *Not a thought.* I mean it's like I just forgot there was even the possibility. You know? And, as for nubile young women— you're the only woman I have seen since I said goodbye to that girl at the airport. So where *is* everybody? I mean: It's like you and I really are the only two people on earth—apart from all these wait- ers in their camouflage tuxedoes. And why is it that when we're in a situation where we could easily satisfy our raunchiest desires, we don't seem to have any that couldn't be satisfied in a PG movie?"

"You're right," she said. "That's really weird."

"Maybe they've been putting something in our food."

"Or maybe it's . . . You know: Now that we're back here. Maybe it's that we've become . . . *innocent.*"

"How could you have run out?" Charles asked the waiter.

"I'm afraid it's not something we generally keep in stock."

"You can get me spinach sprouts from my mother's garden in New Jersey, but when I ask for the fruit of the Tree of the Knowl- edge of Good and Evil for dessert, you don't have any in stock? That's crazy."

"Perhaps you underestimate the repute of your mother's veg- etable garden."

"But this fruit grows right here on the island. That's what this place is famous for! And you can't get me even one?"

"I'm sorry."

"All right. Forget about it. Just bring me my mother's world- famous rhubarb pie."

The waiter returned minutes later with a slice of pie and two forks. Charles and Eve each took a taste. Charles said, "So what do you think of this?"

"Delicious!" Eve cut herself another forkful.

Charles threw his fork down on the table. "This completely proves my point! My mother hates rhubarb! She's never made a rhubarb pie in her life, and she would never let even one solitary shoot of rhubarb disgrace her garden!"

The next day, Charles and Eve went back into the mountains and, after several hours of arduous hiking, found themselves wandering a sort of terrain utterly unmentioned in the guidebook. Here all the leaves were black or blood sausage purple; many were barbed, and some of the grasses along the trail were as sharp as razor wire. Slate gray clouds hung low overhead and white flurry-flakes swirled between the branches of the trees. Eve, who had several bleeding paper-cut-like slices on her ankles and calves, wanted to turn around, but Charles was determined to find the Tree of the Knowledge of Good and Evil, and was certain this was just exactly the sort of place where it would grow. He pushed through the hostile vegetation, never even glancing back to see if Eve was following.

After a couple more hours they came to the edge of a cinder plain where nothing grew at all. Not far into the plain, some twenty men in camouflage fatigues stood in a row, squinting through the sights of raised AK-47s. Directly opposite these men was a shorter row of perhaps eight other men, also in camouflage fatigues, but with blindfolds over their eyes and their hands tied behind their backs. To one side, midway between the two rows, stood the white-haired man whose photograph had been carried by both groups of demonstrators: Spinelli.

He was holding a riding crop held high over his head.

Nobody moved.

And, still, nobody moved.

Everyone was waiting.

Charles and Eve never saw the riding crop jerk toward the

ground. And the sound of the guns was lost in the thunder of their own feet, the blasting of their lungs, the rattle and hiss of the lethal foliage.

They hadn't been running more than a few seconds, however, before the air warmed to a perfect eighty-two degrees Fahrenheit and the vegetation once again became thoroughly benign and conventionally green. Not long afterward, they came to a valley where a waterfall plummeted hundreds of yards in long, slowly shifting plumes to a clear pool, from which Charles and Eve drank deeply, and in which they washed away not merely their blood, but the wounds from which the blood had seeped. When they emerged from the far side of the pool, a waiter was standing next to a table set with a Tuscan-spiced carburetor (or trout), and a bowl of fettuccini with clam sauce, which happened to be the meals Charles and Eve, respectively, had most been craving. Once they had taken their seats and begun to eat, each without a word to or glance at the other, the waiter brought them tropical cocktails of unusual potency.

"There's something terribly wrong here," Charles said.

The waiter seemed momentarily disconcerted, but when he finally spoke, it was with smug self-assurance. "I am very sorry, sir. Is there anything I can do?"

As this was the very waiter who had lied about the rhubarb pie, Charles saw no reason to hold back. "We've just seen eight people executed by a firing squad. Not twenty minutes ago. In the cinder plain on the other side of this woods."

The waiter's disconcertment returned. He said nothing.

"Spinelli was there," Charles continued. "He was the one who gave the command to fire."

At the mention of Spinelli, the waiter's jaw dropped, and a dull "oh" escaped his lips.

"How could this happen?" said Charles. "Here of all places?"

"Doubters," said the waiter. "Didn't believe in Paradise."

"What do you mean?

Charles received no answer because, at the very instant the question left his lips, a flower of gore appeared in the temple of the waiter. He dropped heavily to the grass and disappeared into the bushes, as if reeled in by a fishing rod.

"Would you care for dessert?" asked his replacement.

Charles had to pin the new waiter's arms to the ground and Eve had to sit on his chest before he would finally admit, in a terse whisper, that the execution had taken place. When his interrogators expressed their outrage, the waiter said, "This is Paradise, for Christ's sake! For the first time since Creation, human beings can live in perfect contentment. Are we just going to piss that all away?"

"Perfect contentment?" shouted Charles. "Dead bodies?"

"Casinos?" shouted Eve.

The new waiter hissed: "You think anything gets done in this world without a little compromise? Get real!"

"There are no firing squads in Paradise," said Charles.

"That's academic bullshit!" said the waiter. "This place used to be hell on earth: Elephantiasis! Rampant immorality! Now look at it. Don't you think that's worth a little sacrifice, even if the sacrifice is not always voluntary?"

A gunshot sounded, but no flower of gore opened in the waiter's temple.

Spinelli himself stood not ten yards away, arm raised straight over his head, a smoking pistol in his hand.

The customs agent from the airport was striding toward Charles and Eve, clutching their passports in one hand and a pistol in the other. "I'm afraid you're going to have to come with me," he said. "These documents are forgeries."

As he spoke, perhaps a hundred AK-47-bearing soldiers in camouflage fatigues emerged from the vegetation, the bare-bellied young woman with the pert smile among them.

Leaves burst into fragments and bullets gashed tree trunks, ricocheting with warped pings.

Somehow Charles and Eve managed to make it down to the beach, where they found an idling motorboat anchored just beyond the breakers. "Hurry!" shouted Eve as she waded into the foam, but Charles was running toward a huge, slender-trunked palm that leaned right out over the water, a gigantic lobed nut hanging just below its disheveled fronds. At the very instant Charles drew up beside the tree, the nut fell, disrupting the waves with a craterlike splash.

Watching the nut after it had bobbed to the surface, Charles had to admit that it looked remarkably like the tip of a penis. But once he was actually holding it in his arms, it was incontrovertibly a woman's pelvis.

———◆———

Spinelli and the new waiter were roasting hot dogs in a campfire on the beach. "Why can't some people leave well enough alone?" said the waiter.

Spinelli pulled his stick out of the flames. The skin of his hot dog, glossy with oil, had only just begun to pucker. Not quite ready. Back into the fire.

"It's always the comfortable ones," said the waiter. "They never know how good they've got it."

Once more Spinelli examined his hot dog. Now its skin was puckered all over, crispy-black in a couple of places.

"They're going to ruin it for everybody," said the waiter.

"Don't worry," said Spinelli. "It's all part of the plan." The hot dog steamed as he drew it toward his lips.

He took a bite.

"Perfect!"

———— ◆— ————

"I think they just wanted to get us off the island," said Eve.

"Maybe," said Charles.

"What do we do now?"

Charles pointed at the largest of the humpy islands that had once been empurpled in the sunset. "Well, I guess we should start by heading over there and reporting Spinelli."

Just at that moment the outboard motor spluttered and fell silent. Eve tugged several times on the starter cord; so did Charles.

There was no spare tank of gas on the boat. No oars. No sail. No compass. No shelter from the sun, which was anything but mild now that they were away from the island. No bottles of water. Nothing but:

Charles.

Eve.

A gigantic nut.

A hatchet.

Charles and Eve took turns clinging to the back of the boat and kicking in the water, but none of their efforts kept them from drifting out into the open sea. Paradise had vanished completely from view. Even the largest of the humpy islands was now hard to distinguish from clouds on the horizon. Charles and Eve were so thirsty and exhausted that schools of transparent pollywogs were swimming around their heads.

————————

Despite the heave and fall of the waves, Charles was able to split the nut exactly in two with the first blow of the hatchet. Rushing to keep any precious coconut-like milk from spilling, he scooped up the two halves and gave one to Eve.

It turned out that there was no milk to spill. The center of the nut was soft, granular, white. Charles scooped some out and put it into his mouth.

His lips twisted and his brow became gnarled. "Sand!" He spat over the gunwale. "It tastes exactly like sand!" He spat some more and wiped the coarse grains off his lips.

"What else did you expect?" said Eve. "The book said it wasn't very interesting."

"No," said Charles. "That's not how it is. It's really *disgusting!*"

Eve looked down at her feet. Charles did too, and then at his own feet, which were resting in a rapidly rising puddle of water. At first he thought his prayers had been answered. But then he saw the spurt of water over the wedge-shaped hole that, apparently, his hatchet had made in the hull of the boat.

Eve stamped her foot over the hole, but the water continued to rise.

"I don't think that's going to work," said Charles.

"What else can we do?"

Charles didn't know. Looking toward the horizon, he saw a towering bank of slate gray clouds moving rapidly in their direction. A flurry-flake settled on his right shoulder.

Love

◆

Three days before Christmas, Alice's college housemate fell over dead of a cerebral hemorrhage while cross-country skiing. At the memorial service, on a frigid Saturday in early January, ten people, Alice among them, crowded the dais of a Unitarian church near Boston to speak to a gathering that the tall-windowed, fog gray room made seem pathetically small. Alice told the story of an afternoon during college, when she and the housemate—Katinka—had polished off a thermos of margaritas in a sunny field, then lay on their backs, talking and looking up at the sky, only half-noticing as a cow moseyed over to them, followed by another and, somewhat later, by a third. It wasn't until the sky began to darken, and they had gotten unsteadily to their feet, that they discovered themselves surrounded by some score of cows, who were standing shoulder-to-shoulder, emitting bovine grunts, and watching them with enormous eyes. "Katinka just walked right up to one of those cows," Alice explained, "and rapped it twice with her knuckle in the middle of its forehead. 'Excuse me, madam,' she said, and the cow promptly backed away so that we might walk past. She was fearless, dear Katinka, which is one of the reasons it is so hard to believe she is not with us now."

Next to speak was a lean, broad-shouldered young man with

Slavic cheekbones and wiry black hair that curled crookedly off the top of his head like smoke from a smoldering fire. Alice had not lived in the same city as her old friend for several years, and so did not immediately recognize this young man as Ian, the longest-lasting of Katinka's numerous boyfriends—her "great love," many people said, although she had never been terribly faithful to him, and had finally left him for her married thesis adviser. Ian spoke with wit, tenderness, and eloquence, building toward an evocation of a single instant one blustery evening in Providence, when, without knowing it, he was looking into Katinka's eyes for the last time. "For that infinitesimally small particle of duration," he concluded, "there was no such thing as death, only the two of us on a street corner, shivering, smiling, saying goodbye."

As Ian returned to his seat beside Alice, she knew that, should she even glance in his direction, she would start to cry. Nevertheless, throughout the rest of the ceremony, she remained alert to every shifting of his hands and legs, and to his every caught breath and sigh.

At the reception, glass of wine in hand, Alice went over to Ian. "Oh!" he exclaimed, on hearing her name. "I've always wanted to meet you!"

"Me too," said Alice. She blushed and corrected herself: "I mean, meet you"—although, in fact, Katinka had almost never spoken to her about him.

Alice told Ian that his speech was the only one that had made her cry. Then she asked, "Are you a poet?"

"God no!" He laughed. "I'm a total sellout!" He wrote copy for an advertising company, he explained, but he loved Czeslaw Milosz, and his speech had been partially cribbed from of one of Milosz's poems.

When Ian asked what Alice did, she said she was a waitress, then added that she had been working on her PhD thesis for six years.

"What's it about?" he asked.

She touched her lips with her fingertips, as if at a terrifying thought. "Oh, please! I don't even want to talk about it!"

Ian went to the bar and came back with two refilled glasses. A little later, he and Alice were sitting side by side on folding chairs, eating bruschetta and stuffed tomatoes from paper plates balanced on their knees.

Alice was small, thin-wristed and nearly hipless. She cut her wavy brown hair herself, and it always looked a tangle, even when, as now, she had swept it up in the back, Victorian-style. Her lips were full and so deeply red she never needed lipstick. Her eyes were huge and heron blue. They flitted delightedly over Ian's lean cheeks, aquiline nose, and muscular, expressive mouth, but always fell to her plate when he looked in her direction.

Neither she nor Ian spoke to anyone else the whole evening. When it turned out that they both lived in Brooklyn, he asked, "Do you want a ride? I've got a car."

"That would be lovely," Alice said.

They arrived at her apartment in Greenpoint shortly after one in the morning. She invited him up for coffee and, except for a mid-afternoon brunch, he didn't leave her apartment for thirty-one hours—which is to say, until seven thirty Monday morning, when he had to go to work.

In the weeks that followed, Alice told her friends, "This is it! Ian's the one!" He seemed to feel the same way about her, and she moved permanently into his apartment in Williamsburg four months later.

Her first night in the apartment they got into a fight about who should have the top drawer of the dresser, but after that they settled so smoothly into a domestic routine that Alice sometimes found it hard to believe that this new life of hers was real, that she and Ian weren't just kids pretending to be grown-ups.

With his trim suits, Italian shoes, and six-figure salary, Ian did, in fact, manage a credible impersonation of an adult, whereas Alice, with her thrift shop wardrobe and perpetually depleted bank account, felt stuck in grad student mode. She was particularly humiliated that she couldn't even come close to paying her half of Ian's rent. He would happily have paid the whole rent on his own—which, after all, was what he had been doing before she moved in—but Alice insisted on contributing the same amount that she had paid in Greenpoint, where rents were lower and she'd had two apartmentmates.

"That sounds reasonable," Ian said, the night they reached this agreement. They were at the dinner table, meal over; Alice had cooked. Ian smiled and kissed the top of her head.

For reasons that she didn't fully understand, she wanted to push his face away as he did this. Instead she stood up and carried her plate toward the kitchen. "Help me with the dishes," she said.

It's my damn dissertation! Alice told herself during many a grim four a.m. reckoning. It's killing me! It's destroying the best relationship I've ever had. On several occasions shortly after she moved in with Ian, she dragged her dissertation drafts and notes into her computer's tiny wastebasket, and let her mouse hover over the command "Empty Trash"—but every time she would drag them out again and restore them to their original folders.

The woman who had struggled years over that dissertation was so much more knowledgeable, compassionate, and wise than the waifish waitress in her black miniskirt, or the compulsive smiler who hardly breathed a word at the dinner parties she was taken to by her brilliant boyfriend. That woman, Alice believed, was her real, true self—or, at least, the self she would become, if only she could finish the dissertation.

One night she went into the living room, where Ian was doing his e-mail, sat down beside him on the couch and announced, "I've got something to say." She had been rehearsing this speech for days, and leaped straight into it before she lost her nerve. "I'm quitting my job and moving up to my father's cabin for the summer."

Ian's handsome face alternated between bafflement and hurt. He and Alice had lived together only a month and a half at that point.

"I have to finish my dissertation," she continued. "It's driving me crazy. It's quiet up there. There are no interruptions. I'll be able to concentrate."

"But what about Cape May?" Ian asked—referring to his father and stepmother's offer of their beach house for his two-week vacation.

"I know," Alice said, as if forgoing the Jersey shore caused her real pain (which, in fact, it did, she assured herself). "It's just that I'm turning thirty, and I've got to get this dissertation done so that I can start leading my real life."

The pinch of tension between Ian's eyebrows eased somewhat at the words "real life," for he believed that what Alice meant was not merely getting an academic job—or any other careerlike job—but also having children.

Alice and Ian had not talked specifically about having children together; their relationship was far too new for that. But one of the things that had set them smiling so happily into their mimosas that first brunch after Katinka's memorial service was the discovery that they both loved kids. Ever since, they had been in the habit of voicing a soppy "Aw!" and grinning at each other every time they saw anyone under two and a half feet tall.

"Well, you know," Ian said, twitching his hands helplessly and attempting a smile. "If you feel you have to do that, then that's what you have to do."

The cabin was a ten-minute hike off an old logging road, halfway up a mountain. It had two rooms, electricity, running water (but only cold) and an outhouse. Up until his heart attack a year and a half earlier, Alice's father had used the cabin primarily as an escape from married life. For a couple of weeks every summer and most weekends during the fall, he and two or three friends would load up their cars with beer, and spend their days stalking the woods around the cabin in camouflage overalls, or fishing off an aluminum skiff on the small lake just downhill.

Alice had been to the cabin only a few times as a little girl, but on each occasion she had felt she was living in a child's paradise. She and her two younger sisters would spend whole days building teepees in the woods out of sticks and bedsheets, or playing mermaids down by the lake. Their parents gave them halfhearted warnings, but never actually supervised their play, and hardly seemed to remember they existed, at least as long as they were home for dinner.

What Alice most loved was to explore the woods entirely on her own, sometimes for hours at a time. Never once on any of her expeditions did she encounter another person, neither child nor adult, and so it had been natural for her to feel that every tree, rock, or stream she passed, every vista she looked out over not only existed—in some secret but essential way—for her enjoyment, but, actually, shared in her enjoyment. When she was happy, how could the trees and lake not also be happy? And how was it possible that the mountains did not exult in their own magnificence?

Unfortunately, Alice's mother enjoyed nothing about the cabin, except, perhaps, its extravagant view of the forested slopes and granite peak of Mount Quiddagunk, but that only when her appreciation had been enhanced by sips from the vodka and orange juice she would prepare herself every morning, or from the martinis that her husband would mix for her every evening. She never went for hikes, never fished or swam. All she ever did in the afternoon was nap, mouth open, snoring. "This place gives me the willies," she used to say—and absolutely refused to take family vacations at the cabin after Alice turned ten.

Ian was supposed come up to the cabin every weekend, but canceled his first visit at the last minute because an important client from Korea was making an unexpected trip to New York, and the whole firm had to work late into the night Saturday and Sunday, to get a presentation ready.

Alice was disappointed, but not crushed. She had been missing Ian, especially at night, but, at the same time, her dissertation had been coming along far better than she had ever dared to imagine, and she had worried about how Ian's visit might affect her momentum and confidence. In the end, she hardly gave a thought to his absence, and her work continued to go well, if somewhat more slowly, over the weekend and throughout the ensuing week.

When Ian finally did arrive, just before sunset the following Friday, Alice had a bottle of wine and two glasses waiting on the round picnic table on the deck. She and Ian shared the bottle, watching Quiddagunk go orange and rose, then devoted the whole rest of the night to sex—not eating until two in the morning, when they snacked in bed on apples and peanut butter.

The following afternoon they dragged Alice's father's fishing skiff out from under the deck and carried it down the steep wooded path to the lake. The skiff had a bench at either end, and a large space between for fishing tackle and coolers of beer. It also had two sets of oars, and oarlocks bow and stern, but Alice and Ian decided to share one set, and sat side by side on the rear bench.

Somewhere near the middle of the lake, an affectionate kiss led to other more serious kisses, then some intraswimsuit groping, which ended with Alice lying flat on her back in the skiff's puddly middle, her bikini bottom off in some corner. But when Ian hoisted himself up onto his left elbow so that he might wriggle out of his own swimsuit, the shifting of his weight caused the skiff to lurch up on its right side, which, in turn, caused him to fall against the left gunwale, and Alice to roll on top of him. After a brief interval of thumps, shouts, and metallic clamor, Alice and Ian found themselves surrounded by murky green and strings of silvery bubbles. Rising to the surface at the same instant, they spotted the skiff floating crookedly, upside down, and both started to laugh.

"Way to go, Romeo!" said Alice, aiming a splash at Ian's head.

"Hey!" protested Ian. "You never told me the boat had an ejection seat!"

They circled each other, splashing and laughing, and every now and then came together for a kiss. Alice still wore her bikini top and tee shirt, but had nothing on below, a state of affairs that had decided advantages for each of them—although Alice did hope her bikini bottom hadn't been lost forever; she'd brought only one swimsuit to the cabin.

Ian was telling a story about getting bumped overboard while white-water rafting, when Alice noticed that the gunwale on the more up-tilted side of the skiff was less than an inch underwater. The slightest of waves—it seemed to her—could lift the gunwale high enough above the surface that the air pocket beneath would gasp free, and the whole boat would roll over and drift to the bottom of the lake.

"Oh my God!" she called out. "The skiff's about to sink!"

Ian looked at the boat, then back at her, his lips and brow screwed up in mock incredulity. "No it's not!"

"It might," she said. "What if the air pocket escapes?"

"That wouldn't make any difference."

"Why not?"

"It just wouldn't."

"How do you know?"

"Because that's the way these things are built. They're unsinkable. They've got these blocks of Styrofoam at either end."

It was true that there was a sealed triangular space at the bow that might have contained a block of Styrofoam, but the stern was entirely open. At best there may have been some Styrofoam under the rear seat, but not nearly enough to keep the skiff afloat.

As Alice mentally debated whether to voice her doubts, Ian said, "Let's flip it over."

"The boat?"

"Yeah. Flip it over. Like a canoe. Back when I was in Boy Scouts, we went on this camping trip and they taught us how to flip an overturned canoe. You have to stretch across the bottom and grab the far side. Something like that."

None of this made sense to Alice. Even if Ian could somehow perform the gravity-defying feat of yanking the far side of the skiff into the air, the near side would only scoop up water as it rolled around underneath—which, at the very least, would swamp the boat.

"I don't know," she said unhappily.

"We can do it!" Ian pulled himself over to the cockeyed craft in two strong strokes. "Come on! It'll work if we both do it."

"I don't know," Alice repeated. "Maybe we should just swim it to shore."

Ian wasn't listening. With a swoop of his arms and a powerful dolphin kick, he flung himself across the bottom of the boat and managed to grab the far side, but only with one hand. "Help me!" he shouted. "You do it too!"

Alice watched in alarm as the near side of the skiff was forced deep below the surface by Ian's weight. In the next instant, he shouted "Shit!" and flopped backward. She ducked underwater to escape being hit by him, and, when she rose to the surface, saw the skiff floating exactly as crookedly as before, and not an inch deeper.

"We have to do this together!" Ian said. He flung himself once again across the bottom of the boat, the muscles on his back and ribs rippling though his sopping tee shirt. Unable to grasp the far gunwale this time, he slipped right back into the water, and, yet again, the skiff bobbed into its cockeyed float.

Alice joined in Ian's next several attempts. She was an excellent swimmer, but far smaller than he, and not remotely as strong. The best she could manage was to get her chest onto the near half of the skiff bottom and to claw at the far half with her fingertips. One time Ian grabbed her by her armpit and thigh and shoved her up onto the overturned boat, but the entire purpose of that exercise seemed to have been to expose her bare butt so that he could give her a not entirely pain-free spanking.

She slipped back into the water and pinched his cheek. "We're not getting anywhere."

"You're right," he said.

In the end they had to do what Alice had suggested at the start: swim the skiff the hundred or so yards back to the shore. At first, Ian swam ahead, pulling the boat's dock line, while Alice put her hands against the stern and kicked. But soon they discovered that even a little forward motion caused the skiff's down-sloping bow to cut deep beneath the surface, so they turned the boat around and swam it stern-first—which was only marginally easier.

The second Alice was able to put her feet down on the mucky bottom she leaned her temple against the skiff's dented hull and panted in sobs, worried that she might have seriously strained her heart. Ian was also panting, but only as if he had climbed a flight of stairs. He waited patiently while Alice regained her breath.

They walked the overturned boat toward the dock until the water was shin deep. Then, each taking an end, they grunted, lifted the boat into the air and heaved it over. It flopped onto its belly with a reverberant bang, then skidded sideways like ice in a frying pan, a scrim of peat-peppered water sloshing back and forth under the seats.

No bikini bottom.

"Shit," muttered Alice. And, just at that instant, Ian cried, "Fuck!"

"What's the matter?" she asked.

"The oars!"

Alice looked into the skiff. Both sets were gone, even the pair they had never bothered to extract from under the seats.

This was even worse than losing part of her bathing suit. She could always swim in jogging shorts, but the skiff was useless without oars, and she had no idea where to find new ones.

As she and Ian peered off across the water toward where the boat had overturned, Alice noticed something moving in the high grass at the far end of the lake's western shore. As she squinted, what had seemed a tall, weathered tree stump suddenly morphed into a stocky, gray-haired man, half crouched and looking right at her.

"Christ!" She grabbed Ian by the upper arms and pulled herself around behind him.

"What!" Ian tried to turn so that he could see her face.

"No!" She gripped his arms fiercely, and kept him in front of her. "There's a fucking pervert over there."

"Hunh?"

"This fucking asshole, staring at me."

"Where?"

"Right over there!" She pointed, but by the time Ian looked, the man was gone.

"I don't see anyone."

"He was right there. He ran off into the woods. I saw him."

Ian looked again, then turned toward Alice with an expression halfway between skepticism and bemusement.

"This is so disgusting!" she said. "Fucking perverts in the woods!"

Increasingly bemused, Ian pulled his tee shirt over the top of his head. "Here."

Alice wrapped the shirt around her waist and tied the sleeves at her hip. The shirt hung down below her knees, but still, most of one leg was exposed, and the drenched material clung to her pelvis and thigh like paint.

"Let's get out of here," she said.

They hauled the skiff out of the water and turned it over in high grass. Then, arms around each other's waist, they headed back in the direction of the house. The trail passed through a small grassy floodplain and up a low bluff before entering the woods. At the top of the bluff, Alice stopped and took one final look toward where the man had been standing.

"I don't see anything," said Ian.

"He was there. I saw him clearly. This potbellied old man—in chinos, a white tee shirt, with long gray hair combed straight back off his head." She didn't want to leave Ian the faintest room for doubt. "Disgusting," she concluded.

Ian laughed. "I don't see what's so disgusting!"

"You wouldn't!" She punched his rippling stomach.

"He's out taking a walk, sees this gorgeous, bare-assed naiad standing on the shore of a lake—who wouldn't stop and stare?"

"He's a pervert."

"It's not his fault you're so beautiful!" Ian smiled and patted her butt.

"No!" She yanked his hand back up to her waist. "That's the last thing on earth I feel like right now."

That night they ate on the deck, ringing the table with citronella candles to keep the mosquitoes away. As the light faded, bats appeared, weaving jerky figure eights in the gloaming. Gradually, the sky beyond Quiddagunk turned luminous teal, then navy blue, while the mountain itself became a looming velvet black silhouette. White points of light appeared above its peak, and soon the sky filled with so many stars that Alice became dizzy and had to look away.

Ian was telling her about his mother's grief when his father, a dentist, took up with his twenty-four-year-old hygienist. "Everything I had taken for granted about my mother was just gone. You tell her a joke, and she'd just look at you like you were a Martian. One time I made her a birthday cake, but she wouldn't blow out the candles. She just sat there staring at it, like she didn't know what it was. I had to blow the candles out myself. That just really scared me—like my mother had been kidnapped and then replaced by this weird woman I didn't know. I was just eleven years old, but I felt like from then on it was my job to be happy for her, keep her going, always show her the bright side. And . . . Well . . . It took me a long time to realize this wasn't something I could actually do."

Ian smiled at Alice, but his eyes were sad. She could see the individual candle flames flickering in them, and the wavering glow against his lean cheek and muscular neck. "Oh, babe," she said softly, kissing him.

He moaned and let his hand fall onto her bare thigh, just below the hem of her skirt.

"You're beautiful," he said.

"So are you." She laughed. It was a perfect moment—one of those moments she hoped never to forget.

She told him about her own parents, who seemed to have been kept together only by their shared love of television and alcohol. It had not been uncommon in her household for whole dinners to go by without her parents saying a single word to each other. "But after dinner," she said, "once they got drunk enough, that's when the insults would start to fly. My mother especially. The things she used to say to my father! She was always telling him—right in front of me!—about how guys would be flirting with her—the fathers of my friends!—and how she was too good for him. She'd mock him for the stains inside his underpants. And for like . . . *sex!* I mean totally disgusting, intimate stuff! I used to go upstairs and put my fingers in my ears. But the truth is I don't believe anybody ever flirted with her—this dumpy old lady drunk!" Alice laughed. "I remember one night she was holding her drink in her left hand, so I said to her—'cause I saw that her watch was on her left wrist—I said, 'Mom, what time is it?' She turns her wrist over to look at her watch, and dumps her whole drink into her lap. That was so *mean* of me! She's jumping all around the room, going, 'Oh! Oh! Oh!' and I couldn't stop laughing. I know that was mean, but . . . The thing is, I really hated my mother. For most of my childhood. Just hated her. I don't know how my father could stand her. Somehow he took it. It was like he could reach up inside his brain and turn off the part that noticed her. That's why he drank so much. And he'd just watch whatever was on television. Baseball especially. He was a maniac Yankee fan. He wore his baseball hat everywhere. In the shower, I bet. Probably even in bed."

Alice laughed again, but not really at what she was saying. The whole time she had been talking, Ian had been idly stroking the inside of her thigh, and ever so slowly moving his fingers up to ever more sensitive elevations. She had been pretending not to notice, just as he had been pretending to be doing nothing in particular. But then, just as she started to talk about her father's baseball fanaticism, Ian's fingers reached a place where they could no longer be ignored, so she laughed, leaned forward and, smiling, spoke in a low voice: "You are *very* naughty."

Ian leaned forward too, his mouth so close to hers, she could feel his breath. But, just as their lips were about to touch, there was a crash in the woods.

Alice turned her head to listen: breaking twigs and the rustle of dry leaves. Something heavy was moving through the trees ten or fifteen yards to the right of the deck.

"What do you think that is?" she said softly.

Ian had not budged; she could still feel his breath in the downy hairs on her cheek. "A bear?" he suggested.

"No, seriously."

Now he drew his head back. "I *am* serious. It's a bear."

There was another distinct rustle of leaves.

"Bears always sound like drunks staggering through the woods," Ian said.

"You don't think it could be that guy from the lake?"

"Your secret admirer?"

Alice was silent, listening.

Ian lowered his lips once again, but she put her hand on his chest. "No."

He said nothing, but she could tell from the set of his head that he was irritated.

"Seriously," he said at last. "It's just a bear."

"How do you know?"

"Because I know everything!" He was grinning, but only like a defiant child. "Anyway, even if it is your secret admirer . . ." he slipped his hand up under her shirt ". . . I think we should just give him his money's worth." Once again he moved his lips toward hers, but she pushed him away and stood up.

"Stop it!" she said. "This is serious. The thought of that guy out there really creeps me out."

Ian fell back into his chair, and lifted both hands palms-upward in disbelief. "Jee-sus!"

Alice picked up her plate and hurried inside the cabin.

After a few minutes Ian came in, carrying a tray filled with clinking dishes and the smoking candles.

Alice turned to him, a waiflike sadness in her wide blue eyes. "I'm sorry."

He put down the tray and took her into his arms.

She squeezed him as hard as she could.

They rose around two the following day, had a pancake breakfast, then decided to walk down past the lake to a rock ledge, from which there was normally a postcard view onto the gray roofs and white steeples of the village of Eikenville. The weather was mediocre—drizzle and fog—and they wouldn't be able to see much from the ledge. But they didn't know what else to do in the hour or so before Ian was to leave for Brooklyn.

The trail down from the cabin had grown slippery in the rain, and they had to hold each other's hand to keep their footing on slick roots, muddy inclines, and lichen-covered rocks. A mist hung over the lake, reducing the far shore to modulating smudges of pastel green, yellow, and brown. Crows yammered invisibly in the gray, and a bright lens of water dangled from the tip of every bent-over grass blade.

After the lake, the trail meandered along level ground for about a mile until it veered abruptly to the left and opened onto a stretch of weathered granite that seemed to end in a wall of gray. As they walked across the stone, the fog grew brighter and gained depth, but once they had reached the edge of the precipice, all they could see were mist-dimmed treetops directly below; everything farther out seemed to have been erased.

They had hardly spoken during their walk. Alice had been feeling a weight of sadness at the prospect of Ian's departure, and Ian had seemed lost in his own thoughts, barely responding to anything she said. They had not made love last night—and Alice had blamed herself with a particular ruefulness. Despite having pushed Ian away out on the deck, once they were in bed she could not stop thinking about how his fingers had moved up her thigh. She wanted to run her own fingers down his turned back; she wanted to murmur something filthy into his ear, but somehow she couldn't, and so had lain awake for much of the night.

As they stood on the ledge, looking off in the direction where the view ought to have been, Alice felt as if their silence were hardening around them, and that if they didn't find a way to start talking now, the silence would solidify into real alienation (their relationship was still new enough that she worried one bad day could ruin it). She gestured toward the fog and, after a quick, shy smile, spoke in the singsong voice of a tour guide: "And here we have the picturesque village of Eikenville, first settled in 1785. If you will turn your gaze to the far side of the Millfield River, just beside the old stone bridge . . ." (she pointed down and to the right) ". . . you can see the wrought iron fence on which Phinneas McAllister was impaled in 1835, after falling from the roof of the Congregationalist church, which he was repairing. And, a little bit farther on" (she pointed again), "that copse of beeches, just across from the Exxon station, is where Grandma Kettlebottom succumbed to apoplexy in 1878, and lay there for three days before she was found by a passing chimney sweep, who had noticed an odd smell . . ."

Surprised at how well her improvisation had come out, Alice grinned up at Ian. He kissed her on the nose, but did not meet her eye. Without a word, he turned and started down the trail toward the cabin.

The drizzle intensified as they walked. Their hair was bedizened by hundreds of tiny silver-white water beads. Each branch they brushed dappled their clothing with droplets, and, every now and then, tiny pools that had collected in flowers or cupped leaves would spill onto their shoulders and necks. Their fingers became wet, chilly, red. Their nipples tightened inside their tee shirts, and their sodden running shoes made squeegee noises with every step. Ian took Alice's hand as they crossed a rushing stream, and didn't let go on the other side. Somehow, after that, it was no longer difficult to speak.

They talked about friends whom Ian planned to see for dinner during the week before his return to the cabin, and also about this new band he had tickets to see Thursday night. He didn't say who he was going with, however, and Alice didn't ask. Ian was trustworthy, she reminded herself. He loved her. There was nothing to worry about. She lived in dread of ever seeming "the jealous girlfriend."

As they passed along the low bluff, just above the lake, Ian touched her shoulder. "Look."

He was pointing at the skiff: still exactly as they had left it, belly-up in the high grass—except that now three of the four missing oars were resting on top of it.

"Whoa!" said Alice.

"They must have floated to shore. Somebody must have found them."

"Weird," she said.

Ian drew his breath to speak, but didn't say anything.

"I think it's creepy," she said.

"It's not creepy. Someone did you a favor. That's nice."

Now Alice was the one who didn't speak.

Ian left. The sun rose yolk yellow Monday morning. By eight, plumes of gold-white mist were rising like volcanic exhalations all over the valley. Standing by the deck railing, Alice could feel the moisture against her cheeks. Her sinuses filled with the thin, sweet smell from the pines, and with the deeper, headier scent of heated earth and rot. By noon the mists and clouds had cleared, and the forest was baking under a glaring sun; the cicadas were emitting their ringing racket in every direction, and the birds were silent.

By two thirty, even the shadiest recesses of the cabin were so hot that sweat was running down Alice's nose and neck, and she could no longer concentrate on her work. She changed into jogging shorts and her bikini top, and loaded up a hiking pack with a bottle of cold water, sun lotion, a book (*Anna Karenina*) and her sunglasses. She sang as she descended the trail, her flip-flops keeping a pitter-patter time with the melody.

As she came out of the woods at the top of the bluff, she glanced at the skiff, and saw that there were now *four* oars—in two pairs, neatly crossed—atop the overturned hull. Alice pressed her fingertips to her lips, troubled most of all by the aesthetic arrangement of the oars, which made them into a sort of gift and implied a relationship . . .

"No," she said aloud, shaking her head. "Stop being so neurotic. He's doing you a favor. It's nice." She lifted the skiff and slid both sets of oars underneath.

As she had done almost every afternoon of the last two weeks, Alice spread her towel over the entirety of the bed-size dock, then smeared her face, shoulders, and arms with sun lotion—hesitated half an instant, then smeared the tops of her breasts as well. Tossing the tube of sun lotion onto her knapsack, she stood with her hands on her hips and pretended to be wholly absorbed in the beauty of the woods, the dark-shimmering lake, the pale, hot sky. She made contented noises; she smiled and turned her head left and right, looked up and down, but took particular care never to give the perimeter of the lake more than a cursory glance, especially at the far end of the western shore.

One of her favorite parts of her afternoons by the lake was lying on her towel, eyes closed, waiting for the sun to make her so hot she could leap, without trepidation, into the water. She would listen to the drum of passing dragonflies, to the lapping of the lake waves amid the cattails, and to the sawing croaks of bullfrogs. Her thoughts would wander ever farther astray, becoming ever less rational and ever more infiltrated by dreamlike imaginings. Finally she would drift into a five-minute doze, from which she would awake refreshed, sun-baked, and ready for her swim.

But this afternoon there were no dreams, no wandering of thoughts. She managed to keep her eyes closed, but her ears were alert to every sound that could be interpreted as a shoe raking through dry grass, or a foot-thump on hardened earth, or a cough, or a sneeze, as well as to what she could not help thinking of as looming silences. Finally, deciding that she'd already been hot enough when she came down the hill, she cast aside her sunglasses and flung herself from the end of the dock in a belly-smacking dive.

Sometime after ten that night, Alice pushed herself away from the kitchen table and went out onto the deck. She'd been hunched over the computer for close to five hours. Her back was killing her; her brain was aching and dull. But also she felt weirdly restless. Her dissertation concerned the emergence of child abuse as a social problem in the late nineteenth century, and one of the reasons she had not completed a single draft, even after six years, was that the details of some of the cases she wrote about often left her frantic and depressed.

There was no moon out, nor any stars. All Alice could see beyond the deck railing was a dense blackness that seemed constantly to swirl and reassemble, without ever settling into a definite landscape. The heat of the day was still rising out of the valley, stirring faintly against her arms and cheeks, and within her sleeveless cotton nightie—the coolest item of clothing she owned.

Alice could not recall a night at the cabin remotely as hot as this. She had no fans, and the ventilation in the bedroom was terrible. Perhaps she could sleep in the front room, but even there the air was stagnant, steamy, and smelled of mice.

She went back inside and brought out her cell phone. When Ian didn't pick up, she felt so fiercely irritated, she nearly sent the phone sailing out into the roiling dark. She made a second trip inside and poured a shot of vodka into a plastic orange juice glass.

"That's better!" she said aloud, leaning against the railing once again, but was not entirely sure whether she had spoken only for her own benefit.

All night she'd been hearing noises in the woods: stirrings in the leaves, gentle tappings and, once, something like a grunt; animals, no doubt—birds, squirrels, maybe raccoons—but, even so, she'd been unable to suppress a frightened gasp at every unexplained sound, or to stop her heart from pounding.

She went inside yet again and brought the vodka bottle onto the deck. After her third shot, she could feel beads of sweat trembling on her forehead and upper lip, and she could smell the drips running down her ribs from her armpits.

What she would most have loved would have been to cool off with a midnight skinny-dip, but that, of course, was impossible; she didn't even dare use the outdoor shower—the only place to wash apart from the kitchen sink.

"This is so fucking stupid!" she said, looking down into her empty glass.

Just at that moment, she was startled by her ringtone. She'd left her phone on the kitchen table.

The very first thing Ian said was "Sorry I missed you, babe. My phone was dead and I didn't even know. It's on the charger right now."

This didn't actually make sense; Ian's phone had rung and rung when Alice called, but she let the inconsistency pass because she was so happy to hear his voice.

"Guess what," she said. "My secret admirer found the fourth oar!"

"Really?" said Ian. "Amazing!"

"I know!" she exclaimed. "I couldn't believe it."

"What luck!"

"Yeah." There was a brief silence when she thought of saying something about how uncomfortable the discovery had made her, but she chose not to.

Ian asked how her day had been. "Good," she said, and then she repeated, "Good." She told him about swimming in the lake—not mentioning her anxiety beforehand. She told him about coming across a "tiny meadow" of wild sorrel on her way back from the compost heap, and about how delicious the sorrel had tasted in her salad at dinner.

"And right now," she continued, "I'm out on the deck having a nightcap. It's so hot out here I've got practically nothing on."

Ian made a low, appreciative moan. "I wish I was there with you, babe," he said.

"Me too!" She squeezed her thighs together.

But when she asked Ian what he'd been up to, he was silent a moment. "Oh, you know," he said at last. "Nothing much . . . The usual."

She couldn't help asking, "You didn't see anybody . . . you know, like after work?"

"No way!" he laughed. "After all that not-sleeping you and I did over the weekend, I came right home and just passed out in front of the television. That's another reason I didn't hear your call."

Alice was puzzled that he should talk about not hearing her call, since his phone wouldn't have rung if the battery had been dead, but again she said nothing.

They talked awhile about his work and about the friends he would be having dinner with the following night, and then Alice asked, as if she'd only just remembered, "You're going to that show on Thursday, right?"

"Yeah, man. Can't wait.

"But who're—I mean, you're not just going by yourself?"

"Oh, no. I'll—you know: friends."

Alice drew her breath to speak, but couldn't get her words out.

"There's this guy at work," Ian said. "Doug . . . I told you about Doug, right? Copy editor?"

Alice had never heard of Doug, but said nothing.

"His sister's going out with the bassist," Ian continued. "She got us the tickets. Actually, we're going to be on the guest list!"

"Sweet."

After Ian hung up, Alice remained on the deck, looking out into the blackness, turning her cell phone over and over. Then, not twenty feet below where she was leaning, she heard a distinct, sharp crack—like the splitting of a nut, or the sound of one rounded stone striking another.

She went back inside and latched the deck door behind her.

Her father had a row of hunting and fish-cleaning knives in a wooden rack over the sink. She took the longest and most lethal-looking, and put it on the table beside her bed.

Her night was one long collage of anxious dreams and feverish revelations entirely uninterrupted by sleep. Only when the ashen light of approaching dawn turned the leaves outside her window the color of cooked liver did she fall briefly into a restorative oblivion.

The heat had not relented the following morning and Alice couldn't write—her sentences meandering, vague, and probably false. She gave up at around eleven, packed a picnic lunch and a big bottle of water, and headed down through the woods.

She was too tired to swim across the lake—her normal routine—so, between bouts of reading and napping, she just paddled in the vicinity of the dock, mostly on her back, watching the clouds drift and mutate, and the swallows snatch mosquitoes out of the air.

Around five, the leaves on the treetops began to flutter restlessly in turbulent breezes, and huge gray clouds coasted out of the west, over the mountain behind the cabin. The breezes never touched the bug-dimpled mirror of the lake, but once she had returned to the cabin, she could feel them blowing the hot, mouse-fragrant air out the windows and doors.

She barbecued chicken sausages that had been on the verge of going bad, and ate them on the deck with a romaine salad and a tall glass of seltzer. As the light faded, the breezes began to surge into powerful gusts that she could watch sweeping across the valley, bending the topmost branches of the trees and turning up the bright bottoms of leaves.

After dinner, she brought her computer out to the picnic table, but no sooner had she booted up than one huge raindrop struck her temple and another left a beaded, diagonal oval in the dust across her screen. She returned to the kitchen table and, amid the whispery patter of the rain, had absolutely no trouble knocking her morning's cumbersome sentences into sonorous sense.

Not long after dark, thunder began to rumble in the west, and every now and then the blunt, gray peak of Mount Quiddagunk would flash pink or ice blue. The gusts came so forcefully now that, instead of sweeping from one side of the valley to the other, they hit it all at once, hissing in the trees and causing the house to creak, crack and groan.

Alice had just decided to unplug her computer when everything went white and a slamming blast knocked her half out of her chair. Before she had even fully registered what had happened, the cabin and valley went white a second time, and the instantaneous thunderclap was so loud, her whole body reverberated with it. "Holy fuck!"

Finding herself on the floor, she yanked her computer's plug out of the surge protector, and crouched a moment on her hands and knees, trying to determine if the sound she was hearing was rain or the crackle of a burning tree. Another blast sent her flat onto her belly. "Holy fucking shit!"

Did the cabin have a lightning rod? Would a lightning rod make a difference in a storm like this? She had always heard that a car was the safest place to be in a thunderstorm, but to get to hers, she would have had to run down a steep and slippery path beneath hundreds of tall trees.

Another lightning bolt hit—not quite so near—and she began to laugh, which struck her as odd, even at the time. She had, perhaps, never been rendered so utterly powerless, insignificant, and so absolutely at the mercy of massive and relentless forces, and yet all she felt was happy and wildly alive.

The wind was roaring. Twigs and pinecones were skittering

across the roof shingles, and the rain hit the windows like sand and tiny pebbles. Alice poured herself a vodka and stood in the deck doorway, savoring the pinpoint chilliness of the wind-whipped rain against her cheeks, arms, and knees. But, when a bolt of lightning set every single hair on her body upright, she retreated from the door and poured herself another drink. Taking a seat on the iron-framed bed where she had slept as a child, she flipped open her phone to call Ian, but the service was down—a blackout, maybe, or a transmission tower had been hit. Nothing to do but wait and watch the sky flash lavender and pink and blue.

Soon the worst of the storm had moved beyond Mount Quiddagunk. Alice poured herself one more vodka and went over to the dusty boom box at the end of the kitchen counter. The boom box had once belonged to her, but she hadn't seen it in years. Her father must have brought it up to the cabin—along with a carton of her old cassettes—after she went to college. She put on a tape of eighties music that had been given to her by her high school boyfriend, cranked up the volume, and, vodka glass in hand, started dancing around the cabin, pleased to discover that she could still sing all the words to every song. But then, midway through Billy Idol's "Rebel Yell," the music quit suddenly. There was a brief brown flicker, and then the cabin went so deeply black that the darkness was like a pressure on her eyes.

She stood a moment, listening to the drumming rain on the roof, the water clattering in the gutters and the seething wind, then felt her way along the walls to bed. Nothing else to do. She didn't even wash.

Some number of hours later, she was woken from dreamless sleep by light streaming across her face and Billy Idol crying, "more, more, more!"

The air was so clear the following morning that Alice felt she could make out each individual tree on the slopes of Mount Quiddagunk. Brilliant white clouds with slate-colored bottoms coasted through a deep blue sky. A faint, cool breeze streamed steadily through the cabin, allowing Alice to write with transcendent concentration until mid-afternoon, at which point the temperature had reached the mid-eighties—perfect for swimming.

She called Ian while she was eating dinner, but once again he didn't pick up. (Was this the day he was having dinner with their friends? She couldn't remember.) He returned her call just as she was getting ready for bed, so she went out onto the deck to talk to him, wearing only her tee shirt and underpants. "There are so many stars out tonight!" she exclaimed, twisting in a circle with her head raised. "Zillions! I feel like I am standing on the edge of the whole universe!"

"Great!" Ian said distractedly. "I'm glad you're having a good time."

"So what's up?" Her voice was more subdued. "How're things?"

"Okay. You know. Fine."

"Did you see Maddie and Zach tonight?"

"Uh . . ." He was silent a long moment. "Yeah."

"How are they?"

They were fine too, and the dinner was also fine.

Alice was just beginning to become upset at Ian's strange monosyllabism, when he told her that Maddie was pregnant.

"Oh my God!" Alice exclaimed, and they talked for a long while about Maddie and Zach's complex responses to the news. This was just the sort of conversation that might have evolved into another of their habitual rhapsodies on the cuteness of very small children, but instead they went on to talk about amniocentesis, deer ticks, disgusting omelets, and Zach's near bicycle accident.

Ian broke off the conversation. "I'm sorry I'm so out of it tonight."

"That's okay." Alice was glad to hear him acknowledge it.

"Mr. Soon" (the client from Korea) "hated our presentation.

He didn't say anything when he was here. In fact, he seemed to love it. But then we got this unbelievably vicious e-mail from one of his underlings, accusing us of breach of contract and threatening to go to another company. Everybody's been sort of—you know: thrown for a loop."

Alice was about to make a sympathetic remark when she heard heavy footfalls in the undergrowth just below where she was standing, and a repeated grunting noise.

"Alice?" Ian said.

She crouched and backed away from the railing, whispering tersely into her phone: "Jesus fucking Christ!"

"Alice?"

She continued whispering: "There's someone down there!"

"What?"

She heard another noise—like a foot being lowered carefully through weeds.

"Right in front of me," she said into her phone. "There's someone moving. I can hear him. Right below the deck."

"Alice? Alice? I can't hear you. You're breaking up."

She backed into the cabin and, crouching beside her old bed, spoke louder. "Ian, I'm afraid!"

"What's happening?" Now he understood. She could hear his concern.

"You remember that day? By the lake? The pervert?"

"Your secret admirer?"

She was about to say "He's here" when she heard another heavy footfall, and another grunt. Without even thinking, Alice ran back onto the deck, shouting so loud her voice cracked: "Get the fuck away from me, you goddamn fucking asshole! Get the fuck away! You don't get out of here right this second, I'm gonna blow your fucking head off! I've got a gun! You hear me? I've got a gun."

Alice did not, in fact, have a gun. Her father never left his rifles at the cabin when he was not there. And, in the next instant, something about the emptiness of her threat and the hysterical tone in which she had uttered it made her afraid that she had imagined everything, that there was no one there at all.

"Alice? Alice?"

She'd let the phone fall from her ear. Ian's voice was tiny.

She snapped her phone shut. Listened.

Peepers down by the lake. A breeze passing over the treetops, making a sound like air easing through the teeth of a thousand people—nothing like the noises she had heard. She stilled her own breathing and cocked her head to one side, but even so: No footfalls. No grunts. No gasps. Just peepers and the breeze.

She went back through the cabin, flipping off all the lights so that she couldn't be seen. She picked up the knife from her bedside table and walked toward the deck.

Just as she stepped into the night air, her phone rang. "I'll call you back," she said, snapping the phone shut.

She crouched on the weathered cedar boards, phone in one hand, knife in the other, listening. She heard the long, pulsing hoot of an owl from the far side of the valley. The whispery flutter of a bat passing back and forth over her head. One tree groaning against another.

Peepers. Wind.

She listened a full twenty minutes, but heard no sounds to indicate that anyone was waiting in the vicinity or making a hasty retreat through the woods.

"You okay?" Ian asked as soon as he picked up.

Alice was back inside, the lights still off, all the doors latched, her father's knife in her hand. "You're not allowed to laugh."

"What?"

"Don't laugh."

Ian started laughing.

"Ian, stop! I'm serious."

"I'm sorry." He was still laughing, but took a deep breath and seemed to get control of himself. "Really. I'm sorry. It's just . . ." He had to take another deep breath. "I don't know . . . I was just—you know: *nervous*. I was *worried* about you."

She told him about the noises. She told him what she had been afraid of. And she told him she wasn't sure anyone was there at all. She was trying to sound levelheaded and resolutely honest—the opposite of hysterical.

When she had finished, he said, "Maybe you should just come home."

"No!" At the mere suggestion she felt a plummeting sorrow. "I love it here. My work has been going so well."

Ian sighed heavily.

"You know," he said, "the whole time you were telling me about what you heard, I was thinking that it was probably a bear. Have you ever heard a bear walking through the woods?"

"You've already told me all this," she said impatiently.

"But wait a second." Ian seemed afraid she was going to hang up again. "You know how, when we were sitting on the deck, we kept throwing our fruit pits over the edge?"

Alice made a small, affirmative grunt.

"Have you been doing that on your own?"

"I don't know. Maybe."

"Well, anyhow, what's probably happening is the bear's coming up under the deck because he's sniffed out the fruit pits and wants to suck on them."

Ian sounded so confident of this opinion that Alice could hardly stand it. "It's late," she said. "I'm tired."

"So you've probably got nothing to worry about."

"Have fun with Doug," she said.

"Doug?"

"Doug. Your friend. Your friend with the sister." When Ian still didn't respond, she added, "The sister who knows the bassist."

"Oh," he said. And then he said, "Thanks."

As soon as she hung up, a voice sounded in her head: *He's going to the show with Gwendolyn.*

Gwendolyn was Ian's previous girlfriend. She'd dumped him about a month before Katinka's memorial service, and Alice had always worried that Ian was not really over her. Gwendolyn loved going to shows. The way Ian told it, that was the only thing he and she had in common. Alice, on the other hand, couldn't bear loud music. She hated how all the sounds blurred, and how, afterward, she'd feel as if she'd been beaten up. She'd gone to a couple of shows with Ian, but only under duress, and had stuffed her ears with toilet paper both times.

The following morning Alice tried to write about how the nascent labor movement of the late nineteenth century contributed to the new and increasingly influential vision of children as vulnerable, incompetent, and in need of protection, but all she seemed able to do was load the page with disconnected facts. To clear her head, she decided to take her swim early, before lunch.

She noticed the phlox without being fully aware that she had noticed them, and so did a double take. Yes, there they were, on top of the overturned skiff: a bouquet of some dozen white and purple flowers, held together by a bow made from a long cattail leaf.

Her first thought was: Now Ian will have to admit I'm right. Her second was that she had to get out of there as fast as she could. And her third was that she was damned if she was going to let some perverted old man drive her away from a place she loved. Anyway, she told herself, if the old man had harbored ill intentions, he would have done something already. All he had done, in fact, was make kind gestures. He was harmless; she had nothing to fear.

Standing on the dock, she noticed white and purple phlox growing amid the weeds and grass all along the western shore,

with one of the denser clusters being exactly where she had spotted the gray-haired man. She kicked off her flip-flops, dropped her
backpack onto the splintery wood, and then, not bothering even to
take out her towel, flung herself onto the water.

The cold trilled along her face and ribs, momentarily making
it hard to breathe. But within seconds, she felt no colder than she
normally did while swimming. Why had she never done this before? The shock was good. It had invigorated her, and had gotten
her off to a more rapid start. What a coward she had been! That
was over. Never again.

For a while she actually managed to lose herself in the sensual-
ity of swimming: the gurgling beside her ears, the eddies along her
belly and hips, the spiraling bubbles trailing her celery-pale fingers
as they swung through an evergreen obscurity. But then she began
to think again about the phlox.

Once picked, wild phlox go dull and limp very quickly. The
flowers on the skiff had been bright and springy, clearly picked
only minutes before she came upon them. Perhaps this had been
mere coincidence, but even so, it meant that the old man—or
whomever—was quite likely to have still been nearby when she
dove into the lake, and so could well be watching her this very
minute. If, on the other hand, he had been spying on her at the
cabin, and had raced ahead to pick and prepare his gift—well, then
there was no question that he was watching her now.

She became caught by contradictory impulses: On the one
hand, she wanted to drive all thought of the old man from her
head; on the other, she wanted to demonstrate, through the grace
and efficiency of her stroke, her complete indifference to him. But
the longer she swam, the more rigid and inefficient her stroke became. She felt herself veering to the right, and constantly had to lift
her head to correct her course. Then, one time, she lifted her head
and inhaled a dollop of water, which set her gasping and goose-
honking for long minutes at the center of the lake. So ridiculous!

she told herself. So absolutely stupid! She refused to even glance at the shore.

Once she had resumed swimming, she found that her stroke had gone jittery, and that she was weaker than normal. Several times she wondered if she shouldn't just turn back, but every time she shamed herself into continuing by thinking of Ian, who was never intimidated, never down—happy-go-lucky, always.

In the middle of the night, she had remembered a conversation with Ian the morning of her departure from the city. They had been discussing a friend who was trying to decide on a course of treatment for her breast cancer, and Ian mentioned that Gwendolyn's older sister had just had a mastectomy. Preoccupied by their friend's dilemma, Alice hadn't fully paid attention to what Ian had said. But in the middle of the night, she realized that he could have known about the mastectomy only if he was back in touch with Gwendolyn. This revelation had been promptly followed by a host of unsettling questions: Could it only have been coincidence that Ian should reconnect with his old girlfriend just as Alice was leaving for two months? Had he really been kept in the city by work that first weekend? Was there really a Mr. Soon? (How could anyone have such a preposterous name?) And what about Ian's distraction the afternoon he left the cabin? And on the telephone?

The questions had just kept on coming, eating up her sleep. And, as they recycled though her mind on the lake, they did nothing to improve her swimming. The worst was that, no matter how hard she tried to abide by her normal rhythm of one breath for every three strokes, she never felt she was getting enough air. She started breathing every second stroke, and then for several strokes in a row—but always her lungs felt tight, unable to fully expand. Could the water she had inhaled be blocking some vital air passage? Were some of her alveoli flooded? She knew full well that, were either possibility true, she would still be coughing—but, even so, she couldn't dismiss them from her mind.

Finally she decided to give up and just head back to the dock. A nap and lunch—that was what she needed. She would swim later, maybe. But no sooner had she reversed direction than she was stopped mid-stroke by the image of the old man looking down at her as she swam up to the dock. She saw him with startling clarity, as if in a magnifying mirror: His tobacco-stained teeth, partially eaten away. His eyes exactly the gray of his hair, but with pupils so tiny he looked blind. His leathery brown cheeks bristling with white whiskers. He was smiling. He held out his hand to her. He wheezed.

This image so horrified Alice that she reversed yet again, and swam toward the far shore as fast as she could, her arms chopping and her legs kicking so hard the fronts of her thighs became knotted with pain.

For a while this seemed exactly the right thing to do. Swimming the length of the lake would be a triumph over fear, and would help restore her confidence. But she was too tired to keep up her fierce stroke for long, and once she slowed, she became aware that every time her right arm descended through the water, she would feel a rightward rolling inside her head. After a while, she began to suspect that she actually was rolling in the water, and tried to keep herself steady. But then she discovered that, with the spinning inside her head, she couldn't tell precisely which direction was up and which down, and so had no way of knowing if she was steady or not.

When, at last, the rolling got so bad that she felt as if she were spiraling through the water, she stopped and lifted her head into the air—which only had the effect of transferring the spiraling to the outside world. The trees, the sky, Mount Quiddagunk, the phlox-festooned shores—everything she could see was rotating around her. It didn't matter how often she shook her head, or how rigidly she stared at any single point, the entire world was drifting, inexorably, from right to left.

All at once she understood what was happening: She was having an anxiety attack. She was hyperventilating. The hyperventilation had made her dizzy. And if she didn't stop hyperventilating, she would faint. In the middle of a lake. A hundred yards from shore. She would faint and she would drown.

Over the ensuing minutes, one tiny voice in Alice's mind repeated over and over: *None of this should be happening. You love this lake. You're an excellent swimmer. If you weren't so afraid, you'd have absolutely nothing to fear. How stupid! How unbelievably stupid!* But all the rest of her mind was given over to terror. She forgot how to swim. She thrashed. She screamed. She swallowed more than one mouthful of water, and never felt she was getting enough air.

For what seemed hours, she thought she was making no progress whatsoever toward shore. But then, just when her lungs felt sucked shut from the vacuum inside them, and she thought she had no more strength in her arms, she realized that in only a few more strokes—four, six, ten—she would be close enough to the shore to lower her feet and stand.

And, indeed, seconds later, her feet settled into silky slime. And seconds after that, she staggered through the warm shallows and collapsed facedown onto cool, ticking grass—sobbing, breathless, shamed; so deeply, deeply shamed.

She packed her clothes, her books, and her computer, and hauled her bags out onto the deck—only to bring them right back inside and unpack them.

All of the homecoming scenes that came into her mind were intolerable: She saw Ian's surprise gradually yielding to recognition of her flagrant and stupid cowardice. She saw how his tender consolations would do nothing to conceal his swelling pride at his manly capability. And then, because the earliest she could have arrived home would have been while Ian was at the rock concert, she imagined the apartment door flying open, and Ian and Gwendolyn tumbling in, mouth to mouth, their hands at each other's crotch. Worse, she saw herself watching the green digits on her bedside clock all through the long, grim night and into the first grays and pinks of what would surely be the most awful day of her life.

Why bring that on herself—any of it? All she had to do was endure one night and then Ian would be there; she could return home with him, if she still wanted to, and he would never have to know why.

One night!

She could do that—no, she *had* to do that! How could she live with herself if she gave in, yet again, to her fear? Her groundless, paranoid, stupid, stupid fear.

Once she had unpacked and put away her belongings, she decided to walk to the ledge where she had gone with Ian. She wanted to steady her nerves and just look out onto something beautiful. But when she arrived at the ledge, she was surprised that the view wasn't anywhere as picturesque as she had remembered it. Yes, there were a couple of steeples, but also three gas stations, a strip mall, and, along the river, a long, low nineteenth-century factory with cinderblocked windows and a gaping hole in its roof, through which Alice could look down onto a charred floor and wall and a heap of garbage.

On the way back to the cabin, she felt a certain diminishment of tension between her temples and in her shoulders. Everything's getting better, she told herself. You're back in control. When she got to the skiff, she grabbed the now wilted phlox, ripped off their cattail-leaf bow, and scattered them across the path.

As the western flanks of Mount Quiddagunk went gold and orange, Alice barbecued an elaborate dinner of chicken with an oregano sauce and yellow squash, pausing frequently as she cooked, and then as she ate, to sip from or refill her juice glass of vodka.

"You can do this," she said aloud. "There's no reason why not."

But then the sun was down, and an ever-deepening gloom accumulated beneath the trees and diffused east to west across the sky. Soon everything would be black, and the space where Alice could feel at home would shrink to the quavering oblong of light cast by her citronella candles, and to the incandescently illuminated interior of the cabin. Her head throbbed; her spirits sank ever lower—less at the prospect of the long, anxiety-filled night than at the fact of her anxiety itself. Stupid, stupid, stupid.

Finally she said aloud, "Fuck it! If you want to get out of here—just do it! Stop second-guessing yourself."

No sooner had these words left her lips than the whole night seemed brighter and more welcoming. Yes! The perfect decision! Why hadn't this come to her sooner? Why did she always deprive herself of what she wanted most?

There was, of course, the small matter of those half-dozen vodka shots, but she figured that by the time she had finished packing, rumbled her car down the rutted logging road and traversed the five-mile-long dirt road to the two-lane blacktop (the first place she was likely to encounter traffic), she would be fit enough to drive.

As it was already dark and she didn't want to travel the long, uneven trail down to the car more than once, she only packed her computer and as many clothes as she could stuff into a single suitcase. She could come back for the rest of her things another time—maybe make a weekend of it with Ian.

She was standing on the deck, looking down the steps into a pool of throbbing darkness. Her computer bag was slung over her shoulder; she gripped her suitcase with one hand and, with the other, a high-power, steel-cased flashlight, long and heavy enough to be used as a club. The loudest sound in the night was the pounding of her heart. Sweat trickled in front of her ears and into the hollow at the base of her neck. The metal of the flashlight grew slippery under her fingers.

"It's like jumping out of a tree," she told herself. "Just start, then it's over."

She flicked on the flashlight, and—suitcase against her hip—began to lumber sideways down the steps. Once she was actually moving through the woods, she felt a flutter of panic at the way everything outside the skittering illumination of the flashlight beam was cloaked in impenetrable blackness. But the trail was winding, steep, muddy, and crossed by myriad roots; without the flashlight she couldn't move.

"Fuck it," she said. "Just fuck it."

She got down the steepest incline without incident, and began to feel that the worst was over. Soon she would be in her car, radio on, wind blowing in the open windows. But then she heard the snap of a stick over her right shoulder—although it was hard to be sure amid the raspy wheeze of the suitcase cloth against her leg and her own grunting and panting.

She stopped a second. Hearing nothing but ordinary nighttime rustlings, she resumed her journey. Just get to the car, she thought. Get to the car and go! But then, a few steps farther on, once again over her right shoulder, she heard, distinctly, the swish of a branch passing over something large.

Half out of a desire not to show her fear, half wanting to believe there was nothing to fear in the first place, she didn't alter her pace in the slightest, although sweat began to sting her eyes, and the hand holding the flashlight was trembling. She wished she could turn the beam off so that she wouldn't be marked out so clearly amid the trees, but it was already too late; who- or whatever was following her would know exactly where she was even in pitch dark.

The incline steepened once again, which meant that she was coming to the place where the trail made its final bend around to the logging road. Although it was hard to tell over all the noises she herself was making, she no longer heard any worrisome sounds behind her—no cracks, swishes, rustles or grunts. You are so stupid! she scolded herself. You are so fucking paranoid!

Finally, she was walking along the level stretch just before she would come out onto the logging road; she could even make out, flickering between the trees, the glint of her flashlight beam on the car's windows. But then, all at once, she came to a halt.

Perhaps she had noticed a slight movement, or picked up some subtle sound, but all she felt was a sort of malevolent aura emanating from the blackness beyond the illuminated branches directly in front of her. Something was there, something big, overpowering. Her flashlight beam was quivering. There was a rushing in her ears. But she could not move. Her car was only yards away, but her feet had frozen to the earth. She was helpless. All she could do was wait.

She had enough time to take a shower and put away her clothes before the apartment door opened and Ian entered alone.

"Hello," she said.

As Ian caught sight of her, he looked as if he had been punched in the stomach.

"I came back," she said. She was sitting at the kitchen counter in front of her open computer. She had been browsing Facebook without being able to take in anything she had read or seen.

"You okay?" said Ian, putting his briefcase down by the door. His face was glossy. He had been sweating, and seemed to be having trouble seeing her—drunk, maybe, or just tired. He had come home just exactly when he would have had he left right after the show.

"How was it?" she asked.

"Okay," he answered, but not as if he had actually heard her question. "Fine," he said.

He crossed the room and took hold of her hand, which she had extended to him. He didn't kiss her, only looked at her in a sort of stunned incomprehension.

"Things just got—" She had intended to say "pretty weird up there," but her vision went blurry and she began to sob. Ian pulled her into his arms and pressed her head against his chest. "It's okay, sweet babe; it's okay."

Ian's words, his smell, the feel of his hard chest and strong arms released something in Alice, and allowed her an almost delirious sense of well-being. It was good that she had come home. And being in Ian's arms was good too. He was a good man: tender and strong. And she loved him. How could she have ever doubted that she loved him? She loved him more than she had ever loved anyone in her life.

Alice was lying in bed, looking up at the multiple parallelograms of street glow on the ceiling, listening to the long, low whisper of Ian's sleep-breathing. For hours she had been flipping from side to back to belly to side, waiting for sleep, glancing every now then at the brilliant green digits of her clock, hoping to discover that an hour had passed since her last glance, but finding, always, that it had been two minutes, three minutes, eight minutes.

But then she was back in the woods, yards from her car, at the moment of her utterly pointless panic. Only this time, she could see that there was, in fact, a darkness moving within the darkness behind the scrim of illuminated branches. It was a bear, in a sort of room—a kitchen. The bear was standing on its hind legs, like a man, with its shoulders hunched slightly and its arms out, gunslinger-style, on either side of its body. And the bear was looking at her with an expression of profound irritation, as if she had just done something contemptible, something for which she would never be forgiven.

The Professor of Atheism
Stealing Peaches from Sam Snow

———◆———

It was nearly midnight. Snow had been falling since dawn, and Charles was alone at a borrowed country house high in the mountains, his face moon white in computer glow. Seven words scintillated to the left of his blinking cursor: *Dead Certainty: The Afterlife of the Faithless.* This was the title of the book he hoped would win him tenure at the great Christian university where he constituted the entire Department of Atheistic Studies. He had been working on the book since graduate school, and thought he had fifty-six solid pages.

His heart was pounding. The house was at least a half mile off the road, entirely surrounded by woods, and someone had just knocked at the door.

He waited, sweat on his temples and fingertips. The whispery collisions of wind-driven flakes against the windowpanes. A mouse paw on the tin breadbox. Nothing else. Silence. He'd just imagined it.

No. There it was again, louder this time, more emphatic.

———

Charles was standing at the door. Outside, in the yellow porch light, an old man, wearing only a pink button-down shirt and gray flannel pants, was clutching his shoulders and stamping his feet against the cold. Charles had recognized the old man instantly, but it had taken several long moments for the evidence of his senses to be accepted as fact:

The old man was his father.

"Goddamnit, open the door," the old man said. "I'm freezing out here!"

Charles's father had been dead for thirteen years.

"For Christsakes!" said the old man. "Jesus!"

Charles opened the door, and the old man barreled into the house, trailing tiny whirlwinds of snow.

"What took you so long?" he said. "It's like a hundred below out there! And all that wind!" A massive shudder ascended from the old man's belly, making his cheeks flap and his eyeballs vibrate.

"Dad?" said Charles.

"Aren't you going to close the door? What's the matter with you!"

Charles closed the door.

The old man was slapping his shoulders and rubbing his upper arms.

"What are you doing here?" said Charles.

"What's it look like I'm doing?" said the old man. "I'm freezing!"

"No, I mean—"

The old man was muttering to himself: "Never do it that way again! Fucking idiot!"

One of the many things troubling Charles was that this old man was behaving nothing like his father. For one thing, Charles's father had never uttered a swearword in his life. He had been a cheerful, soft-voiced dentist, whose hands had radiated cleanness, and whose cheeks were always so neatly shaven they seemed polished. This man had silver stubble on half of his upper lip, and a clot of purplish blood at the wrinkle of his jowl.

"Don't say it," said the old man.

"What?"

"That I'm not your father."

"That's not what I was going to say," said Charles.

The old man ignored him. "I just figured this was the only way you would let me inside."

As Charles had no idea what the old man was talking about, he said nothing.

"You know how it is," said the old man. "All that about how no mortal can gaze on my face and live? Well, it's all true."

"What do you mean?" said Charles.

"I'm God," said the old man.

"God?"

"Yup."

Charles sat down on a wooden stool just inside the door.

The old man was holding what looked like a small colonial gravestone. "I've come to give you this new set of commandments. I want you to tell everybody about them. Go on TV. You know. Radio. Whatever you have to do."

Charles squinted at the tablets and saw only two commandments, both in English. The first was the Golden Rule, and the second: "Do not kill anyone unless it is necessary for self-preservation or to save the lives of others." There was a small asterisk at the end of the second commandment, and at the bottom of the tablet, an asterisked footnote: "This should not be construed as support for the death penalty. No death penalty! I mean it."

"How come there are only two?" asked Charles.

"Ah, I was just messing around with you the other time. I was—well, the truth is I was in this really bad mood. Anyhow, just the other day I was thinking, 'You know, things are getting pretty fucking miserable down there. I better go down and give them the real dope.'"

"But why me? I don't even believe in you."

"Okay, so you're having an LSD flashback, or a minor psychotic episode, or maybe you've just fallen asleep over the manuscript of that book you're never going to finish. What does it matter? You believe in my new commandments, don't you?"

"Well, yes." As it happened, when Charles reduced his moral beliefs to their most basic essentials, these two commandments were just exactly what he came up with.

"All right then," said the old man. "It's simple. Go out and preach. I'm placing the fate of humanity in your hands." He gave Charles the tiny gravestone. "Got it? Good. I'm outta here."

More pounding on the front door. Blue daylight. The clock on the night table read 6:00 A.M. Peering between his bedroom curtains, Charles saw that someone had plowed the snow off his driveway and that a limousine, motor running, was parked at the end of his scrupulously shoveled front walk. The pounding continued the whole time Charles was descending the stairs, and grew so forceful that the entire front of the house reverberated and the beams in the ceiling creaked.

On the porch stood a huge blond man in a chauffeur's uniform so many sizes too small that his shoulders seemed to have been pinned together behind his back. About ten inches of bratwurst-colored forearm were visible between his cuffs and gloves.

"Sorry I'm late," said the man. "I had to wait for your snow-plow."

Charles, whose night had been a sleep-free cascade of anxious fantasy, could only respond with an uncomprehending squint.

"You gonna go like that?" The chauffeur gestured at Charles's bare feet and pajamas.

"Go?"

"To the studio."

"Studio?" said Charles.

Now it was the chauffeur's turn to squint uncomprehendingly. "Yeah, studio. I'm supposed to take you to the studio."

Charles shook his head. "I'm sorry. There must be some mistake."

"Oh, shit!" said the chauffeur. "Excuse my French." He took a tiny notebook out of his pocket, checked the address and Charles's name. When Charles confirmed both, the man looked even more baffled.

"Sorry," said Charles. And then he said, "Could you just wait here one second? I'll be right back."

"Sure," said the man.

Charles had gone to relieve his bladder. He was only half finished when the phone in the next room began to ring.

"So what's the problem?" a gruff voice asked without even bothering to say hello.

Having hurried from the toilet perhaps a split second too soon, Charles was occupied by a distressing wetness descending his left leg. "Uh," he said.

"Aren't you the guy who made the amazing discovery?" the man on the phone said.

"What?" said Charles.

"Hold on a minute." Charles heard a riffling of papers. "Yeah," said the man. "It says right here. You're the guy who saw God in a burning bush and got the new Ten Commandments."

"Not really."

"What do you mean, 'Not really'?"

"I mean no."

The man exhaled impatiently. "You didn't see God in a burning bush?"

"No."

"There are no Ten Commandments?"

"There are two."

"Two?"

Charles told him what they were, not forgetting the footnote.

"Hunh," said the man. "Ten, two—what's the difference? The main thing is we got a whole show scheduled around your discovery, and if you're not in our studios pronto, you get sued for breach of contract."

The woman who buzzed Charles through the glass door was wearing a set of 1950s telephone operator earphones, complete with mouthpiece. She had to unplug herself from a giant console so that, still wearing the earphones, she could come around from behind her desk and shake Charles's hand.

"Thank you for agreeing to be on our show, Professor," she said. "We understand how very difficult it must be for you to wrench yourself away from your students and research."

"No problem," said Charles.

The woman was about seventy, and her face had been lifted so many times all of her teeth were visible when she smiled.

"Nice shirt," she said.

Charles had put on trousers, a jacket and tie, but, in the interest of saving time, had left on his pajama shirt, which was covered with stars, quarter moons, and rocket ships. Something in the woman's smile told him this might not have been a good idea.

"I'm afraid the show is about to start," she said. "We have to hurry."

She turned about-face and strode toward another set of glass doors, placing one stiletto-heeled foot directly in front of the other, as if she were walking a tightrope.

The glass doors opened automatically. As Charles followed her into a long corridor, he said, "Excuse me?"

"Yes?" She glanced over her shoulder but didn't abate her pace in the least.

"Nobody's told me what show I'm going to be on."

"Lamb Chop," she said.

"Lamb Chop?"

"Right. *The Lamb Chop Show.*"

On either side of the corridor were what looked like the windows of museum dioramas. Behind most of the windows were bare, three-quarter-size offices, with up-tilting floors, single wooden desks, and single metal filing cabinets. But some of the windows looked into equally spare bedrooms, in one of which a fat man—elephantine on the child-sized bed—lay sound asleep.

"What's *The Lamb Chop Show* about?" asked Charles.

"Exactly what it sounds like," said the woman. "Lamb . . ." She lifted her hand into the air and let it fall like an axe. "Chop!"

"Oh," said Charles.

Charles was alone in a room that contained a giant television camera, a pair of spotlights, a stool, and very little air. The room was so hot his nostrils dried with every breath, and so silent that the high-pitched whine in his ears—what he thought of as the dial tone of his consciousness—was deafening. After sitting on the stool for a few minutes, he tried to open the door, but it was so firmly locked it might have been painted on the cinderblock wall. His hand was still on the knob when the door was shoved inward and a man, wearing the same antique earphone set as the receptionist, hurried into the room.

"Oh, hi," Charles said.

The man ignored him, went behind the camera, and came out carrying another pair of antique earphones. "Put these on."

As soon as Charles had done as instructed, a very efficient-sounding young woman spoke into his right ear. She thanked him again for being on the show, and explained that the host was in an entirely different studio, in a place called In-toot-ten-not—although Charles wasn't at all sure he had heard her clearly.

While he was listening to this young woman, the cameraman came up to him, held out both hands, and flicked his fingers in what was the gestural equivalent of the word "gimme."

"What?" said Charles.

"Give him the tablet," said the efficient young woman.

"Oh." Charles picked up his briefcase and withdrew the tablet, which he had wrapped in several layers of newspaper.

The cameraman tore through the wrapping, then looked up at Charles with bewildered irritation. "What's this?" he said.

"That's all I have," said Charles.

"This is just a giant mudpie!" said the cameraman.

He was right. The tablet had deteriorated shockingly overnight.

"This is worthless!" The cameraman threw it into a trash basket.

"Don't worry," the young woman murmured into Charles's ear. "We've got another one."

The cameraman turned on a fan that blew so forcefully it set Charles's hair and tie wriggling horizontally.

"That's just for effect," said the young woman.

"Oh," said Charles. Then he asked, "Do you mind telling me what *The Lamb Chop Show* is about?"

"Not enough time," she said. "You'll see." Then she told him to ignore the studio monitors and look straight into the camera. "That's right," she said, "just like that." She paused, and when she spoke again, her voice was distinctly lower and her lips seemed to be moving just beside his ear. "You're looking good," she said. "*Really* good. I *mean* it."

The face of *The Lamb Chop Show*'s host filled the monitor, but Charles was so affected by what the young woman had just told him that all he heard of the host's introduction was its final words: "...high atop Mount Sinai."

Now Charles's own image was on the monitor, but, instead of sitting on a stool in a cinderblock room, he was standing on a windblown crag, the dark, flame-illuminated clouds of a volcanic eruption directly behind him.

Charles heard the host's voice in his left year: "Good morning, Professor."

"Hi," said Charles, and a moment later his image on the monitor said, "Hi."

Then Charles watched his televised face take on a senile vagueness. This was because the young woman was whispering into his right ear: "Beautiful! You're looking great!"

The host said something like, "Stealing peaches from Sam Snow."

"Excuse me?" said Charles.

"Excuse me?" said his image on the monitor.

"I said," the host repeated, "thanks for agreeing to visit *The Lamb Chop Show*."

"Just ignore the monitors," said the young woman. "They're on a delay."

"Uh," said Charles. Then to the host: "No problem."

"I understand," said the host, "that God has revised his original commandments."

"Well . . . Uh . . . Sort of, I guess."

"Do you mind telling the folks at home what the new commandments are?"

"Sure. Okay." As soon as Charles began to recite the words he had read the previous night, a tablet exactly like the one the old man had given him appeared on the screen. After a while, the camera zoomed in and Charles was able to read the words as he spoke them, even the footnote, which was in smaller print than the rest of the text.

"But *why*, Professor?" The host's voice had begun to echo, as if it were amplified inside a cave. "*Why* has God replaced his original commandments with only these two?"

"Well, I don't know. Maybe it's just that these really are the most important moral principles. I mean, when you think about it, everything else kind of flows from them."

"Thou shalt have no other gods before me?"

"Well, maybe not that one."

"Thou shalt not make unto thee any graven image?" The host's voice had grown even louder, and the cave in which he was speaking seemed to have tripled in size.

"Well, maybe not that one either."

"But WHY? What did the Lord God say unto you? What were his reasons?"

"I'd rather not bring God into it, if you don't mind."

"NOT BRING THE LORD GOD INTO IT! BUT THESE ARE GOD'S OWN COMMANDMENTS!"

The host's voice had become so loud that Charles tried to rip the earphones off his head.

"No! Don't!" said the young woman. "You're doing beautifully. This won't last much longer."

"HOW CAN YOU POSSIBLY TELL US TO LEAVE GOD OUT OF IT?"

"I just think that these commandments kind of make sense all on their own. You don't really need God to—"

"DON'T NEED GOD!"

"Not really. Not to—"

"THAT'S ATHEISM!"

"Just say it," the young woman told him.

"What?" Charles said under his breath.

"Just tell him you're an atheist. This is great! You're brilliant!"

"Well, actually," Charles said, "I *am* an atheist."

The sky behind Charles had gone lurid orange and beet red. An enormous boom shook the studio walls, and his stool heaved beneath him, having been lifted by the cameraman, who had scuttled across the floor. As the cameraman scuttled back, he winked at Charles and gave him the thumbs-up sign.

"THIS SO-CALLED *PROFESSOR*," the host was saying, "THIS BLASPHEMING *DEVIANT* THINKS THAT HE KNOWS MORE THAN *THE CREATOR OF HEAVEN AND EARTH*! THIS *LIAR*, THIS *FORNICATOR*, THIS *CHILD MURDERER* WOULD HAVE US BELIEVE GOOD AND EVIL ARE MATTERS OF MERE *OPINION*!"

There followed a series of televised images Charles would never quite be able to make sense of. It seems that shortly before she died, his mother gave testimony regarding his practice of wiping snot on the undersides of furniture. In the court artist's rendering, his mother had whiskers and pointed, furry ears. A grainy video, purportedly taken of him in high school, showed him dancing naked in the bathroom and making copulatory hip movements. The president of his university, interviewed right in *The Lamb Chop Show*'s In-toot-ten-not studio, denounced him as a notorious plagiarist. A female student pulled down her underwear to show where Charles had burned her with cigarettes. A steam locomotive tumbled off a dynamited trestle, and an FBI poster of Charles with a Hitler mustache claimed that he was wanted for the crime of "Vehicular De-elevation." A torchbearing crowd was shown chasing him down a European street, his shadow reeling crazily against a castle wall. And finally, while the host cried out, "PURLOINER OF PEACHES! DEFILER OF SNOW!" a half-dozen billyclub-wielding policemen burst through the studio door and dragged Charles off his stool and down the corridor. The last monitor image he saw as he passed the receptionist's desk was of yellow gothic letters over volcanic clouds: "COMING NEXT . . . THE EXECUTION!"

Charles was lying on his back. Night had fallen. A frigid wind tore at the streetlight overhead, causing it to shudder and sway. A diminutive mountain range of sooty snow was heaped against the bulks of parked cars. Globs of trampled ice, like plastic amoebas, glinted dimly up and down the sidewalk. The billyclub-wielding police, all actors, were huddled by the stage door, sharing a joint, laughing.

Charles got to his feet. "Is that it?" he asked the cops.

"That's it for us," one of them said.

Charles tucked his hands into his armpits, shivered and said, "I think I left my coat inside," but none of the cops seemed to hear. They all had their heads rocked back in silent laughter.

The stage door was locked tight. He banged with his fist. No one answered. He walked down the sidewalk and around the corner, looking for the main entrance. Although the studio turned out to occupy an entire city block, and although Charles walked all the way around it, he did not encounter a single doorway more welcoming or less locked than the one he had left. By the time he had completed his circuit, he was so cold he had to grind his teeth to keep them from chattering. The actor-cops were gone, but a naked woman was leaning against the wall exactly where they had been sharing their joint. She too was smoking, and, as Charles approached, she took a last toke and flicked her joint into the gutter.

This was yet another bit of sensory evidence that took a while to coalesce into fact.

But once the woman had shoved off the wall with her hips, there was no longer room for doubt: She was real and she was walking in his direction on six-inch stiletto heels—the only adornment on her impossibly beautiful body.

Charles started to remove his jacket. "That's all right," she said. "You need it more than I do." And indeed, as she drew near, Charles saw not the faintest evidence that she was cold, not one single goose bump. On the contrary, her body seemed to radiate heat. Even before she had touched him, he felt his face and the front of his shirt and pants grow warm, as if he were standing before a blazing fire.

She put her arms around him and pressed her pelvis against his. It is probable that even in bare feet she would have been taller than he, but in her heels, she had to lean over to whisper into his right ear, "You were so good in there! *Really* good. I *mean* it."

"Oh my God!" he said, drawing his head back so that he could look into her face.

She laughed and kissed him. Then she kissed him again, her tongue getting involved this time. Soon her hands were moving all over his body, and his were moving all over hers, and he had forgotten about the cold, or the possibility that anyone might see what he and this extraordinary woman were doing. He had never known such intense desire. Several times his knees buckled, and waves of erotic ecstasy extinguished his consciousness.

"Let's go to my place," she said at last. "It's not far."

They walked side by side down the block, her hand inside his pants, cupped around a buttock, and his arm across her back, his fingers lightly stroking the outer swell of her breast.

"You know," she said after a while, "I wasn't entirely telling the truth before."

"When?"

"Just now. When I said you were so good in there. You weren't good at all, really. You were terrible. A real idiot, in fact. And, for a while there, I was getting pretty pissed off."

Charles stopped. His hand fell from the woman's breast. "What are you talking about?"

"I gave you a simple task. Go out and preach my new commandments. I placed the fate of humanity in your hands."

Charles let go of the woman entirely. He tried to step away, but she restrained him with the hand inside his pants.

"The truth is, you utterly blew it. And, for a while there, I was feeling . . . well, pretty wrathful." She lifted her free hand in front of his face, her thumb and index finger a quarter inch apart. "You came *this close!*" she said. "*This* close!" She laughed and stroked his cheek. She kissed him on the nose. "But . . . Well, it's the old story. I look at you and . . . as vengeful as I sometimes think I ought to be, I'm just too damned merciful. You know what I mean? And loving. Loving, especially." She had turned to face him again. She closed her eyes. "Hmmm, *loving!*" she said.

Her arms were around him, her pelvis against his.

He was kissing her, and running his hands up and down her back and over the splendid ovalescence of her buttocks. Between waves of mind-erasing ecstasy, he thought, "Holy shit! I'm making out with God! And, maybe, in a few minutes, if all goes right, I'll be making *love* with God! No—I'll be *fucking* God, for Christsakes! *Whoa!* Talk about sacrilege!"

Then a little later he thought: "But wait a second! Isn't God male! Does this mean I'll be fucking a man! Can that be true? Will it mean I'm actually gay? Holy shit!"

And not long after that: "Who gives a fuck what it means! You know? I mean, *whoa!* I mean, what the fuck does any of that matter? Besides, I don't even believe in God!"

In that very instant his teeth resumed chattering. His pants had fallen to his ankles, and he was alone on a windy street, in an empty city he had never visited before. He didn't even know its name.

Sawed-in-Half Girl

I don't know how long I was walking but I think it was days. I can tell you that mostly between the towns it was grass. And Indians. And some kind of men. I don't know what kind of men they was. They look like regular men, but they got this smell: It's like pond ice. And when it gets in your head, it gets all of you cold and you don't know what to do. Regular men want to take things from you, or they want you to do things for them. But this kind of men don't want nothing. You know how when you do something, even if it's a really good thing—like you help out baking cakes for the other boys—you know how a part of you always thinks it's a mistake, wants to bust it all up, make it like you never did it? These men're like that. They're God thinking he made a mistake. 'Cause you can give them everything you got and they don't even notice. I mean, if you're the one who pokes the needle in the baby's eye or you're the baby, it's all the same to them. They just want revenge on you for being born. When I catch smell of one of these men I light out before I can't do nothing else. I just . . . I don't know . . . Lie down in the grass. Jump out the window. Put my coat over my head so I don't have to smell that smell. These men is how come I'm near blind in one eye. And it's so hard for me to do the private. I don't mind the Indians, though. They just want to sell you stuff.

Well, by the time I got to the town there warn't much left of the day but a little green on the edge of the sky and a little pink in the clouds higher up. Just enough light to make the houses seem bigger than they really was, and the fields behind them like they was hardly there at all—except you knew they was there 'cause all the bugs and toads in them was making a noise that's like the noise inside your head only it's in a million of pieces. There warn't nobody on the streets, and I was glad of that 'cause then I could move fast and didn't have to hide behind bushes or barrels or nothing. Mostly I like to come into a town in the daytime 'cause you can always get a baker to give you a pie if you do a little work for him. Or the grocer will give you apples out of a barrel. Or pickles. Sometimes they give me jerky, which is good, 'cause I can take it with me and it keeps me going for days. One time it was an oyster. But if they catch me after dark, that's when they say I'm "skulking." They say, "I see you skulking," or, "Why you skulking?" And that means I'm going to get a beating or if they got a jail there it means I'm going to spend the night on a couple of planks and get nothing to eat till morning, and maybe nothing then neither. The first time somebody said I was skulking I thought they meant I was hunting for skulls and I was scared to learn that people did such a thing. But that was back before I knew anything.

What was strange about this night is it warn't only the streets that was empty it was the houses. I must have passed six houses before I saw one with a lamp burning. And then I passed six more before I saw another, and then I began to wonder what kind of a bad-luck town that was that everybody cleared out when the fields was still green and the houses didn't look any older than I was.

I was heading for the tavern 'cause that's the only place a boy is likely to get some work at night, or maybe some old drunk will just take pity on him. But then I saw what the cause of all the empty houses was. The stable was lit up by one hundred lanterns and most the whole town was in there sitting on benches and chairs and upside-down buckets. And the preacher was preaching some kind of gospel I never heard before. He said, "I am the master of in between . . . Mine is the kingdom in the blink of an eye." And I was happy 'cause revival meetings is the best place when you're hungry, 'cause someone's always selling hot corn and doughnuts and such, and no one's very particular about food when they're saving their soul, so there's always plenty to eat. And that's just how it was that night: Ears of corn with nary a bite taken out of them, exactly where they always is, on the right side of the door (I don't know why nobody never throws them on the left side), and all I had to do was knock off the bits of straw and wipe off the mud. Some of them was even warm still. And I'll tell you, I was about content as I ever been, 'cause I don't think I had one thing to eat in about two days.

But that's when I saw the woman with fire in her hands. She was standing up there with the hundred lanterns all around her. And her shoulders was up and her hands was out flat on each side of her like someone just asked her something and she said, "I have no idea!" Only there was these flames of fire dancing in the palm of each of her hands. And the preacher was holding a torch and calling her "darling" and "my own true love." Then he just about swallowed that torch, and the next thing it was this big ball of flame coming out of his mouth. And he's just doing that over and over and blowing balls of flame at the woman, and I was so sure he was about to set her on fire that I couldn't hardly look except I couldn't stop myself. Then she just clapped and that was it. The fire was out in her hands and his mouth, and the torch was smoking in the bucket and all the people in there—mostly they was men, but they was women in there and children too—and every one of them was hollering like they was crazy. Mainly it made me think of when you're trying to slit a pig's throat and it's jumping every which way and the knife keeps going in the wrong place and the pig is hollering so loud it's like he wants to holler himself right out of his own life. That's what that hollering in that stable was like to me. And everyone was stomping and carrying on and banging their hands together. Even the women and the little children. And that's when I began to notice that I was wrong. This warn't no revival meeting. Or if it was, it was some kind of devil's revival. 'Cause I never heard shouting like that. And such carrying on. Not even at the orphanage. And the man kept saying, "Oh my love . . . Oh my darling and my dear . . . Oh how I love you so much . . ." And then I knew the worst was coming, 'cause I could see it in the woman's face. It was like he already cut her in two and the expression on her face was the expression of a woman who knows she's already dead. But still, she did what he said. He was saying, "the sages of India." He was saying, "the mirages of turkey man." And the woman did what he told her to, even though she still had on the face of her own death. And she got into that box and she lay down with her head out one end and her feet out the other. And she kicked once, but it warn't no good. She couldn't move. She was stuck. And she lay there with her face all white and her mouth looking like it was going to scream, only in her eyes you could see she knew there was no point, it was all over. It's the look in a pig's eye once the hollering has stopped and his blood is splashing down into the pot. She knew it was coming and she was just going to let it happen. And all the time the man was saying, "Do you know I love you? . . . Do you trust me? . . . Just close your eyes so gently, my darling and my love . . . Soon it will be over . . . You have nothing to fear . . ."

Screams went up all over when he took out that saw. And then every single person, all at once, went "Oh!" And he laid that saw across the box and commenced to cut. And for a long time there warn't nothing in that big room of dust and light but the sound of groaning wood.

That's when I noticed it: pond ice. And that's when the I-don't-know-what-to-do started to get me. But only part of me. The other part knew I was about to lose my mortal soul. And that part told me I had to light out of there so fast I couldn't let my feet touch the ground. But I just stood there, helpless as that woman. Helpless as everybody in that barn. Until finally he killed her and he pushed the two halves of that box apart. And half the people was screaming and the other half was like pigs hollering, stamping the straw and the dust.

I didn't stop running until I reached the creek and the cold was up to my waist and I couldn't hardly shove my knees against the water and lift my feet over the rocks. On the far shore I was just about out of breath and didn't know which way I should run 'cause I didn't know where I was. The moon was already up and bright enough to see that there was a big old willow standing there like a gray old lady completely covered by her hair. I figured if I climbed up inside that tree no one could see me and I would be safe for the night. And that's what I did. I stuck myself between two big black boughs and I was in there so tight I didn't have to worry even if I fell asleep—which I didn't plan on doing 'cause I wanted to be out of that devil town soon as it was light. Also, from where I was setting I could see all the way back to the stable, which was still shining through all its cracks, and it sounded like people was laughing in there even though that man killed that woman right in front of their eyes. And I figured that was just something else I had to get used to, something else I learned about this sorry life.

And then nothing happened for a while. And then I guess I did fall asleep, 'cause the next thing I knew the stable was all black and I could hear a woman singing softly like she was singing to a baby. I warn't sure if I could hear all of her words but it sounded like she was singing, "Oh, beautiful one, I can tell you what you're dying for." That was it. That was all she sang. Those same words, over and over. "I can tell you what you're dying for." Except for one time when she sang, "I can tell you what—" And then she grunted and there was a clank of metal on rocks and then splashing. Then another grunt and she started to sing again, only this time she warn't singing to a baby. It was more like she was singing to a soldier and maybe she was holding a gun to his head. Then her voice started to get quieter 'cause she was walking away from the creek. And when I turned around to see where she was going, I saw that just beyond the last stringy branches of the tree there was a lit-up window and an open door. That's when I noticed something about her voice. And when she got to the door and I could see her against the light, I saw the same thing about her dress.

She came out to the creek three more times, every time singing that same song or the same part of it. Then she went inside and she stayed inside but she didn't close the door, and I had to climb down out of the tree just to make sure I could believe my eyes.

When I got to the window, she was sitting at a table with a lantern on it, holding a chicken leg in one hand and peeling little strips of meat off it with the other. She'd hold them little strips up over her head and tilt her head back and drop them into her open mouth like she was a little bird feeding herself worms. And she just did that over and over, peeling that chicken leg like plucking petals off a flower until it warn't nothing but a stick. Then she threw it away and ripped off another piece and put more strips into her mouth the same way. She had a big mouth, but she had skinny lips and they looked like they had a hunger all their own, like they was just trying to coax that chicken out of her fingers with a whole dance of little nips and licks until suddenly it just dived down her throat and it was gone. After a while she wiped the grease off her lips on her hands, and her hands on each other, and she went over to the fire to look down in this big pot, leaving most a whole chicken on that table all by itself. More chicken than any one person could eat. And there was a hunk of bread there too and a bottle of whiskey and a tiny glass she been refilling from time to time.

Well, finally that chicken smell got so powerful it was like this giant hole inside my stomach and I couldn't help myself. I did exactly what I told myself I warn't going to do: I knocked on the open door. She was on her way back to that pot but she turned around with that dead face of hers again and she told me what you doing here and if you don't get away this instant I'm gonna shoot you dead I swear I will. And I told her I'm sorry ma'am, it's just I ain't had nothing to eat in so long I can't help myself and if there was any work she wanted me to do I'd be much obliged if I could just have a piece of that chicken or maybe some of that bread. And then she asked me how old I was and after I told her the dead face went away and she said, "You can come in. I got some work maybe you can do. But first you got to eat. You're so damn skinny, if you walked in front of that fire I bet I could see right through you."

So I sat down at that table right across from where she was sitting and she pushed her plate and the chicken and the bread over at me and she said I could have it all if I wanted, she was stuffed.

"What happened to that eye?" she said. "You got such a pretty face but that eye looks all funny. Something happened, right?"

I didn't say nothing. She shook her head like she just thought up a secret but didn't say nothing neither. Then she gave the plate a little push.

Well, I promised myself that I wouldn't have more than two bites, but once I got started it was like I couldn't stop. And the whole time I'm piling up bones there on the plate she's watching me like she thinks I'm just something to laugh at. And she's taking sips from that little glass, her face getting redder and redder and shinier all the time. Finally I ate enough that I could ask her what I been thinking ever since I saw her by the creek: "I thought that man killed you."

That's when she finally did laugh, rocking her head back with that big mouth of hers open. She was missing half her teeth. "You mean the Amazing Mancini?" she said.

"In the stable," I said. "He was like a preacher."

Another laugh. And a hoot. Then she said, "That was my sister." Then a little bit later she said, "His wife."

"He killed his wife?"

"Wasn't nobody got killed. There's two of us."

I just shook my head and took another bite of that chicken.

"It was the same," she said, "when he put her in that box on one side of the stage. Then—*Alakazam!*—she walked out of the box on the other side. That was me."

I was working on the rib cage now. One by one I pulled the bones out of my lips and piled them on the plate. She poured herself another glass and finished it with one little click of her throat.

"Didn't it hurt?" I said. "With that saw?"

She smiled and shook her head. "It was a trick," she said. "It was my sister. I'm just the feet. She's the head." Then she looked at me funny, and then it seemed like she thought up another secret. "Look. I'll show you," she said. And she picked up the lantern and took my hand and led me around the table and into the next room, only it warn't really a room; it was more like part of the outside. It smelled of horses. And it was filled up with boxes. I saw the torch the man was holding. And the bucket. She waved her lantern around in the air and I saw the box the man made her lie down in, and it was back together. I saw the white line where the wood was cut. That's when I realized that there warn't no blood. The man cut her in half but there warn't no blood. That's when I thought maybe it was time for me to go. "Just a trick," she said. "See! The Amazing Mancini isn't so amazing. He's just a liar!"

"Thank you for the food," I said. "But I got to be going. Thank you kindly."

And she said, "Aw." And then she said like she wanted something, "You don't want to leave me all alone." And then she said, "I got some work for you. You promised you would work."

She took me back into the room with the fireplace, where a big pot of water was boiling. She gave me the bucket she been carrying and told me she wanted me to fill the tub. There was a screen that had three parts to it and it was made of cloth, red with a little bit of green. And behind the screen was a bathtub and a folded towel and a block of soap sitting on the floorboards. The bathtub was already half filled with water. And, while I filled it the rest of the way with the water from the fire, she closed the door and put the bar across it. And then she told me that I could finish the chicken if I wanted or I could have myself a drink, and she went behind the screen and I could hear the sound of her feet. Then fingers moving on cloth. Then there was some splashing. Then I heard her say, "Ah." And, "That's so good. That's just right." Then there was just quiet and some more splashing.

Well, I told myself that soon as I put the water in her tub I would just walk out that other door into the room that warn't a room, and I would say "Thank you," and I would just go on my way by the moonlight as far as I could. But it was just like when I knocked at the door. Something was making me do the opposite of what I knew I should do. So I just sat down at that table, but I didn't eat nothing. I couldn't. And I just waited. 'Cause I knew something was going to happen. And all I could do was wait for it. My hands was shivering.

After a while, she said, "You know, there's one more thing you can do for me. One more thing that would make everything just perfect." She waited for me to say "What?" but I couldn't say nothing, so she just said, "If you could just pour me one more glass and bring it around here, that would be perfect. Then I'd have just about everything I could want." Then a little later she said, "Go on. There's nothing to be afraid of." And after another little bit: "I got nothing to hide." And after that: "I'm not going to bite your head off."

So finally I poured her the glass and I brought it around to her. But my hands was shivering so much I shook most of it right out the glass. She told me to put the glass down on the floor near the towel. Then she told me there was one more thing I could do for her. I could wash her back for her, right down there at the part she couldn't reach, 'cause that's the only part of her body she couldn't touch with her own hands.

Well, I warn't looking at her, so I didn't notice that she was holding out that block of soap until she hit me on the side of the leg with it. So then I took the soap out of her slippery hand and she leaned forward and I started to do what she told me to do. That's when I noticed she been talking about how skinny I was but she must have been most as skinny as me. Her muscles was just like a bunch of straps and bandages under her skin. I could see every one of them, and all of her ribs too.

"I'm just about sick of this life," she said. " 'The invisible girl.' That's what he calls me. Well, I'm just about ready to disappear for real. Every town we come to, soon as the show is over, he's off to have dinner with the mayor, some banker, or he's off carousing at the saloon till the roosters crow. Him and Clara. His assistant. The sawed-in-half girl. The rematerialized. And I have to hide out all by myself in the hotel, or in some shack like this. One time I had to spend the whole night in a barn with the donkeys and the mules. It's 'cause I'm his secret. Anybody sees me and Clara in the same room, they know he's just a big faker. 'You're the secret of my success!' he told me just tonight. 'That's what I pay you for!' I'll tell you what he pays me for: He pays me not to exist!"

When she said that, it got her so full of anger that she just threw herself back in the tub and a whole lot of the water went out onto the floor.

"Look at me!" she said. "Do I look like I don't exist? Do I look like the invisible girl to you?"

And this time I did look at her a little bit, and she was like a gray cloud beneath the water, a gray cloud with dark places and a red face.

"Look at me," she said. But this time her voice was quieter. "Go on."

So I did what she told me to. I was on my knees in the water she splashed and I was still holding that block of soap. I looked down at her but she didn't look up at me. I saw that she had a woman shape. I could see the woman parts of her just below the skin of the water. And I could see the private. That part of her was very dark, and very deep down in the water. That part really was almost invisible.

"'Why can't I be the sawed-in-half girl?' I told him. 'I can do it just as good as her. Why can't I get a chance?' And he said, 'Clara's my wife.' And I just laughed in his face. Seems like he thinks when he married Clara he married me too. Leastways, that's what he thinks every time her back is turned. And she knows it too. That's the real reason I'm always left behind. That's the real reason I'm the invisible girl. The girl who doesn't exist. 'Cause that's what *she* wants me to be."

Then she knocked the soap out of my hand and pulled my hand under the water.

"Give me your hand," she said. "There," she said. "You can feel I exist? Right? I'm just as much a woman as her. You can feel—" And then she stopped talking in the middle of her own words.

She was holding my hand on her. And it was a feeling that warn't like a feeling I ever had before. And she was holding my hand real hard. Then I started to think about my mother. I don't think I thought about my mother since I was hardly more than a baby. But then I started to notice how this woman and my mother was the same. And I remembered how one time when I really was a baby my mother took me into a bathtub with her and it was just like this. And I was sitting between her feet. Laughing. It was a real good time. And I think it's just about the only good time I can remember with my mother. But maybe I'm wrong. I don't hardly remember nothing about my mother at all.

For a long time she didn't say nothing, just lay there with her head back and her eyes closed. After a while she moved a little, said, "Thank you." She was quiet a little longer and said, "That was . . ." But she didn't say what it was. Then she opened her eyes and stood up.

"Now it's your turn."

"What?" I said.

"Now it's your turn. You need a bath more than I do." She was spilling water all over the floor, but she didn't do nothing. She didn't pick up her towel. She just let the water run all over her. And drip off of her. "Come on," she said, and she took her wet hands and undid the top button of my shirt. "Get out of them clothes. I bet you ain't had a bath in weeks. Come on. Let's get you washed and maybe we'll wash them old clothes too." She just stood there, looking at me and laughing. And when I didn't do nothing, she got me out of my clothes herself. Then she made me sit down in the bathtub.

That's when I saw it. The red line across her stomach where he cut her in half. It was just a little bit above her belly button. This red line. Or pink line. And it hardly looked like she was cut at all. It looked like she was so completely healed that in a few minutes that line might not be there anymore. And then I remembered what she said about being the feet. And I wondered if maybe it was that she was the bottom half of the sawed-in-half girl, and she just growed herself a new top. And I wondered if her sister was the top half and she growed herself a new bottom. And then I wondered what would happen to me if I got cut in half and grew into two people. Would I be the same me in two different heads? Would I be thinking two different thoughts at the same time? Or would one of those two mes be the good me and the other be the bad? And what about if one of them died? Would the one that was left still be alive or would he be dead in some way and just not know it?

She pushed my head under the water. Then she made me lay my head back and she started rubbing that block of soap around on it. Then she was rubbing her fingers in my hair and she said, "You sure are a pretty boy! I just can't believe it. Here I am all by

myself and this pretty boy comes to me right out of the night."
Then she pushed my head under the water again. After that she
made me just lie there even though the water was cold. And her
hands was running all over my body. And finally her face was right
up next to my face, and I could feel her breath blowing on me and
it smelled half like what she been drinking and half like something that came from deep inside her body. And she started doing
something with one of her hands and sometimes it was gentle and
sometimes it hurt. "I want you to feel good," she said. "You're such
a pretty boy I want to give you what you want. Doesn't this feel
good? Isn't this what you want? You're such a pretty boy, most ways
to being a man. Isn't this what you want? Come on. I'll give you
anything you want. Anything. Don't you like this? Just tell me what
you want. Come on. Just tell me."

She just kept saying that to me over and over. And after a while
I thought there was something I wanted but I couldn't say it to
her. I didn't want to stay in that bathtub no more. I just wanted
to get up and go. But there was something I wanted. There was
something that kept coming into my mind. Finally I just said, "I
can't tell you."

That made her happy. She got a big smile on her face and she
said, "What?"

And I said, "No."

She said, "Come on."

And for a long time I didn't say nothing and she kept asking
and finally I told her.

"What you want to do that for?" she said.

"I don't know."

"Is that really what—" But she didn't finish her question and I
didn't answer. Her hand stopped.

"All right," she said. And she pulled me out of the bathtub, and
she led me back across the room and I was dripping all over the
floor and so was she. So then we was out in the room that warn't

a room. She didn't bring the lamp but she seemed to see just fine. Everything was black for me. I heard the hinges, and then she said, "All right." She sounded angry. It was like she was saying, "Hurry up."

"We don't have to."

"Get in," she said.

And then she helped me. I couldn't see nothing. But she lifted my one foot over the edge, and then she held me while I lifted the other foot myself and climbed in. It was a lot smaller in there than I thought. I found the holes for my feet, but I couldn't find the one for my head. But that was all right. I didn't want my head out anyway.

"Do you want me to shut the lid?"

"Yes."

She did.

After a while she said, "I have half a mind to go away and just leave you here." But she didn't. And then she said, "Is that good enough? Are you happy now? Is there anything else you want?"

And there was, but I couldn't say it. I wanted her to do it all on her own. If I had to tell her, then it just wouldn't be the same. She could never do it. And I wanted her to do it. I wanted her to crouch right where she was standing and put her arms around the box and bring her thin lips right up next to the wood and say to me, in an angel voice, just like the preacher said to her, "My love . . . My darling . . . Oh, how I love you, my beautiful one . . . Trust me, my darling . . . Trust me, my dear . . ." That's what I wanted.

I Think I'm Happier

❦

Ithink I'm happier than I used to be, my father said.

Oh, Christ, Dad!

Why shouldn't I be happier? Haven't I got the right?

For Godsakes! I said.

He was silent the rest of the way home.

He can't come in, said the ticket taker.

Why not?

Because he's disgusting. He'll drive away the other customers.

Come on. There's nothing he can do about it. Anyhow, isn't his ticket as good as anybody else's?

Just tell them at the booth. They'll refund your money.

My father touched my elbow. That's okay.

No, I said. This is a matter of principle.

I slipped the ticket taker a fifty, and he said, Sit all the way in the back on the right side. And leave before the credits start.

When he was alive, my father had been a rock. This square presence at the head of the dinner table. This dark silence. This sharp eye. Swift judgment and swifter punishment.

The main reason I didn't recognize him when he first came

170

back was his manner. I was on the bus, coming home from work, and he sat down beside me. The first thing I noticed was the smell, and I was about to get up and move to another seat when he said my name.

How you doing? he said.

Excuse me? I said.

It's me.

Oh my God! said my wife when he followed me into the house.

I don't know what to do with him, I said. He doesn't seem to have anyplace else to stay.

Her eyes widened, then narrowed.

Well, you know, I said. It's not like he can move back into his old place.

He can't stay here! Absolutely not!

What about the basement?

As usual, my father cried all the way through the movie. That was beautiful, he said as we hurried out of the still dark theater. That part, he said. You know. When the girl found the rose in the bathtub—

My father couldn't finish because he had started to blubber.

I *am* happier, my father insisted.

Great, I said.

Why does that bother you? he asked.

It doesn't bother me.

He just looked at me with his one eye.

It's just that you're always talking about it.

I'm sorry, my father said.

Forget it.

It's just that, before, I didn't realize how unlikely everything is. I never understood the extent of coincidence. You know? Absolutely nothing has to be this way. There is no reason any of this has to happen. And yet, here it is! It's a sort of miracle.

My father had been the great engine driving our lives. We had all been afraid of him, and yet we depended on him for everything. I'm not just talking about money. I'm talking the known universe. I'm talking dead certainty. When my father got that look in his eye. When he said, You park your bicycle behind my car, I'll run it over. When he said, You worthless scumbag. When he said, You hear me? You hear me? Or do I get the belt? Well, then everything was simple. Choice equaled zero. And when he came down out of the bleachers after the game, that slit of a smile, that brick hand on your neck, that Way to go! Well, then, the whole world had been re-created and you along with it. There you were: Driving the Oldsmobile. There you were: King of the dinner table.

I always thought I'd come back as a dog, my father said.
    Hunh?
    A dog. You know: A dog. Woof. Woof.
    You always hated dogs.
    No I didn't.
    Servile scavengers, you always said. Born to be whipped. You said that.
    It was night. The streetlights were buzzing. Trees loomed over the illuminated interiors of the houses like mute giants. There was the sound of a trickle echoing in a culvert. There was the sound of our footsteps. And there was that clicking. That click-click, click-ity-click.
    My father said, I always thought when I came back my life would just be. You know. A big romp in the park with my tongue hanging out. All that stupid barking in the night for no reason. Sniffing the assholes of my buddies.
    You're not making any sense, Dad.

Running squirrels up a tree. Charging into a crowd of pigeons. Waiting for you to throw that stick with my big, snaggletooth smile and my eager, dimwit eyes.

Click-clickity-click. That's how it always was when I went for walks with my father. Click-click-clickity-click, click-clickity. There were always at least two or three dogs following behind us, sometimes whole packs. All of them: heads lowered, ears back, fangs bared. No barking. Maybe a rumbling growl deep in a furry throat. Every now and then one of them would lunge at him, sometimes getting a piece. That's why I always carried the stick. I had to beat them away. I would swing at them as hard as I could. I really hated those beasts. I wanted to kill them. Seriously. I wanted to crack their skulls.

I never thought it would be like this, my father said.

It was the first time my father met my wife. We were at his place. I went to the bathroom. When I got back she gave me this stare. In the car on the way home she said, Don't you ever leave me alone with him again.

What do you mean? I said. I had thought the evening had gone fairly well, all things considered.

When you were in the bathroom he said to me, You look like you have a tight cunt.

Are you kidding!

That's what he said. I couldn't believe he was saying it at first. Then he said, It's nothing to be ashamed of. A tight cunt is good. I've always been partial to tight cunts.

Jesus Christ!

Don't you ever leave me alone with him again.

Phillis would laugh and laugh.

My father would attach his finger to his nose and wiggle it. He would put his feet on the ends of his arms and his hands on the ends of his legs. He would stick his tongue out of his empty eye socket. Phillis would chortle and bang her plastic cup on the tray of her high chair.

More, Da-da! More!

He would twist his head around backward and walk into walls. He would attach one leg to the end of the other, and his arm to the end of that leg, and his other arm to the end of the first, and then he would wriggle across the floor like a snake.

Phillis would laugh and laugh.

Great kid, he told me when she had been put to bed.

My wife would leave my father's food at the top of the steps. Three times a day she would put a bowl or a plate and a glass or a cup on the topmost step and close the door. And every time she opened the door again the bowl or plate and the glass or cup would be gone. We would go to bed. And every morning when she got up, the sun would be shining through the kitchen window onto the dish drainer, where all my father's plates, bowls, cups, and glasses from the previous day would gleam in splendid cleanness. But always there would be those mauve and yellow smears on the floor in front of the sink, and lingering traces of that smell.

When that girl picked up the rose, my father said, what made me so sad was that she didn't love him. She thought she loved him, but she didn't. And he didn't really love her, although he didn't know it. Deep down inside they were too practical, just looking out for themselves. But they didn't know it and they wouldn't have believed it if they had known it, and they wanted so much to be in love, but they weren't. And that's what made me so . . . so—

Hold on a second, my father said.

And when he had pulled himself together, he seized hold of my upper arm and brought his teeth up next to my ear.

Practical and love, he said. They are exactly the same thing.

And love is exactly the same as death. But the human mind is incapable of grasping these simple facts. The human mind, he said, is a wad of chewing gum on a bed knob.

My father told my boss that I had an inflatable woman in my briefcase. And you know that little business of yours with the captain of the cheerleading squad? my father said to my boss. Your wife knows all about it. My father opened up my boss's desk drawer and started pulling out papers. Look at this, he said to me. He's got a private Swiss bank account. And here are two tickets to Curaçao.

You're fired, my boss told me.

Why? I said.

You shouldn't have brought him in here.

But he's my father! I said. He follows me everywhere.

Doesn't matter. You've shown very poor judgment.

Security arrived. They led me down the hall by my elbows. A little later they came out carrying my father in a wheelbarrow, and dumped him into the trash.

Well, at least that's over with! my father said, flicking a piece of eggshell off his shoulder.

I was sitting on the curb, looking at a centipede in the gutter.

Aren't you going to thank me? my father said.

The centipede was missing half a dozen legs on its left side.

What's the matter? my father said.

Why did you do that, Dad? It was a good job and I was making good money.

My father's face became cloudy with pity. He shook his head, then released a sigh that was like wind blowing over a treeless prairie.

Machines ticked and hummed beside his bed. Rain tapped at the window. My sister had just left the room, and I was all alone with my father. He hadn't spoken in days. He had hardly moved. I was

175

looking out the window, down at the rain-glossy street, when I heard his voice: Are you deaf?

Dad?

Are you deaf? Speak to me!

Those were his last words. After that he was silent.

No, said my wife. Not with him staring at us.

He's not staring at us.

Yes he is. I can feel his eyes.

I got out of bed. I turned on the lights.

Look, I said. He's not anywhere in the room.

I opened the closets. I even pulled open the drawers.

Do you see him anywhere? I said. Look.

I turned the wastebasket upside down.

He's not here, I said. See? We're completely alone.

A used tissue drifted to the floor.

He's right outside the window, my wife said. He can see us. Turn off the lights.

In the morning there was a note on the kitchen table: Phillis is with me. When he's gone, you can give me a call, and then we'll see.

Why are you still here?

What do you mean?

You can't stay here.

What are you talking about?

This isn't your time, Dad. Your time is over.

I know that.

So?

So, what?

Why are you here?

Don't you understand?

Understand what?

I'm waiting for you.

I just looked at him.

That's why I'm here, he said.

What are you talking about?

I'm waiting for you. That's what this is all about. I thought you knew that.

Waiting for me?

I'm your father. What else do you expect me to do?

Waiting?

You'll see. It's a lot better than this. None of this matters. This is all a sort of mistake. You'll see.

And then my father began to laugh. He laughed so hard he started to cough. And then to gag. And then his bones made a sort of wet clatter as he hit the floor. But he was still laughing. He couldn't stop.

The Professor of Atheism
Department of Refutation

—◆—

Could Charles conceivably have been granted tenure without anyone having told him? The heading of the memo read MANDATORY TENURED FACULTY MEETING (ATTENDANCE REQUIRED), and just beneath were twelve names—eleven of venerable, long-tenured professors, and the twelfth, at its alphabetically predetermined position, Charles's.

The smooth surface of the memo was coarsening with moisture in the vicinity of his fingertips. His hand was quivering. No matter how many times he reread the list, his name did not mutate or vanish.

Was it possible he had forgotten?

For one beautiful instant he envisioned a life of perfect financial security, in which his work was acclaimed by review journals the world over and he was happily married to a graduate student half his age. Her name was Evelyn, or perhaps Ingeborg, and they had three children, each so buoyantly loving and joyful that their pudgy pink feet hardly touched the earth.

In the next instant he was forced to confront the obvious:

A mistake, a moment of absentmindedness.

His disappointment was indistinguishable from self-loathing.

Charles had been reading the memo in the corridor of the Divine Retribution Department at one of our great Christian universities. The meeting was in ten minutes. Babette, the departmental secretary, was hurrying down the corridor in Charles's direction, clutching a stack of lavender folders against her belly with both arms, a pair of half-lens glasses dangling around her neck from a redeployed rosary chain (now fifty, Babette had spent her entire youth as a nun).

"Pretty funny," Charles said, without being able to impart the faintest inflection of mirth to his lips or voice.

"What?" said Babette.

"The list." Charles held up the memo. "Look." He tapped his index finger next to his own name.

Babette squinted at the list with an expression of faintly puzzled irritation, neither hand free to lift her glasses. Then she said, "Ted wants you all there. It's an important meeting."

Babette was gone—hurrying off to the conference room. You? thought Charles. All? As he watched her recede down the corridor, he noticed that the back of the shapeless gray shift she had worn every day for as long as he could remember was open in a long V from her shoulders to midway down her buttocks, and loosely laced with thick pink ribbons. He could detect no trace of underwear.

Charles was not, in fact, a scholar of divine retribution. Technically, he was in the Department of Atheistic Studies, but as he comprised the entire faculty of that department, he had been lumped into Divine Ret. for bureaucratic purposes. Thus he had never really felt comfortable at departmental gatherings of any sort.

The conference room was loud with academic gossip. Charles

waited a long while just inside the door, certain that, at any second, one of the venerable presences at the noisy table would cast him a condescending glance and mouth the words "tenured faculty only." But when at last one of the professors did glance toward the doorway, she only nudged her neighbor and the whole room fell silent.

"Uh," said Charles.

He was about to apologize and retreat, when Reginald Zaighlidi, holder of the Greenfield Chair of Eternal Damnation, smiled and said, "Hey, Charles!"

"What's up?" said Elizabeth Gar, the eminent inquisition-studies scholar.

"Uh . . . Hi," said Charles.

Conversation resumed as Charles walked into the room, but seemed decidedly muted. Also, although no one looked at him directly, he had the impression that everyone was observing him out of the corners of their eyes. The only available seat was the one directly to the right of Ted's still vacant chair at the head of the table. As Charles sat down, the man in the next chair over gave him a startled glance, uttered an almost inaudible "Congratulations," then flushed and looked away.

A lavender folder and a four-inch-thick school-bus yellow book had been placed in front of every seat. As no one was speaking to him, Charles picked up the surprisingly heavy tome and was disconcerted to discover his own name in red letters on the cover. The book was entitled *Every Known Delight: Gullibility and the Invention of Believability,* and in the lower right-hand corner of the cover was a gold sticker reading "Pulixer Prize Winner."

Charles had no memory of writing this book. The title wasn't even faintly familiar. Turning the book over, he saw a postage-stamp-size photograph of the author, which, after a moment's scrutiny, he realized was a bad reproduction of the photo on his driver's license.

Pulixer Prize? Charles thought. *Pulixer?*

With feigned casualness, he flipped open the cover and found his name once again on the title page, and on the following page he found a moving dedication to his parents. There was only one word on the next page, however. The same word was on the page after that, and on the one after, and, as far as Charles could tell, on every single one of the book's 962 pages. Only one word. Smack in the middle of every page. That word was "grapefruit."

Charles slammed the book shut, and glanced up and down both sides of the table. To his great relief, no one had the book open, and, as far as he could tell, not one single copy had been shifted from its position diagonally up and to the left of the lavender folders.

"I didn't write this book!" Charles protested to himself. "I'm writing a completely different book!" Try as he would, however, he could not remember the subject of the book he was writing—even though he was pretty sure he had been working on it since graduate school.

Ted stood at the head of the table, his huge red face radiating institutional beneficence. "As I am sure most of you already know," he said, "thanks to the brilliant arguments of our esteemed colleague . . ." (he smiled, and gestured toward Charles) ". . . the university has decided to permanently discontinue its affiliation with Christianity, and to dedicate itself to the eradication of superstition in all forms, especially organized religion. From now on, our department will be known as the Department of Refutation of the Too Good to Be True."

"Here! Here!" cried Reginald Zaighlidi.

Charles was given a prolonged standing ovation.

As Charles stood beside his desk, holding his head with both his hands, he heard a knock at the door. Before he could move or say a word, a beautiful black-haired graduate student slipped into his office and closed the door behind her. "Excuse me," she said. "I hope I'm not interrupting."

"No," said Charles, lowering his hands. "No. That's okay."

The graduate student's hair was so deeply black it seemed to absorb light. Her eyes were exactly the blue that reflected off the backs of ravens and certain flies.

"Good," she said, a coy smile on her lips.

She crossed her hands at the bottom of her shirt and lifted it up over her head. Then she began to unzip her pants.

"What are you doing!" cried Charles.

"Don't you want me to?" The girl seemed hurt.

"Of course not! I mean . . . This . . . This is . . . Highly . . . Inappropriate!"

"No it's not." Her pants were now around her ankles. She was exactly as underwear-free as Babette.

"Get dressed!" Charles cried. "Quickly! If anyone were to come in here now, I'd be fired in a flash."

"Oh, Charles!" She laughed.

As Charles didn't see anything funny in the situation, he only stared at her.

"The *dispensation*?" she said, wiggling her pressed-together thumb and forefinger in the air as if they held a piece of paper. "Remember?" She kicked one foot free of her pants leg and shoe.

"Dispensation?"

"God, Charles! What's the matter with you? The *dispensation*! The university charter has been rewritten to grant you an exemption from the Faculty Code of Conduct. It specifically stipulates that you are free to do whatever you want with female students."

Charles made a small bewildered noise.

"Jesus!" The student shuffled past him, dragging her crumpled pants with her one shod foot. "Look," she said. She pulled open his bottom desk drawer and stepped aside. In the place where he had always kept the paperwork regarding his university health insurance and pension, he saw two sets of handcuffs (one plain steel, the other wrapped in crimson fur), a bullwhip, a black leather mask, a ball and chain, an assortment of plastic and latex devices the purposes of which he could only dimly imagine, and several hundred condom packets in a multitude of colors and sizes.

He closed the drawer.

"You know what," he said. "I don't think I'm quite . . . Well . . . *Ready* for this today. Sorry." The graduate student was now completely undressed and sitting on the corner of his desk. "So if you don't mind," he said. "I think I need to be alone."

As it was mid-January, and the campus had been under a foot of snow when Charles had come to work that morning, he was not prepared to emerge from the newly renamed Department of Refutation Building to find a row of lofty palm trees rattling in a balmy breeze. Children were shrieking in the distance. He heard the whumph of what sounded like an enormous animal crashing to the earth. A beach ball rolled past, followed by a wet, naked child. There was another whumph.

After no more than six steps, Charles had to undo his scarf and open his overcoat. A dew of itchy sweat had settled across his brow. He felt short of breath, and noticed that there was an extraordinary amount of sand scattered on the brick-paved campus walkway. Rounding the corner of his building, he found himself on a wide white beach that stretched for miles into a sun-gilded sea haze. Kids were running. Kites were flying. Turquoise waves struck the mirrored sand with reverberant whumphs and sent sheets of hissing foam racing toward the feet of sunbathers.

The sunbathers were all women, and all astoundingly beautiful. From one hazy horizon to the other, the beach was littered with gorgeous young women on brilliantly colored towels. A few of the women were in bikinis, a few were topless or nude, but most were wearing business suits and heels. Some rested their heads on briefcases, and others were leaning against carry-on bags or even full-size suitcases. Luggage was heaped everywhere. The air was dense with the smell of baking leather and nylon, which gave the beach something of the feel of an airport during a pilots' strike. A substantial proportion of the young women were asleep, but many of them smiled groggily at Charles as he walked past, or made kissing gestures with their lips. A few—especially those farthest away—waved to him wildly, as if he were a long-lost friend.

Charles stopped three times: first to remove his overcoat and scarf, then to remove his tweed jacket and his tie, finally to take off his shoes and socks. He carried all of these clothes in a big ball against his chest, and, for some reason, they seemed to get massively heavier as he walked. His feet sank ever deeper into the hot sand, his back ached, his biceps burned, sweat began to dribble into his eyes, and his breath came in ever more raw-sounding pants. He had not walked for very long, however, before he came to a bamboo and palm-thatched structure, underneath which he saw tables, chairs, a jukebox and a bar. The jukebox was playing "Hotel California."

As Charles ducked into the shade beneath the thatch, the bartender cried out, "Charles, my man, how's it going?"

As far as Charles could remember, he had never seen the bartender before, but he answered, "Fine."

"The usual?" the bartender asked.

"Sure," said Charles.

He had hardly taken a seat when the bartender set an enormous frog-shaped chalice on the table. Inside the frog's upturned and gaping mouth was a luminous orange fluid from the depths of which rose white bubbles of dry-ice steam.

"Thanks," said Charles.

The bartender stared at Charles a moment. "You okay?"

"Well," said Charles, "actually I'm a bit confused."

"Confused?"

"Yeah. This has been a really weird day."

The bartender laughed, but when he saw that Charles was serious, he said, "What do you mean?"

"It's just that so much stuff has been happening. I mean good stuff. I mean unbelievably good stuff. But. I don't know. I just can't quite make sense of it. You know? It's like I've died and gone to heaven."

The bartender shrugged. "So?"

"Hunh?"

"So, what else do you expect?"

"What?"

"You know. Heaven's heaven. What else should it feel like?"

"What?" said Charles.

The phone at the bar had started to ring. "Hold on a second." The bartender trotted athletically between the tables and chairs, grabbed the phone on its fourth ring and said, "Ye-allo!"

While Charles was waiting for the bartender to finish his conversation, a man carrying a brushed aluminum briefcase sat at the next table. Charles leaned over and said, "Excuse me."

"Yes." The man had a very thin, up-arching mustache, as if a pair of plucked women's eyebrows had been transplanted to his upper lip.

"Have you noticed anything strange about this place?" said Charles.

"What do you mean?"

"Well . . . The bartender just said something very strange to me."

"You mean about his schnauzer?"

"Uh," said Charles. "No."

"What?"

Charles couldn't bring himself to repeat what the bartender had said. So finally he ventured, "Everything here just seems a little too good to be true."

"Of course it does."

"Why do you say that?"

"It's our reward."

"Reward?"

"You know, eternal reward. It wouldn't be a reward if it was just like it was when we were alive."

Charles had to take a deep sip of his drink. He swallowed and sat motionlessly for a very long moment. "Alive?" he said at last.

"Are you all right?" said the man.

"Alive?" said Charles.

The man just stared at him.

"Are you trying to say," began Charles. "Are you . . . I mean, do you mean that I'm . . . we're . . . that you're, you know, *dead*?"

"Of course," said the man. "How would it be eternal if we weren't all dead?"

A naked woman with something like a transparent lampshade over her head explained to Charles that this beach was proof of the existence of Divine Justice. "Only in a just universe would the good be eternally rewarded for their virtue," she said.

Charles wasn't so sure he had been good enough to deserve eternal reward, but didn't say anything.

The woman seemed to know exactly what he had been thinking, however, and said, "You wouldn't have been awarded the Nobel Peace Prize if you weren't good."

"I *didn't* win the Nobel Peace Prize," said Charles.

"Of course you did, everybody knows it." A newspaper was lying on the woman's beach towel. She picked it up and handed it to Charles. "Look." Above a black-and-white blow-up of his driver's license photo was a banner headline: PROFESSOR WINS NO-BELL PRIZE.

"No-*Bell*?" said Charles.

"Congratulations!" said the woman. She pointed at his shirt pocket, where Charles found a brass medal depicting the Liberty Bell behind a circle crossed by a diagonal line.

"But it's not real!" said Charles. "None of this is real."

"Of course it's real! This is the ultimate reality. All the rest of it—that was just illusion! *Maya*. We're all out of the cave, man! This is *it*!"

Charles passed a man carrying a gigantic blue fish under his arm. A little later he saw Elizabeth Gar constructing a small bouquet by slipping the stems of daisies into the upturned anus of Reginald Zaighlidi. Both Elizabeth and Reginald were entirely naked and so deeply engaged in conversation that they didn't even notice Charles. More surprisingly, perhaps, neither of them was older than thirty-five, despite the fact that not much more than an hour previously they had both been in their sixties.

Charles looked up and down the beach. It was filled with children, teenagers, twenty- and thirty-somethings, but no one middle-aged or elderly. Charles had been forty-six when he got up that morning. Now he had no idea how old he was.

"Hi, Charles!" It was the black-haired graduate student. She was still carrying her clothes in a bundle under her arm.

Embarrassed by the way he had treated her in his office, Charles didn't know what to say.

She looked hurt, having misinterpreted his silence. "It's me! Ingeborg!"

"Of course," said Charles. "Sorry."

She smiled at his apology in a way that made his throat thicken in anticipation and his heart flutter like a trapped bird, but just as she was about to speak, a muscular young man with curly gold hair jogged up and brushed the sand off her bottom.

"Bye!" Ingeborg called over her shoulder as she and the young man walked off arm in arm.

Charles's sister was sitting on the edge of the boardwalk, slapping the crook of her right arm with two fingers of her left hand. She had a rubber tube tied just below her biceps and a hypodermic needle rested on the weathered wood beside her.

"It's okay," she told Charles. "This is my reward. I can do it as much as I want now." She picked up the needle and stuck it into her arm, giving Charles a goofy grin as she pushed in the plunger.

"How you doing, Charlie?" she said, once she'd removed the needle.

He sat down beside her on the boardwalk and said, "I've been better." But she didn't hear him. She was lying on her back with her eyes closed and a faintly nauseated smile on her lips.

She was sixteen, the same age she had been the last time he saw her. But she looked much better. Her skin had cleared up. The brown smears were gone from under her eyes. Even her broken front tooth seemed to have mended itself.

After a while, she called out his name as if she was surprised to see him. He looked around and smiled. She held up both arms— one of which still had the rubber tube on it—and said, "C'mere! Gimme a hug!" This is what she had always said to him when she was four and he was eight.

Charles leaned back onto one elbow and wrapped his other arm around her shoulders, giving her a hug that she returned with surprising ferocity. "Oh, Charlie," she said, "I've missed you."

He was going to tell her that he had missed her too, but then he felt her fingers tugging at the zipper of his pants.

"Hey!" He sat back up.

"Come on, Charlie!" She sat up herself. "You know this is what you've always wanted." She reached for his zipper again, and he pushed her hand away.

"What are you talking about?"

"You think I didn't notice those horny little eyes of yours staring at me through the bathroom window?"

It was true that it had been possible to crawl along the porch roof from his bedroom window to the bathroom's.

She continued: "I didn't say anything because I liked you staring at me. I used to imagine it when I masturbated. I used to imagine you coming in through the window and, you know." She drew closer to him and put her hand into his pants, which somehow she had managed to open.

She breathed into his ear: "You know what I mean?"

Charles's own breath was beginning to fragment. His sister's hand was around his penis, which was doing what it traditionally did when clasped in a female hand.

"So now we can," his sister murmured in his ear. "You know . . . Right? There's nothing to stop us."

Charles pushed her hand away a second time and stood up, yanking on his zipper.

"That was all your imagination!" he said. "I was never out there on the roof."

"Oh, Charlie!" she cried after him as he walked away. "It doesn't matter anymore! If it feels good it doesn't matter!"

Charles couldn't remember if he had left his briefcase and winter clothing at the bar or by his sister. He was, in any event, walking in bare, sandy feet along a suburban street that he soon realized was the street on which he had grown up. Everything seemed a little bigger than he remembered it—even the children's toys scattered on the lawns—as if he were looking at it all through binoculars. After a while, he came to his house and saw his father—thirty-five years old—sitting on the yellow porch swing with his hand inside the shirt of Ludmilla Simic, also thirty-five, the hygienist in his dental office. They were kissing. But there was also a fat, naked man with a hairy back kneeling between Ludmilla's legs with his head under her skirt.

The television was on in the living room, but no one was watching it. In the kitchen, Charles found his mother sitting at the table playing solitaire. She too was thirty-five, the age she had been when Charles was seven. The last time he saw her she had been fifty-two, hanging outside her bedroom window, a king-size sheet knotted around her neck, her face black, her tongue sticking out, and an expression in her eyes that Charles had never been able to get out of his mind.

Sunlight was streaming through the kitchen window. The coffee machine was making the hoarse splutter that signified it had finished brewing. There were two cups on the counter, and a small pitcher of milk. On the sparkling grass outside the screen door, gleaming ropes of water droplets were arcing off the ends of a rotating sprinkler.

"Mom?" Charles said softly.

His mother looked up, her hand on the next card in her pile. "Hi, Charlie!" She drew the card, looked at it, and placed it on one of the shorter rows spread out on the table. "How are things?"

"Okay, I guess."

"Isn't this great!" said his mother. "We're all together again!" She was smiling fiercely, but Charles could see that expression in her eyes. He looked away.

"What are you doing here, Mom?"

"This is my eternal reward," she said.

"But . . . You know . . . I thought . . ." He was thinking of the prohibition against suicide, but couldn't bring himself to mention it.

His mother, however, knew exactly what he was thinking, as she always had. "It's because God loves me!" she said. And, because she also knew the next thing that came into his mind, a sorrowful and disapproving expression came onto her face.

"Oh, Charlie," she drawled. "If there were no God, none of this would be happening, would it?"

"But this is all craziness!" said Charles. "It doesn't prove anything."

"That," said his mother, "is a matter of opinion." She drew another card and spent a long time studying it before she put it down.

———

Charles heard a shout from outside. It was Jimmy Higbee, the older boy who had lived next door for most of Charles's childhood. Charles had never liked Jimmy, but had probably spent more time with him than any other friend. The truth was that Charles had never had many friends; neither had Jimmy, and the two of them had kept each other company out of sheer loneliness. Jimmy had been killed in the first Iraq war, but Charles had never gotten the details.

"Hey! Douche bag! Come out here!"

Charles stuck his head out the back door, but didn't see anyone, either in his own yard or Jimmy's. A grayish cloud was moving across the sun, turning the light a rusty orange. Charles smelled smoke.

"I'm over here!" called the voice. "Over here!"

Only when Charles was standing on Jimmy's driveway did he notice someone in the open garage, but it was too dark inside for him to be able to see whom.

The cement floor of the garage was glossy, wet. Red rivulets ran out onto the tarmac of the driveway, and were flowing hesitantly in Charles's direction. A cat was hanging from the rafters inside the garage, a cord around its neck, its golden eyes stilled mid-shriek, its intestines, pink and viscous, spilling from its sliced-open belly. Just behind it hung a rabbit, its brown eye glinting like a button, its belly also sliced. As Charles stepped closer to the garage, he noticed hundreds of other similarly strung up and gutted animals, maybe dozens of other cats and rabbits, but also parakeets, pigeons, robins, snakes, assorted rodents, a groundhog, and at least one small dog.

Although most of the animals were perfectly visible, the figure in their midst was in such deep shadow that Charles could see only his bare shins and his flip-flop-shod feet, curiously immaculate on the shimmering red.

"Hey, Charlie," said the voice. "Long time no see."

And when Charles neither came closer nor spoke, the voice added, "It doesn't matter. None of them have souls."

It was getting dark. Way out on the water, practically at the horizon, the flowerlike pink machines that Charles had heard some people refer to as God were turning ocher in the dusk light. Up in the hills it was beginning to be possible to make out the flicker of bonfires against the walls of the biggest houses. A beefy man with slicked-back hair grabbed Charles's arm and put a cold stone into his hand. "Here," the man said. "I'm too tired."

"What?" said Charles.

"Over there!" the man called out as he ran down the road. "Over there!"

Charles looked in the direction in which the man had been pointing and saw a noisy crowd along a low wall. The people kept bending over then standing up and raising one arm in the air. They were throwing things over the wall. Stones—like the one Charles was holding in his hand. There were fist-size stones lying everywhere. Some people picked up and threw them one at a time. Others gathered baskets of them, then flung them one after the other, in rapid succession. Most of the time it was impossible to make out anything that the crowd was shouting, but every now and then the cacophonously overlapping vocalizations united into an "Ohhh!" or an "Ooooh!" or a "Yay!"

The crowd was so dense that it was a long time before Charles could squeeze through and discover that the wall surrounded a circular pit, about thirty feet deep and wide. On every side people were shouting and flinging stones at two shadowy figures below—a man and a woman, Charles thought, but he couldn't be sure. The couple staggered haphazardly as they tried to escape the falling stones, their hands over their heads. Just at the moment Charles stepped up to the wall, a stone struck the woman on her shoulder, and her arm went suddenly limp. To Charles it looked as if she was howling in pain and supplication, but if so, her voice was utterly drowned out by a loud and extended cheer of the crowd. She gathered up the injured arm in her other arm, and thereby left her head utterly unprotected.

As a man nearby drew back his arm to hurl another stone, Charles grabbed his wrist and cried, "You can't do this!"

"I have to," said the man. "They're sinners!"

"No!" cried Charles as the man lifted his stone again. "You'll kill them!"

"What are you talking about?" said the man. "They're damned! This is how they'll be for all eternity!"

All at once Charles recognized the woman in the pit: It was Ingeborg, her black hair disheveled and wet-looking, blood streaming off her face onto her cradled arms.

"It's what they deserve!" said the man.

The extremely tall man in the blue suit was carrying Charles's over-coat, tweed jacket, and one of his shoes. The other extremely tall man—also in a blue suit—was carrying Charles's briefcase and tie. "Come with us!" said the first man. When Charles neither budged nor said a word, the second man transferred Charles's briefcase to the hand that held his tie, and grabbed Charles by the collar. "Let's go," said the man.

It was dark. The only light was from the bonfires in the hills. The two men dragged and shoved Charles down the road.

"What are you doing?" said Charles.

"There's been a mistake," said the first man.

"You're not supposed to be here," said the man dragging him by his collar.

Charles could not reply. His collar had suddenly been wrenched so tight he could no longer breathe.

The road went right up to the edge of a cliff and just ended—as if it had once led to some other destination from which it had been cut off by geological cataclysm. The first man threw Charles's clothing and shoe over the edge, then took out a flashlight and shined it into the empty space, apparently checking to see where Charles's things had landed.

"Okay," he said after a moment. He grabbed Charles by the upper arm.

The second man tossed Charles's briefcase and tie after his other belongings, and then the two men dragged him right to the edge of the precipice. Charles made no effort to resist. He knew it was pointless.

The ruptured road was dark, but what lay beyond the rupture was vastly darker. Charles could see absolutely nothing, but seemed to perceive a sort of falling away, as if space itself were rapidly expanding in front of him—which sensation, he suddenly realized, must have been the origin of the expression "yawning depths."

"Hold on a second," said the first man. "You don't deserve this." The man ripped the No-Bell medal off Charles's shirt and tossed it backward.

Charles heard a tiny clink on the pavement behind him, and then realized—from the lurch in his stomach, the wind whipping the hair off his forehead and whistling through his extended fingers—that he was falling, belly-first, ever more rapidly.

Not long after his descent had commenced, something hit him hard on the back of his head. At first he thought it was a stone, but then he saw—in the flashlight beam shining down on him with surprising brilliance—that it was a copy of *Every Known Delight*. A slight cross-draft was blowing, and so the book remained open directly in front of Charles's eyes, and he realized that he had been wrong: There had not been only one word on each page. In fact the pages in front of him were crammed tight with words to their narrow margins. And it seemed to Charles that if he squinted, he might be able to read the book. Indeed, the first of the words was just beginning to come into focus when the flashlight beam shut off. After that Charles heard paper fluttering. He reached out again and again, but the book always eluded his grasp.

Disappearance and

————

The cormorant, it is said, can foretell the hour of your death.

The first thing Tim noticed was the hiss of feather against feather, and a certain salt mustiness. It was a cormorant. Its feet were still wet, and left beaded tracks in the middle of the plastic tablecloth. Cormorants always look affronted, their beak tips higher than their heads, their inflated feather-and-bone breasts, the way they look at you with only one beetle green eye. This bird was no different.

Brown glint on skull top. Tick of talon accidentally hooked through plastic cloth, extracted.

What surprised Tim was her voice; there was nothing hinge-squeaky about it, no rasp of rounded stone against rounded stone, nothing remotely aquatic. If an oak had a voice, it would be her voice: pale of hue, frank and efficient, the voice of endurance without shame.

The whole while the cormorant spoke, Tim had been looking down into his coffee cup.

"Got that?" she said when she had finished.

How was one to respond?

"If anything doesn't make sense, just ask. That's what I'm here for."

He wished she wouldn't move her head that way: first one eye and then the other—fast as a blink. That beak always pointing at the ceiling. The way the bend slid up and down her neck, like an arc on an oscilloscope.

"That's okay," he said.

He felt that he had let her down.

"The only rule is that you can't tell anyone," she said.

"Why not?"

"Because then they would know." The bird seemed to think this was self-explanatory.

"Oh," he said.

"Right, then," said the cormorant, duck-footing it to the table edge. "If you would be so kind."

Tim opened the kitchen door onto a morning like other mornings: Dew on the fiddleheads twinkling copper and aquamarine. Sun puddles the size of dinner plates striking the birch trunks and trembling beech leaves. That faint mist like a variety of not seeing very well.

"Thanks," said the bird at his feet.

"Don't mention it."

First there was a considerable expansion of wing and a sound like nylon on nylon. After that there was a buffeting of his bare knees, shins, and feet by wads of air. Then the cormorant was only a bird in the blue. A tiny, horizontal wiggling. A trembling dot. Nothing.

His wife was the one who should know what the cormorant had said. But if he told her now, she would only think she was dreaming. He put her cup of coffee on the night table. "Morning," he said.

His wife's name was Ava. Once she and Tim had been sproingy, like bent twigs, like gymnasts. Now they were resilient, in the manner of moss on the forest floor, in the manner of water muscle flexing against brook stone. It was a natural development.

Polly and Chanticleer were huddled in their quilts on their bedroom floor. They made small peeping noises as Tim shook their shoulders; they covered their faces with their forearms. His children were so light. If you threw them into the air, they would drift slowly to the ground, rocking like snowflakes.

"Rise and shine!" he called out as he yanked up their blinds. "Rise and shine!"

"God, Dad!" said Polly. "You sound like a cereal ad!"

"Shut up, Polly!" said Chanticleer.

"Breakfast is on the table!" said Tim.

"Barf me out!" said Polly.

"Jeeze, Poll," said Chanticleer.

"What's that smell?" Ava asked, eating a piece of toast over the sink, already in her stewardess uniform, her carry-on against her knee.

"What smell?" asked Tim.

He had decided not to tell her. What difference would it make? What could she possibly do?

"Like a tide pool," she said. "Like duck breath."

He nodded at her carry-on. "Where to today?"

"Abu Dhabi," she said. "Boring. Don't wait up."

Eleven fifty-six p.m., he thought.

The children were off to school: Polly with her backpack that stank of cigarettes, Chanticleer lugging his briefcase on a trolley. They reminded Tim of bubbles as they rose toward the top of the hill—aimless, multicolored, unrestrained. They called out to each other.

They shouted insults. Then, at the hill's crest, they seemed simultaneously to leap off the earth's edge. All that lingered afterward was the subsiding echo of Polly's laugh.

As a child Tim had learned to tell the difference between disappearance and loss. Disappearance is best defined as the occasion for reappearance; loss is the diminishment of life. The problem was that Tim had only learned this lesson in a way; in another way he hadn't learned it at all, and so, during all of his days and years, even his most joyful hours had contained minutes of sorrow.

It was a short walk through the woods to the ornithology lab. Where the path got boggy, he could leap from stone to stone. Even the trees sported lichen. Spiders drifted on yards-long strands. Philosophers tell us that the clearest measure of our isolation in the universe is a pair of infinities: the first between the photons for green and our perception of the color, and the second between our perception and the word by which the color is known. That is all well and good, but Tim was grateful, nevertheless, for the coincidence of light and leaves that morning, and for the leaf-fluttering wind, and for the heat of the May sun on the bed of pine needles, for their sweet musk. It was in such isolation that he constructed himself; and as he walked into the meadow that was what he did; and he did it again as he walked through the thick glass doors of the ornithology lab, and so on and so on . . . I live in the constant unfolding of a miracle, he reminded himself.

Loss and loss and loss.

"Doctor?" said the volunteer, whose teeth had begun to push her lips apart.

"Hunh?" said Tim.

And then he said, "Sorry."

He replaced his wrinkle of disconcertion with the frown of authority. He made a note on his clipboard: *Bill-bite. Unfortunate but expected, treatable.*

"I'm sending you to Orthodontia," he declared.

"Thank you," she said.

He gestured at her collar with his pen.

She unbuttoned her shirt enough for Tim to see the cirrus of down that covered her chest.

"Nice," he said. "Beautiful."

Then she rolled up her sleeves so that he could examine her nascent pin feathers: auburn, soft—like infant hair, oiled and combed.

"Perfect!" said Tim. "How are the flying lessons?"

"I haven't started yet."

Tim made a note on his pad.

Susurrus and jay-clink. Olive brown, slug yellow, and robin's breast red. The head-cleansing scent of ants.

Tim filled paper cups so that he could watch the bubbles rise like jellyfish in the water cooler by the staff lounge. Twelve full cups in a crowd at his feet. Fourteen. Eighteen. Twenty-seven.

Tim?

Tim?

Everything okay?

Loss and loss and loss.

People were talking in Celia's presence, so she decided to go see for herself. Celia was a woman whose entire life revolved around one monumental fact. She was transparent, poor Celia; she was naked in public. The whole world could see that inside Celia's mind there was a shrine, and on the throne in that shrine sat a medium-size man with sandy brown hair, fog gray eyes, and an unimpressive chin: This was Tim.

And thus it was that Tim had been having a degrading effect upon her marriage for years.

She dreamed of him nightly: They shared a gondola in Venice, but then the canal caught fire. She held his penis in her hand, but between her legs she had gone blank as a Barbie. They were astronauts together, in a glass globe floating toward the moon, and the moon was exactly the same as their globe but opaque and alight, and when they collided with the moon, either the moon or their globe would crack—but maybe not; maybe she and Tim would drift right past the moon, and then just drift and drift and drift.

Tim had trouble remembering Celia's name. At various points he had called her Cynthia, Cecelia, Cecily, and Jane.

"Everything okay?" she asked. Tim stood alone on the observation deck, his pants legs flapping, his hair perpendicular to the left side of his head.

"What?" said Tim.

"Windy day," she shouted.

The air beyond the railings was dizzy with swoops, barrel rolls, knife-winged hoverings, and dives.

Tim pointed.

"I was just remembering," he said, "that I first got interested in ornithology because I wanted to become a barn swallow. If free will had ever been more than a myth, I would be out there right now, weaving flight paths with my buddies, cheeping in joy at my incomparable skill."

Celia, who well understood what it was to have been born into the wrong life, touched Tim at his elbow and asked, "Everything okay?"

"I am trying not to feel pathetic," he said.

Celia wanted to kiss him. She knew that if she could just summon the strength, she could save him—and save herself—with her limitless love.

"Me too," she said.

"Suppose you had been told by a reliable authority the exact minute of your death," said Tim. "What would you do?"

"This," said Celia, leaning forward and kissing him on the lips.

But that was not, in fact, what she did.

What she did was say nothing, look choked, shrug her shoulders, and wince.

"I've been thinking about that all day," Tim said. "And I've been thinking that the only thing I would do would be to keep on living the life I've lived."

Celia gulped. Her head twitched. Her eyes went shiny and red.

"It's not as easy as you would think," said Tim.

The cormorant duplicates its upper half in the lake. When the cormorant merges with its own reflection, both cease to exist. Where once swam the cormorant swirls a dimple in the sky. Beak-first emerges the snake-headed, snake-necked, night-colored bird. Perky. Superior. Dumb as a post. The cormorant dives again to return with a carp—long as a flip-flop and twice as thick—clutched in its slender, hook-tipped beak. Wait a second—what *is* our friend the cormorant doing? Note how the fish head and fish tail jerk violently with every shake. Note the sharpness of the beak hook. All self-replicating beings of cellulose or flesh must one day surrender that essence distinguishing them from stone, air, and empty space. The fish is metallic orange, and then, as it flips toward the sun:

flashing gold. In fact, the jaw dislocates. "Welcome, my darling," says the expanding darkness. Now watch carefully: Note how the bird's throat is roughly three times the thickness of its head. Note how that thickness descends until it merges with the bird's sleek body. Well done! Well done! You've earned your rest, Mrs. Cormorant. Cork bobbing; beak under wing.

"At exactly eleven fifty-six p.m.," the cormorant said. "Double one, five six."

"Lucile?" said Tim. Then a moment later: "Oh God! I am *so* sorry."

Tim's days had been pickles in a barrel. Had been ninety-nine point nine-nine-nine-nine-nine percent interatomic space. They moved with the slowness of thunder lizards petrifying on a red plain. *Fssst!* Have you ever seen a shooting star? Like that, from birth to this instant. A succession of windows onto impossible landscapes. Like grape after grape tossed into the air, mostly bouncing off the teeth, nose, and chin to roll in the dust. Like having to masquerade as a eunuch in a harem. Barn swallows snatch microbites of clear-winged protein with every swoop, twist, and free fall. They are always hungry. Why, then, should we be different? All of Tim's days could be measured on the scale of desire. What Tim could never figure out was why there had to be, around every corner, this big guy with callused knuckles and an unsavory disposition. The hoot of a great horned owl multiplying in the leafy wood.

"I have always spoken with the owls," Tim said. "They are so cold. They have known such sublime sorrow."

Chanticleer's bathing habits were verging on the repulsive. Already the world had shown Polly manifold discourtesies, and her brother often had to cart her home on his trolley. Pizza or blood sausage? "Jesus, Dad, have you no sense of proportion!" The mechanism by which his children prevailed in life consisted primarily of attitude, solidified with a sort of paste made by masticating sassafras root, vole's blood, and a gray-green mold commonly found on the stem scars of blueberries. Ignorance helped. Pass the juice. The gray arcs beneath Chanticleer's fingernails, and a certain pong that would waft across the table. What his kids were, really, was a sort of mechanical fog that, directed by randomly generated algorithms, could assume an infinite assortment of shapes. More pizza? Homework? Bedtime? They made their mistakes, but their bodies were so soft, miracles of pertness. And, oh, what a dream it had once been to place his lips upon their warm infant heads! And, oh, what a dream simply to breathe those molecules in!

"Bedtime!" said Tim. He chased his children from the table with a broom. "Bedtime!" He batted them aloft, and they reversed midflight like badminton birdies as they arced through the air to their quilts.

Each bridge became the foundation for the next, but none ever reached the other side. The other side was, in fact, only one postulate among many. "Bedtime," Tim said. Now he was a coyote. Now he was a redtail stationary in the wind. And his dead father, drunk again, was rolling in the grass outside the basement door—and Tim was out there too, as bat wings carved the darkness overhead, and the night was so very gentle, if needled occasionally by mosquitoes. There were worse things, Tim reflected, than to be lying on a picnic table on this first summer night of spring. He had done this so many times before. He should have been afraid of what the cormorant had told him, and he was, but he had lived his whole life at the edge of winking out. You know that instant just as the dark dwarf beside the road is becoming the bush in the headlight, but hasn't yet? It was just like that. All of it.

Double one, five six.

If truth is only a variety of falsehood, that left Tim to choose between faith and fear.

Eleven fifty, said Tim's watch.

"There you are," said Ava. She lay down beside him on the picnic table. Night was over them, a sort of canopy—eons across, and constantly expanding.
  "You're home early," Tim said.
  "No headwinds."
  "Ah."
  She had taken his hand. From the coolness of her fingers and palm, from their suppleness and weight, he could deduce her entirety: This body so known to him. Its every fragrance and split. Her habit of coughing as she entered a room. Long ago she had climbed the steps into his attic and leaned a ski pole against the wall. It was still there.

The sky in which the stars hung grew ever larger, ever larger. The stars became brighter, lonelier, chromatically rectified; there were more of them every time, and there was more and more room for the breezes. If a woman could be a season, Ava would be late summer, after the orioles have gone, when the robins are getting restless, and the geese.
  "It's nice out," said Ava.
  "Yes," said Tim.
  "But chilly."
  "A little."

"I'm going back inside for my sweater."
"Don't," he said.

There it was again: the owl's solitude in the mouse-filled night.

Eleven fifty-five.

It was a practiced move: the letting go of hands, the simultaneous head-lifting and backward rotation of arm. And it ended, as it
nearly always had, with her head on his shoulder and him breathing the warm air riding close to her skull. And all that while, the
night sky had continued to hurtle away from the earth, making
more room for stars. There were new ones every instant, thousands
of them, and each was a pinprick gem, an incandescent speck, a
microscopic leap of light. Star after star after star. This couldn't
keep happening. If it did, the whole night sky would soon be white.

Eleven fifty-seven.

Eleven fifty-eight.

Tim began to snore. Ava's elbow between his ribs. "What?" said
Tim. There it was again: that long, cool cry.

Eleven fifty-nine.

Elodie

—◆—

1

The cousin came into town sometime during the night of February 6th; no one knew exactly when. A noise woke me. A muffled cry. I crossed the room to peer through the glittering ice forest on my window. A plain of white stretched all the way to where mountains heaved over the horizon like a frozen wave. There was no moon that night, but the cold had so thoroughly wrung moisture from the air that each star shone like a green beacon at the end of a tunnel, and cast enough light that every snowflake had its glittery tilt, and every shadow had a razor edge.

You know how you can tell when everyone has just been talking about you? That's how it was the morning after the cousin had arrived. When the receptionist saw me, she looked as if she were swallowing a burp, and then she said, "Hi." The sales director seemed to have forgotten why he had come into my office. He was holding a file, which he slipped onto my desk. "Close this out," he said, and left without looking at me. That's how it was that entire first day—as if suddenly everybody had to make up a whole new way of being around me, and they weren't doing a good job of it.

Of course, I had no idea what it was at first. All I knew was that things kept going wrong. Every purchasing agent I called seemed to be away from his or her desk, and they never returned my calls. When I tried them a second time, it was the same story all over again. Finally I got Todd from SaltEarth on the line, but he only laughed at everything I said, as if I had caught him just exactly as he was transferring the company's cash reserves into his own bank account. "So what'll it be, Todd, another thirty gross?"

"Whoo, boy!" he said, and then just laughed.

"We've got a special on this month," I told him. "Renew your order and you get fifty percent off on our new Devil-Kid penlights."

"Ho!" he said, and then went totally silent.

"Todd?"

"Sorry," he said. And then he said, "Listen, things are pretty crazy around here. Maybe I better call you back."

"Sure," I told him.

I never heard from him again.

At lunch Hal and Joanie kept giving each other glances. They were like a couple who had decided to divorce but didn't want anybody to know yet. We talked about what happened last night on *Fifty World*. We talked about where we would go on our summer vacations. Hal told us he had brought home another springer spaniel from the animal shelter, and Joanie said she knew a parrot who could say hello in twenty-seven languages. It was a normal conversation, except Hal and Joanie hardly seemed to be paying attention to what they were saying. "What's up, guys?" I said at last.

"Nothing," said Joanie.

"What do you mean?" said Hal.

They cast each other glances made of solid lead.

Joanie drew a smiley face in the beaded window fog, then wiped it away.

When Joss and I walked back from the movie, it was so cold that every sound had a clink at the end, as if it had frozen in midair. Our arms were intertwined but there was no harmony in our movements. With each step our shoulders banged, as if we were two logs drifting in the same current. In the movie a wife had caught her husband cheating and pretended she didn't know. I told Joss that was the only thing about the movie I couldn't believe, and she said, "But isn't that just what your wife did?"

I had never told Joss about my wife. I had never even mentioned I had been married.

When I was silent a long time, Joss said, "What?"

"How did you know that?" I said.

"What?"

"About my wife."

"What are you talking about?"

"I never told you about my wife."

"Of course you did."

"No I didn't. You think I wouldn't remember if I had told you about my wife?"

"How else would I know?"

When I got home, my breakfast dishes had been washed and there was a bed of orange-fluttering coals in the stove, even though I had been away for more than twelve hours. The door had been double locked when I came in. I checked the back door and all the windows. Locked. Each and every one.

The following morning, on my way into work, I saw the cousin disappear around the corner. Her hair was still brilliant red—after all these years. When I got to the corner, all I saw was the long concrete flank of an indoor parking lot and, across the street, the soot-blackened brick and chicken-wired windows of a moving company. Empty sidewalks.

But at last I was beginning to catch on.

2

I was twelve the first time the cousin came to visit. She was French, the daughter of an aunt who had moved abroad after college. She was traveling with her school choir, and my mother went to pick her up in the city. The crickets had built a dome of sound around our house, and, at a certain point, that dome was pierced by the crunch of tires on gravel. The crunch ceased, but was followed by the mutter and tappety-tappety-tappety of an old motor, which ceased in turn and was followed by the squawks and slams of two car doors, then my mother speaking a French that sounded as if it had been constructed out of cardboard and twine, and then a different French that was like birdsong played on a wooden flute.

A knock on my door.

"Come," said my mother in her normal voice. "Your cousin is here."

"No," I said.

"Please," said my mother. "She's very nice."

"No."

"You have to." My mother was becoming flustered, not exactly angry. "It's not polite."

"I don't want to," I said.

"Why not?"

"No."

"She speaks beautiful English."

"I don't care."

Another, more forceful knock, this one rattling the door in its frame. "Let me in," said my mother.

"No."

A little later my big brother kicked the door on his way to the bathroom. "You idiot! She's gorgeous!"

I didn't say anything.

After a clamor of pots and dishes: four voices outside the window, four door squawks, four slams, a sound like a snare drum hammered with mittened fists, the crunch of gravel diminishing until I was once again alone under that dome woven by the crickets.

The second time the cousin came I was in college. "What's wrong?" my girlfriend said.

"Nothing."

She took my hand and spoke softly. "I can always tell."

"Oh, God," I said.

I told her how the cousin had come back to town. I told her how I was sitting all by myself in the audience at the music hall. How my hands were sweating. How waves of dizziness kept kicking through my head and warping the world. I told her how I recognized the cousin instantly by her radiant red hair, how her voice was the only voice I heard, how it was like the shriek of the hawk as it closes its wings and hurtles toward the rabbit, and like the shriek of the rabbit as it watches the hawk grow gigantic in a flash. How the sound filled my ears and beat upon my brain until everything went black. How when I awoke I was alone in the lofty darkness of the music hall, except that the cousin was sitting beside me. How she took my hand in her hot fingers, how she kissed my hand and stroked it and said in a voice that was like birdsong on a wooden flute, "Now you know. I am so sorry." She kissed my hand again and then she said, "Nothing will ever change."

My girlfriend just looked at me and didn't say a word.

"I wanted you to hear it from me," I said. "I wanted to tell you before people started talking."

She still didn't say a thing. It was almost as if her face had disappeared from around her eyes, as if her eyes had become two blue marbles resting on a shelf.

After that I had to leave. It took many years, but I built a new life for myself in a new city. What is any life built out of? Mostly the hope that today's dream will be tomorrow's fact. That's what makes a box of furniture a home. That's what turns two rows of faces into a dinner party. Every day a birthday—a celebration of the one who is not here yet. Or of the one who is here, but who is not behaving quite like himself. That's what forgiveness is made out of. We forgive because we think we're going to get. We all look toward the door waiting for the knock, for the door to open, for our real lives to begin.

You take a street, with an assortment of driveways and trees, and you glue it to a job, which, in turn, you glue to a circle of variously agreeable people whom you call "my friends." You plug in a dentist, a doctor, a mall, a view from a hilltop onto an eternity of rust and gold in the autumn, cloud blues and grays in the winter, and green-green-green in the spring. You plug in a "special someone," whom perhaps you replace with another "special someone," whom perhaps you also replace, until finally you end up with a "wife," who is really only another way of saying "life," whom you plug into a landscape with palm trees, white sand, and transparent water that deepens to turquoise as it approaches the sharp horizon, whom you plug into a candlelight dinner, whom you plug into an earnest conversation under a kitchen ring-light. And so on and so on—which is mostly what I did, and mostly it all held together, humming along fairly nicely, until the inevitable occurred: the beating upon the brain, the lofty darkness, the silence, the face vanishing around a pair of eyes.

So, again, I had to leave—moving farther north, then farther and farther, until I glued a job to a field and a set of distant mountains, and I plugged in a succession of days and nights, a favorite song and some movies, to which I glued Hal and Joanie and Joss.

3

This time when the receptionist saw me she only looked, and then she looked away. Hal seemed startled. "Hey, man!" he said. "How's it going!" His eyes darting from corner to corner, ceiling to floor to window—everywhere except where I was.

"Same old, same old," I said.

"Yeah, man," he said. Then he slinked his head between his shoulders and lifted his palms helplessly. "Catch you later, man," he said.

"Yeah, man. Catch you later."

And then I was alone in my office, computer light blue on the walls, the loudest noise the electric trickle inside my hard drive. The clouds outside were the color of sodden ash. In a moment snow would start to fall. By afternoon everything would be white.

Joanie kept folding and unfolding her paper napkin. She would turn a square into a triangle, then a triangle into a smaller triangle, and that into a triangle half its size and so on until the thickest fold would bulge and begin to fray, and then she would reverse the process, until she was back to the lip-smudged square, which she would smooth with both hands on her thigh until the time came, once again, to turn the square into a series of diminishing triangles.

"Hal's gone home sick," she had told me as we left the office. "Headache," she had said. "Migraine."

But now as we sat looking out the food court window at the slush tracks in the parking lot, at the snow-stippled windshields, at the giant flakes rocking like tiny rowboats in the air, she said, "I'm worried about Hal. He tells me his head feels like it's going to break in half. But he doesn't have any other symptoms; no numbness, no neon squiggles. He's not even sensitive to light. I mean, that just doesn't sound like a migraine to me. My mom had migraines all her life. And what he's got doesn't sound like a migraine."

She stopped talking. When I didn't say anything, she started talking again.

"I keep telling him he should go to the doctor. But he won't go. 'What's a doctor going to do?' he says. 'Get rid of your migraines,' I say. And he says, 'They'll just tell me to take aspirin and I'm already taking aspirin—so what's the point?' 'There are much better drugs than that,' I tell him, but he still won't go."

She stopped again, and again I said nothing.

"What I really think, though," she said, "is that it's all that E he's popping. And the K. I think it's affected his brain. I'm worried it's giving him a brain tumor. But of course I can't say that."

And when I still didn't say anything, she said, "Hey, Mr. Spaceman, you hear one single thing I just said?"

"Sorry," I said.

"What's the matter with you?"

"I don't know. I guess I just didn't know what to say."

She gave me a look like I was something she'd just bitten into and didn't like the taste of.

"The two of you," she said. "I'm worried about both you guys."

There was a time before I met Joss:

Joanie and I had spent an afternoon apple-picking. Then we had gone for burgers at Mack Johnson's, and we had both had a couple of beers. And then we were standing in the parking lot under a green and orange and purple sky, and she had said, "Well!" And I had said, "Well!" We both laughed, and then it seemed there was nothing left for me to do but kiss her. So I did. She was small. She had black eyes and round little cheeks, and a little body that was also round in places. And when we had finished, she said,

"Now what?" I thought for a while. I kissed her again, and then I said, "Maybe we shouldn't rush into things." She thought for a while too. Then she said, "Maybe you're right." A week later she introduced me to Joss, her best friend from high school, who had just moved to town.

"Sorry," I said as Joanie and I sat looking out the food court window. Snow. Snow. And more snow. And then I said, "Don't worry. Don't."

But she just kept looking at me.

I plugged Joss into my life. Joss with the long waist and the sideways eight bottom. Joss whose father, when she was six, drank a bottle of vodka and drove his car into a frozen lake. Whose mother died of pancreatic cancer eleven years later. Who pigeon-wobbled her head when she danced. Who loved new potatoes more than any other food on earth. Who ran the yoga class at the Excellence Center, and was so flexible she could fold over while standing and smile at me from between her knees. Who had lost most of the enamel on the backs of her teeth after twelve years of bulimia. Who could only have an orgasm if she was drunk, but not too drunk. Who had a nose that got thick in the middle before it came to a point, and who could make one eye look up and the other look down simultaneously. I glued Joss to an afternoon on Tremper Creek, to my burgundy Subaru, to the smell of rose water, to the children I had never had. I glued us both to a life of cold summers and crystalline winters, to a life of cognac after dinner, one movie a week, basil and tomato salads, spaghetti and meat sauce.

Clouds of steam over the gigantic silver pot. The air was dense with the smells of garlic and cumin and broccoli. Classic rock thump-deedled from the small black radio. Joss lowered a tongs-clipped wad of dangling spaghetti onto a plate and covered it with glossy, red, particulate sauce. "Here," she said, holding the plate out in my direction.

"I'm not hungry," I said.

The plate hovered in midair, trembling slightly as she tried to figure out if I was joking.

"Are you sick?" she said.

I took the plate and brought it to the kitchen table. I sat down.

Joss sat beside me, our two plates steaming beneath our faces. The scratch, the flare, the elongating candle flame. How the air around the flame seemed composed entirely of transparent fibers—silk-thin, but see-through. The velvety darkness of the wine rising exactly to the widest part of the glass. That was a rule for Joss. To the widest part and no farther. Joss had a lot of rules.

"I have to tell you something," I said. "You are not going to like it, but I have to tell you."

She lowered her fork to her plate. She spoke my name. It hovered in the air, trembling. My name in the form of a question.

"Something bad is going to happen," I said. "You have to know that. I am going to hurt you."

Her eyes widened. Her mouth became a sort of space around her bared teeth. "Don't talk like that!" she said. "Why are you talking like that?"

So I told her about the cousin. I told her the cousin was family, my flesh and blood. I told her that I loved the cousin more than life itself.

More. Than. Life. It. Self.

Joss followed me out into the snow. She was barefoot. I heard her call my name weakly as I slammed my car door. Then, for an interval, the night was loud with motor noise and wind. Millions of heavy flakes dove toward my windshield, then swooped up at the last instant. Front door. Double-locked. But this time a fire was roaring in the stove. My breakfast dishes gleamed on the plastic rack. The back door was locked too, and all the windows. The wind leaned against the side of the house. The window frames rattled. Inside the walls beams ticked. A moment of silence. The wind regathering.

Then the rocking chair beside the stove moved. Ever so slightly its runners arced onto their own reflections in the polished floor-boards. Another silence. I knew that the cousin had been here. I knew that she had placed her right hand on that chair. And what is more—and this came to me all at once, as certainty, as simple fact—I knew that if I spoke, she would answer.

"No," I said.

"I'm so glad you're home," she told me.

"I don't want to," I said.

"Now," she said, so very, very softly. She was speaking in the voice of the chair, which was also the voice of birdsong on a wooden flute. "Now it's our time."

"No."

"It had to happen," she said, "and now it has. Finally."

"I don't want to," I said.

"Why not?" The runners on the chair arced forward, but only enough to make me stare at them so that I could be sure they had moved. The wind tore at the corners of the house. "We've never had any choice," she told me. "Not ever. Not really."

"No," I said.

The Professor of Atheism
Glue Factory Bowling

———◆———

Yesterday the gutters had been ankle-deep in slush, but today sunshine poured through every window and filled the streets; magnolia, apple, and cherry blossoms scented the breeze, and all the young women were out displaying their winter-pale abdomens and the triangular hollows between their breasts. Charles had spent the last week in his dim study, trying to make sense of hundreds of pages of notes, false starts, and scribbled four a.m., inspirations for his magnum opus, *Faint Hope: Hyperbole and Unpredictability in the Etiology of Apostasy,* and had just come to the conclusion that if he did not flee his apartment that instant he would suffer a self-induced ontological catastrophe. He swept all the papers off the top of his desk into his open briefcase and ran out the door without having bothered to shave or brush his teeth, and only discovered that he was wearing mismatched shoes—one plain black, one brown and wing-tipped—as he was hurrying down the sidewalk.

Blobs of sunshine wobbling over a shady lawn speckled with pink petals. The happy shrieks of toddlers on a slide. The distant thwack of baseball against bat. Charles was seated cross-legged on the grass, the elements of his book arrayed about him in fourteen piles, each held in place by a small stone or chunk of concrete. And, not ten yards away, a young woman lay belly-down, her head and shoulders lifted studiously over a hardcover book, the pages of which she flipped at regular intervals with a finger moistened on the tip of her tongue. Charles was doing his best to look the brooding intellectual, but, in fact, hadn't a single erudite thought in his skull. He was wondering how he might respond were the young woman to look up at him, shake aside her golden hair, and smile. He was wondering whether he ought to, in fact, ask her for the time or what she was reading. It seemed to him that the first thing to do was attract her attention, so he commenced a campaign of somewhat louder than normal throat-clearing. Every now and then he would pull a piece of paper out from under one of the stones and say, "Right!" or "Of course!"—also in a slightly louder-than-normal voice. After a while he began to wonder if the best way to attract her attention wasn't to make some sort of broad gesture—say, to stretch out his legs and lean back on one elbow with Byronic languor. Or maybe it would be better if he did a few calisthenics. Charles could do forty push-ups without panting. Perhaps she would be impressed by his blend of physical and intellectual prowess.

Shouting. People running. A huge crowd had formed just beyond the young woman, two angry voices rising from its center. "Iambic upchucker!" one shouted—or so it seemed to Charles. "Glue factory bowling!" shouted the other. First two voices, then only one. The crowd was mostly silent. The young woman licked her finger and turned a page. Seeing his chance, Charles passed so close to the young woman she might have reached out and grabbed his ankle. She didn't. She was biting the tip of her finger. He had just reached the edge of the crowd when, with a low, collective, off-key moan, it exploded, leaving Charles the single person closest to the two men who had been at its center. One of the men, in his fifties, with the hulking shoulders, barrel neck, and shaggy head of a minotaur, had placed his foot on the wrist of the other man—or boy, really; he couldn't have been older than seventeen—who was flailing in the dust with all three of his remaining limbs, and making an almost inaudible, puppylike whimper. The man was informing the boy that he was a piece of shit and a bitch-faggot. He told the boy that he was going to rip his balls off and shove them down his throat. As far as Charles could tell, these threats, delivered in the low growl of an articulate digging machine, were entirely serious. He looked around. No one was doing anything. Nothing but a horrified form of glee on the faces of the reconvening crowd. The man's foot was set so firmly on the boy's wrist it was hard not to imagine mashed bones. "Hey!" shouted Charles. "Hey! Stop that!" The man was informing the boy that he should never have been born and would soon wish his mother had aborted him. "Hey, goddamnit!" Charles said. As no one else seemed prepared to do anything to help the boy, Charles lowered his shoulder and rammed the man's beef-fragrant, cinder-block-solid gut.

At first Charles thought his assault had had no effect, but then it became clear that the man's equilibrium had been disturbed just enough for the boy to wrench his wrist free. There was another low moan from the crowd, followed by a very loud noise and the sudden evaporation of the man's weight from Charles's shoulder. The man lay in the dust at Charles's feet, a red-burbling hole at the center of his chest. An instant later there was another loud noise and another red-burbling hole a short distance to the right of the first. Then a piece of his cheek separated from the rest of his face. Charles had just formulated the intention of running for his life, when he heard a gigantic but utterly arhythmic drumroll and the boy also collapsed, burbling red into the dust. Men in blue suits were striding through the cheering crowd. One of them pushed Charles to the ground while another yanked his arms up behind him and encircled his wrists with steel. A gob of warm saliva struck Charles's cheek.

It seemed that the barrel-necked man had interrupted the boy as he was about to commit a heinous crime against a twelve-year-old girl. The man had knocked the boy's gun from his hand and had been immobilizing him until the police arrived. Where was the victim? Charles wondered. Where was the gun? He hadn't seen either anywhere, but several members of the crowd identified him as the boy's accomplice, and one provided a detailed description of how Charles had been holding down the screaming girl while the boy engaged in a series of complex maneuvers involving his zipper and gun. A powerful wind began to blow. As Charles was lifted bodily onto the shoulders of the police, he watched every one of his fourteen piles scatter across the lawn and into the bushes, trees, and river. The studious young woman had vanished, although Charles thought he could make out the impression of her pelvis, legs, and elbows in the new grass.

"So you're a professor," said the man in the white shirt. "What subject do you profess?" Charles hesitated a moment before answering, "Atheism." Then he added, "I'm an associate professor in the Department of Atheistic Studies."

The man rocked back in his chair, slapped his thighs and laughed. "Amazing!" he said.

As Charles wasn't quite sure what the man in the white shirt—a detective, presumably—found so funny, he said nothing.

"Do you have tenure?" asked the detective.

Charles admitted that he didn't.

"Good," said the detective. "Good. I think we can help you with that."

"What do you mean?" asked Charles.

"I take it you're a man of principle," said the detective.

"Uh," said Charles.

"I mean that you don't believe morality merely a matter of dictates from God."

"Well, no."

"Perfect. Absolutely perfect!"

Charles blinked.

"Most people," said the detective, "don't really take moral dictates very seriously. Thou shalt not worship false idols? Honor thy mother and father? Covet not thy neighbor's wife? I mean, come on! You know? But ends, means, the greater good! Rationality! Consistency! The categorical imperative! Now, those are things you can really stand on! Am I right?"

"Uh," said Charles.

"I mean, you know: reason. *Principle!*" The detective leaned forward and unlocked Charles's handcuffs.

"Thanks." Charles rubbed his wrists, which were red and dented at those places where his bones came closest to the surface.

"You're just the man we've been looking for!"

The detective unlocked the door to the closet-size room where they had been talking. "Come," he said. "And let's see what we can do about that little matter of tenure."

Half a dozen doors and gates had to be unlocked, and at least as many corridors traversed before Charles and the detective were standing in an elevator that descended so slowly it seemed not to be moving at all. After an immeasurable length of time, the doors wheezed open, and Charles was informed by a stenciled sign on a cinder-block wall that he had arrived at

SUB-BASEMENT C-7
ACCOUNTABILITY DIVISION
DEPARTMENT OF JUST THIS

"Just This?" asked Charles as they hurried past.

The detective jerked his thumb at the sign. "Accountability! That's what this is all about. Consequences. Can there be effects without causes? Causes without effects? Of course not! Does anyone really believe that the tree falling in the forest makes no sound? Nonsense! Who wants to live in a world like that!"

More gates. More doors. Clink-clank of huge keys in giant locks. Hydraulic hisses. Implacable slams echoing down ever-longer corridors. The air smelled of motor oil and cooked dust, and got hotter and hotter with every step. Charles cupped his hand over his nose to keep his sinuses from drying out. Every breath seared his throat.

At one point they passed a chair with gunmetal shackles on its arms and front legs, a corona of gleaming pincers around its back, a square plate studded with needle-sharp spikes beneath it, and an assortment of meat-grinder cranks mounted on its sides. On closer inspection Charles saw that one of the cranks was designed to elevate the studded plate so that the spikes would pass through holes drilled in the chair bottom. He couldn't tell what the other cranks did, but the points of the gleaming pincers were so sharp they were invisible.

"What is that?" asked Charles.

"A consequence," said the detective.

Ted Sanders, the chairman of Charles's department, was sitting naked on a stool in the middle of an empty room. The ceiling and floor were concrete, and three of the walls were unpainted cinder block. The fourth, on the far side of Ted, consisted of galvanized steel shutters such as rattle down nightly over storefronts in bad neighborhoods. Ted greeted the detective with an expression of queasy solicitude, but when he caught sight of Charles something between disconcertion and abject terror took over his face. But then he smiled, crossed his legs tightly, and extended his hand. "Hey, Charles. How's it going?"

Charles shook the proffered hand. "Hey, Ted."

"Lloyd," said the detective.

Charles thought the detective had cleared his throat.

"Lloyd Rassmussen," the detective said.

"Lloyd?" said Charles.

"Lloyd Rassmussen. That's his real name."

"Ted?"

"Lloyd Rassmussen. He murdered his first wife by means of vivisection, with no other anesthetic than a balled-up sock in the mouth. It took several hours. Then he killed their six-month-old son by submerging him up to his neck in bleach. That took most of a day."

"Stop!" shouted Charles. "Jesus Christ!"

"Rassmussen! The Rassmussen murders!"

Ted's smile had evolved into something like a wince. His head had sunk lower than his shoulders.

"Where have you been?" said the detective. "The Rassmussen murders were all over the news in the nineteen seventies. He escaped to the Indian Himalayas for five years, then returned under an assumed identity, bought himself a PhD from a Texas degree mill, and eventually installed himself as the chairman of your department."

Ted pointed at the detective, then spiraled his finger beside his own temple. Droplets of sweat quivered all over his face.

"I've got proof." The detective handed Charles a cream-colored, cushiony family photo album. On the first page was a formal wedding portrait showing a boyish Ted in a tuxedo, his arm around a bony, hollow-eyed, ostrich-necked young woman in a wedding dress several sizes too big for her. Then Ted and his bride cutting a cake. Then the couple with arms intertwined, sipping flutes of champagne. Holding hands in front of the Eiffel Tower. Sitting side by side on the bench of a rowboat in a mountain lake. Then the bony woman grinning and looking down at a bump of a belly. Then the belly so big she has to hold it up with both hands. Then the baby pictures. Scores and scores of baby pictures. Followed by what Charles first thought was a page from a medical textbook, except there was Ted, grinning, his glasses speckled with blood, and the young woman—his bride—her mouth stretched wide by a balled-up sock, an expression in her eyes impossible to describe.

Charles flung the album across the room. He thought he was going to vomit.

"I've reformed," Ted told Charles. "I've lived a whole new life. I've devoted myself to good works. Tell Captain Sharp how well I ran the department. Tell him about my sense of humor. The office parties. The piñatas. Tell him how I've reformed."

"Reformed! Hah!" scoffed the detective (the name Captain Sharp was etched on a silver pin attached to his breast pocket; somehow Charles hadn't noticed). "Give me a break!" Sharp looked directly into Charles's eyes and spoke in that nonvoice that was the voice of Charles's own thoughts: "Why do you think you've never been able to publish a single one of your papers? It's because every time you sent one out, he would write to the journal telling them not to publish you."

"I just happened to be on the review committees," said Ted.

"He would tell them you were a plagiarist and a child molester," said Captain Sharp. "He would threaten them with lawsuits and public exposure."

A motor began to hum. There was a loud clank, and the bottom of the steel shutter lifted from the concrete floor. The room filled with the eye-watering stench of Clorox.

Captain Sharp handed Charles a rusted, needle-tined pitchfork of just the sort that folksy restaurant chains like to hang from their walls and ceilings. "Go on," said Sharp, making a jabbing gesture in the direction of Ted, and nodding out the now open shutter at what appeared to be an endless aquamarine swimming pool.

Charles seemed capable of nothing more than a wide-eyed, open-mouthed stare.

"Come on!" said the detective. "There have to be consequences. The moral fabric of the universe has been rent. It is time to repair it."

Charles said "I," then he said, "I mean," and then he said nothing.

Captain Sharp wrenched the pitchfork from his hands. "Look! It's easy!" He jabbed Ted in the ribs, causing him to leap from the stool, tremors passing through his flaccid buttock- and belly-flesh, his shrunken genitals bobbing like a cluster of acorns.

"No!" Ted wailed. "I'm sorry! I didn't mean it!"

Sharp jabbed Ted a second time and he fell to the floor, blood streaming profusely from the wounds in his side.

Sharp put the pitchfork back in Charles's hands. "Your turn." When Charles did nothing more than stare uncomprehendingly at the dripping tines, Sharp added, "Do you want this to be a world in which evil has no consequences? A man can torture his wife and son to death and it's like nothing happened? Does that kind of world make sense? Would you bring children into that world?"

Sharpe shoved Charles in the direction of the cowering Ted.

Kneeling in the puddle of his own blood, Ted wailed, "Please, Charles! I didn't mean it! It was an accident!"

"I thought you were a man of principle," Sharp told Charles. "I thought you knew the difference between evil and good."

The pitchfork clattered to the floor.

"Christ, you're hopeless!" said Sharp, grabbing the pitchfork before Ted could reach it.

There was a bit of noise and a fair amount of blood, but it took only a minute for Sharp to prod Ted into the aquamarine pool.

"Bleach," Sharp told Charles, leaning the pitchfork against the wall. "It's what he deserves."

"Watch out," said Sharp, once they were back in the hallway. A stalactite of oozing yellow hung from the concrete ceiling and made a glossy puddle on the floor. "I don't know why they never get around to fixing that."

Ted's shrieks were more muted out in the hallway, especially once the door to his room slammed. But even so, Charles kept his fingers in his ears.

Sharp pulled open the next door down. "This one will be easy for you." Before Charles had a chance to object, Sharp shoved him into the room and locked the door behind them.

This time there were two people in the room: a man in a white shirt, examining a clipboard (Lieutenant Spoke, according to his silver name tag), and a redheaded woman seated on a stool with her back to Charles.

Charles had not seen this woman undressed in more than twenty years. Then she had been merely chunky, now she was decidedly obese, balanced on her stool like a pear upon a thimble, and her once glossy mahogany-red hair had become ragged and gnarled, like rusted steel wool. But even so, Charles recognized her in an instant: She was Margo, his ex-wife.

"Everything your lawyer said about her in court was true," Sharp informed Charles.

At the sound of Sharp's voice, Lieutenant Spoke dropped his clipboard to his side and gave a three-fingered salute; Margo cranked her head around, caught sight of Charles, and lowered her gaze to her shoulder.

"Actually, it was worse," said Sharp. "Remember your wedding night? When she and your best man exchanged identical grins across the dinner table?"

Charles didn't speak, but it was obvious he was reliving the scene.

"Blow job in the bathroom," said Sharp. "She swallowed."

"Tell him about the IV," said Spoke, looking at his clipboard again.

"Remember the day your father died, and the nurse found that kink in the IV tube?" Sharp nodded in Margo's direction.

She looked up at Charles, eyes wide, lips pursed in contrition. "Sorry, Charles. I was just. You know. Fiddling. I was just so anxious that day. I mean upset."

"Don't fall for her poor-little-me bullshit!" warned Sharp. "She's a certified sociopath, with a master's degree in con artistry."

"What are you doing here, Margs?" Charles asked.

"I don't know." She sighed heavily and looked down into her lap. "I think it might have been suicide."

"Barbiturates and an entire bottle of vodka," said Spoke. "Also, in her note she named you as the person who had driven her to it."

"I was out of my mind then," she said. "In fact, I had already finished most of the vodka when I wrote the note."

A hum, a clank, and a rattle. The steel shutter was rising from the floor. Sharp was holding a long-handled pitchfork, points up, like the farmer in *American Gothic*.

Spoke read from a long list of Margo's transgressions, most of them being lies of various sorts, with a surprising number involving small animals. Also it seemed that she had been in the habit of masturbating during her high school algebra class, and had been an accomplice in a liquor store robbery when she was seventeen. As it turned out, she had actually had *four* affairs during her three-year marriage to Charles (not counting her wedding-night interlude with Richard, Charles's best man); Charles had always thought there had been only two. And, finally, it seems that she had, indeed, known what had happened to the football Charles had won when he was eleven at a Punt, Pass and Kick contest (punctured with a kitchen knife and crammed down the garbage disposal with a broom handle).

"What you have to understand," said Sharp, "is that, when it comes to damnation, the quantity of sins is generally more important than the quality."

The steel shutter had been open for quite some time now. The room looked out onto a vast pit of snarling wolves with unusually large mouths. Some of the wolves were snapping at one another's throats, drawing blood, filling the air with shredded fur. But most were gathered in a noisy, roiling pack just in front of the room, some leaping so high it was possible to hear their yellow canines tearing at the air, and to look down their liver-colored throats. Margo was huddled in a corner at the far side of the room, her stool clutched, legs to the fore, in front of her. She had always been terrified of dogs.

"Here's your chance," said Sharp, holding out the pitchfork to Charles. And when Charles refused to take it, Sharp added, "This isn't just a matter of restoring justice, but of righting your own soul, and regaining your dignity."

"Remember," said Spoke, "this is the woman who told a whole table of your dinner guests that you couldn't tell the difference between your dick and your pinkie and neither could she."

Charles let the pitchfork be put into his hands, but after giving it a moment's contemplation, he threw it to the wolves, whose huge teeth clanged against its tines and instantly reduced its handle to splinters.

"Do you believe this guy?" said Sharp.

"Loser!" said Spoke.

"Hypocrite!" said Sharp.

Spoke shook his head, grinned, then moved so suddenly Charles hadn't an instant to duck.

Eventually Charles understood that what he had been taking for a lunar landscape was, in fact, a concrete floor strewn with ash and cinders. In all likelihood, those very same cinders were the source of the pointillist irritation on his left cheek and ear. Also that green metal tower was most probably the leg of a bed. Someone was laughing. Charles pushed himself up and found he was sitting in the center of a small stone room—a jail cell, really, or a dungeon—lit only by a single beam of snow-colored light angling down from a horizontal slit of a window. Margo was sitting on the bed, and the beam of light fell across her ear and cheek. She was the one who had been laughing.

"Oh, Charlie!" She shook her head. "You haven't changed a bit!"

Following her gaze, Charles noted, for the second time that day, his mismatched shoes.

"What happened?" he asked.

"We're in Hell," she said matter-of-factly.

"No. I mean. You know. With Spoke?"

"Oh . . ." She waved her hand dismissively. "They can't do anything without their pitchforks. They'll be back in a few minutes, I guess." She patted the bed beside her. "What are you doing sitting on the floor?"

Charles got to his feet, discovering in the process that every inch of his body hurt, as if he had fallen down a long flight of stairs. He brushed the ash and cinders off his clothes and cheek, and out of his hair.

Margo was wearing a floor-length, tube-skirted aquamarine dress, with a row of tiny orange pom-poms on each shoulder and a deep neckline revealing the tremulous convexity of her plumped-together breasts. This was the same dress she had been wearing when Charles first met her in his high school algebra class—or had it been at his cousin's wedding? His German cousin. Ulrich. Amazingly, the dress still fit Margo perfectly. He had been wrong when he had imagined she had gained weight. She was model-thin, and her sunset-colored hair fell in a silky cascade.

She took hold of his hand. "Thanks," she said, looking into his eyes and smiling sadly, adoringly. "That was very brave of you. You know: what you did."

"Don't worry about it."

"Oh, Charles!" She sighed. She was still looking into his eyes, and he knew she wanted him to kiss her.

He did. Then he kissed her again. And again. Eventually he slid his hand through the neckline of her dress. She sighed once more, and began to sink backward onto the bed.

"Wait a second," said Charles, removing his hand.

"What?"

"We've got to get out of here first."

"We can't."

"We have to," said Charles.

Margo tugged at her neckline, then pulled her dress off her shoulder and placed Charles's hand on top of her exposed breast. "We're damned, Charles. This is it—for all eternity." As she kissed him she laughed softly. "It's not so bad, really. At least for the time being."

"How can we be damned?" He pulled his hand off her breast. "That doesn't make any sense. I mean, I'm not even dead yet."

"Of course you are! You wouldn't be here if you weren't." She tried to lift his hand again, but he wouldn't let her.

"No. I'm not. I'm really not."

"Are you sure?"

He thought for a moment, and said, "Yes." Then: "Yes, I *am* sure." But, in fact, he was remembering the arhythmic drumroll and the red burbles, and he became so agitated he had to get up from the bed. "We've got to get out of here!" he said. "*Now!* Before they come back." He was striding toward the cell's rusted steel door.

"It's locked," said Margo. "Believe me. I've tried it a million times."

The door simply melted away before Charles's hand, like the darkness when a light is turned on. He looked out into the hallway. Empty. Utter silence. Even Ted's shrieks had ceased . . . No. Wait a second. He did hear something. But very quiet. He listened again. There it was: the plink, plink, plink of the stalactite of yellow ooze.

Charles was to go first. Margo would follow. "But don't look back," she said. "You know? Just in case. Things always go wrong when the guy looks back. Promise me you won't do it."

"Okay," said Charles.

"Do you promise?"

"I promise."

Margo tugged her dress back up onto her shoulder and shoved her breast inside. "Let's go."

Charles had no idea whether to turn left or right, but went left on impulse. Coming to a T-shaped intersection, he went right, then left at the next T, and so on, each cinder-block corridor getting shorter and shorter, until finally he made a left and bumped straight into a door. He turned the knob and found himself on a busy city street, loud with traffic, rusty gold with evening sunshine.

A hand gripped his upper arm. Margo was holding herself up as she slipped her bare feet first into one high heel, then the other.

"You okay?" asked Charles.

"Fabulous!" she said. "Wonderful!"

Between the joyous avidity of every one of her features and the whiskey-colored glow of the setting sun, Margo looked more beautiful than she ever had during all the years Charles had known her.

"Wow!" she said, shaking her head with delight. "I can't believe it!"

"Pretty damn good!" said Charles.

She kissed him on the cheek. "Thanks, Charlie. I'll never forget this. I'm so glad we ran into each other."

"Me too," he said.

She smiled, winked, and waved. "Gotta go! See you later!"

She turned and, in a matter of seconds, had disappeared amid the bobbing heads and shoulders of the pedestrian crowd. Charles watched a long time after she was gone, hoping he might glimpse her farther up the street. But he never did. And if she ever looked back to catch a last glimpse of him, he was never to know.

Based on a True Story

—◆—

1

"Just take a look at it." F.D. slid the script across his desk. Rain was falling in gray sheets outside the window, the sky growing lower and darker by the second. "You'll never get another part like this," he said. "Never in a million years."

The first thing I noticed was that the script had been printed on pink paper.

The second thing was the title: *The Robbie Radkin Story.*

I was speechless.

"Do the gods love us or what!" said F.D. And when I still couldn't speak, he added, "Diana's been wanting to do this film for years. And of course she wants you to audition."

I flipped through the script. There were a few names I didn't recognize, but all the main people were there: my mother, my father, Jimbo, Josette, and, of course, Beth.

"I mean, talk about getting your career out of the dumps!" said F.D. "I mean, talk about golden opportunity!"

Just at that instant the sheets of rain, the ginkgo branches, and the muddy construction site across the street flashed purple-pink, then brilliant white; there was a tearing blast, as if the sky had been ripped in two; the room went dark.

"What was that?" said F.D.

"But suppose you don't get the part?" Beth asked me at dinner that night. "Wouldn't it be terrible if Quint or Brad or somebody like that got it instead? I mean, what would happen to your career if it got around that Diana didn't think you were good enough to play yourself? Maybe you should refuse to audition. Maybe you should say it's beneath you."

The scene Diana chose for the audition was a gift: I'm working on the cleaning deck of a fishing trawler off the Aleutians, and the first mate comes to tell me my father has died. "Thanks," I say. "It hurts. But I'm not bleeding. I can stick it out."

All the other actors auditioning for my part tried to imbue these words with various forms of restrained, manly grief. I was the only one who knew the truth: that with all the noise on the cleaning deck, I had thought the mate was asking about the cut I'd given myself with a scaling knife. Thus I was the only actor who spoke the lines with a good-natured smile that slowly morphed into saucer-eyed confusion.

"Brilliant!" Diana called out from the darkness between the lights. "That's just what I'm looking for!"

That night Beth and I split a bottle of champagne and stayed up late, relishing the notion that we could finally redo our bathroom. The big question: Clawfoot or Jacuzzi?

When we woke in the morning, our daffodils were bent to the ground by an inch of frozen slush.

A founding theorist of the "Time Is Truth" school of directing, Diana wanted to shoot the main action of the film in the order in which the events actually occurred. Thus, we started with the flashbacks: the time Josette and I got stoned in my high school bedroom, my solitary journey by thumb and rail across Europe, my long, lonely nights in the psych lab, giving electric shocks to white rats, and, of course, my innumerable trips to the 7-Eleven to buy cigarettes and Diet Coke.

My whole life I have suffered from a recurring nightmare in which I am standing alone with a violin on the stage of a crowded concert hall. The truth is that I am tone-deaf; I can't put one note after another without setting my own teeth on edge, and this dream always ends with the anguished cries of the audience as I begin to draw my bow across the strings. Shooting those flashbacks, however, turned out to be exactly the opposite sort of dream. It was as if I were back in that concert hall but, instead of noise, my bow extracted music of such transcendent beauty from the violin that the audience began to levitate, the ceiling melted away, and golden sunshine poured down onto the stage.

I'm not quite sure why that was.

No doubt the props and sets helped—that blue-eyed rat, for example: astoundingly accurate. Ditto the prison cell in Prague with the bare foam mattress and the mint green bars. But most amazing of all was my high school bedroom.

As a kid, I could never bear to leave the stones I had kicked home from school out on the street, so would carry them inside and put them in the bottom drawer of my desk. I couldn't help myself. I did this for years. The desk on the set of my high school bedroom may have been just slightly smaller than the original, but was otherwise such a perfect copy that, the first time I saw it, I half expected the bottom drawer to be filled with stones. "Go ahead!" the design coordinator said as he saw me hesitate. I pulled the drawer open and, sure enough, it was filled to the brim with road gravel.

Everything else in the room was just as perfectly copied: the Little Richard posters taped to the ceiling, the melted model airplane in the closet, even the battered *Playboy* hidden behind the dresser. Every time I made a new discovery, I would cast the design coordinator an astounded glance, and he would merely shrug and suppress a happy smile.

That night, at a local pub, I asked him how he'd gotten everything so right.

"Dumb luck," he said, but didn't meet my eye.

But then, a Guinness and a half later, he leaned close to my ear and spoke in a yeasty whisper: "You want to know the truth? Freedom of will is mostly illusory. In reality, we have very few choices."

And maybe he was right.

It is certainly true that the instant I stretched out on the bed in that perfectly reconstructed room and began sharing a joint with the full-figured and pheromone-charged Josette Kish (played with deft understatement by Melissa Spivic), I was firmly in the grip of fate: seventeen all over again and paralyzed by the equally emphatic urgings of fear and desire. It seemed as if there was no other way I could ever be.

The other thing about those flashback scenes was that I had no specific memories of the events they re-created, and so had few ghosts to contend with as I acted. Every line seemed to be coming out of my mouth for the first time ever, and every gesture seemed spontaneous, heartfelt, and possessed of that impregnable self-assurance of all things real.

The main action of the film, however, consisted almost entirely of the most dramatic events of my life, and these, of course, I remembered all too vividly. The result was that almost every scene I did was haunted by its original, and I was constantly feeling—especially during Beth's and my courtship—as if I were betraying my own life. This was true, not only when my performance strayed from what had actually happened, but even more so when it was exactly right.

I'll never forget the day—this was weeks earlier, before we'd all flown to Dingle to begin shooting. It was the day of the Montefiore Dust Storm, in fact. Fantastic winds were tearing at the eaves, our neighbors' houses were lost in sand-colored dimness, and tiny jets of talcum-fine particles were sifting through the window casings and settling like a yellow radiance on the nearest furniture and floorboards. Beth had no tolerance for such weather. The dust particles had infiltrated her brain, she said, and the shrieking wind had stripped the insulation from her nerves. And so it was that she came to be lying in our darkened bedroom with a cold washcloth across her eyes when the doorbell rang. I was in the kitchen cleaning a trout.

Not wanting Beth to be disturbed by a second ring, I dashed across the entire house, my hands silvered with fish scales, and pulled open the door. There, standing on my front stoop, her midnight black hair horizontal in the wind, was the most beautiful woman I had ever seen in my life.

"Hi, Robbie," she said, holding out her hand. "Miranda Wilkes."

One of the many things that had made F.D. think *Robbie Radkin* a blessing for my career was that the legendary Miranda Wilkes had signed on to do "Beth." I had never met Miranda before—although we had said hi over the speakerphone in F.D.'s office. What amazed me, as she stood on my doorstep, was how much she looked as she always did at the Academy Awards and on the covers of supermarket magazines. I'd never seen an actress who looked so exactly like herself.

"Pleased to meet you," I said.

I held out my right hand, but yanked it away the instant before our fingers were to touch.

Her perfect face was marred by a wrinkle of disconcertion.

I showed her my silver palm: "Trout."

"Ah," she said. "Fascinating!" She lifted my hand to her nose and gave it a delicate sniff—after which her beauty was fully restored.

"I've been a huge fan of yours," she said, "ever since *Pie in the Sky.*"

The fact that Miranda Wilkes even knew the title of one of my films so overwhelmed me that I could only blush.

Sand was stinging my cheeks and eyes. A tiny dune was accumulating against one wall in the entryway.

"I hope this isn't a bad time?" she asked.

"No. Of course not."

That midnight black hair. Those huge brown eyes in which countless male stars had gotten lost.

Miranda Wilkes blinking against the dust and the wind.

"Sorry!" I said. "Would you like to come in?"

"Thanks!"

She barged inside before I could step out of the way, and walked straight to the center of our living room. "I just happened to be passing by," she said, "and I thought, 'Why not stop in and say hello to Robbie?' Is Beth around?"

I went upstairs to rouse Beth and to wash the trout off my hands. When I returned, Miranda was standing with her back to me, examining a copy of Beth's high school yearbook. Where she'd found it, I couldn't imagine. I hadn't seen it in years.

Hearing my footstep at the door, Miranda swiveled around, smiling brightly. "Amazing!" she said, gesturing at the room. "This is nothing like I imagined it!"

Not quite sure what she meant, I merely said, "Oh?"

"From the script, I mean . . . I guess I was thinking: Minnesota farm girl. You know? Butter-churn lamps? Red-checked tablecloths? Curtains with little white pom-poms on the bottom? Ridiculous, ridiculous! This is so much better!" She did a slow pirouette, taking in the beige walls, the beige rug, the Navajo sand paintings. "That's why I love this business!"

When Miranda barged past me at the front door, I had thought she was considerably smaller than Beth. But when the two of them were finally shaking hands, I saw not only that they were, in fact, exactly the same height, but that they looked into each other's eyes with identical pained squints and uneasy smiles.

Miranda stayed for dinner, of course—we wouldn't hear of her going back out into that savage weather—and by the end of the meal I realized that she had acquired Beth's habit of clasping her hands horizontally just below her chin to indicate she had something important to say, and that her laughs ended with just exactly the wiggly squeak that had so endeared Beth to me back in our Buffalo days.

Everybody knows about the extraordinary depth with which Miranda studies the characters she portrays, so I suppose it will come as no surprise to hear that we agreed she could have dinner with us twice a week until she and I departed for Dingle, that she could join us on our anniversary camping trip up at Scopes Lake, and that she and Beth would travel to Saint Cloud together so that Miranda could get to know Beth's parents and Jimbo firsthand.

The wind had ceased, the streets were invisible, the entire neighborhood seemed to have been dropped onto a sandy beach, and a million stars glinted like crystal flecks in the lofty darkness. I was standing on my doorstep, waving goodbye as Miranda drove off in her famous backfiring Toyota. I was smiling. I was calling out, "So long! See you soon!" but I was so filled with gloom that I could hardly keep my hand in the air. All I wanted was to slump to the ground and lay my head against my knees.

When I had first heard that Miranda Wilkes was going to be my leading lady, I had consoled myself with the thought that, at the very least, I would have a massive head start on getting into character. But that night, as her taillights receded, trailing corkscrews of red-tinted dust, I realized that, in fact, I had no advantage over her at all, that unless I worked day and night, and was blessed by unparalleled good fortune, I would be vastly outshone on the screen by Miranda, and come across only as the palest and most stilted imitation of myself.

From then on, Miranda and Beth went to the grocery store and gym together several times a week. Miranda also started helping Beth down at the nursery, and turned out to have a serious green thumb for ornamental grasses.

One afternoon Miranda took Beth to her own hairdresser, and when the two of them arrived at our house for dinner, Miranda's midnight black hair was exactly Beth's shade of red, and cut in bangs at the front and shoulder length everywhere else, just as Beth's had been since the day I met her.

A week later, when the three of us rendezvoused at a miniature golf course, Miranda was wearing tinted contacts that perfectly matched Beth's slate blue eyes, and was also wearing exactly the same green jeans and baggy purple sweater as Beth, even though both women insisted that they had not exchanged one word about wardrobe beforehand.

That was the first time I had to make a conscious effort to keep Beth's and Miranda's names straight. It was also when I realized, after one near slipup, that henceforth I would have to forswear giving Beth affectionate bottom-pats whenever Miranda was around—a resolution that turned out to be surprisingly difficult to keep. But my most disconcerting realization came when I noticed that any time either of them would knock her ball into the cup, she would hoot, hop on one leg, and wave her opposite knee in the air. Despite myself, I couldn't remember who had been the originator of this little ritual and who was copying it, and I began to wonder if I had ever really known my wife at all.

Things only got worse.

At the airport after Beth and Miranda's trip to Saint Cloud, I was watching them walk toward me down the tunnel from the plane, their heads bobbing and shoulders swaying so identically, and their expressions of weary expectation so perfectly twinned, that it wasn't until they had given me simultaneous kisses on opposite cheeks that I was able to tell them apart. . . . But that wasn't the bad part—I'd already grown well used to that sort of confusion. What really distressed me was the realization that one of these two women was the creature of flesh and blood to whom I had been married for close to a third of my life, and the other one was the perfect Beth—Beth as she ought to have been, and as she was, in fact, in my most romantic memories and imaginings of her.

I was so disconsolate as I drove us all home that I nearly swung the car into the oncoming traffic.

I love Beth—I really do! I love her, love her, *love* her!

That's what I told myself that whole afternoon and evening, and for weeks thereafter—but it made no difference.

Miranda invited me alone to the Kasbah Club. We sat on giant throw pillows made from Persian rugs. We sampled hashish from half a dozen hookahs and stuffed hundred-dollar bills into the golden girdles of belly dancers. Through our first couple of Moroccan martinis we mainly traded industry gossip, but then Miranda leaned across her pillow, put her hand on my thigh, and asked me to tell her ten things that Beth had never confessed to anyone but me. When the first two items on my list turned out to be things Beth had, in fact, told Miranda, I was forced to get much more down and dirty.

I came home that night to find Beth lying on the couch, watching television with sunglasses—clearly suffering another of her headaches. I was grateful I couldn't see her eyes, but, even so, I could hardly bear to be in the room with her—my dear, sweet Beth, who had rabbited on so trustingly during countless postcoital middles of the night and who, on more than one occasion, had turned to me with hollow eyes, believing that I was the one person on earth to whom it was safe to confess her deepest shame.

2

Miranda and I were on our way to Dingle. Once through the security gate, she tugged at my elbow and said, "There's something I have to tell you." She fixed me squarely in her gaze and—for an instant, but only an instant—looked nothing like my wife. "From now on," she said, "I *am* Beth Radkin. Until the final take of that final shot of our hands clasping on that speedboat fleeing Hong Kong, I *am* your wife, the woman you love and to whom you are bound by solemn vows. Miranda Wilkes doesn't exist. Nor does *that other woman*"—which was how she would refer to Beth from then on. "Do you understand?" she asked.

"I do," I said.

Somewhere off the coast of Nova Scotia, as we were picking our way through our MSG-marinated chicken dinners, Miranda turned to me with exactly Beth's most impish grin. "You know," she said, "when I asked *that other woman* to tell me ten secrets about you, she mentioned that, on your first trip to Europe together, you had sex in the airplane's bathroom."

I laughed. My face went hot. All I could say was "Wow!"

"Do you mind telling me how that happened?"

I laughed again. "Well, the main thing, I guess, was that we'd only known each other about a month. But probably it also helped that, when we were having our dinner, we ordered a couple extra bottles of wine."

"Let's do that!" said Miranda.

We did.

An hour or so later, she wiped herself and pulled up her underpants. "Thanks," she said. "I got a lot out of that. Things are really falling into place."

Miranda disappeared while I was waiting for my suitcases at the baggage claim, and I didn't see her again for the whole week we shot the flashbacks. I didn't see her, in fact, until the cameras were already rolling during the blizzard scene in which I first meet Beth. Not coincidentally, this was also the scene in which my performance began to be haunted by my memory of the events I was trying to re-create.

The first problem was that I wasn't drunk.

The night I met Beth I had been so profoundly intoxicated as I staggered along the path outside her dormitory that, even with my coat wide open and my shirttails flapping in the wind, I had hardly noticed the cold. Alas, neither Diana nor Miranda wanted anything to do with soap flakes in Dingle, so the snow on the set was real and the entire soundstage (a converted hog barn on a working farm) had been refrigerated to twenty-two degrees Fahrenheit. Once the fans got going, the artificial blizzard was, in fact, indistinguishable from the one it was meant to represent—which would have been fine had my internal furnace been stoked with "Mystery Punch" and half a bottle of tequila. Instead, by the time the cameras started rolling, my teeth were chattering so ferociously I wasn't sure I could pronounce my lines.

The second problem was the two bare feet sticking out of the snowdrift in front of me.

And the third: the toppled black stiletto heels, already half buried by swirling flakes, lying on the walkway.

This was all wrong. Beth's feet had not been bare that night, but shod—and in fluffy slippers, not stilettos. She also had not been wearing a tight black strapless minidress, but a bathrobe and flannel nightgown. And she had not been drunk, nor had she been to the party I had just left. On the contrary, the only reason she had ended up in that snowdrift was that she had been leaning out her dorm room window, shouting at a bunch of partygoers, and her hand had slipped on a patch of ice.

As these inconsistencies mounted, I grew increasingly irritated and finally enraged: This isn't my life! It's just a collection of crass clichés! A shameless sellout! An assault on my integrity!

My concentration was shot. All I could think about was what to say to Diana. Did I dare walk off the set? Should I get F.D. on the phone?

But then Miranda spoke her first line, and everything changed.

Having knocked her head during her fall, Beth had been watching a whirlpool of stars as she lay in that snowdrift, and had been more than a little frightened when I loomed suddenly over her. Thus the first words she ever spoke to me were "Holy shit! What happened? Who are you?"

As for me: So drunk I was seeing two of everything, I found it impossible to believe a semidressed girl had simply fallen out of the sky. Thus my first words were "Whoa! Hold on a second! This is crazy!"

The screenwriter got the lines right, but Miranda could hardly have interpreted them more inaccurately. There may have been some disorientation in her "Holy shit!" but not a trace of fear. On the contrary, when I pulled her up out of the snow, her glittering eyes fixed eagerly on mine and the corner of her mouth lifted in a smirk of inebriate lust.

"Whoa!" I said, but far more softly than I had spoken this syllable to Beth.

And when Miranda said, "What happened?" her smile only broadened, as if she couldn't believe her luck.

She was flushed, clearly freezing, the snow oozing aesthetically down her bare shoulders and chest.

"Hold on a second," I told her, opening my coat and drawing her inside to keep her warm.

I hadn't done this with Beth.

Miranda's face was so close to mine that when she murmured mischievously, "Who are you?" I could feel her breath on my lips.

"This is crazy," I murmured in return.

Then I kissed her.

243

Not only had I never come close to kissing Beth that first night, this kiss had not even been written into the script.

After we had held it for a while, Diana shouted, "Cut!"

Her brow was wrinkled. She clutched her chin between her thumb and forefinger, and went so completely motionless she might have been a photograph of herself.

"That was interesting," she said at last. "But let's try it again— *without* the kiss."

While the stagehands reconstructed the snowdrift and swept away our footprints, Miranda and I wrapped ourselves in woolen blankets and went off to the lounge to sip sweet, milky tea in front of a gas fire. I was soon so warm I had begun to sweat, but Miranda was still visibly shivering.

I held out my blanket to her. "Here, Randi, you take it."

She kept staring into the whispering orange grid as if she hadn't heard me.

I shook the blanket next to her shoulder: "Miranda?"

Still she didn't respond.

Finally, I remembered: "Beth?"

She turned to me with a happy smile, took the blanket and said, "Thanks, Bo-Bob!"

Bo-Bob is one of Beth's love names for me.

And Miranda's happy smile exactly duplicated the one with which Beth had woken me the morning after we first made love.

I tried to smile in return, but ended up with a guilty wince. My throat went fluttery with nausea; my saliva turned to paste.

We did four takes without the kiss, and then three more with it. With every repetition I became more self-conscious, and found myself speaking my lines increasingly as I had actually said them to Beth. This was clearly throwing Miranda off. At first she just forged ahead with her typical brilliance, but after a while, whenever she said the line "Who are you?" I could see her eyes—behind their lusty glint—searching mine with genuine uncertainty.

As we walked back that evening toward the adjoining thatched farm cottages that had been rented for us, Miranda slipped her arm through mine and said, "I think that first take was a keeper. Diana seemed very excited by it."

I heaved my shoulders and sighed.

"What's up, Robbie Bo-Bob?"

"Nothing. I guess I got a little self-conscious there toward the end."

"Happens to the best of us." She smiled, lifted my hand and gave it a little pat.

"Not to you."

At that moment, we happened to be in a grassy field so luxuriously green it glowed. The sun was setting, and the sky was an enormous dome of conch pink modulating to lavender and indigo. A steady wind blew skeins of silver, orange, gray, and gold cloud from the western to the eastern horizon. A nightingale sang at the top of a massive live oak. The clip-clop of horseshoes on cobblestones sounded from the bottom of the lane.

Miranda had stopped walking and was looking up at me with just exactly Beth's most loving expression. The streaming clouds were reflected in her eyes. Her cheeks were flushed such a luminous pink, she might have been lit by a candle from within. She was Beth and only Beth, and yet her entire expression was so thoroughly suffused with a movie heroine's just-before-the-climax "I-believe-in-you" radiance that had she looked up at me an instant longer, I might have swooned at her feet.

She punched me gently on the jaw and gave me one of Beth's goofy grins. "C'mon," she said, "I've got a Mexican pot roast waiting for you in the oven."

Mexican pot roast was my absolute favorite of Beth's dishes, but Beth had never cooked anything so extravagantly delicious as the meal Miranda placed before me.

After our baffled encounter at the snowdrift, Beth and I had made our way to our separate dormitories without bothering even to exchange names, and did not see each other again until a week later, when we both happened to take a one-day underwater photography workshop. For most of the first hour of the class, we merely cast each other increasingly less furtive glances across the swimming pool, and didn't have a chance to speak until the instructor assigned us to the same darkroom.

I closed the door and heard Beth's voice in the total obscurity: "Isn't there supposed to be some kind of light on in here?"

There followed a joint fumbling along the wall that resulted in several unintended collisions of fingertips, shoulders, and forearms.

Beth was the one who finally found the switch.

For a long moment, all we could do was grin at each other in the red gloom. Then she winked and said, "Do you believe this!"

I flicked the switch off again, and it was not long before we had found each other with our mouths.

So here's the problem: When I cast Miranda increasingly less furtive glances across the swimming pool on the set, I was not really acting. Nor was I acting when I stood grinning at her in the red spotlight, and even less so when the light turned blue and it was time to press my lips on hers. Our kiss evolved into a passionate if intermittently comic love scene (an elbow in a developing tray, a tottering enlarger, bouncing film spools), and not a single instant of it was faked.

My mouth swiveled on Miranda's. I breathed her breath and wrestled her tongue. My hands rose and fell along the length of her body, inside and out of her bathing suit, and her hands roved inside and out of mine. Everything was just as it had once been with

Beth—except that no woman's body has ever possessed such delectable convexities and concavities as Miranda's, and no woman has ever known so well how to convey desire with a grunt, a sway, or a lingering touch. It was not long before everything disappeared—the cameras, the crew, the lights, the wooly microphones—and any memory I had of Beth or my entire previous life faded with them. Nothing existed in this world but Miranda's body and the delightful effects that body was having on mine. And soon this too was gone, and ours was the perfect nonexistence at the center of a box of mirrors: desire reflecting desire reflecting desire . . . and so on to infinity.

But then, in the midst of an adjustment of lips and groins, I happened to open my eyes and found myself looking into a gaze it was impossible not to think of as Beth's.

Perhaps you can imagine how disconcerting this was.

It wasn't so much that I felt caught-out in adultery—although, for half a second, that was exactly what I did feel. It was more my sudden recognition that Beth had not, in fact, disappeared, that Miranda had never truly eclipsed her, that were it not for Beth's ineradicable essence, everything I felt under those red and blue lights would have been trite, superficial—barely rising above the momentary excitation of pornography. I had undervalued my wife. I had failed to realize that Miranda's erotic urgency derived its depth and force from its juxtaposition to Beth's edgy, wallflower insecurity, that even Miranda's perfectly formed breasts would have been far less miraculous apparitions had they not also, in some complex way, belonged to that girl from Saint Cloud who liked to clean her ears with paper clips, who had once, when she was little, sent her hamster into cardiac arrest by feeding him a chocolate kiss, and who, the night I came home from my first audition feeling talentless and full of shame, had taken me wordlessly into her arms, patted me three times at the center of my back, then three times again.

"*Robbie?*" said Diana.

"You all right?" said Miranda.

"Why don't we try that again?" Diana suggested.

And we did, twenty-three more times, until finally everyone agreed it would be better to quit for the day and have another go in the morning.

That night Miranda and I stood face-to-face at the foot of her bed. She was naked; I was in my boxer shorts and socks. I had tears in my eyes.

"I know it's hard," she said. "But you've got to get through this—okay? You'll see. It won't be so bad. Just remember, we're only developing our characters. There's nothing personal about it. It's all professional—I *promise*."

Then she gave me another of Beth's goofy grins and tapped my nose with her index finger. "Got that, Bo-bob?"

I didn't know what to think.

I didn't know what to do.

"Sure," I said.

And then I attempted a classic leading man's soul kiss. When that didn't work, I tried an open-handed breast mash with a combination pelvic twist and single buttock crush.

"No, no, no!" said Miranda. "I want to do it the way we *always* do it. You know: the way you do it with—" she didn't finish her sentence. "Tell me what I like." She ran her finger down the middle of my chest. "Am I a moaner or a shouter? Tell me if I moan or shout. Tell me all the things I like the most, and let's do that."

And then I was touched by genius:

I lied.

I thought of everything Beth liked, and told Miranda she liked the opposite. I thought of all the things I had always enjoyed, but Beth had never had much of a taste for—and Miranda and I did them. As the night wore on, I got more and more creative: I threw in a few minor perversities and then some acts only top-flight acrobats and contortionists could have pulled off—and Miranda accomplished them all with aplomb. There was one moment when she pulled back her head and gave me a skeptical squint, but I just said, "You only asked for ten of that other woman's secrets—she's got hundreds! She's an extremely complex individual."

"Tell me everything," Miranda said. "I want to know it all."

Miranda was such a fast learner that the following morning we were able to do three more takes of the darkroom scene without my being reminded even once of my wife. "Brilliant!" Diana cried after the first take. "Perfect!" after the second. "I'm smelling an Oscar!" after the third.

The spelunking and med-school scenes were next—and these were difficult, for obvious reasons. But if anyone noticed, no one said a word, and Diana seemed happy. Then finally we got to the Singapore shark-farming sequence, and things really started clicking. Every single take of every single scene was a surprise, and every one of them seemed better than the one that had preceded it.

What can I say? It was all due to Miranda Wilkes's brilliance. The Beth Radkin who gradually came into being as a result of my steady stream of lies could hardly have been a more incoherent assemblage of contradictory characteristics, but Miranda was not only able to make this impossible woman seem vibrant and real, her every word, gesture, glance, or vocal tremor was so profoundly nuanced and so brilliantly on point that I always knew exactly how to feel and what to do. By simply following Miranda's lead, I uncovered fascinating dimensions of my own character I had never imagined before.

Everything I had feared from the start ultimately came to pass: On the rushes each evening I was the palest reflection of Miranda's galvanic genius, but it didn't matter, because I knew, during each and every moment of our filming, that I had never acted so well.

And I also knew—and this is the main thing, really—that I had never felt so profoundly and ecstatically alive.

After that first night in Miranda's bedroom, I moved permanently out of my thatched cottage and into hers. Every morning I would come down to the kitchen to find Miranda sitting at the table, sipping black coffee and waiting for the toast to pop. We would walk over the fields to the soundstage, holding hands and chatting idly, and return home the same way every evening. Sometimes we'd have dinner in our kitchen, sometimes we'd go out to a restaurant, a pub, or a disco. Our sweat would mingle on the dance floor, or amid the disheveled sheets of our bed, and in quieter hours of the night I'd listen to the noises Miranda made in sleep, or I'd draw my face next to her shoulder and breathe the warm air close to her skin.

Then, in the morning, it would start all over again.

What was there not to love about that life? Why would I ever want such a life to end?

The problem was that *Robbie Radkin* was a love story. The problem was that after all of Beth's and my breaking up and making up on three continents, Beth got that rare blood disease that only made her look more poignantly beautiful and vitally alive the closer she came to death. The problem was that the movie's climax was that moment in the Shanghai hospital (before the arrival of the Bavarian aroma therapist) when Beth and I, believing her every next breath might be her last, realized that we had been born to love each other, that nothing on earth had ever been or would ever be as beautiful as our love. The problem was Miranda's stupendous talent.

The moment Miranda looked up at me from that hospital bed, her slate blue eyes glimmering in Asian AmberTone spotlight, she would know nothing and believe in nothing but the transcendent glory of Beth's and my love. All of those nights and mornings at the thatched cottage would be gone, all of those sultry and lascivious gazes we had cast each other across the disco dance floor, all of our proclamations of love, our merry teasing, our conversations about children, retirement, the wisdom of investing in Tuscan real estate—all of this would be obsolete, nonexistent. That lump-in-the-throat embrace on the windy cliff-edge above the raging Atlantic, that afternoon of cavorting with puppy Labradors in waist-high wheat, that climactic moment of inspiration in the glowing green field beneath the conch pink sky: zilch, obliterated, cigarette ash out a train window.

By the sheer force of Miranda's talent, Beth's and my love would not merely be made compellingly palpable, it would be magnified, glorified, canonized. With a perfectly calibrated blinking-back of a tear, with a scintilla's tremble of her lower lip, Miranda would elevate my love for Beth into something so resplendently pure that whole nations would be ready to die for it, and by its grace alone might the human species seem deserving of redemption. To betray such a love would be an unfathomable atrocity. This is what Miranda would believe as she brought it all into being. This is what every member of her audience would believe—and I would believe it too. I would be powerless before the force of her performance. Were I to deny what Miranda had made so dazzlingly real I would only become contemptible to myself.

"Rob!" Miranda cried. "Robbie! Wait!" I had charged off the set and out of the hog barn. I was striding down a muddy road, through a field of rust-stained sheep and house-high boulders. The hay-scented wind battered my ears. The sky was enormous, the sun arc-lamp white and low over the hills.

"Rob! Robbie! Robert!"

I heard the patter of Miranda's flip-flops on the mud behind me, but I didn't look around.

"Robbie! Rob!"

I lowered my head, plunged my fists into the pockets of my tennis shorts, and redoubled my pace, hoping Miranda would tire out or get disgusted and leave me to my misery and rage.

But she didn't.

She was no longer calling my name, but the flippity-flap of her footsteps grew ever louder behind me. The road dwindled to a couple of ruts, then to a single path, and Miranda kept coming closer and closer, until I could hear her feet tearing through the yellow grass to my right and see, out of the corner of my eye, her pink, striding shins and the flapping skirts of her kimono-style hospital gown. Her wind-tousled hair flashed orange in the low white sun.

"Robbie! What's wrong?"

I didn't answer, but slowed my pace as she linked her arm in mine. After a while, I moved over so that there would be room for both of us on the path.

"Robbie, please!" She squeezed my biceps against her ribs.

"I don't want to talk about it!" I said.

And so we walked in silence for more than an hour. The sun set below the hills as we descended into a valley, then rose as we mounted the other side—but only for a while: Soon the western horizon had taken on many of the colors of Miranda's hair, and we passed cottages, towers, and stone crosses—all mottled with a yellow lichen that only grew more luminous as the light faded. We were honked at by tiny cars on winding roads. The sky turned from scarlet to rose to purple. By the time we came down to a small sandy beach between looming bluffs, the Northern Lights were wavering gently over the sea—radium green curtains that seemed to start a mile in the air and rise forever. Waves hacked, whumphed, and hissed. Out on the water we heard the Munchkin bleats of leaping dolphins. Every now and then we caught sight of a greenish smear on a sleek fin-tip or arching back.

We were huddled side by side on the sand for some minutes before Miranda finally said, "So now are you going to tell me?"

"Oh, Beth!" (I'd grown used to using that name for her. I no longer winced, no longer felt guilty.)

When, after a long moment, I still hadn't said anything, Miranda gave me a soft kiss on the cheek and murmured into my ear, "It's okay, Robbie Bob. Everything's gonna be all right."

"No it isn't," I said. "I can't do these scenes. I'm not going to be able to finish the film."

"Of course you are."

"No. I can't."

"Why not?"

There was a huge whumph, and a sheet of ticking, green-tinted foam slid up the sand to within inches of our bare feet.

"Because it's all a lie. I don't love that other woman and I never have. I know that now. I didn't before, but now I do, and everything is different."

"I don't see why."

"Because this film is the story of my life, and I don't want to lie about my own life, not to myself, not to the world, and especially not to you."

"But why do you think you are lying?"

"Because I don't love that other woman. I love you!"

"And I love you, Bo-Bob. I've never loved anyone else."

I couldn't speak.

Miranda gave me another soft kiss on the cheek. "You are the only man I have ever loved, and I love you with all of my heart."

"Oh, Beth!"

I pulled her into my arms, and for a long time—our mouths otherwise occupied—neither of us said a word.

"So you see," Miranda said at last. "None of that matters."

"What do you mean?"

"That other woman. Whatever happened with her—it doesn't mean a thing. This movie isn't about her. It's about you and me. It's about *our* love. *I* am the woman you will be kissing. *I* am the woman you will marry. Nothing else matters. Only my love for you, and your love for me. That is not a lie."

Another silence.

She loosened the strings of her hospital gown and we made love on the beach. Then we swam out to where the dolphins cavorted and squeaked. The radium curtains waved overhead and the water was so cold my limbs felt glazed with ice. I had never been so cold before, and never so full of feeling: I was alert to every cell of my body, to every twitch, tingle, and hum of every single nucleus and mitochondrion.

We got lost on the way home and arrived at the hog barn at dawn, just as the shooting was to commence for another day. With no more rest than a doze on the beach, and with nothing at all to eat, we did all the hospital scenes straight through. By the time we were done, the cameraman was wiping his eyes with his shirttails, Diana was sobbing on the phone to her mother, and the Bavarian aroma therapist—whose name was Doug—was so choked up he couldn't speak for a day.

After Beth's miraculous recovery, there was little more to shoot than a quick, wrap-up montage: Our rainy wedding in Saint Cloud, the opening of my first big film, *Kung Fu Kickboxer*, assorted shots of Beth and me clowning with penguins, camels, and baby seals, and finally that scene on the speedboat as we fled Hong Kong across Victoria Harbour, and zoomed out into the South China Sea.

The rear projector and the fans had hardly been turned off before I knew exactly how things were going to go. Without a word, Miranda clambered down from the boat and went off to the toilet. When she came back, her hair was still red, but her eyes were chestnut brown. (I'd forgotten about the contacts.)

That night, when we all went down to the pub for a final blow-out, she went home with the bartender.

In the morning, I noticed that the bathtub was stippled with drops of deep purple. Miranda was sitting at the kitchen table with her cup of coffee. Her hair was midnight black, her suitcases stacked neatly by the door.

I put a couple of slices of bread in the toaster and she put her empty cup in the sink.

"Well," she said, turning to face me, both arms at her side, almost as if she were standing at attention. "I guess this is it."

"I guess."

I'd forgotten how beautiful she looked with her dark eyes and hair. So much more beautiful than she had been as Beth.

"So what's next for you?" she said.

"Oh . . . I don't really know. Go home, I guess."

And when she didn't respond to this with even so much as an eye flicker, I asked, "You?"

"Saint Petersburg," she said. *Anna Karenina.*

3

"You've changed," said Beth. We had been kissing. But now we weren't. We were in bed, clothesless.

"What do you mean?" I said.

"I don't know. You've changed."

"I'm just tired," I said. "Long flight."

Her slate blue eyes went dark. Her chin wrinkled. I tried to distract her with digital stimulation, but she pushed me away and went to the bathroom. When she came back she said, "I'm too tired."

"Please," I said.

"Maybe tomorrow."

The drought had worsened during my absence. The sky was sandy yellow, the sun coppery and dim. Although it was the middle of

July, all the leaves on the trees had gone rattly and brown, and most of them had blown away. Bare branches wailed in the ceaseless wind. The hedges on either side of our yard were box-shaped concatenations of gray wire, penetrated by off-white eddies.

Beth was nursing her black coffee at the kitchen table, waiting for the toast to pop.

"Hey, Robbie-Bobbie-Bo-Bob!"

"Hey, Betheroo!"

We both smiled.

But when I kissed her, it was like kissing the seam of a Naugahyde pillow.

"It's good to be home," I said.

She lifted her cup and smiled a second time. But when she'd finished her sip her smile was gone.

That night she served me Mexican pot roast for dinner. It tasted like hot, wet dust.

"I'm sorry," she said.

"It's delicious," I said.

"No it's not!" she said. "It's terrible!" Her eyes had gone teary, her lower lip was trembling.

"I love it!" I said.

She pushed back her chair and fled the room.

It was dark. I was standing with my forehead against the door. Beth walked up behind me. "What are you doing?" she said.

I turned around. I smiled. "I'm going for a walk," I said. "I won't be long. I just want a breath of air."

Her eyebrows buckled dubiously; then she handed me a garbage bag. "Get rid of this," she said.

The bag was empty except for the uneaten portion of her Mexican pot roast.

———

"This is ridiculous!" I told myself as I leaned into the wind. Despite the dark, I was wearing sunglasses to protect my eyes, and had my tee shirt neck pulled up over my nose so I didn't have to breathe the dust. "I'm an *actor*," I thought. "I should be able to feel *anything*—especially what I actually do feel. All I need is something to work with—just one sliver of memory, just one mote of emotion, and I can build a whole character."

I tried to think of love, but all I could see were the skeins of silver, orange, gray, and gold clouds streaming across Miranda's upturned eyes.

I tried to think of passion but all I could see was the aesthetically melting snow slipping down Miranda's shoulders and across the convexity of her breasts.

"Beth!" I told myself. "Think only of Beth!"

But no, that was Miranda smiling at me across the brim of her coffee cup. That was the corner of Miranda's mouth rising in such sweet anticipation at the sound of popping toast.

The sunglasses did no good, nor did the squinting. My eyes were stinging from the impact of wind-driven particles. My throat was coated with a film of chalk. It was so hard to see that I didn't even know I had walked up to my neighbor's house until I had opened the front door.

"No," said Beth. We were clothesless in bed. I had just given her my classic leading man's soul kiss.

"What?" I said.

I gave her a gaze so profoundly smoldering that I could almost smell the singeing of body hair. Then I gave her one of those emphatic pelvic grinds that, though they inevitably occur just below the lower left-hand edge of the screen, always enable movie audiences to feel the limitlessness of the man's desire and the grateful parting of the woman's thighs.

"No," said Beth, pushing me away.

"No what?" I said.

"I can't."

"Can't what?"

"Go on doing this."

"What?"

"Living a lie."

"What do you mean?"

She was silent a long time. Twice she opened her mouth to speak but no sound came out. Her eyes grew enormous and began to glimmer in the candlelight. Her lower lip began to tremble again, and I felt an almost irresistible desire to give her another pelvic grind.

"Quint," she said.

"Quint?"

Quint was my brother. So was Brad. We were triplets. Identical. Quint had been the cute, shy guy in Beth's Anglo-Saxon poetry class way back during our Buffalo days, before Beth and I met. That's whom she had thought she was making out with that first time in the darkroom. (The screenwriter had left that detail out of the script because he thought it was just too complicated. Diana had agreed.)

"I'm sorry," Beth said.

"About what?"

"You know. I mean there's always been this—" She couldn't say the word. "—between Quint and me."

I couldn't speak. I thought I was going to vomit.

"I mean, nothing ever happened. I promise. It was just . . . You know. We had this—" She still couldn't say it.

Her lips were dry. She wet them with her tongue. I watched the tip of her tongue slide left to right, then slip back into her mouth.

"So then, while you were away, he sort of stopped by and . . . Well, I guess one thing just sort of led . . . to another."

———

Stoic silence. Guilty entreaty. More stoic silence. Manipulative gestures of affection. Outbursts. Fists against the mattress. Candle dashed to the floor. Window-rattling rage. Sadistic confessions. Miranda Wilkes's Nobel Prize for fellatio. Quint's presence in Hong Kong during the entire filming of *Kung Fu Kickboxer.* ("Why did you think I was so happy to see you go off in the morning?") Moments of white blindness. Moments of startling lucidity. Fierce rationality. Weariness. Apology. Four a.m. fatalism. Resolution. Tender fury.

Divorce?

No. Not yet.

Separation.

Do we really have a choice?

I'm sorry.

I'm sorry.

No, *really*—I am *so, so* sorry!

Good night.

It's good *morning*!

A last kiss. Another last kiss. A third. A hand sliding down a back. A lifting thigh. Tongue against tongue.

By the time it was over all the covers had been kicked from the bed. One sheet trailed across the floor to the bedroom door. There was a pillow on the dining room table, a chair lying on its side. Beth and I were leaning up against the wall in the living room, rug burns on our knees, mouths swollen, our sweat evaporating in the morning chill.

For the first time in weeks there was no wind. The sun rose pink rather than scab red.

The sky was sky blue.

"Oh, God," sighed Beth.

She was holding my hand. She gave it a squeeze.

"I know," I said, lifting her hand to my lips. "I know."

The Professor of Atheism
Magnum Opus

—◆◆—

As it turned out, Charles was guilty; he bore responsibility for all the world's iniquity within his own person. That's what the men told him. "This is the only way justice can be served," they said.

It happened in a basement room, filled with ancient, yellow-eyed, turkey-fleshed old people who expressed their disdain for Charles with their green- and rust-colored sputum. There was no trial, no process, nothing to prolong either hope or despair. After the excruciation at the centers of his palms and in the arches of his feet, after the blade between his ribs and the cracking of his clavicles, there was a period of darkness.

And then he was outside the orange brick building—arches and turrets; Anglo-American, circa 1860—his progress more horizontal than vertical. He could already see the difference. In window after window, people were being helped out of chairs, or up from their knees. Couples were embracing while children jumped up and down on the beds. It was clear to Charles that this was a spontaneous response. Nobody knew why they were doing what they were doing, or even that what they were doing was anything more than whim, mere good mood. But it was occurring simultaneously, over and over, in apartment after apartment, home after home, nation after nation. Eventually people began to notice the change in the light, the unseasonable freshness of the breeze. They came to their windows and, ultimately, spilled out onto the streets.

The verticality of Charles's motion had increased, and the bloody soles of his feet were now several dozen yards above the heads of the promenading citizenry. Every now and then some-one—most often a child—would look up at him for a few seconds, not more than a minute, and never with more interest than would be occasioned by the sight of a runaway balloon. Even these few curious souls had better things to attend to. They had their happy lives, all those newly fascinating people strolling around them, people they had seen every day but never really noticed. As Charles drifted over the square in front of City Hall he saw a heap of weap-ons—gray and silver and black and olive drab. Men and women with megaphones were announcing that trucks were on their way from missile silos and that all the weapons of the earth were to be launched into space, where they could do no harm.

And after that Charles was out over the gray sea, which, as he climbed, became silent and then motionless, the only detectable movement being the slow dispersal of foam created by massive waves. And then not even that was visible and the sea came to seem merely a metallic skin between the green, yellow, orange, and white mottling of the land.

And then as Charles passed through the last evanescence of the atmosphere into the total vacuum of space, he felt cheated that he should have had to leave the earth at this beautiful moment, when it seemed, at last, to have become a place where it might actually have been possible for him to live.

Then there were stars everywhere, the earth itself only a blue-green flickering point of light—then nothing.

For a while his ex-wife rose beside him. She had become an-cient, not a tooth in her mouth, her once full red hair clinging to her skull like strands of Spanish moss; yet he recognized her by a particular fluidity of her movements. She said, "I know you want me to say that I never stopped loving you, Charles. I wish that I could. Perhaps I loved you once. For a while. I'm not sure."

After that, she was silent, drifting ever farther away. And when she was gone, Charles found that he missed her more than he had at any time since the days when their marriage had first begun to go wrong.

He rose higher and higher, even though height was a concept that no longer had meaning in the realms where he was traveling. He passed star after star, galaxy after galaxy, and then untold galaxies of galaxies until, at long last, the universe itself became a speck of white brilliance, then finally diminished to such a minute point that he blinked and it was gone.

Time too no longer had meaning, and yet Charles couldn't help experiencing his existence as persistence—with the most essential element of his persistence being his loneliness, not just for his wife but for all the people he had loved and left behind, and for those he might have loved had he been better and luckier—and even for those whom he might have been able to love now, were he still on the earth he had perfected by leaving.

But the longer Charles traveled, the more clearly he came to realize that his dreams had always been hopeless, that it had simply never been his destiny to live in a world that was simultaneously good and real.

Aunt Jules

◆—◆

1

Bryan was the cellist in a string trio that had gotten a drummer, gone electric, and played rock songs quoting slyly from Bach and Beethoven. Nobody sang. Julianne heard them at the Crypt, the coffeehouse in the basement of the campus chapel. After the show, she went up to Bryan to let on, in a way she hoped sounded musically intelligent, how much she had liked the set. One thing led to another, and Bryan invited Julianne and her boyfriend to a party at the house he shared with the group's violinist and two other guys. The house had a stereo with speakers the size of filing cabinets, a beer-filled refrigerator, and a brass cuspidor heaped with sinsemilla.

As sunrise slowly turned the sky lavender and rose, Julianne, her boyfriend, and Bryan were sitting in lawn chairs at the bottom of an empty swimming pool, discussing Sartre and the nature of the self. Julianne tended to think of her "true self" as somehow separate from the rest of her, as a tender and idealistic creature hiding out, not merely from life's barbarities but from her own thoughts and emotions. Bryan insisted with passion and eloquence that the self was nothing other than the totality of one's actions upon and reactions to the world in each new instant of being. It was one of those conversations that would leave Julianne feeling profoundly changed, even if she could never articulate precisely how or why. In later years, all she would remember of the exchange would be the mischievous delight in Bryan's pale blue eyes, and the way his long black hair framed his cheekbones and narrow jaw. She would also remember the slappy echo of their laughter against the concrete walls of the pool.

Julianne's boyfriend became the singer in Bryan's band, and so she ended up spending many a night at the house, cramming pinches from the cuspidor into a bong or brass pipe, talking and talking, and sometimes dancing. She loved to dance, especially with Bryan, who made up for a lack of grace by exuberant athleticism. One night, after a bottle of vodka had made its way several times around the living room, she and Bryan crouched on the floor with crossed arms and did a Cossack dance, while their friends clapped, laughed, and shouted "Hey!" every time either of them leaped into the air.

Later that night, Julianne found her boyfriend alone on a couch, pointedly avoiding her gaze.

"Hey you!" she said, dropping into his lap.

He said nothing, and still wouldn't look at her.

"Don't you know you're the only one for me?" she said.

He grunted unhappily, but was smiling, so she pulled his head down and stuck her tongue into his mouth.

That summer, Julianne and her boyfriend moved out of their dorms and into the house's dining room, where they slept on a mattress they'd found on the street. The landlord refused to fill the pool, because it leaked—or so he claimed—and he even went so far as to remove the handle from the spigot under the diving board and to surround the pool with DANGER and NO TRESPASSING signs. One day, when the thermometer topped ninety before noon, Bryan, Julianne, and their friends decided to "liberate" the pool by filling it with a garden hose and holding a skinny-dipping party. Julianne's sister, Claire, happened to be visiting that weekend, and, sometime around one a.m., Julianne noticed that both Claire and Bryan had vanished from the party. She was not to see either of them until the following morning when they came down to the kitchen, crusty-eyed and tousle-headed, with red, swollen mouths.

Claire was eighteen, nearly three years younger than Julianne, and had always been the more studious of the two sisters. She was slim and blond, with a dancer's poise—although she didn't, in fact, like to dance. Julianne, by contrast, was cursed by big bones and thick ankles. Her belly and hips were fatless and firm, but even so, she seemed bulky and almost masculine in her carriage. Her eyes were beagle brown, and her hair was the color of chestnuts, but so lank it always looked wet.

After breakfast, the two sisters went outside for a solitary talk and found the pool drained but for a greenish, trapezoidal puddle, in which floated a few black leaves and a pair of boxer shorts. Julianne and Claire took seats on the end of the diving board and let their bare feet dangle in the emptiness.

"So?" said Julianne.

At first Claire could only blush and smile shyly. But soon the two sisters were embarked on an extended discussion of Bryan's manifold virtues, during which—Julianne noted—Claire was constantly laughing and squeezing her thighs together.

At one point Julianne threw her arms around her sister and exclaimed, "This is exactly what I hoped would happen! You guys are perfect for each other!"

In September, Julianne's boyfriend, who had already graduated, left to work on an oil rig in the Gulf of Mexico. He sent her a postcard from New Orleans, of a cowboy riding a bucking crayfish, but, as he hadn't put his address on the card, she couldn't write back, and never heard from him again.

Rather than find a new singer, Bryan decided to break up the band. He was a senior and wanted to devote himself to studying for the LSATs. Julianne too was applying to graduate school—in medieval history—and so she and Bryan fell into the habit of studying every night at the same oak table in the library, then returning to the house and having a couple of beers in the kitchen. Bryan was admitted everywhere he applied, but decided to forgo Harvard and Yale in favor of Berkeley, where Claire was an undergraduate. Julianne was admitted to only one school, the University of North Carolina at Chapel Hill, but considered herself lucky, given her decidedly sorry grades, and believed she would never have been admitted even to this one program had she not done supremely well on her GREs—an achievement she would always attribute entirely to Bryan's influence.

After law school, Bryan got a job with the ACLU, and he and Claire moved to New York, where they found an apartment on West End Avenue with a view of the Hudson from its bathroom. Claire became a language arts teacher at a public middle school a few blocks away, and discovered she was pregnant on Halloween.

The last day of classes, she returned to her apartment flush-faced, with a pounding headache, and her belly so enormous she could no longer see her navel. Her due date was in less than a week, but she and Bryan had been so overwhelmed by work that all they had done in the way of preparation was stack her baby shower gifts in the "maid's room" off the kitchen. As she stood in the doorway of this dim and musty little chamber, her whole life seemed utterly wrong: She'd failed as a teacher; her students had learned nothing; Bryan didn't love her; and how could they possibly have been so irresponsible as not to have prepared for the baby! The aspect of this grim moment that would haunt her thoughts for years to come was that, on some profound level, she didn't actually care about any of these terrible possibilities. She seemed, in a split instant, to have become fiercely bitter and cold—a creature of pure rage.

Thus it was that Julianne, fretting over her dissertation in Chapel Hill, received an emergency summons to New York.

On Julianne's second day in the city, she and Claire were rolling butter yellow paint onto the walls of the maid's room when Claire dropped her roller to the newspaper-covered floor and clasped her belly with both hands. "Feel that," she said, lifting her shirt. Julianne placed her fingertips against her sister's weirdly distended abdomen and found it as hard as a wooden globe. "That's a Braxton Hicks contraction," said Claire. "I've been having them for a couple of weeks. But this one really hurts."

Julianne told Claire to lie down for a bit, and Claire waddled from the room, with one hand on her back, the other cupped beneath her belly. About forty-five minutes later there were shouts from the bathroom. Claire's water had broken and the contractions had suddenly become so fierce she thought she would vomit—which, indeed, she did: once in the cab on the way to the hospital, and again as she and Julianne hurried though the emergency room door.

Bryan had been taking a deposition in Albany when Julianne phoned, so it was four hours before he rushed into the recovery room, looking worried, bewildered, and so young. At that moment, Claire was being examined by her doctor, so Julianne was holding the bundled-up baby in her arms. "Yo, Bryan!" she called across the room. "There's somebody here I think you should meet." The little boy's name was Zachary. His eyes were the muddy blue of all newborns, but his hair was chestnut brown—exactly the color of Julianne's.

Julianne and Bryan rode a cab home from the hospital at about eleven that night. They cracked a bottle of champagne, then spent the next few hours painting the nursery, assembling the crib and changing table, and filling the new dresser with unbelievably tiny clothes. When at last everything was in order, they walked down the hallway together and stopped in front of Bryan's study, where Julianne would be sleeping on a foldout couch.

"Thanks," he said, leaning one shoulder against the doorjamb and smiling wearily.

"Oh, man!" said Julianne. "This is so exciting! I don't think I'm going to be able to sleep."

"I really appreciate it," said Bryan. ". . . Your being here, I mean."

He took hold of her hand and, when she didn't pull it away, he leaned over and kissed her on the lips.

Afterward, Julianne and Bryan talked long into the night.

They agreed that sleeping together had been less a choice than a sort of destiny, something that had actually been meant to happen long ago.

"I've always loved you," said Bryan.

Julianne wanted to say that she too had always loved him, but couldn't because she was crying. Bryan confessed that he had wanted to make love with her from the very moment she came up to him at the Crypt.

"Why didn't we?" she asked.

"I don't know," he said. "It was stupid."

"It would have been so much better then."

Bryan sighed. "Oh, God."

They admitted that what they had done was wrong—even if they did not feel entirely culpable. But they also agreed it wouldn't change anything, since neither of them loved Claire any the less. The longer they talked, the better they felt, with the result that, as the light behind the blinds turned powder blue, they made love a second time.

A little later they sat face-to-face on the bed and resolved, with a sadness so full it verged on joy, that they could never give in to their feelings for each other again.

"It would be so destructive," said Bryan.

Julianne closed her eyes and shook her head. "I couldn't live with myself."

At the hospital, they found that Claire had a low fever. The nurse gave her Tylenol, but her fever returned during the afternoon and her obstetrician recommended she spend another night in the hospital—"just in case." Julianne and Bryan glanced at each other across Claire's bed, then looked instantly away. When, sometime later, they dared to look at each other again, they affirmed—through sustained and sober gazes—the inflexibility of their morning's resolution.

In the cab home, however, Julianne found it impossible not to let her knee fall against Bryan's, and he seemed unable to keep his hand from sliding up the inside of her thigh. This time their sadness in the morning was nothing like joy. Neither of them knew how they would ever be able to face Claire. Julianne went to the hospital first, but only to tell her sister that she had gotten a phone call from her thesis adviser, that something had come up, that she had to rush back to Chapel Hill. "I'm so sorry!" she said. "I know I shouldn't be doing this. I am so, so sorry!"

Claire was astounded by how much she resented the change in her life. No more could she and Bryan spend an idle Sunday morning browsing the *Times,* then go out for brunch, or for a walk, or to a museum, and end up at a restaurant, or a jazz club, or meeting friends at a bar. Everything had to be planned; everything had to be negotiated; everything had to be worked around the inflexible routines of feeding, diapering, bathing, and bedtime. Even the simplest of social engagements—coffee with a friend—took so much organization they hardly seemed worthwhile. Claire would scold herself: "Babies are helpless. What else did you expect!"

She didn't blame Zachary, of course. She loved him with a passion she could never have imagined before. The mere sight of his perfect little lips or his tiny fingernails could make her go all weak inside, and she knew she would be willing to die for him. But, even so, there were days when, in the midst of maternal duties, she would be gripped by such a wild restlessness she thought she might be going insane.

It did not help that Zachary was a poor sleeper and could not bear to be left alone in his crib. For the first few months of his life, Claire never got more than two hours' sleep in a row, and, on many a night, she had to pace her street-lit apartment with her fretful infant on her shoulder. More than once she actually fell asleep as she walked, and woke only when her knees buckled and her shoulder hit the wall.

One terrible four a.m., when Zachary was less than four weeks old, diarrhea leaked from his diaper in such quantities that it not only saturated his stretchy but penetrated his sheets and quilt. In her fury, Claire wiped, poked, and scrubbed the tiny boy far more forcefully than she ought to have. She knew exactly what she was doing, but could not restrain herself. She was dabbing the last yellow clumps from the crenulations of his scrotum when all at once Zachary's whole body jerked and went still. After a moment, his face turned purple-red and his upper lip began to quiver. But before he could release the cry building up inside him, Claire was shouting, "Shut up, you fucking little bastard! Shut the fuck up before—"

The rest of her sentence was lost in her own sobs and Zachary's catlike yowl. She cried so hard she couldn't see. Her tears fell onto her hands and Zachary's ruddy, trembling shins.

Although Bryan's life had been far less affected by parenthood, he too seemed traumatized, his face always a cloud of worry. He fulfilled all of his agreed-upon duties—he shopped, cooked, diapered, and handled the first and last feedings of the day—but always joylessly and with just barely restrained irritation. He was never jokey or affectionate anymore. He never kissed Claire unless she kissed him first, and he never said, "I love you." When his day was finished, he would drop exhausted into bed and immediately shut his eyes. On those rare instances when Claire made the noises or gestures by which she signified desire, he would only roll away with a sigh.

Claire was too humiliated by the state of her life to talk about it to anyone but her sister. Julianne, however, let her down completely. She seemed incapable, on the phone, of anything other than bright greetings and trite aphorisms, and fled all serious conversation with obvious horror. One night, after hanging up, Claire complained to Bryan: "Julianne's not even listening when I talk. It's so bizarre! Sometimes I think she's only doing an impersonation of herself."

Bryan stared into space a moment, something like nausea on his brow and lips. "She's probably just tired," he said at last, and went back to scribbling on a legal pad.

What Julianne most hated about calling Claire was the possibility that Bryan would answer. This happened twice during the first week of Zachary's life. Both times Bryan sounded extremely happy to hear her voice, and just as disappointed when she immediately asked for her sister. As she listened to him cross the apartment to tell Claire who was on the phone, she would find herself vividly remembering the smell of his hair and chest, the rhythm and weight of his body, the muscularity of his tongue. She had to bite her knuckle to drive these memories away and to keep her sorrow out of her voice.

After that first week, Julianne called only during the day, when Bryan was at work. She kept promising she would visit, and kept finding excuses not to. Claire was understanding for a while, but soon started meeting Julianne's excuses with grunts and silences.

That year, Julianne spent Christmas with her parents in Philadelphia, while Claire and Bryan went to his family in Minnesota. The two sisters spoke by phone on Christmas Day, and Claire had just told Julianne how she and Bryan had to go straight back to the city because of his work, when all at once her voice rose an octave: "Hey, Jules! Zachary's six-month birthday is on the thirtieth. Why don't you pop over for a little celebration?"

Julianne had to struggle some moments before she could say, "That would be wonderful!" Then she added, "If you'd like, I could even babysit on New Year's Eve, and you guys could stay out dancing until dawn!"

Claire and Bryan greeted Julianne with shouts and laughter, and for a while she wondered why she had been so afraid to visit. There was, however, an odd moment, just after all the greetings had been exchanged, during which everybody seemed to be avoiding everyone else's gaze, but that ended as soon as Claire ushered Julianne down the hallway into the living room to see little Zachary, and Bryan went to the kitchen to get a bottle of wine and three glasses. Conversation at dinner went smoothly, although from time to time Julianne would notice either Claire or Bryan giving her a searching glance, and she would have to lower her eyes to her food or take another sip from her wine.

At the end of the meal, Claire brought out half a birthday cake, in which she had stuck half a candle, and all the adults sang a song in which "half-y" was substituted for "happy." Zachary seemed oblivious throughout the entire ceremony—until its concluding cheers, at which his eyes grew huge, his lower lip stuck out, and he began to wail in abject terror. Claire took the tiny boy for a feeding in the peace of his own bedroom, and Bryan and Julianne cleared the table.

They were standing side by side at the sink when Bryan said, "You know, I can't stop thinking about you."

"Don't." She gave him a firm glance.

"You're right," he said.

"We can't do this."

"You're right. You're right. I'm sorry. I just wanted you to know."

"No," she warned. Then she wiped her hands with a dishtowel. "I'm going to go see Claire."

She found Claire sitting in a rocking chair, nursing Zachary in the amber illumination of a teddy-bear-shaped lamp.

"Hello, beautiful!" Julianne said, lightly stroking her sister on the back of the neck. "Is it okay if I just sit here with you for a bit?"

Claire only smiled—but it was a smile that Julianne couldn't help but associate with the thousands of beatific Madonnas she had seen in her researches and travels. She took a seat in a child-sized red plastic chair, and reflected that her sister really was beautiful: rounder than normal, but flushed and healthy and so clearly content to be holding her infant in her arms.

At first Julianne found it difficult to look at Claire's massive, vein-laced breast, but the longer she sat in that quiet and cozy little room, the more she came to appreciate the resilient fullness of this most female of forms, and the pleasing symmetry with which it was echoed by Zachary's round pink head. But more than anything else, Julianne felt the beauty of the simple fact that Claire was nourishing her child from her own body. As ordinary as this act may have been, it was so unlike anything Julianne had ever imagined in her little sister that it seemed like magic—a true miracle.

When, at last, Zachary had slipped into a satiated sleep, and his still-puckered lips—glossy with milk and saliva—had fallen away from his mother's equally glossy nipple, Claire placed the little boy, with his diapered bottom up, at the center of his crib, and Julianne pulled the star-speckled quilt up over his shoulders. Out in the living room, Bryan was sprawled on the couch, watching a video of *Atlantic City*. He offered to turn the movie off, but Claire said, "No. This is perfect! I'm pooped." She joined him on the couch. Julianne sat in an easy chair by herself.

At bedtime, Claire hugged Julianne and said, "I'm so glad you're here!"

Bryan gave her only a curt wave as he left the room, and didn't meet her eye.

Julianne fell instantly asleep on the foldout couch in Bryan's study, but was startled awake sometime in the depths of the night by the creak of floorboards just outside her door. She knew from the timbre of the creak that it had been caused by something heavy—by a man's weight. Bryan was standing out in the hall. She knew that for a fact, and could not breathe as she waited for the knob to turn and the door to push inward. When, a moment later, she heard another creak farther down the hall, and then the familiar susurrus of Claire's bare feet crossing the kitchen linoleum in the direction of the nursery, Julianne fought back tears by repeating over and over, "This is *stupid*! This is *so* stupid!" She hardly slept the whole rest of the night, and got up with Claire at dawn.

After breakfast, when Claire asked, "Want some practice changing a diaper?" Julianne only scowled at her as if she had just made an extremely rude noise. "I was only thinking . . ." Claire said. "You know—about your babysitting."

"Jesus, Claire!" Julianne rolled her eyes. "It's not exactly rocket science."

Claire squinted at her sister under a lowered brow, but said nothing.

Later, when Zachary seemed unable to settle into his nap, and only lay in bed wriggling and making noises of complaint, Claire said to Julianne, "How about we bundle him up and take a walk in the park? He always goes to sleep in his stroller."

"Not the *park*!" said Julianne. "I hate the park! Why can't we take him to the Met? I mean, this is New York, for Godsakes!"

"He's not very good in museums, I'm afraid."

"That's because you indulge him too much. If he doesn't learn to accommodate your needs from time to time, he's going to grow up an unbearable narcissist."

Claire stared at her sister in shocked silence. "Since when are you such a child-rearing expert?"

"Who said I was an expert? It's just obvious, isn't it?"

Not long afterward, Claire discovered that Zachary had a fever of one hundred and one, and realized that he had an ear infection. That was the end of their New Year's Eve plans. Although Julianne insisted that Claire and Bryan should still go out—at least for a little bit—they only shook their heads. They would be too worried, they said, and they'd feel too guilty. So all three adults spent the rest of the day coaxing Zachary to suck antibiotics and Baby Tylenol from droppers.

When, at last, his fever had receded and he seemed to have settled into a sound sleep, Bryan ordered a take-out pizza, and they all sat down to watch *Chinatown*. But the FBI warning hadn't even vanished from the screen when Zachary woke, shrieking in pain. Bryan put the movie on pause; Claire went to soothe the poor little boy. Then, minutes after she returned, new cries rose from the nursery, and this time it was Bryan's turn to go off.

When this routine had repeated for the fourth time in less than an hour, Julianne said to Claire (Bryan was the one attending to Zachary), "Man! I pity you guys! This is torture!"

Claire had been staring exhaustedly into the air. But now her forehead darkened and her voice was sharp: "Would you cut it out!"

"Cut what out?" said Julianne. "I was just expressing a little sympathy."

"Come on, Jules! You've been such a bitch all day!"

Julianne started to protest, but stopped because she knew her sister was right.

"Look! Nobody forced you to visit us. If you don't want to be here, you shouldn't have come."

"I *do* want to be here."

"Then why don't you act like it?"

All at once, Claire rose from the couch and began striding back and forth before Roman Polanski's frozen sneer, which trembled behind lines of static.

"All right!" Julianne said. "I'm sorry! But it's not such a big deal!"

"It *is* a big deal!" Claire stopped mid-stride and stamped her foot on the floor. "*You're* the fucking narcissist, you know that? Not Zachary—*you!*"

"Claire—"

"Let me finish!" She was pacing again. "You think I *like* this? You think I'm stopping the movie every fucking five minutes and eating goddamn cold pizza just to give you a hard time? Not everything in this world centers around you! You know that? Can you get that into your skull! I go into that room because that's my baby boy, and I love him, and it's my duty as a mother. That's what I *am* now: A *mother!* Nothing can change that. And if you can't live with that fact, then you better not bother coming around here anymore!"

Julianne was quiet a moment, then said, in a soft voice, "I'm sorry, Claire."

She said nothing else. All at once, it seemed best that Claire should think her merely selfish and spoiled. Perhaps—in the long run—that would make everything easier.

Julianne fell in love with Peter, who was in the psychology graduate program at Chapel Hill. When she got a job teaching medieval history in Maine, he moved with her, and spent a solid year doing nothing but working on his dissertation. Sometimes he would get cabin fever, drink a quarter bottle of vodka, and tear off down the road in their antique Toyota at ninety miles an hour. The plan was that when he got his PhD he would find a job within commuting distance of Portland, but he ended up taking a position in Albuquerque, and Julianne found that she was more than willing to let him go.

A month or so after Peter's departure, Julianne commenced an on-again-off-again affair with a married sometime lobsterman named Clement, who did odd jobs to make ends meet. He first came to her house to repair her porch, and over the years put on a new roof; stripped, sanded, and polyurethaned her floors; and built her a patio out back. Although Clement's attentions were anything but reliable, they did help blunt her loneliness—so much so that she would one day wonder whether they hadn't, in fact, sapped her of the desperation necessary to go out and find somebody more compatible and full-time—real husband material.

She published one book, a deconstruction of the controversies regarding the historicity of King Arthur, but did not get tenure. When Claire's and her father died, she used her share of the modest inheritance to open a bookstore in Portland, which ended up being fairly successful, especially once she added a children's section. She developed a circle of good female friends, consisting of neighbors, a couple of ex-students, and her former therapist, who discontinued treatment when her marriage broke up and she needed a best friend. Every now and then, although with diminishing frequency, a new man would come into Julianne's life. "Summer weather" was how she came to think of these men: lots of sun and heat, followed inevitably by dark clouds and thunder, and sometimes by an extended, dispiriting drizzle.

She was a devoted aunt to Zachary, Megan, and Jonah. She never forgot a birthday, and always spent Thanksgiving with Claire, Bryan, and the kids, first on the Upper West Side and then at their new home in Cobble Hill, Brooklyn. Every August, the kids would come up to Maine to spend two weeks at her beach house on Peaks Island. Occasionally Claire and Bryan would come along for a few days, but mostly—with Julianne's encouragement—they took advantage of the kids' time with their aunt to go off alone on canoeing trips or to Europe. This tradition lasted for eighteen years, and ended as, one by one, each of the children reached that stage of adolescence when it became intolerable to be ripped away from friends merely to spend solitary weeks staring into tide pools and swimming in the frigid Atlantic.

Julianne's relations with Claire were generally cordial and sometimes intimate—especially during late-night telephone conversations—but never truly close. Julianne knew that this had something to do with the reserve of anger that had built up between the two of them during the first year of Zachary's life. But mainly she thought it was a matter of simple busyness, geographical distance, and that regimentation of emotion commonly referred to as growing up.

Her relations with Bryan were also cordial, but increasingly formal. He never again said a word about their two nights together, and never again was there any real erotic tension between them—although Julianne did notice that he scrupulously avoided kissing her hello or goodbye. He also got into the habit of calling her "Aunt Jules," even when the kids weren't around.

Julianne didn't mind that Bryan had grown remote. It seemed natural under the circumstances, and even desirable. He was a good husband to Claire, as far as Julianne could tell, and a good man, who worked tirelessly for civil rights and freedom of speech, and argued three cases before the Supreme Court. Julianne was glad that she knew him—glad simply that he existed on this earth.

Her hair turned completely gray in her forties. She grew stout, and her face went red—from exposure to the harsh Maine weather and from her fondness for wine. To celebrate her fiftieth birthday, she took a trip to India and Sri Lanka, and traveled every year thereafter to a different part of the world: Patagonia, Vietnam, Russia, New Zealand . . . Thus it happened that she was crossing the Sahara in a truck caravan when Bryan died of a neglected flu that had turned into pneumonia. He collapsed at work, and spent two days in the hospital on oxygen and intravenous antibiotics. He was only fifty-five.

Julianne got the news at an Internet café in Casablanca, but wasn't able to return to the United States until the day after Bryan's funeral. She offered to come straight down to Brooklyn, but Claire said, "The house is full of people, and I've got so many dishes of lasagna stacked up in the fridge that I don't know what I'm going to do with them all.

When I'm really going to need company will be this summer. It will be the first time I have ever been up in the country alone."

2

After the six-hour drive from Portland, Julianne had been too tired, her first night at Claire's country house, for more than small talk over a light dinner of cheese, salad, and the very good bottle of Vacqueyras. Still, as she and Claire bade each other good night in the hall outside their bedrooms, Julianne gave her sister a long, hard hug and said, "You know, I've never loved anyone more than I love you." This realization had come to her in Casablanca as she read Zachary's e-mail, and she had resolved on the plane home that she would tell Claire how she felt at her first opportunity.

"Thanks," Claire said. "That means a lot."

Claire smiled warmly, but then her smile turned off. She looked down at the floor and took a step backward, her hand settling on her doorknob.

After a moment she repeated, "Thanks." Then she said, *"Really."* And then: "Sweet dreams."

They were standing in an overgrown field between two disintegrating barns. The air was loud with the jingling of crickets and the long, robotic cries of cicadas. A crow flew overhead, its black-brown wing feathers making a textured hiss as they cut the air.

Julianne's legs were itching. Sweat glinted in the down on Claire's temple and cheek. A grass fleck was stuck to her upper lip. The sun was high and yellow-white, and the entire sky seemed to radiate heat like the walls of an oven.

"Ugh!" Claire said as she dropped an ostrich-egg-size stone into the wheelbarrow. "Every inch of my body is crying out in pain!'"

"It feels good," said Julianne.

Claire rubbed her wrist across her brow, leaving a small brown streak. "Maybe."

"This is what our bodies are made for," said Julianne. "It's good to use our muscles this way."

"No. You're right. It's just . . ." Her gaze grew vague. She didn't finish.

Julianne was silent a moment. Then she tapped her own forehead with her index finger.

"What?" said Claire.

"Mud. When you wiped your forehead."

"Oh." Claire lifted the front of her tee shirt to wipe away the mud and sweat. Despite having had three children and commenced menopause, her belly was trim, even muscular, and showed only the faintest trace of middle-aged crinkliness where it strained a bit against the waist of her cutoff jeans.

As well as Claire had kept herself, however, she wasn't anywhere near as strong as Julianne. She trembled visibly when she lifted a heavy stone, and couldn't even budge the wheelbarrow when it was full. Julianne felt positively manly around her sister, which was odd, because Claire had always been the athlete when they were kids—the gymnast, the marathon runner in high school.

Julianne tossed a last stone into the wheelbarrow, then grabbed hold of the handles and dug the toes of her jogging shoes into the loose soil. Gradually the barrow's one wheel surmounted a lump of dislodged sod and she was able to move along the path tamped down by previous journeys to the edge of the stream. The stones slid from the wheelbarrow with a resonant hacking sound.

Steering the empty barrow back toward her sister, Julianne asked, "Why didn't you ever do this before?"

"Oh, I don't know." Claire was resting her hip against the handle of her upright shovel. "This house was always the place where we came to relax. Bryan worked so hard during the week. All he wanted to do when we got up here was play. You know? Anything that smacked of work—even a vegetable garden . . . Well, he just didn't want to do it."

"You could have done it on your own."

"I guess." Claire looked thoughtful. "The thing is," she said, "he always wanted to play with *me* . . . And I always wanted to play with him, too." A smile twitched on her lips and vanished.

Neither sister spoke for a long time after that.

The clouds leaned over the tops of the hills like the petrified spume of an enormous wave. Julianne was sitting in the shade of a young locust tree on the edge of a rectangle of brown earth that she and Claire—after three hours of hard labor—had still not been able to rid of stones. From Julianne's vantage point, the stones were as thick as chocolate chips on a brownie. It was depressing.

"Here I am!" called Claire, coming down the hill from the house, carrying a glass pitcher in one hand and two paper cups in the other.

"Gimme, gimme, gimme!" said Julianne. "I'm parched."

Claire handed Julianne the two cups, then knelt in the long grass while she filled them one after the other.

The tea was sweet and very cold.

"Whoa!" said Julianne. "I needed that."

"Me too."

Claire sighed heavily. A catbird called from the vines covering the side of one of the barns. The fronds of the huge old willow beside the stream swayed and hissed in the breeze.

"So how's it going?" said Julianne.

"Oh . . ." Claire began, but then said nothing.

"You seem . . . You know. I mean you seem not too . . ." Julianne didn't finish either.

"It's been three months. And every month has been a little better. From what I hear, that's about . . . Well, you know." She took a sip from her drink.

"Yeah."

"So it's easier. It's definitely easier. I'm starting to sleep through the night. Most nights now, actually. Though I still can't bring myself to sleep on his side."

Julianne puckered her lips sadly.

Claire smiled. "I've sort of been making that a goal. When I feel free to just stretch out my legs, when I can sleep smack in the middle of the bed, that'll be a sign that I'm on the road to mental health!"

Julianne made a small laugh.

"But I'm not ready yet. I . . ." She shrugged. "I can't."

"Of course."

Unexpectedly, Julianne felt her own eyes grow hot with tears.

She glanced down into her empty cup, and then at the spume-like clouds, which had all lifted above the hillside and now looked like a row of bedraggled blue-white commas.

"Oh, Jules!"

"Sorry." Julianne wiped her eyes with her thumb and forefinger.

"Oh, sweetie!"

"Don't mind me. I'm okay." She forced a smile.

Claire watched her sister fondly for a moment. Then she said, "You've had to deal with it too, of course."

"Yeah, but—"

"No. I feel bad. I've never said a word. I've never asked you how it's been for you."

"Ah, well." She shrugged. "It's true. I've always loved Bryan."

"I know." Claire looked Julianne straight in the eye.

"I mean. You know. As a brother," Julianne said. "As a friend."

"I know what you mean." Claire was still looking her in the eye.

"Oh, shit! Oh, shit! Oh, shit! Oh, shit!" Julianne had just fallen backward into the "swimming hole"—a chest-deep pool in the stream beneath the willow—and her splash sent small waves hissing into each grassy bank. "I can't tell you how wonderful this feels!"

282

"I know! I can't wait!" Claire was standing with her arms twisted up behind her as she wrestled with the clip of her burgundy bra.

"I don't remember the last time I went skinny-dipping!" Julianne said. She was floating on her back, looking up into the silver-green leaves and black boughs of the massive willow. "It feels so good!"

"I'm coming!" Bra, at last, on the heap of her other clothes, Claire was stepping tentatively through the high grass to the water's edge.

This was the first time in decades that Julianne had seen her sister naked. Claire's skin, of course, was no longer as firm and smooth as it had once been; there was the faintest puckering just below her waist and in her thighs, but, basically, she was as slim and lithe as she had been in her twenties, her teens even. She still had that dancer's figure and those modest, shapely breasts that had always reminded Julianne of peaches.

As soon as Claire had both feet planted firmly at the stream's edge, she dove and surfaced just beside Julianne. "God!" she cried. "Don't you just feel the tiredness melting out of you?"

"And the heat!" said Julianne.

"And the heat!"

For several moments the two women only paddled on their backs, making contented noises, savoring the easing of all those muscles made stiff by five hours of hard labor and hot sun.

Then Claire said, "Of course, this would be just the moment Craig Tyler would come walking down the path to see how I'm doing!"

"Who's Craig Tyler?"

"He's this old guy, this retired cop. He lives up the hill. Everybody here knows everything about . . . what happened. And ever since I got up here this time, Craig's been coming around to make sure I'm okay. It's sort of sweet. He brought me a bag of apples the other day, and some maple syrup he made himself."

"Do you think he's sort of nosing around?"

"Maybe. Who knows? The idea has occurred to me."

"Well, that's not so bad!"

"God, no! Jules! He must be nearly seventy!"

"So what! In *principle*, I mean. It's not bad that men are noticing you. I mean, Claire, you are an incredibly beautiful woman! Of course men are noticing you!"

"Oh, I don't know."

"You *are*! You're gorgeous! I wish I looked like you."

"Oh, Jules. You're lovely."

"Let's just not go there!"

"He wasn't the perfect father, that's all."

"What do you mean?"

They were standing on the end of Claire's front porch, having just walked up from the swimming hole. Their clothes were clammy and clinging to their still cool bodies. The sun was low and the light falling on the lawn and the trees across the road was tinged with gold. The bits of sky visible through the treetops were a deep blue.

"He wasn't there. He was always traveling. But even when he was there, he was never completely with us. The phone was always ringing. He always had briefs to read or prepare. And then e-mail came along. And then the *BlackBerry*! That damned thing might as well have been grafted to his fingertips! So it was mainly up to me—the kids, I mean. In many ways ours was a surprisingly traditional marriage."

"But you always taught."

In response to this, Claire only crinkled up her nose, as if at a bad smell. "But the main thing was Jonah. Bryan was always too hard on Jonah. I'll never forgive him for that. It wasn't good."

"What do you mean?"

"Well . . . Jonah was kind of an accident. We never intended to have more than two children. And I think Bryan sort of resented him from the start. Of course, Zach and Meg were part of it too: I mean, as much of a handful as Zach could be, especially when he was a teenager, I think Bryan always saw Zach as his alter ego . . . because Zach played guitar and everything. And because of that rock band of his. And even when Zach was really fucking up—like getting caught with marijuana at his high school dance, and flunking every single course the spring semester of his junior year . . . I don't know. I think that, in a weird way, Bryan *liked* that Zach fucked up. I think Zach was exactly the kind of person Bryan secretly wished he could be himself: happy-go-lucky, taking things as they came. Bryan was always this incredibly wound-up guy. He never relaxed."

"He *became* that way," said Julianne.

"No. That's how he *always* was. Even in college. Even when we first met."

This was not at all what Julianne remembered, but she decided not to say anything.

"Then, with Meggy," said Claire. "Well. What can I say? It was just this classic father-daughter thing. They had that really sweet, kind of jokey-teasey relationship. And she was always so good at everything! So he was just incredibly proud of her." Claire smiled; Megan was an environmental lawyer working in San Francisco. "So after those two, it was like Bryan had no more room left in his heart. He was always pestering Jonah. Lecturing him. And harassing him about the cello. God, Bryan could be such a Nazi when it came to that cello! He'd sit in the hall outside the door when Jonah was practicing. And when he heard a mistake, he'd barge in and say, 'No, no, no! That's not how it's done. You have to do it over. Let me hear you do it over.' I don't know why he was like that. It was clear from the beginning that Jonah would never have a concert career. He just didn't have the talent, the natural feel for it. It was killing him. I'm *serious* about this. Completely serious! He told me just the other day that in high school, when he was playing football, he never put tape on his fingers, because he hoped that he would break them. And there were times when he would intentionally catch the football the wrong way, so that he'd . . . So that he wouldn't have to practice the cello anymore. So that he could just quit."

"God! I never knew."

"And then." Claire's voice thickened, and for a moment she couldn't talk. When she continued her voice was calm, but the pacing of her words was measured and her pronunciation unusually precise. "When Bryan died, Jonah was the first one at the hospital, of course." Jonah was a journeyman architect in Manhattan, and lived alone in a walk-up on the Upper East Side. "Bryan was still lying there on the bed. And . . . Well, it was a great help to me, having Jonah there. But still . . . It was the strangest thing. As soon as they wheeled Bryan out of the room. And we were . . . You know: alone. Jonah said to me. It was the very first thing out of his mouth. He just said, 'Mom, do you think I could have Dad's Casals records?' You know: that famous set of the solos?"

Julianne nodded. "With the autograph."

That collection of Bach's solo cello suites had been Bryan's most prized possession in college. His cello teacher had taken him backstage after one of Casals's performances, and Bryan had gotten the album autographed in person.

"So, of course I said yes. There was something so . . . so . . . I just couldn't believe it would be the first thing he would ask for. The first thing he would *say*! And then, just the other night, he called me, and we had this three-hour conversation. And he told me that he's playing his cello again, that he's practicing for hours every night—every *single* night! And he said . . ." Once more her voice became thick. "That the reason he does it is, when he's practicing, he feels . . . that Bryan is in the room with him. 'I'm keeping Dad alive,' he told me."

Claire's eyes glistened with tears. Julianne took her hand, but Claire shook off her grasp.

"I'm worried about him," said Claire. "I don't think it's healthy for him to be playing that stupid cello. I wish he'd stop."

Julianne already knew about Claire's worries. As far as anyone could tell, Jonah—who was twenty-five—had never had a girlfriend, and didn't seem to have any real friends. He had acquaintances and workmates. When he was in college he'd had roommates. But never, since he was very little, had he had a best friend, or even someone who would count as a good friend. The whole family wondered, of course, if he was gay, but he showed no sign of that either. He was just an enigma. A disturbing mystery.

"Oh no!" said Claire, a sudden mischievous smile on her lips.

"What?" said Julianne

"Don't look!" Claire grabbed Julianne's hand. "Pretend to be talking to me. That's Craig Tyler coming over the hill. He's slowing down."

Despite Claire's command, Julianne turned toward the road and saw a brand new metallic silver pickup slowing to a stop. The charcoal-tinted side window rolled down, and a kindly looking white-haired man reached out his hand and waved. "Hey, Claire! How's it going?"

"Hey, Craig!"

"I see you been working on that vegetable garden of yours."

Claire lifted Julianne's hand into the air—like a referee holding up the arm of the champ after a boxing match. "This is my sister! She's helping me!"

"Hello there, Claire's sister!"

"Hi!"

Craig smiled for a moment and said nothing. Then he rocked his hand in a slow wave, said, "See you girls later!" and drove off.

"See us later!" said Claire. "What's that supposed to mean?"

"I think he's nice," insisted Julianne.

Claire just smiled and shook her head.

"He's not even all that bad-looking. I bet he was handsome when he was young."

"Oh, please, Jules! Not yet. I'm not ready for anything like that yet!"

"Mouth like a hatchet chop," Julianne said, studying her own face in the mirror. "Ugh." Then she put on the half smile that had long been the expression she most liked to see reflected back at her, even though she wasn't sure it ever crossed her face at less self-conscious moments. She'd gotten burned out there in the barnyard, despite wearing a straw hat and slathering herself with lotion. But that was okay; the red evened out her complexion, diminishing the intensity of the sunspots on her cheeks and the broken capillaries in her nose. She combed her gunmetal gray hair straight back off her forehead, and, for the fun of it, put on some lipstick: "Autumn Rose," read the sticker on the bottom; although the truth was that the color was closer to congealed blood. Still, Julianne liked the way it brightened her brown eyes, and how it contrasted with her hair.

Claire was slicing a deep red and robust-looking tomato at the kitchen counter. "I thought we'd have a tomato salad," she said without looking up. "First of the season!"

"Yum, yum! My favorite."

Now Claire looked up and smiled.

"What can I do?" said Julianne.

"You can start by opening a bottle of wine."

Because Julianne knew that Claire preferred white wine, she went straight to the refrigerator, where she found two bottles of a New Zealand sauvignon blanc and a muscadet. She chose the muscadet.

When she turned around, Claire had both hands over her face. The knife was on the cutting board, next to the tomato.

"Oh, Claire!" Julianne put the bottle down on the counter in preparation for taking her sister in her arms. But Claire pulled her apron up over her face and fled to the kitchen table, where she sat down and leaned over so far she seemed about to lay her cheek on the varnished wood.

After a moment, she lowered her apron and sat back up. "I'm sorry," she said, her eyes still running with tears.

"That's okay." Julianne also sat at the table, but didn't touch her sister. Not yet.

"It's just . . . What you said: 'What can I do?' That's what Bryan would always say. And I'd always tell him . . . I'd say, '*You can open a bottle of wine.*'" Once again, Claire covered her face with the apron, and this time began to sob heavily.

Julianne put her arms across Claire's hot shoulders, kissing her hair and her temple again and again, saying, "My lovely little sister! My poor Claire! My poor, lovely Claire!" until finally Claire let herself be drawn into an embrace and sobbed even more deeply.

Eventually, she pulled her head back. "Oh, my! I thought I was over that." Her face was swollen, her eyes red and still wet with tears; there was a trail of glossy mucus between her nose and her upper lip.

Julianne got up from the table and came back with a box of Kleenex. "Here."

"Thanks." Claire blew her nose, then pulled out another tissue and wiped her eyes and cheeks. She blew her nose again.

She was smiling: a tight, crumpled smile that seemed mainly intended to hold back more tears. After a moment she sighed and took hold of Julianne's hand with her hot, wet fingers.

"It's so good of you to be here. I'm so grateful." The smile got tighter; she took a deep breath. "It's just . . . It's just that . . . I thought it would be better to have some company. But instead, it's just bringing back so many memories. Because it's so like having him here: being in this house with someone I love."

Claire didn't resume crying. But Julianne knew that in two seconds it would be her turn to sob helplessly.

She got up from the table.

"Okay," she said. "Let's *do* something. Let's get out of here and go someplace you would never have gone to with Bryan. Never in a million years."

They were at John Redmon's, a bar and grill that Claire had probably driven past a thousand times. There were always dozens of cars parked along the road in front of it, and the people Claire had seen on its front steps or standing by their car doors always seemed to be having a good time. Inside, the restaurant was more or less what the sisters expected: pine paneling, antique rakes and pitchforks hanging from the ceiling, and ads for nineteenth-century elixirs on the walls. The burgers were fine: thick, juicy, and charcoal-grilled, with fresh lettuce and a slice of ripe beefsteak tomato on top, but the wine tasted like Mr. Clean mixed with Kool-Aid. After one sip each, they'd sent their glasses back and ordered margaritas. "You deserve it," Julianne had said when Claire hesitated at a second round. "Besides, we can take a walk before getting in the car."

Claire smiled and patted Julianne on the hand. "I'd forgotten how much fun you are!"

Now both of the glasses from their second round were empty. Claire's eyes were glazed and her lips had settled into what easily could be described as a stupid grin, but she seemed more relaxed and more genuinely happy than Julianne had seen her in years.

Julianne picked up her glass and rolled the edge through the puddle of condensation that had collected on the table.

She put her glass down. "I've got a question."

"What?" said Claire, her gaze and grin both becoming more focused. After a moment, her grin altered slightly, into something signifying curiosity.

"I was wondering about what you meant before," said Julianne. "When you said that you knew . . . I mean, when I said—"

"That you loved Bryan?"

"Yeah." Claire's gaze was now thoroughly alert and serious. Julianne had to look away.

"I just meant that you and Bryan had been best friends. And that over the years . . . I mean, he and I had been together for *thirty-four* years. And you'd known him even longer. That's all. That's all I meant."

"Oh." Julianne looked up again.

Claire was examining her, an appreciative but perhaps slightly patronizing expression on her face.

"What?" said Julianne.

"Nothing. Just . . ." Claire picked up her empty glass and let a last drop run down onto her tongue. She put the glass down, shrugged, and looked Julianne in the eye. "It's just . . . also . . . that I know."

"Oh," said Julianne. Then, after a moment, "Know what?"

"What happened between you and Bryan. When Zach . . . When I was in the hospital."

Julianne's mouth had gone completely dry. She couldn't look at her sister, or speak. Finally she said, "How long have you known?"

"Ten years, I think. Maybe nine."

"Wow."

Julianne was responding less to what had just been said than to the fact that this conversation was finally taking place.

Claire reached across the table and lightly stroked the back of Julianne's hand. "It doesn't matter, Jules. Not anymore. I'm not sure it ever really mattered."

"Oh, Claire!" Julianne squeezed her sister's hand. "I have felt so bad about this! I hated myself when it happened. There was just no excuse. I did it, and I knew I shouldn't do it. But afterward, I did everything I could to make sure it wouldn't happen again."

"I know."

Julianne was silent. So many thoughts were passing through her mind that she was having trouble paying attention to what she and her sister were actually saying.

"Bryan told me," Claire said. "He told me all about how you wouldn't talk to him. How you wouldn't be around him. He took all the blame onto himself."

"Well, he wasn't being fair. To himself, I mean. I don't even remember exactly how it happened. But I do know—"

"Shhhh."

Julianne looked up. Claire was grinning, but not happily.

"It's over," she said. "Water under the bridge. Let's just forget about it."

Julianne took hold of her sister's hand with both of her own and squeezed hard.

"I was mad at you when I first found out," Claire said.

"Of course! Jesus! How could you not be?"

"But then I started remembering things. How upset you were when you came to say goodbye to me at the hospital. You kept saying 'I'm sorry!' over and over. I should have known just from that, I suppose. And then how you never came to visit." Claire shrugged and looked at the ceiling. After a long moment she said, "But the truth is I had much more pressing things to think about at the time."

"What do you mean? When?"

"Ten years ago. When Bryan told me."

"Why? What was happening?"

"That was not exactly the best time in our marriage. We were in couples counseling. Bryan had been . . . Well, actually there'd been a whole bunch of affairs."

"Shit!"

Claire shrugged.

"Listen," said Julianne. "I think we need another round."

292

Claire shrugged again, and smiled dubiously. "You go ahead."

"You sure?"

"I've had enough."

Julianne looked for the waitress, but she wasn't in sight. "Forget about it." Then Julianne looked at Claire: "God! That must have been awful! Do you want to talk about it?"

"I don't mind. That's water under the bridge too."

"*Affairs?* A whole *bunch* of affairs?"

"Yeah. Well. As you know, Bryan was a pretty charming guy. Nice-looking. Funny. Doing this incredibly good work. And he was always traveling. So, you know . . . The usual deal! Everywhere he went, there was always some attractive young law clerk, or legal secretary, or reporter. It seems that women just couldn't resist him."

"Did you know?"

"Well, that's the sixty-four-thousand-dollar question!"

"What do you mean?"

"The truth is that I both knew and didn't know at the same time. I mean, there were all these obvious signs, but I kept not coming to the obvious conclusion. Then one day I came across something I couldn't explain away." She put her finger on the rim of her glass and ran it around clockwise, then counterclockwise. "It was almost like Bryan wanted to get caught. In fact, he said he did. He was tired of lying. He was tired of leading this double life." She almost knocked her glass over, but caught it before it hit the table. "So . . . One day I go into his office. In the house, I mean. At home. And there's this letter lying open on his desk. And of course I can tell right away that a woman wrote it. And then I see it begins, 'Dearest Sweet Thang.'"

"Sweet *Thang!*"

"I know! And she wasn't even from the south. So, anyway. There was nothing ambiguous about this letter! She was . . . Well, she was writing about how she'd been remembering all the things they'd been doing, and how she couldn't wait to see him again."

Claire crumpled her lips. "Actually, what she wrote is that she'd been masturbating."

"Oh, my God!"

"In some ways that was very hostile of Bryan, to have left that particular letter out."

"I'll say."

"Bryan had this affable presentation. But he also had these deep wells of anger. Like what I was saying about Jonah. Anyway, the worst of it is that this woman's not just some piece of ass on the road, she's a junior attorney in his own office. And it turns out that they'd been having this serious affair for five years. And I mean *serious*. She'd been talking about having babies. They'd taken these trips together. To Paris and Rome—all on 'business,' of course!"

"How did you find all this out?"

"Well, the first thing is, when he came home that night I told him I was getting a divorce, and I was kicking him out of my house and out of my life, and I was never going to let him see the children again. And then, after that, it was time for the theatrics. He got down on his knees and apologized. Tears in his eyes. He said it was over. *Really* over. So I said, 'Okay, if you agree to go to couples counseling, I'll think about it.' So we did. And he really was serious about it. And, fortunately, when he broke up with the girl, she got so upset, she not only left the ACLU, but moved to London!"

"Where's that waitress?" said Julianne. "Have you seen that waitress?"

"I just saw her. A minute ago. She just walked through."

"Jeeze!"

"I know. I'm beginning to think I want one too."

"So anyhow?"

"So anyhow," Claire said. "We were in therapy for about a year. And Bryan, in his typical way, was fanatically devoted to it. He not only fessed up completely about this affair, but he told me about all the other women. And how he'd been angry, and insecure, and just sick of himself. And how all he'd really been doing was trying to prove his masculinity to his dead father! And then one day, we had just left therapy, and he said he had something to tell me, but he only wanted to tell me in private. And he told me about you. And about how he was sorry, and he wished it had never happened, and that you did too."

"Jesus."

Claire raised her hand, but the waitress didn't see her and walked into the kitchen.

"So how was it afterward?" said Julianne. "I mean, I never had a clue that you guys had any trouble."

"I'll tell you one thing: All that drama did incredible things to our sex life. I mean, we were like teenagers again! But these incredibly knowledgeable teenagers! These . . . Well, I won't go into it." She laughed. "But after that, things settled down. Became normal again. In some ways things were better. Much better. We knew a lot more about each other. We were more honest, and tolerant—of ourselves as well as each other. And I truly believe he never cheated on me again. But even so . . . If you want to know the truth, I've never forgiven him for what he did. I loved him. I would have given my life for him. I mean that completely seriously. *I would have given my life.* But I never forgave him. Until the day he died. I just couldn't. It was beyond me." Claire stared at Julianne grimly across the top of her empty glass.

"And what about you?"

"Me?"

"Did *you* ever do anything?"

"Me?" She frowned. "No. Not then."

"Not *then*?"

Claire smiled and shook her head. "Well, believe it or not, there was this dentist."

"Dentist!"

"Dentist. This incredibly sexy dentist. Up here in the country.

It was only a few years ago. A big chunk of one of my wisdom teeth cracked off. So I went to see him, mainly just to see if I could wait until I got back to my regular dentist in Brooklyn. So he comes into the examining room, and there was just this *unbelievable* electricity between him and me. I don't know what it was. From the second our eyes met. We could both feel it. It was just like this incredible magnetic *pull*. Anyhow, he was also a photographer. And he had all these amazing photographs that he'd taken all over the world. The Taj Mahal. Machu Picchu. You know. Places like that. So when he was escorting me back out to the waiting room, I just said . . . I mean, it was the most brazen thing I'd ever done in my life! I just told him, in this sultry voice, 'I'd like to see more of your photographs.' I couldn't even believe I was saying that. Anyhow, he knew exactly what I meant. So we exchanged numbers. And when Bryan went back to the city a couple of days later, I called him up."

"And?"

"We had dinner. And then. Well, all we did was make out passionately in his car."

"Nothing else?"

"No." Claire frowned.

"How come?"

"He was married, for one thing. And. I don't know. It's kind of strange French-kissing a dentist! You know? I mean, you're always wondering if he's examining your teeth with his tongue."

Both sisters laughed.

"But the main thing," said Claire, "was that I didn't actually want to go through with it. I mean, I'd seen how it had been for Bryan, and, mad as I was at him, I just didn't want to go through that myself. Things were finally going well in our marriage. I didn't want to wreck that up either."

Claire shrugged, the palms of both hands turned upward, signifying helplessness. Then she clapped her hands loudly and kept them pressed together as if she were praying.

"And that was that!" she said.

Just at that instant the waitress arrived.

"Hi." A giant man, teddy-bear-shaped, was standing beside their table. His hair was buzz-cut, glinting gray. His eyes, at the top of his meaty cheeks, were squinty with amusement. He was one of those men—Julianne knew many like this in Maine—who seemed to find almost everything they came across in life to be curious, surprising, and good for a laugh; although in Julianne's experience that attitude was primarily a cover-up for shyness.

"Oh, Pete! Hi! Wow!"

Claire seemed positively startled by Pete's arrival at their table. She also seemed to be having trouble focusing on his face. She'd finished her third margarita and her cheeks were flushed, making her blue eyes seem brilliantly pale—the color of moonlight on snow.

"Pete, this is my sister, Julianne."

The giant man nodded but didn't say anything.

"Julianne, this is Pete!" Claire swept back her arm as if she were making a presentation on stage. "Pete's a genius! He's done all the repair work on our house."

"Genius!" Pete grunted bemusedly. "Well, I don't know."

"Pleased to meet you!" said Julianne.

When Pete shook her extended hand, she noticed he was missing the tip of his index finger, down to the first joint.

"Pleased to meet you too," he said, and then his general air of amusement seemed to go up a notch. "Boy, you sure do look like your sister!"

Now it was Julianne's turn to grunt bemusedly.

"No, it's true. You're practically twins. I could pick you out in a crowd as Claire's sister."

"Well, thanks," said Julianne. "I'm flattered. Claire's much more beautiful than I am."

Pete showed all of his teeth and made a small laugh, but didn't bother to correct her.

Neither did Claire.

"How's Amanda?" Claire asked. "And the baby?"

Pete's expression clouded. "Ah, well. You know. Not much we can do now except wait."

It seemed that his daughter, who lived in Alaska and was married to the skipper of a fishing trawler, had recently given birth to a child who might be deaf and blind. "It's still too soon to tell. The doctors did the examination and . . . Well, they can't find anything physically wrong. I mean, the little guy's eyes just look normal. And his ears. They did like these MRIs of his ears. And they're normal too. Structurally. A hundred percent. It's just that he . . . Well, we did this kind of experiment on him when I was there. You know how babies, when there's this sudden loud noise, how they—" He jerked both hands outward, as if he were clawing at something.

Claire made a sympathetic noise.

"So we'd—you know: bang on a pot right next to his head. And . . ." Pete's face filled with pain. "*Nothing*. He'd just lie there. Sort of sleepy. Happy as a clam, I guess. And it was the same thing with his eyes. Most people think babies are born blind. They're not. It's just they can't control their eyes yet. That's why they're always making those weird, space-alien expressions and everything. But not little Chuck. He just sort of lies there and stares. Doesn't matter what you do. He just looks hypnotized."

"How old is he?" asked Claire.

"Two and a half months."

"Well, that's still . . ." She didn't finish her sentence.

"Yeah." Pete sighed. "Most babies are—you know: already focusing by now."

Julianne asked, "Is there any possibility that it could be neurological?"

"Well, yeah. That's another thing. Nobody knows. Too soon. Nothing we can do but wait."

Pete seemed suddenly so miserable that Claire slid aside in the booth, and patted the bench beside her.

"Thanks."

He lowered himself to the bench and they talked some more about Amanda and her husband, about the strain little Chuck's apparent problems were putting on the marriage, especially since the husband—big Chuck—was off at sea so much. "But you know," Pete said, the amusement coming back into his face, "she just loves that little thing to death! It's a godsend. You know? Makes it all bearable. Amanda just loves that little critter more than anything else. It's impossible not to. You take a look at him lying there, and you just *love* him. You know? That's just how it is. But it's beautiful. Love like that."

The longer Pete talked, the more Julianne could see the handsome face buried beneath his meaty cheeks. His eyes were dark and intelligent. He had high cheekbones, with a Slavic tilt, and a forceful chin. Were he to lose ten or fifteen pounds he could be something close to movie star handsome. Not that he was all that fat. By far the largest portion of his bulk was brawn. Julianne watched the muscles of his forearm as he gestured in conversation: They made her think of flexing bridge cables. His arm was as thick as her leg.

"Well, I bored you girls long enough," Pete said, putting his hands down flat on the table. "I just came over to say hi."

"No," said Julianne. "We weren't bored."

"Really," insisted Claire.

"It was . . ." Julianne began. "You know: nice."

"Well." Pete leaned back in his seat, in preparation to standing up. "I left my beer waiting at the bar. Edward too."

Both women followed his gaze to the bar, where a skinny man—probably in his mid-forties—with a long, dark ponytail nodded in their direction and gave a hip-high wave that, to Julianne's eyes, seemed tinged with irritation.

"Invite him over," she said. "Why didn't you tell us he was waiting there? Poor guy!"

Pete seemed to find Julianne's invitation deeply funny. "Well, I don't know," he said after he'd finished laughing. "You mean it?"

He was looking at Claire, but Julianne answered, "Sure we do!"

"Really?" He was still looking at Claire.

She seemed to have found something interesting in her glass. But after an instant, she lifted a distracted smile to Pete. "Sure," she said. "Of course."

"All right then." Pete stood up. "What are you girls drinking?"

"Margaritas," said Julianne, with a happy smile.

Claire looked hesitant a moment, then said, "I'll have a coffee. You know." She smiled without meeting Pete's eyes. "I'm the designated driver."

The following morning, Julianne would remember that when Pete put Claire's coffee down on the table, he said, "Irish." Claire only took a few sips from the drink, and Julianne finished it—much later, when it had gone completely cold. She seemed to remember that they had stood at the bar for a while, talking with many different people, and that Claire had a gin and tonic. Or maybe it was only soda water. Julianne wasn't sure if she herself had any more to drink, but she probably did.

Edward was an electrician, and he took night classes at Rensselaer Polytechnic. He had been married twice and had three children, one of whom worked for him. At some point in the evening, the music on the jukebox got very loud, and Julianne retained a vivid memory of dancing in a group to "Brown Sugar," and of thinking how good it was to dance again, and how she hadn't lost her knack; she could still do all her moves, although maybe she couldn't dip down quite so low to the floor—she didn't even dare try. She also thought about how strange it was that, although Claire had never been the most limber of dancers, now she seemed almost pathologically stiff and restrained. Her hips hardly swayed, and she held her arms up rigidly beside her shoulders, as if they were in casts. But even so, at one point, Julianne leaned her head next to Claire's and said, "Isn't this amazing!"

Claire answered only with a happy, open-mouthed smile.

"Nothing's changed!" Julianne said. "We're still exactly the same!"

Then there was an ambiguous period in Julianne's memory. She remembered a scuffed, grimy chicken-wire tile floor, and the brown-bordered cracks of an extremely old porcelain toilet bowl. She also remembered her arm wrapped around Claire's neck, and Claire's arm across her back. Somebody had opened a car door, although she had no idea who that person was, nor did she recognize the car. She remembered a tree lit by a yellow plastic sign. But after that there was a very long stretch of nothing. Not even blackness—just nothing. And it was accompanied by the impression—although this must have been from *after* the period of nothing—that a lot of time had passed. She remembered noise. And cold. And an odd pattern of deep blue and speckled white that she eventually realized was a starry sky. It seemed to be jiggling, and periodically dark, ragged masses would shoot across it, and sometimes it would disappear completely. Her shirt was flapping in a cold breeze. Something pressed up, then sank away beneath her back and then there was a metallic rattle all around her.

That was what did it: She was on the bed of a pickup truck, lying flat on her back. The shooting black things were passing trees. Once she figured this out, everything seemed rather pleasant. She'd been feeling nauseated, but the nausea went away. She marveled at the fact that the sky seemed to stay completely still while the trees moved. She even liked the feeling of the wind blowing down the length of her body. Then all at once the whole sky lurched counterclockwise, and then continued to spin, even though she knew the truck was driving straight along a road. She worried that she might vomit.

Another period of nothing ended in heat and a sort of rumbling. Now the trees were just as still as the sky, and blocking most of it. She heard a click, click, click. Perhaps a turn indicator. Maybe they were stopped at a red light. As she waited for the truck to start moving again, she heard a long clear tone, halfway between a low whistle and the moan of a ghost. A few seconds later—this time from the other side of the truck—she heard another long, low tone, filled with such sorrow and loneliness that it sent a weird chill through her entire body.

Owls.

In the coming years, whenever she was served lettuce, zucchini, or tomatoes from Claire's vegetable garden, Julianne would remember their conversation about Bryan, and the great generosity of her sister's forgiveness. But she would think that the conversation had taken place in the garden, or, rather, in that rectangle of earth and stones that would one day become the garden. John Redmon's Bar and Grill would all but vanish from her memory, except for a dim sense that one night she and Claire had gotten so drunk they had to be driven home by someone they barely knew. Julianne would remember that person had been a man, but he would never have a name or face.

The only moment of that entire first visit after Bryan's death that would survive with nearly pristine clarity in her memory was when she was lying in the back of the pickup truck. She would not remember why she was in the pickup, nor that she was drunk. But she would remember the long, low hooting of owls in an otherwise soundless night. First one owl, then another, then a third, and then, almost immediately thereafter, maybe a dozen more owls, near and far, on all sides of the pickup truck—with one, perhaps, calling from a branch directly overhead. She would remember that she had been transfixed, and even afraid, but also that she had never heard anything so beautiful or pure. And for the rest of her life, she would consider herself to have been, in that moment, the beneficiary of the most extraordinary good fortune.

Acknowledgments

—◆—

Thanks, first of all, to the many good friends whose conversation, advice, editing, and own inspiring work has done so much over the years to turn this daunting business of putting one word after another into an adventure and a joy. I want to thank, in particular, Daniel Judah Sklar, Becky Stowe, Bill Logan, Ellery Washington, and Bill Warner. To all of those who I do not have room to list here, please know that I am grateful for every word we have exchanged over coffees, beers, glasses of wine; on subways, street corners, mountainsides; while swimming, walking, jogging, bicycling, or lying in haystacks and looking up at a French moon.

It has also been my great good fortune to have been able to work on these stories with several wonderful editors: first and foremost, Wylie O'Sullivan at Free Press, but also Willing Davidson, Carolyn Kuebler, Andy Hunter, and Scott Lindenbaum. Thanks, too, to Martha Levin and Sydney Tanigawa.

Many thanks to my determined and unrelentingly enthusiastic agent, Jennifer Lyons, without whom this book might never have found its way between two covers. I also owe a great debt of gratitude to the Corporation of Yaddo, the MacDowell Colony, and the Virginia Center for the Creative Arts, where several of these stories were written.

This book is dedicated to my mother, who I had so hoped would live to hold it in her own hands, and whose presence can be felt in my every word and image. I also want to express thanks, one last time, to two great teachers who died while these stories were being written: Kenneth Koch and Leonard Michaels. I would never have become the writer I am without their inspiration and encouragement. Their presence too can be felt on my every page.

Thanks also to Simon and Emma Benedict O'Connor, constant sources of amazement and joy, not just the most loving of children, but the most fascinating and dearest of friends. And finally I want to thank Helen Benedict, my first and best editor, my adviser, coconspirator, and partner in all struggles, who has kept me sane these many years and given me my greatest happiness.

Permission Credits

—◆—

Several stories in this collection are reprinted with the permission of the journals in which they first appeared:

"Ziggurat," *The New Yorker*
"White Fire," *TriQuarterly*
"He Will Not See Me Stopping Here," *Denver Quarterly*
"Bestiary," *New England Review*
"Man in the Moon," *Conjunctions*
"Love," *Electric Literature*
"Sawed-in-Half Girl," *Antioch Review*
"I Think I'm Happier," *Threepenny Review*
"Disappearance and," *Conjunctions*